"THERE'S NO WAY TO WIN THIS WAR."

Gerber watched the performance, then returned to his meal.

"Aren't you going to respond?" asked Morrow, staring at the captain.

"I have nothing to say."

"I don't believe it."

"The problem," said Gerber, "is that the man is right. We won't win this war. Not because we can't, or because the VC and NVA are strong. It's because we won't."

"Tony?" said Morrow.

"I'm staying out of this," said Fetterman.

"Robin," said Gerber, "I showed you and anyone else who cared to watch how it could be done. You win this war by taking it to the enemy. We can do it because we have a nearly endless supply of technological advantages. Helicopters, jets, trucks, cluster bombs and people sniffers. And we have good soldiers. Use all that and the VC and NVA would be overwhelmed."

"But we don't," said Morrow.

"And that's because we can't attack the real enemy," said Gerber.

"And who's that?" she asked.

"The bureaucrats running the war."

VIETNAM: GROUND ZERO™

EMPIRE

ERIC HELM

A GOLD EAGLE BOOK FROM
W☰RLDWIDE®

TORONTO • NEW YORK • LONDON • PARIS
AMSTERDAM • STOCKHOLM • HAMBURG
ATHENS • MILAN • TOKYO • SYDNEY

First edition January 1990

ISBN 0-373-60504-8

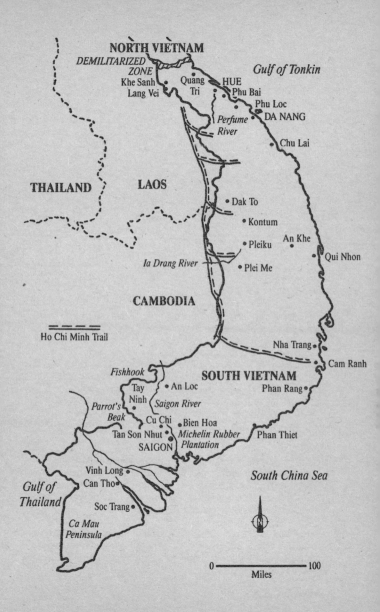

VIETNAM:GROUND ZERO™

EMPIRE

PROLOGUE

CARASEL HOTEL
SAIGON
REPUBLIC OF VIETNAM

"There's no way to win this war," said the man, waving his beer around as if it were a banner. "Just no fucking way."

Special Forces Captain MacKenzie K. Gerber, who had been listening to the slightly drunk civilian, started to stand up. Master Sergeant Anthony B. Fetterman reached out and put a restraining hand on Gerber's arm. "Let it go, Captain."

Gerber slipped back into his chair and stared at the civilian. He could tell that the man wasn't simply a soldier in civilian clothes blowing off steam. He was a reporter, drinking with his cronies, making pronouncements without knowing the facts. The long hair and the gaudy clothes gave him away.

Gerber had met these types before, and it burned him the way they were always spouting off, never mind distorting the facts when they filed their stories.

"Someone should say something," said Gerber.

"No, sir," said Fetterman. He picked up his beer, drank and then glanced at Robin Morrow. "You tell him."

"Oh, no," said Morrow. "I'm not getting involved. Besides, I won't be able to change his views."

"Fucking military will keep this thing going just as long as they can, refusing to admit they can't win it," said the drunk. He was pounding the table to emphasize his point.

Fetterman shook his head. He was a small, balding man. His skin was tanned and his heavy beard gave him a Hispanic look. He didn't look like a soldier, but he was the deadliest man Gerber had ever met. He could slide through the jungle without leaving a sign of his passing, could find the enemy on the darkest night and could eliminate that enemy before anyone was aware that he was around.

But he was a good-natured man who was slow to anger. He usually ignored the opinions of those he found irrelevant, and that included the majority of the news media attempting to report the war in Vietnam. Now he was trying to keep Gerber out of trouble by not letting him react to the drunken opinions of a narrow-minded civilian.

"Robin," said Fetterman, "maybe you should take the captain out of here."

She grinned broadly. Even though she was a reporter, she had spent her share of time in the field. She had seen the war from the smoking ruins of a Special Forces camp that had barely survived an attempt to overrun it. She had seen the war from the trenches, had bullets whine over her head and had used a pistol to defend herself as the enemy ran through that same Special Forces camp.

She was a tall, slender woman who had nearly reached her thirtieth birthday. Her brown hair was sun-bleached and touched her shoulders. Her green eyes sparkled as she watched Gerber trying not to listen to the man. She wore a light blouse and a short skirt. Sweat beaded on her upper lip as she waited for the evening breeze to pick up.

"Want to dance, Mack?" she asked.

Gerber turned and looked over his shoulder at the miniature dance floor. Surrounded by potted plants, it looked like a clearing in the jungle. On the far side, near the French doors that led down into the air-conditioned portion of the restaurant, was a mahogany bar staffed by two men who were busily making drinks. Four sweat-soaked Vietnamese waitresses, all clad in low-cut, tight blouses and short, almost nonexistent skirts, were rushing the finished drinks to the waiting customers scattered around the rooftop bar.

The dance floor itself was jammed with men dressed in civilian clothes or jungle fatigues. A few wore khaki uniforms. The women, some of them Americans who worked at the embassy or were assigned to cultural missions, were wearing dresses in a variety of colors. A few Vietnamese women wore the traditional *ao dai* while others sported Western garb. They ranged from those who looked like refined, educated women to those who were obviously there because the men had money to spend on them.

"Too crowded," said Gerber. He wiped at the sweat beading on his forehead. "Too crowded and too hot."

"I'm telling you like it is," yelled the drunk. "They fuck around and fuck around and no one has a clue about what he's doing. Money down the drain and kids getting killed because they don't know what the fuck they're doing."

"That's it," said Gerber. He shoved his chair back and stood.

"Captain," said Fetterman.

"Mack," said Morrow.

But Gerber was moving across the floor. He stopped directly behind the drunk, hesitated, then tapped him on the shoulder. "I want to have a word with you."

The man tried to turn in his chair, couldn't make it to the right, then tried it to the left. He tilted his head back, looked up at Gerber and grinned. From Gerber's appearance, a youngish man with short brown hair, deeply tanned skin, and blue shirt and khaki pants, the man knew that Gerber was a military officer. It was almost as if the clothes Gerber wore were an unofficial, off-duty uniform. Ninety percent of the soldiers dressed in the same fashion.

"Got a problem?" asked the drunk, slurring his words.

"Nope," said Gerber calmly, "but you do."

"Why don't you back off, chief?" said one of the other civilians. He wasn't quite as drunk.

Gerber stared at the man until he dropped his eyes and then said, "You've been over here spouting off, and I thought it was time someone set the record straight."

"This is a private conversation," said the drunk. He tried to grin and failed. It looked as if he were sneering.

Gerber grabbed a chair from another table, spun it around and dropped into it. He was aware of everything that was going on around him. Aware of the muted music coming from a tape recorder near the bar, the speakers hidden by the potted plants; the quiet, distant boom of artillery as the Americans and the Vietnamese carried on fighting the war; and the heat and humidity, along with the stench from the streets below them. It was almost like a scene from a dream—the outer edges wrapped in darkness and a charcoal-gray that tapered to a brightness in the middle of his vision.

"You know nothing," said Gerber. "You have no idea about it, and I don't think you should state opinions until you have all the facts. That's the problem with all of you. Hear a few key words, make an overflight of a battlefield and suddenly you're an expert on the war."

"Look, chief," said the reporter. "This is a private conversation, so why don't you invite yourself out?"

"Don't you want to hear conflicting opinions?" asked Gerber.

"No. We just want to be left alone."

The drunk waved a hand as if signaling for a time-out. "Let's hear what the chief here has to say. Might be enlightening...." He had trouble pronouncing the last word. He tried it a couple of times, shook his head and then just let the sentence trail off.

"I am telling you that the war can be won," said Gerber.

"Nope," said the reporter. "Absolutely no way."

"I can think of two words that prove you're wrong. Nazi Germany."

"What in hell does that have to do with anything?"

"It proves we can beat them into the ground if we decide we want to. We can destroy their industrial base, as flimsy as it is. We can eliminate their port facilities, their airports, their roads and railways, making it impossible for them to receive equipment and ammunition, and ship it into South Vietnam."

"Policy won't allow that, chief."

"No," agreed Gerber. "I was just letting you know that we could win, if they'd allow us to."

"Then, if it will make you happy," said the reporter, "we'll say that given the current policies, there's no way to win this war. Not when the enemy is employing the guerrilla tactics he does, and our side doesn't have the popular support of the people."

"Not true again."

"Shit, chief, why don't you get out of here." The man shoved back his chair and started to stand.

"You sure you want to do that?" asked Gerber calmly.

"There are four of us here."

Gerber nodded at the drunk. "Three. And if I can't take the three of you, then I deserve to get the shit kicked out of me."

The reporter dropped back into his chair. "Just leave."

"This war can be won," said Gerber. "We have the tools to do it. Even given the current policy, the restrictions on our side, the war can be won."

"Anything you say."

"No," said Gerber. "You're not going to get off that easily."

A shadow fell across him and Gerber turned, looking up into the face of Fetterman. "I think it's time we got out of here, Captain."

"Sorry, Tony, but I want to show these men they've been handed erroneous information."

"Can't be done by talking, Captain," said Fetterman.

"That's right," said the reporter. "You can't convince us by talking about it. So far all the American Army has done is show us it can't win."

Gerber stared at the man but said nothing. He knew what the man said was too true. The American Army, when it had the chance, had beaten the VC and NVA. But there were all the little skirmishes where the VC hit and ran, much like the Plains Indians had done a century earlier. They decided when to fight and where to fight, while the U.S. Army granted all the advantages to the enemy.

"Captain," said Fetterman.

Gerber nodded and stood up. "You're right, Tony. Can't be done by talking." He stared at the reporter. "And you're right, too. We haven't shown that we know how to win."

"Then you see our point, Captain," said the reporter.

"I have no choice, because you haven't been shown our side of it."

"An intelligent officer," said the reporter. "Don't see many of those. Why not let me buy you a drink to show there are no hard feelings?"

"No, thank you," said Gerber.

"Too good to drink with us?"

Fetterman answered for him. "No, sir. We're on our way out. But if we meet you again, I'll be more than happy to drink with you. I never turn down free booze."

"What's your name?" Gerber asked the reporter.

"Meyers. Daniel Meyers."

"Okay, Meyers, once we have something to show you, I might give you a call."

"All right, Captain . . ."

"Gerber. MacKenzie K. Gerber. Army Special Forces."

Now Meyers laughed. "Should have known. All you Green Beret types are sensitive. Play to the press so that the image isn't tarnished."

"I'll let that one go," said Gerber. He turned to Fetterman. "Let's get out."

As they moved toward their table, where Morrow now stood waiting, Fetterman said, "You accomplish anything?"

"No."

"You feel any better about it now?"

"No. But someone had to stand up for our side."

When they reached Morrow, she said, "Well, at least you didn't start a fight."

"No reason to start a fight," said Gerber. "I just wanted to inform them of another opinion."

"Now what?" asked Fetterman, hoping to divert the conversation to something safer.

Morrow moved closer to Gerber and took his arm. She leaned forward, pressing a breast against him. "I think I'm getting a little tired."

"Ah," said Fetterman. "So am I. I'll leave you two, if you don't mind, and hit the sack."

"Breakfast tomorrow, Tony?" asked Gerber.

"Not too early," said Morrow.

"Not too early," repeated Fetterman. "I'm not in any mood to get back to work right away."

As they stepped through the French doors, Morrow looked at Gerber. "Your place or mine?"

"Yours. That way no one will be able to find me except Sergeant Fetterman, and he won't interrupt."

"Tomorrow then," said Fetterman. He disappeared into the crowd.

Morrow watched him go and then slipped closer to Gerber. "People are beginning to talk."

"Let them," said Gerber.

They used the stairs to walk down to Morrow's room. Gerber stood in the dim hallway, waiting while she unlocked the door. As she threw it open, he said, "This is a hell of a way to fight a war."

Then he thought about that, and the words of the reporter came back to haunt him. The American Army hadn't shown anyone they knew how to win, and now he was ducking into a hotel room with a woman. It wasn't his job to dictate policy or to initiate action. His job was to do what he was told to do to the best of his ability.

Still, there was something to what the man had said.

Then Gerber was in Morrow's room, and she turned and pulled him close, kissing him hard, her tongue darting in and out of his mouth. Gerber's thoughts of the reporter and his accusation vanished. All he could think of was Morrow and what she was doing to him.

1

FORT POLK, LOUISIANA

Brigadier General Billy Joe Crinshaw stood at attention in front of TV cameras, reporters, friends, associates and family. To Crinshaw's right was Lieutenant General Richard Wilder, and to his left was his young wife, Jennifer Crinshaw. The room was cramped, hot and bright, but Crinshaw hadn't noticed any of that. He blinked into the bright lights, and although he didn't want to, found himself grinning.

Wilder, a short, stocky man, wore a dress-green uniform with three stars gleaming on his shoulders. He wore his decorations above the left breast pocket. They were mainly awards for meritorious service. He wore jump wings, but there was no star or wreath above them indicating he had completed the minimum five jumps. Sweat glistened on his forehead and bald pate, dripping down to soak the collar of his poplin shirt.

Relishing the attention, Wilder faced the cameras. "It is with great pleasure that I announce the promotion to major general of General Crinshaw."

The flashbulbs went off like the strobing of machine guns in the triple-canopy jungle. Crinshaw grinned, showing pearly teeth.

"I can't reach, dear," said Jennifer Crinshaw.

Crinshaw glanced down at his wife. She was five-six, and Crinshaw, at six-four, towered over her. Her short brown hair was brushed straight, her eyes dark brown and her features sharp. She had thin lips and a pointed chin and wore a light blue silk blouse and a short skirt that showed most of her thigh.

Still grinning, Crinshaw bent down so that his wife could pin the second star to his shoulder. When she finished, he straightened and then dipped the other way so that Wilder could fasten the star to his other shoulder.

"Give her a kiss, General," yelled one of the reporters.

Crinshaw was only too happy to oblige. He leaned down, kissed her on the lips and then cupped her backside with one of his huge hands, pulling her skirt even higher. A couple of reporters could tell that she wore no stockings and that her panties were bright red. One of them took a picture of that, focusing on her rear.

"What now, General?" asked a reporter.

Crinshaw broke the kiss and stood tall. He faced the reporters, aware of the sweat dripping down his sides. Like his wife, he had dark brown hair, cut short, and brown eyes. But his features were fleshy, his nose broad and long, his skin dark.

Wilder glanced at Crinshaw, whose name had appeared on the list of officers rotating back to Vietnam.

"Assignment?" one of the newcomers called out.

"I haven't been given my assignment yet," said Crinshaw, lying for security reasons.

"When do you leave?"

Jennifer Crinshaw took one of her husband's hands in hers. "Much too soon," she said.

"How long have you two been married?"

"Six months," she said.

"What do you think of all this?"

She looked at the reporter, suddenly afraid. She knew the American media were hostile to American involvement in Vietnam. Their articles were less than supportive. Anything she might say could be twisted around to throw a bad light on her and her husband.

"I'm very proud," she said noncommittally.

"Proud of what?"

She swallowed. "His promotion."

"Gentlemen," said Wilder, holding up both hands, "our public information officer has a handout for you. It gives the details of General Crinshaw's career and education. Some of you might be interested in the fact that he played tackle on the Georgia Tech team. Many of your questions will be answered there."

"Getting him out of here before he can say anything?" shouted one of the reporters.

"Nope. We have a small reception planned and we're late for it already."

"Congratulations, General," said one of the reporters.

The PIO, a captain, stepped forward. "Gentlemen, come with me."

The TV people began to unplug their lights and cameras while the print reporters took a few final pictures. Crinshaw, his wife and Wilder slipped from the rear of the room. Once out of sight of the reporters, Crinshaw spun Jennifer around and kissed her again, deeply, his hands squeezing her breasts.

"I wish you didn't have to return to Vietnam," she said breathlessly a moment later.

Crinshaw looked down into her eyes, which were now brimming with tears. "I know. I wish I could stay with you, but I have my orders."

But that wasn't what he was thinking. He was remembering a Special Forces captain who had made him look bad. He was remembering how MacKenzie K. Gerber had fucked over him repeatedly. And he was thinking that now he had the juice to do more than get even. Staring down at his wife, he could think only of the ways he could get even with Gerber. Even with his wife crying silently, he could think only of Gerber.

IT WAS A DARK NIGHT, the stars and moon obscured by low-hanging clouds. Overhead came the rumble of jet engines and the pop of rotor blades. NVA Lieutenant Tuyen Van Thien lay in the deep grass at the edge of the jungle and watched the open ground in front of him.

Thien was twenty-two years old. He had been in the South for only three weeks, but had spent a year there when he was eighteen. As a young enlisted man, he had learned now to fight the war. He had learned that it wasn't a question of surrounding the Americans and overwhelming them as his father had done with the French at Dien Bien Phu, but of meeting them in small engagements, fighting them and then running. It was a question of hanging on long enough for the Americans to tire of the war and decide to go home.

Clutching his AK-47, he watched the vacant rice paddy, waiting for the first signs that an American patrol was nearby. He'd been there for two days, and might be there for two more, the members of his platoon scattered in a loosely organized ambush, waiting for the chance to hit quickly, kill two, three or four of the American aggressors, and then vanish into the night. For two days he'd been waiting for the chance to put into operation the things he had learned during his first year in South Vietnam.

Thien was a slight man, weighing no more than a hundred pounds. He was only five feet three inches tall, with jet-black hair and dark brown eyes. He had a round face, a broad, flat nose and a round chin. In the South he wore black pajamas rather than green fatigues. The black pajamas were the uniform of the VC. He was wearing it to confuse the Americans, if they saw him.

Confuse the Americans, kill them and then run off to fight another day. That was the plan. Never give them a chance to retaliate. Never give them a chance to fight back—a concept he had learned during his first tour and one that had been taught to him again and again while he was in the North.

There was a sound in the distance. Not the booming of artillery that randomly rained down, killing indiscriminately, and not the roar of the aircraft that filled the skies. This was a quieter sound, coming from the rice paddies that were spread out in front of him.

Thien stared into the darkness, turning his head slowly and looking out of the corners of his eyes. Vision was better that way. He could see the charcoal shapes of a farmer's hut, a clump of trees and a single water buffalo tethered to a pole set in the ground.

The dikes were short black walls. Flashes of starlight reflected from the water in the rice paddies. There was movement out by the hut—a man or woman near the mud-and-thatch structure.

Thien slipped his weapon forward, the barrel pointed in the direction of the hut. He studied the shape, waiting for it to take on features, but it stayed close to the mud walls, finally disappearing inside. Definitely the farmer.

There was a rustling near him, and he turned to see one of his men lean close. "Comrade, there is nothing here."

"Patience," said Thien. "Patience is our ally. Our weapon against the Americans. It's our only strength."

"The men think we should move to the South, closer to the highway."

Slowly Thien turned his head and grinned. "This isn't a democracy. I'm in command here. We'll wait and allow the Americans to come to us."

"Yes, Comrade."

The man slipped away, returning to his hiding place. Thien glanced out over the rice paddies. The Americans might not appear for days, but Thien knew they would eventually. Shifting around only exposed his men to attack by the American technology. Helicopters, fighters and artillery would kill them if the Americans spotted them too early. Staying hidden was the key. He would teach his men just as he had been taught so many months before.

He grinned again, knowing he would win. The Americans didn't understand the war. There was no way they could win it.

2

FORT POLK, LOUISIANA

The window was open and the curtains were fluttering in the late-evening breeze. Crinshaw, still wearing his dress-green uniform, kept glancing out of the corners of his eyes to see the second star perched on each shoulder. It wasn't nearly as thrilling as seeing the first one pinned there, but there was an almost erotic attraction to it. He had leaped another hurdle. Many men reached brigadier general and then retired, the star a reward for a lifetime of work. A few climbed to major general, and Crinshaw had now joined that elite group.

He watched as Jennifer puttered around the small kitchen. It was a brightly lighted room with glass-fronted cabinets displaying her well-used china, the glasses bought at the five-and-dime store and a small stock of canned foods. Jennifer was at the sink, leaning forward slightly so that her short skirt rode up in the back, revealing her thighs. He stared at her legs and wondered if she knew he could see all the way to her red panties.

She glanced over her shoulder and grinned at him. "I'm about done here. Why don't we go into the other room?"

"I'm happy right here," he said. The floral-patterned chairs that surrounded the kitchen table weren't all that comfortable, but then the view was perfect. He watched as she pulled another dish from the soap water, rinsed it and put it into the wire rack on the counter.

Now he grinned. Normally she wore shorts or jeans when she did the housework, but then today was special. He had a new assignment and a promotion and there was talk of a tour at the Pentagon when he finished in Vietnam. It could be said that his star was rising again. Gerber, the bastard, along with his fellow renegades in the Green Berets, had nearly destroyed his career, but it was now back on track.

No, he told himself, he wouldn't think of Gerber and those other bandits who called themselves soldiers. He would study Jennifer's legs. He would stare at the soft, lightly tanned flesh on her thighs, and her round bottom in the light silk of her bright red bikini panties.

She leaned forward as far as she could, her legs straight and her skirt pulled way up. She hovered there, over the edge of the sink, seeming to reach for something just beyond her grasp. Finally she stood up straight and turned, looking right into his eyes.

"Well?" she asked.

Crinshaw felt a stirring. Jennifer knew exactly what she was doing. As he studied her, he noticed she had rolled the waistband of her skirt over, shortening it even more. She was trying very hard to attract his attention without coming right out and saying it.

"You've finished with the dishes, finally," he said.

"Yes, I've finished."

Crinshaw stood. "Then let's go into the living room and see what's on TV."

"Fine," she said as she grabbed the dish towel and dried her hands.

As they walked through the door and down the short, narrow hall that led to the living room, he suddenly understood why she had insisted they have dinner at home. At the club, or in one of the nicer restaurants, there would have been people coming over to congratulate him. Friends, colleagues and fellow officers would have monopolized their time. This way they were alone, and she could play her little seduction game.

Crinshaw turned on the television, saw that it was too late for the news and left it on a western. He dropped into his chair and glanced over at Jennifer. She was sitting on the couch, her legs crossed and the hem of her skirt hiked up. She had unbuttoned the top three buttons of her blouse and had opened it up, showing the rise of her breasts.

He tried to watch the western. He tried to concentrate on the action, but couldn't. The six months since the wedding had made it impossible. He still didn't know her well enough to ignore her attempts to seduce him. He was still vulnerable to them.

Now she uncrossed her legs but didn't keep her knees together. Instead she spread them, forcing the short skirt higher until it concealed nothing. She smiled at him, looked down at herself and then casually slipped her hand inside the waistband of her panties.

"Well?" she asked again.

"A little blatant, don't you think?" said Crinshaw.

"No."

Crinshaw shrugged and watched her hand. She pulled it out and then unbuttoned the rest of her blouse. Leaning forward, she shrugged it from her shoulders, letting it fall onto the couch behind her. Now bare to the waist, she sat back and used the fingers of her left hand to stroke her thigh, her eyes on Crinshaw, watching his reaction.

"You win," he said finally, trying to stand.

"Oh," she asked innocently. "What do I win?"

"Anything you want," said Crinshaw.

Now she stood, smoothed her skirt and then reached around to unzip it, slipping it over her hips. "Anything at all?" she asked as she moved toward him.

"Yes," he replied, wrapping his arms around her and pulling her close. He felt the smooth skin of her back and felt her press her hips against him.

"Now," she said. "Right here and right now."

Crinshaw, forgetting about his second star, forgetting about Gerber, forgetting about the western on the TV, lifted her off her feet and gently placed her on the floor. With his right hand he tugged at her panties, sliding them over her hips and down to her knees.

"Took you long enough," she said.

Crinshaw stopped for a moment. "I was enjoying the show."

"It's time to pay now," she said, her voice husky.

"Gladly," Crinshaw said as he fumbled with the buttons of his uniform.

WHEN CRINSHAW GOT UP the next morning, he was surprised to find that his knees and elbows were bruised and scraped. That was the problem with marrying a woman fifteen years younger than himself. She had a resilience that he could only dream about now. The floor was harder and his joints were stiffer. She could leap up, while he had to struggle not to show the pain that rapid movement gave him.

While he dressed in fresh khakis, the two stars gleaming on his collar, Jennifer sat in bed watching him, the sheet wrapped around her waist. "Going to work, huh?" she said.

"Someone's got to earn some money around here."

She tossed the sheet aside so that he could see that she still wore nothing. "You sure about that?"

Crinshaw bent close to her and brushed her lips with a kiss. "Definitely."

"Okay. I could make you some breakfast. I know the secret for frying bacon. Do it naked."

"I'd like to see that, but I've got to get into the office early. First day now, and I don't want to start off on the wrong foot."

"You've been here for nearly a year," said Jennifer.

"But this is the first day with the new star. I want to make it a good one."

"Okay," she said.

Crinshaw moved to the dresser, took his keys and dropped them into his pocket. "See you tonight."

"Tonight," she said.

Crinshaw walked through the house and then opened the front door. Parked at the curb, partially shielded by two flowering bushes, was an Army staff car. The driver, a young spec four, was leaning against the front fender, waiting patiently, his eyes on the front door.

As the general approached, the soldier moved to the rear of the car and opened the door. He stood there at stiff attention, saluting, and when Crinshaw was close, said, "Good morning, General."

"Good morning." Crinshaw climbed into the rear and waited until the driver was behind the wheel. "Take me to headquarters."

"Yes, General."

The driver started the engine and Crinshaw leaned back. He glanced to the right at the tree-lined street with its neat houses. Not exactly the best place in the world to live, but better than many. Almost everyone living there had a job at Fort Polk. Many of them were high-ranking officers who used their quarters allowance to build equity in the houses. With a constant rotation of men into the training command

and then back out, it was easy to sell a nice house and make a few thousand dollars in the process.

They drove along past the tall pine trees that always surprised Crinshaw. He had thought, on coming to Louisiana, that he would see real trees with leaves. Instead there were evergreens, and he had learned to hate evergreens.

They drove through the front gate at Fort Polk. An MP dressed in pressed khakis came out of the small white shack that guarded the road. He saw the plaque with two white stars set where the license plate would be on a civilian car, and saluted.

They drove up to the big white headquarters building, which was situated on a semicircular drive. It gleamed in the morning sun. The dark green tile of the roof seemed to absorb some of the light. There were bushes and trees and a flagpole.

The driver stopped and then got out of the car so that he could open the door for the general. Crinshaw got out and stared up at the two-story building, feeling that he was seeing it for the first time.

As he walked up the sidewalk and then climbed the steps to the doors, he saw two men, one of whom was General Wilder. "General Crinshaw, we have to talk."

"Certainly, General."

They walked up the steps, and a major opened the doors. The entryway of the air-conditioned building was carpeted and painted a light green. There were bright lights on the ceiling and pictures of the infantry in action on the walls.

"My office," said Wilder.

Crinshaw hesitated. "What's the problem?"

"My office."

Crinshaw followed Wilder down the hallway to a dark wooden door with bright brass fixtures. Wilder opened the door and gestured at the chairs.

Crinshaw entered and moved toward the leather chairs set up in one corner as a conference area. He sat down and glanced at the coffee table, which held recent copies of *Infantry* magazine, the *Stars and Stripes*, the *Army Times*, and *Newsweek*. There was a leather couch to the right, and on the wall above it a framed painting of Fort Polk.

Wilder's desk was across the room, set near the bank of windows. There were two chairs in front of it and a high-backed one behind it. The in and out baskets on the desk were empty, and the green blotter held a single file folder. The curtains were drawn so that the room was dark. Rather than open them, Wilder turned on the lights.

"Can I get you something to drink?"

"A little early for that," said Crinshaw.

Wilder grinned and opened a hidden refrigerator. He held up a glass jar of orange juice. "I wasn't thinking of anything alcoholic."

"Orange juice would be fine."

Wilder poured a glass, handed it to Crinshaw and then filled one for himself. He carried it to the conversation area, sat down on the couch and sipped. Finally he said, "That's a pretty little wife you've got there."

"I was lucky to find her."

"Where *did* you find her?"

Crinshaw took a long sip of his juice. "Is that important?"

"Oh, hell, no. Idle curiosity."

"Well, then, I was home on leave and she was working in a bar. Waitress. I couldn't believe it. She's too smart to be wasting her time working in a bar with a bunch of horny drunks grabbing her ass."

"What's she going to do while you're overseas?"

Crinshaw shrugged. "She's thinking about finishing her degree in journalism and then trying to find a job using it. Something in the print area."

"Christ," said Wilder.

"I know," said Crinshaw. "But she understands. She's slightly afraid of television reporters. I figured that having someone well-versed in their techniques might help us learn to deal with them. Well, help her deal with them if that becomes necessary."

"Maybe," said Wilder. He finished his juice, leaned forward, put the glass on the table and then sat back. "I've got some bad news for you."

Crinshaw suddenly felt himself grow cold. First the questions about his wife and now bad news. Someone had made a mistake and he'd have to give back the second star. Someone had investigated his wife and learned that she had protested the war in Vietnam. Sweat suddenly beaded on his forehead.

"General Hiller in Saigon has sent a TWX asking if you can relieve a week early."

Crinshaw nodded slowly, and then understood the questions about his wife. Would she understand his sudden departure for Vietnam after being promised an extra week?

"I could be ready to go in two, three days," said Crinshaw.

"I think we could arrange an early R and R in Hawaii so that you can see her again quickly."

Crinshaw rubbed his face and tried to run down the things he had to do before he left. He grinned as he realized that everything that had to be done could be done at long range on his orders. He had an aide who could do it. Jennifer could help him do it.

And he didn't have to pack. Once in Vietnam, he could draw everything he needed from supply. Three days left.

"Naturally you can have the rest of the time off, with the exception of a couple of hours for a briefing. We'll get you a military flight out of here so that you don't have to put up with civilian air."

Crinshaw finished his juice and sat there holding the glass in his hand. He stared down at the deep green carpeting and tried to work his way through this. It wasn't that much of a problem, because he expected to be gone in a week anyway.

"I suppose I should head on home then."

"What's Jennifer going to do?"

"Put the house up for sale and then join her parents. Davis can help her."

"Why don't you go?" said Wilder. "I'll let you know when we get the briefing ready."

Crinshaw stood. "I thought you had bad news."

"That was the best I could do on such short notice. Hope it doesn't wreck your plans."

Crinshaw nodded. "If that's all, General . . ."

"That's all." He hesitated for a moment, then added, 'I called your home, but you'd left already."

"You didn't say anything to Jennifer, did you?"

"No. Just told her that I'd talk to you when you arrived here."

Crinshaw held out a hand. "Thanks for everything, Dick."

"You give them hell in Vietnam, Billy."

"I plan to." He paused, then opened the door and walked out into the hallway. Stopping for a moment, he looked up at the ceiling. Things were accelerating. And then he grinned. "Gerber, I'm on my way."

Then, feeling almost as good as he had when they'd pinned the extra stars on his shoulders, he left the headquarters building. He knew Jennifer would be disappointed, but she would find a way of making the last three days something to remember. Something that would hold him for the year he had to serve in Vietnam.

3

BINH LONG PROVINCE
NORTH OF SAIGON

As the sun came up, Thien saw the first activity that suggested the enemy was close—shadows moving in the distance on the other side of the farmer's hut. Two, then three men were walking at the very edge of the jungle, barely visible as the sun's rays began penetrating the thick vegetation.

The size of the enemy unit grew until Thien counted twelve men, each carrying an M-16, with the exception of one man who had an M-60 machine gun. They came out of the jungle, staying on the rice paddy dikes. It wasn't a disciplined unit, more like twelve men strolling through the countryside, maybe hunting for wild turkey or deer. They seemed to be unconcerned about the danger around them.

Thien glanced slowly to his right and left, where the members of his ambush unit were still waiting. Now, in the growing light of the morning, he could see their shapes where they rested. One man was lying on the ground among the roots of a giant teak tree, his AK held in his left hand. On the other side of him was another soldier stretched out behind the compact RPD machine gun, his assistant next to him already slowly, quietly, slipping the ammunition from the ammo can.

The men were ready.

But the Americans weren't. They spread out, sat down along the dikes and passed around a canteen, each of them drinking from it. Then one by one they lighted cigarettes, smoking and talking and ignoring everything around them. One of the men stood up suddenly, pointed, and the others turned to look. They watched as a Vietnamese woman left the hut, stopped near the door and waited.

"Hey, *mama-san*," yelled the standing man. "You make boom boom?"

There was a hoot of laughter, and another of the men yelled, "Come on, *mama-san*. Make *beaucoup* bucks. *Beaucoup.*"

The woman stood there staring, as if paralyzed with fear. She was joined a moment later by a younger woman with long black hair.

"Oh, yeah," yelled the standing American. "Come to *papa-san*. We make *baby-san*." The man began to walk toward the Vietnamese women.

"Hold it," said one of the other Americans. "Leave the locals alone."

"Jesus, Sarge."

"I said to knock it off."

The man sat down again, glanced at the women and then was silent. For several minutes the Americans stayed where they were, smoking and eating the C-rations pulled from the rucksacks they wore.

"That's it," said the sergeant. "Let's move out."

One man licked the last of his food from a white spoon, stuck that into the pen pocket of his jungle fatigues and then tossed the empty can into the rice paddy. He stood up, his weapon at his hip. Pulling the trigger, he missed the floating can and then flipped the selector to full-auto. He held the trigger down and sprayed the rice paddy with nineteen rounds. The water leaped skyward under the impact. When the bolt of his rifle locked back and the water settled down, the can still floated, having survived the fusillade.

"Jesus Christ," snapped the sergeant. "Knock it the fuck off."

"A little target practice," said the soldier.

"Just knock it off. And take the point."

"I've had the point."

"You've got it again, and you'll stay out there until you learn to use your head."

The man pulled the empty magazine from his weapon, glanced at it and then put it into the bandolier. He took a loaded one out, slipped it into the well and tapped the bottom to make sure it was seated properly. He then used the charging handle to chamber a round.

"Go," said the sergeant.

The man moved toward Thien and the waiting NVA soldiers. As they wormed their way along the rice paddy dikes, Thien could see their faces better. The sun had peaked over the tops of the trees, and the ground was now bright. Long shadows grew from the Americans, the hut and the dikes, shifting patterns that made the landscape look unreal.

Thien knew he didn't have to instruct his men. They were ready. The moment the Americans had appeared, they had flipped off the safeties of their weapons and set out their grenades. The instant he initiated the ambush, the air would be filled with shrapnel and bullets.

The Americans came closer, and the two Vietnamese women disappeared into their hut. Birds squawked overhead and there was a chattering of animals in the jungle. Otherwise the scene was peaceful, serene.

And then all hell broke loose.

Thien pulled the pin of one of the Chicom grenades and threw it at the American patrol. It landed with a quiet splash. The American sergeant turned toward it and then dived off the dike. "Grenade!"

Thien opened fire, raking the closest paddy dike. One of the enemy staggered under the impact of the bullets. He stumbled to the rear, blood blossoming on his chest and stomach. He dropped his rifle without firing it and then toppled to the right, falling into the rice paddy with a splash, his blood staining the water crimson.

Other Americans jerked and staggered like puppets whose strings were controlled by angry children. They fell off the dikes and into the paddies. One man knelt and opened fire with his M-16, but he was cut down. Blood sprayed as he fell forward onto his face.

Thien was up on one knee, aiming his shots now. He hit a man who tried to crawl away. One of his other rounds plowed into the body of a wounded American. Around him the AKs of his soldiers were hammering. The RPD barked in short bursts. The ground near the Americans erupted into muddy geysers.

The sergeant still survived. The barrel of his M-16 poked over the top of a dike. He fired quickly. Thien heard the rounds snap overhead and ducked instinctively, returning two shots that slammed into the dike.

Suddenly the American sergeant stopped shooting. A quiet settled over the battlefield. A man groaned in pain, a low distant sound drifting across the open paddies.

There was movement out there, a slight rustling as someone crawled along the side of a dike, stirring the water. Thien stood, but couldn't see the man.

But he did see the destination. The radioman lay on his back at the junction of two dikes. The radio antenna was bent, and there was a wet smear down the man's side. He still held his M-16 in his hand, but he was obviously dead.

Grinning, Thien sighted on the radio. He squeezed the trigger. The man jerked as the round smashed into the radio. Thien kept firing until his weapon was empty. Then, changing magazines, he tried to spot the lone surviving American.

One of his soldiers stood up and moved out into the growing brightness of the early morning. He stopped at the edge of the jungle, studying the scene in front of him.

There was a single shot and a short scream. Thien's soldier flipped back, rolled onto his stomach and was still. Blood spread over the dark green of his fatigues.

Firing erupted from the trees, raking the rice paddies. Water and mud fountained. The bodies, sprawled on the dikes or floating in the water of the paddies, were hammered, shot to pieces. They bounced and danced under the impact of more AK and RPD rounds.

Thien moved forward cautiously, watching the ambushed patrol. When he realized there was no return fire, he yelled, "Cease fire!"

Slowly the shooting died away and again it was silent. Thien knew one of the Americans still lived. The man had ducked down behind the dikes.

"American soldier," yelled Thien in broken, heavily accented English. "American soldier. You quit or you die."

There was no answer.

Thien grinned. Well, he wouldn't have surrendered, either. The Americans, he knew, would torture him for information and then kill him anyway. Better to die like a soldier with a gun in his hand than be executed.

Thien studied the situation in front of him. The sun was higher now, and the scene was starkly lighted. The bodies were covered with blood. Flies, drawn from the jungle, swarmed on the dead, their buzzing sounding like distant chain saws.

Thien pointed to two of his men, motioning them to the right. Two others moved to the left. Everyone stayed inside the tree line, using the cover as they worked their way around to flank the lone American soldier.

Thien waited for the American to make a move. Firing broke out to his right. Bullets slashed through the morning air and hit the top of a dike. There was a movement and then return fire—M-16 against AK-47.

Over the top of the dike, Thien saw the tip of a helmet. He aimed his weapon carefully and squeezed the trigger. He missed, but the bit of helmet disappeared.

From the east came the sound of rotor blades—American helicopters, probably loaded with more soldiers. He didn't think the trapped man had made a radio call for help, but it was still a possibility. With the coming of the sun and with the bodies sprawled in front of them, the advantage was slowly slipping away. The American would have all the help he needed in a few minutes. Thien had to end the situation as quickly as possible.

"American soldier. You quit or die."

"Fuck you," came the reply.

"American soldier," yelled Thien, not because he had anything to say but because he wanted to keep the man's attention focused on him. "American soldier!"

The sound of the helicopters was louder now. Thien still couldn't see them, but they would pop over the treetops any moment now. They had to kill the American quickly.

There was a rifle shot and then another. Two of his men ran from cover out of the jungle, splashing through the knee-deep, mud-choked water of the rice paddy.

The American opened fire. One of Thien's men spun and fell, disappearing from sight. The other dived forward toward the protection of the low dike.

But that was all the opening Thien needed. He had the American in his sights. He pulled the trigger and saw the bullet strike in a crimson explosion of blood. The American dropped into the muddy water and didn't move.

Thien wanted to order his men to strip the bodies and take the weapons. He wanted to order them to fire rounds into the heads of every man lying out there to make sure they were dead, but the helicopters were too close. The helicopters would bring more Americans, or gunships, or jets. The small victory he had won would be stolen from him.

"We go now," he yelled, waving a hand and pointing to the rear into the thick jungle behind them. "Let's get out of here."

The man in the rice paddy stood up, water dripping from his body. He reached down, grabbed the collar of the man the American had killed and dragged him toward the trees.

The roar from the choppers was louder than ever. Thien raised a hand to his eyes to shade them, certain that the enemy aircraft would appear any moment. If he didn't get his soldiers out of sight, they would be chased the rest of the day. "Come on," he yelled. "Move it."

The other members of the patrol were gathering their equipment. The assistant gunner was trying to pick up spent shells. Then one man darted from the trees. He ran along a dike and leaped toward the body of one of the Americans, grabbing at the M-16 there. He hauled it free and then used his knife to cut away the bandolier of spare ammo.

Now it sounded as if the choppers were going to land on top of them. Thien slipped deeper into the shadows. He yelled at the men, trying to get them to hurry, to get out of sight.

Then the first of the choppers appeared. It crossed the clearing and suddenly banked. They had spotted the dead men lying in the open.

"Come on," yelled Thien. He started to the rear, forcing himself to move slowly, carefully. He didn't want the American flight crews to know he was still in the area.

One of his men ran past him, disappearing into the shadows of the triple-canopy jungle. Two more joined the first. Thien halted, turned and looked back at the ambush site. It sounded as if more helicopters had joined the first. The sky was filled with them, as if they were buzzards flocking to the scene of a kill.

Firing erupted behind him. Thien dived for cover and rolled to the right, next to a tree. For an instant he was afraid he had been seen by the Americans. Then he realized they were just firing into the jungle, trying to draw return fire.

Again he was on his feet, hurrying away from the ambush. The sounds of the helicopters were fading behind him. The shooting at the clearing was sporadic. He knew American soldiers would be landing soon.

But none of that mattered now. They had sprung the ambush and killed all the Americans. They had lost only two men, both of them killed through their own stupidity. In the long run the ambush was a success.

Ten minutes later he slowed. The squad formed around him and they took a break. If the Americans operated true to form, it would be late afternoon before anyone started to search, and that search would last only until dark. No concentrated effort would be made.

Thien grinned at his men and held up a thumb, the way he'd seen the Americans do when he'd watched them from the tall grass near their fire bases.

A very good mission, he told himself.

4

MACV-SOG COMPOUND
TAN SON NHUT
SAIGON

Gerber sat at the rickety table inside the plywood-lined room and studied the maps spread out in front of him. The light came from a fluorescent fixture hanging over the table. An air conditioner, built into the plywood wall, struggled to keep the room cool, but it was failing. Gerber had taken off his jungle jacket and had hung it over the back of the metal chair. His OD cotton T-shirt was sweat-soaked.

"Captain," said Fetterman as he entered the room and set a Coke in front of Gerber.

"Found it, Tony," Gerber told him.

"Found what?"

Gerber picked up the Coke, drank from it, then turned to face the master sergeant. "Found the right place for the experiment."

Fetterman shook his head. "I think you lost me somewhere on that last turn."

"Okay," said Gerber. He took another drink of Coke, then set the moisture-beaded can aside. "You remember that reporter last night suggesting that we don't know how to win the war?''

"You're not still worried about that, are you?''

Gerber ignored Fetterman's question. "He was right, to a point. We haven't demonstrated that we know how to win this war. That doesn't mean we don't or can't, just that we haven't shown anyone we can.''

"Yes, sir,'' said Fetterman noncommittally.

Gerber stood up and then bent over the map. "I've isolated a single province where there's been Intel reports of VC and NVA activity. A place where we can establish that there was an enemy presence.''

"Yes, sir.''

"There's an abandoned camp here,'' said Gerber, pointing at the map.

Fetterman moved closer and looked down. The terrain was uneven, varying from near sea level to hills five hundred feet high. There was triple-canopy jungle and areas near the river valleys where farmers had rice paddies. An Loc was the largest city. Xa Thang Binh and Loc Ninh were the other two villages marked on the map, but there were indications of smaller, scattered hamlets, as well as some plantations.

"As you can see,'' said Gerber, "we've got Highway 13 running into the province along with a couple of other, less well-maintained roads, plus a railroad if we should need one.''

"Okay, Captain,'' said Fetterman. "Looks good on paper, but what's the point?''

Gerber leaned back and laced his fingers behind his head. "I want to put an A-detachment into that abandoned camp to reestablish it, then upgrade to a B-detachment and bring in two or three other A-detachments and clean out the whole province. Eliminate the VC and NVA presence.''

"Christ.''

"It can be done," said Gerber.

"Yes, sir. Have you coordinated this with anyone?"

"Not yet."

Fetterman saw a file folder sitting on the table near the map. "That the Intel summaries?"

Gerber rocked forward and grabbed the folder. He pushed it toward Fetterman. "Gives you a rundown of the enemy activity in the province. They have a presence, but not a strong one. We're not really there, so they're not really there."

Fetterman opened the folder and scanned the contents. "Says here the province chief might be working with the VC. That seems to be an obstacle."

"Not really. If you read further, you'll see that his nephew is in the pocket of Saigon and is itching to take over."

"You going to assassinate this guy?"

"Oh, hell, no. We'll just move in and let it be known we're not happy. Let the family fight it out."

Fetterman fell silent and read the folder. Gerber finished his Coke and tossed the empty can at the wastebasket in the corner.

"Looks like the enemy could field a company, maybe a reinforced company with no trouble."

"Yeah," said Gerber. "That's what I thought, too. The thing that bothers me most is the proximity of the Ho Chi Minh Trail. For the first week or so we'll need good surveillance of it. Maybe get Maxwell to arrange something for us."

"I notice that Highway 13 heads right into Cambodia." Fetterman grinned. "The NVA could drive out of Cambodia to attack us."

"Ironic, isn't it?" said Gerber. "If we find ourselves in trouble, we could blow up the bridge here, north of Loc Ninh, or here, near Ap Canle."

Fetterman closed the folder. "Looks like we'd have time to get the camp established before the enemy could hit us, if we start with the abandoned camp at Xa Cat. You have any idea about its condition?"

"Sits on the top of a hill that dominates the landscape around it. The bunkers and buildings were destroyed when we left, but if we land early in the morning, we could have a perimeter established by nightfall."

Fetterman nodded and studied the map again. "What's the jungle like?"

"Most of it's triple-canopy. Trees two hundred feet tall. Open areas around the rivers and a few plains exploited by the farmers."

"Support?"

"Regular Army at An Loc, Loc Ninh and a half-dozen fire bases that could help us if we needed it."

Fetterman closed the folder and dropped it back onto the table. He stared at Gerber, wondering what the Captain was thinking. He'd noticed since he'd come across the beach at Omaha during the Normandy invasion that things had changed. Strategy and tactics during the Second World War had been left to high-ranking officers and politicians. In Korea field-grade officers had planned missions and the overall military commander had defied the political leaders. True, MacArthur had been relieved, but the precedent had been established. Now, here in Vietnam, captains were planning strategies. Gerber had worked out a wild plan to take over a single province. If Fetterman read the situation right, it meant Gerber was on the verge of setting up his own empire in Binh Long Province, and with a few breaks he'd pull it off.

"You cleared this?"

Gerber shook his head. "Still in the planning stages. We'd need to assemble the A-team, find us a company of strikers and then get the logistical support we'd need. Weapons, equipment and food."

"Minh has command of a battalion at Ap Tan Hoa, south of here. He could be persuaded."

"Kepler is still loose here. We'd need Bocker for commo and Boom-Boom for demolitions."

"Boom-Boom handled weapons," said Fetterman.

"That's right," said Gerber. "I meant Sully Smith."

"Yeah," said Fetterman. "Especially if you want to drop one of those bridges. He'd be disappointed if we let someone else do it."

"T.J. is with Bromhead at Song Be. We could steal him. Who else?"

"That would give us a good core," said Fetterman. "We couldn't divide the team, and we'd have trouble if someone got sick or killed, but that would do it. We could bring in Santini and maybe pull in a couple of guys from here to round things out."

"Yeah, though we don't need to worry about that yet."

Fetterman hesitated, then asked, "Captain, are you sure this is a good idea?"

"What do you mean?"

Fetterman shrugged. "Have you thought this thing through all the way?"

"Tony, we've been here for what, six months? And what have we done in that time? Covert missions that seem to have no impact on the war effort. Fuck around in the north or Cambodia, stop the enemy temporarily and then get out. Charlie filters back in and nothing's accomplished. Nothing tangible's accomplished. This is a way to see some positive results."

"But, sir," said Fetterman, "that's not our job."

Gerber smiled. "You've been to the Unconventional Warfare School. You've sat in on the lectures and the classes telling us we have to see the overall picture. Now we get to Vietnam and we have all these generals and colonels telling us we don't know the big picture. That's a load of crap. That's what Meyers, the reporter last night, told me."

"So you're going out on your own to establish your own little empire?"

A look of anger flashed across Gerber's face. Then suddenly he was calm. "That's it exactly. Are you in or out?"

"Hell, Captain, you know me. I'm in."

"Good. Now, we've got a hell of a lot of work to do. I want to hit the field tomorrow morning if possible."

WHEN THEY BROKE UP, Fetterman walked out into the blazing sunlight of the tropical afternoon, carrying his M-16 with him. The air was wet and heavy and coated him with sweat within seconds of stepping out. Ragged black stains formed under his arms and down his back. He pulled out his sunglasses and put them on, then stood and blinked until his eyes adjusted.

His task was simple. He walked around the edge of the building, a low one-story structure with a tin roof and sandbags, until he came to the jeep he'd parked there earlier. He stared at it for a moment and then decided to leave it where it was. There weren't many parking places at Hotel Three, and there was no guarantee the jeep would be there when he returned.

He angled across the hot tarmac, feeling the heat burn through the soles of his jungle boots. When he reached the road, he stepped over the white chain that formed a border. As he walked along, he thought about his plan for a quick flight out to see Minh to ask him to supply a company of strikers for their new camp. Temporarily. Until they could form their own strike companies from the locals.

There was no reason for Minh to refuse, unless he had something else going on. If that was the case, Fetterman could always head out to Moc Hoa where the Mike Force was based. He could get a company there, though he'd prefer to use Minh's troops if he could.

He reached the small gate, where an air policeman stood guard, keeping the Vietnamese out of the area of the World's Largest PX and Hotel Three. The guard nodded as Fetterman passed through it.

He walked along the chain-link fence across the street from the PX. A group of soldiers stood around the entrance, but none of them went in. Fetterman kept walking and passed the movie theater entrance. It was a real theater, with seats and popcorn, and not just a sheet hung on a wall.

He walked around the corner, up the street and entered a large gate. Hotel Three was on the other side of it—an expanse of grass and concrete pads for helicopters. Three, with their rotors tied down, were lined up next to the fence that separated the helipad from the rest of Tan Son Nhut.

The tower was near the gate. It was a tall wooden structure that allowed the controllers to see the helipad and the operations on the airfield. Under it was the terminal. Men who wanted flights out to their units, and flight crews coming in, checked there to see what had to be done.

Fetterman entered and glanced at the men sitting around on a variety of broken-down furniture. The soldiers were all youngsters. Teenagers. Boys who had graduated from high school a year before. Boys whose biggest problem had been getting their hands inside their dates' clothes. Now they were waiting for rides out to base camps and fire bases so that they could engage other young men in war.

Shaking his head, Fetterman moved to the waist-high counter that blocked off one end of the waiting room. Behind it was a white board indicating the haphazardly scheduled flights. Nothing was going directly out to Ap Tan Hoa, but that wasn't surprising.

"Can I help you, Sarge?" asked the young man working behind the counter. He had shaggy hair, a *pistolero* mustache and a peeling face and wore an OD T-shirt that looked as if it had just come out of the washer. If Fetterman had to guess his age, he would have said the kid was no more than fifteen.

"Need to get out to Ap Tan Hoa."

The kid turned and looked back at the scheduling board. "Nothing going there. I can get you out to Cu Chi and maybe Duc Hoa. You talk to the pilot and maybe he'll take you on out to Ap Tan Hoa. That's not far from Cu Chi. Give him a little more flight time."

"When's the flight leaving?"

"Guys went over to the PX about an hour ago. I imagine they'll be back any minute."

Fetterman nodded. "Pencil in my name."

"Sure. Sergeant? . . ."

"Fetterman."

"I'll let you know when they're ready for takeoff."

Fetterman turned and walked over to the waiting room. There was an empty chair near a dirt-streaked window. He sat down to wait for his flight.

WITH FETTERMAN GONE, Gerber stood up. He pulled on his jungle jacket and buttoned the four buttons on the front of it. Then he turned, picked up the map and the Intel folder and grabbed his M-16 from the corner where it rested. As he left the room, he turned off the lights.

He exited the SOG building and walked out to the parking area. Unlike Fetterman, he climbed into the jeep, treating the hot seat with care. He unlocked the padlock and chain looped through the steering wheel and dropped them onto the floor, then started the engine and twisted in the seat so that he could back up. Spinning the wheel, he pulled out of the lot and drove down the street that Fetterman had used minutes before.

Gerber turned off the road and followed another that took him through a different area of the base. He drove by two-story buildings with sandbags around the ground floors. These were white-and-green buildings that could have been on any base in the World had it not been for the sandbags. Gerber was glad he didn't have quarters on the top floor of one of them, and wondered if the attics of the buildings were lined with sandbags. The roof would detonate the mortar or rocket and the sandbags would absorb the shrapnel.

He continued on until he came to the huge brick building that Crinshaw had built on Tan Son Nhut a year or so earlier. It was the same building where Crinshaw had tried Fetterman and Tyme for murder, and the scene of Gerber's triumph over the general. They had mousetrapped him so that he had no choice but to release Fetterman and Tyme, or rather, drop the charges against them.

Gerber smiled as he remembered the confrontation. He, along with Morrow, had gathered information of illegal activities that would have topped Crinshaw if he hadn't dropped the charges against Fetterman and Tyme. Before they could get that arranged, though, Fetterman had escaped from LBJ and then sprung Tyme. They had gotten to Bangkok.

Crinshaw had DEROSed after that. From the moment Crinshaw had left South Vietnam, Gerber's life had been easier. A Special Forces colonel had been promoted to Crinshaw's position, and he understood the needs of the Green Berets. Soon after that he received his first star.

General Bruce Platt had only one tour as a Special Forces officer, but he wasn't like some of the men coming into the Special Forces now. He had gone through the Unconventional Warfare School and had participated in a few covert missions. He understood the needs of the Green Berets. He understood that it was sometimes necessary to slip out of the confines of normal warfare to defeat an enemy who would use anything possible to win.

Gerber pulled up in front of the headquarters building. Two flagpoles were set in the center of the sidewalk. The American flag fluttered on one pole, and the South Vietnamese banner was on the other. There were flowers in a small garden at the base of the poles, and a Vietnamese man crouched there, weeding them.

Gerber locked up the jeep, retrieved his weapon and the files and walked up to the doors. He opened them and was hit with the first wave of cold air. Passing through, he got to the second set of doors and opened them. It was like stepping into a meat locker. It was so cold that he shivered as he stood there for a moment, letting his body acclimatize.

The walls near him were painted light green. There were posters on the walls, the same ones he had seen over at MACV Headquarters. One poster showed a beautiful Vietnamese woman holding an AK. The caption read The Enemy.

There was green tile on the floors and white tile on the ceilings. To his left was a single door that stood open so that he could see the large room beyond it. A counter divided the room, and a half-dozen clerks sat back there waiting to help.

He moved down the hallway to a T-intersection and then to the stairs that led up to the second floor. Moving down the hallway, he came to a solid oak door. Without knocking, he opened it and stepped in.

Two desks faced him. Behind one sat a Vietnamese woman who was supposed to be a secretary. Gerber knew she couldn't type or file and could barely communicate in English. She was there because of the treaty agreements with the South Vietnamese. The Americans, for their use of South Vietnamese soil, had to hire Vietnamese workers whether they could do the job or not. At least the woman looked good. Most of them didn't even have that qualification.

Behind the other desk was a master sergeant in starched fatigues. Balding and graying, he had bright blue eyes and fleshy features. He was lightly tanned, indicating he didn't get out during the day very much.

"Like to see the general," said Gerber.

The sergeant glanced at the calendar near his blotter. "He has a meeting in a few minutes."

"Won't take long."

"Yes, sir. Please wait."

The sergeant stood, opened the door behind him and leaned in. There was a quick, muffled conversation and then he turned. "Go right in."

"Thanks."

Gerber entered the inner office. It was paneled in dark wood. A window opposite him had an air conditioner built under it. Platt was sitting behind his desk, his back to the window. There was a small rug on the floor and framed pictures on the wall, most of them scenes of South Vietnam. An American flag took up one corner.

As Gerber entered, Platt looked up and waved him into the office. "Have a seat."

Gerber sat down and pulled the magazine from his weapon before leaning it against the side of the chair. He then looked at Platt, waiting for him to finish.

"Hang on a second, Captain," said Platt. He was a big man, at least six-four, and weighed over two hundred pounds. His hair was thinning slightly and was turning gray. He wore a khaki uniform with a single row of ribbons above the pocket, all of them combat awards. Finally he put down his pen and looked at Gerber. "Now, what can I do for you?"

"I've been looking at the abandoned camp at Xa Cat and at the infiltration of enemy soldiers and supplies from Cambodia, and feel we should reopen it."

Platt leaned back in his chair and studied Gerber. "Making policy decisions now, Captain?"

"No, sir. Made a few observations and thought we could change the situation with a minimum of effort. Six or seven American soldiers and a full company of South Vietnamese strikers."

"Let me see what you've got," said Platt.

Gerber handed over the map and the Intel reports that he had brought with him.

Platt glanced at them and nodded. "When did you plan to get in there?"

"If we can coordinate the aviation assets, the supplies and the manpower, we could be in there tomorrow at dawn."

"Pretty fast."

"Yes, sir, but then there isn't much more that we have to do. There are fire bases around, a helipad, and the procedures for this have already been established."

"What do you want from me?"

Gerber grinned. "Your approval."

Platt looked at the map and then at the folder. "There's one thing you haven't mentioned. One thing you may not know. The VC, or maybe I should say the NVA, are massing for another push toward Saigon. They want to see themselves on TV again. A camp where you want it would be right in the middle of one of the major infiltration routes."

"Makes us important," said Gerber.

"You know," said Platt, "if you hadn't come in here with this plan, I would have had to find someone to command a unit to be deployed into that area. Aviation assets and the supplies are already dedicated."

"Then it's a go?" asked Gerber.

"It's a go."

Gerber rocked back in his chair and started to grin. Suddenly he wondered what he had gotten himself into. He couldn't help feeling that he had been manipulated.

5

AP TAN HOA, RVN

The swirling cloud of red dust settled slowly. Fetterman hesitated in the rear of the helicopter and then dropped onto the sunbaked ground. Two strikers, short Vietnamese wearing tiger fatigues and holding M-1 carbines, watched from a flimsy-looking gate of gray wood and rusting barbed wire. There were bunkers of green rubberized sandbags on either side of it.

Fetterman moved around to the cockpit and stepped up so that he could shout at the pilot. "How long can you wait?"

"Ten minutes," said the man. "I might be able to get another flight out here in about an hour."

Fetterman nodded. "Wait the ten minutes, and if I don't show, take off. I'll be out here in an hour for the flight home."

"We'll do what we can."

Fetterman stepped down and turned toward the gate. The Vietnamese guards were still standing there. Neither showed the slightest curiosity in the helicopter or in Fetterman. He walked toward them.

The camp, an abandoned French fort, was a three-sided affair with six strands of barbed wire around it. The walls were low, only two or three feet above the ground, with sides that were slanted to deflect bullets. The stone used to construct it was dark brown, standing out in stark contrast to the surrounding light browns, reds and greens. There were firing ports with thin slits for the defenders, and trenches connected the bunkers with the command structure in the center of the fort. Towers stood in each corner, manned by guards supplied with machine guns and searchlights.

As Fetterman approached the gate, one of the soldiers opened it. He stepped back, as if Fetterman frightened him. The other asked, "You want?"

"Captain Minh."

"Huh?"

"Dai Uy Minh."

"Ah. You follow." The man whirled and trotted off across the open field in the center of the fort.

The living quarters, equipment storage and armories were all underground, leaving as little as possible aboveground for enemy gunners or snipers. Crossing the field, Fetterman felt exposed. It wasn't a feeling he had in American camps or in the jungle. Here there was nothing between him and the single clump of coconut and banana trees half a klick to the north.

The man disappeared into a hole in the ground. Fetterman reached it and stepped down into the narrow passage. Ducking down, he smelled the odor of freshly turned earth. Dim light came from a single bulb at the end of the narrow corridor. If it weren't for the concrete floor and the propped-up ceiling, Fetterman might have thought he'd fallen into a VC tunnel complex.

The man entered a room and Fetterman followed. Again he had to step down, but this time the ceiling was higher and the room larger. Light poured in through a slit high on the wall that opened to the outside.

Minh sat behind a flimsy field desk painted dark green. There was a filing cabinet to the right and a table to the left. In front of the desk were two chairs for visitors. The floor was dirty concrete, and one wall made of cinder blocks was stained red by the dust. The others were made of thick planks that bled sap.

Minh looked up when Fetterman entered, stared and then slowly smiled. He came to his feet and held out a hand. "Master Sergeant."

Fetterman, ignoring the Vietnamese striker, stepped across the room to shake Minh's hand. "Dai Uy."

"I haven't seen you since I escaped from that camp so long ago." His voice was quiet, modulated and had a definite British accent. His training had been at Sandhurst in Great Britain rather than in France. Minh, typical of the Vietnamese, was a short, thin man with jet-black straight hair and almond-shaped dark brown eyes. He was clean-shaven and wore a tailored uniform with black tiger stripes on it. Fetterman knew that Minh was one of the few truly professional Vietnamese army officers. Unlike so many others who had bought their ranks, he had earned his.

Fetterman laughed, remembering the smoking ruins of the camp that he and Minh had fought to defend. He couldn't remember the name of it. The VC and NVA had wanted to take the camp, and it had seemed that the defense was going to collapse. Some of those caught on the walls had found themselves surrounded and had to escape and evade. Fetterman, Gerber and a force of Special Forces and Vietnamese strikers had holed up in the redoubt, holding off the enemy until help had arrived.

"Ran out on us too soon," said Fetterman.

"Had no choice," said Minh, still grinning.

"There are always choices," said Fetterman.

"You going to hold this one small indiscretion against me forever?"

Fetterman glanced at the chair, and when Minh nodded toward it, he sat down. "I think you can be forgiven," said Fetterman, "providing you help me out."

Minh sat down and continued to grin. "I should have known you wouldn't come out for a strictly social visit, old boy."

Fetterman propped his M-16 against a chair. "That's the trouble with this, isn't it? No time to visit old friends unless it's all business."

"Would you care for something to drink?" He didn't wait for an answer, but opened a door and took out a bottle of Beam's Choice.

Fetterman laughed. It had been a ritual at the old Camp A-555. Everyone shared in the Beam's. Fetterman leaned forward, snagged the bottle and opened it. He sniffed the contents, tilted the bottle to his lips and drank deeply. Lowering the bottle, he looked into Minh's eyes. "That's smooth."

Minh accepted the bottle, took a drink, then set it aside. "What can I do for you?"

"Not wasting any time yourself."

Minh shrugged, a gesture he had learned from the Americans. "There are things I need to do. Things only I can take care of."

"I understand," said Fetterman.

"So, what can I do for you?"

"I'd like to borrow a company of your best strikers."

Minh laughed. "For how long?"

"Probably no more than six weeks. Until we can get our own force trained and established."

"When?"

"I'll have to coordinate with Captain Gerber, but we'll probably have the aviation assets here in the morning."

Minh nodded. "How is Captain Gerber?"

"He's fine."

Minh was silent for a moment, then asked, "Just what is going on here?"

That was a question Fetterman wouldn't answer for just anyone. Too many of the Vietnamese let too much information slide so that the enemy heard it. The saying in Saigon was that whatever the South Vietnamese knew, the VC knew.

But Minh was different. He hated the Communists and knew that if they won, thousands, maybe millions would die. He knew that the first order of business would be to round up everyone who had ever fought against the Communists and eliminate them. He would do nothing to help the enemy.

So Fetterman said, "We're going to put a camp in the middle of an infiltration route north of here."

"And by doing that, you'll slow down infiltration of arms and supplies to the enemy, making my job here easier."

"That could happen, too."

"What do these men have to take in the way of equipment?"

Fetterman shrugged. "We haven't really thought about that. How about a basic load of ammo and rations and supplies for a week? We'll get in resupply long before that, or we'll have to get out."

"They'll have the same when they're returned?"

Fetterman understood what Minh was asking. He wanted to know if the men would be given a basic load of ammo and supplies for a week when they returned. If they were, it would mean that none of the supplies would come out of Minh's stocks.

"Certainly."

"All right, then," said Minh. "I've got a good company that I'd like to see get some field experience. You can have them."

"Great. Only one other thing. I'll want to meet the liaison officer."

"No problem. You're looking at him, old sport."

Fetterman chuckled. He couldn't help himself. It was the combination of Minh's clipped British speech and his enthusiasm, along with the prospect of working with the Vietnamese officer again. "That'll be fine. Captain Gerber will be happy, too."

"Then let's get to work."

Fetterman nodded, stood up and grabbed his M-16. "Let's."

GERBER LEFT THE MEETING with Platt, figuring there must be something else he could do. It was hard to believe he would be landing in the field in twelve hours without any briefings, weapons checks and planning sessions. Normally a mission took two weeks to get into the field. Usually a team would be isolated for a week of intensive study before the kickoff.

But this wasn't a covert operation. They'd be landing with a group of Vietnamese strikers into a camp that was already partially built. Artillery and air support was as close as the radio. It was an operation to put in a camp. It didn't demand the rigid security or planning that many other missions required.

He left the building and walked out to where his jeep waited. Stopping short of the flagpoles, he watched as the Vietnamese gardener continued to work there. Gerber wondered just what could take so long. The flowers at the base of the poles didn't look all that good, and the small garden wasn't all that great.

Man must be a VC, thought Gerber. He probably hung around the building all day, watching to see who came and who left so that he could report it to someone in Saigon.

Gerber watched the man for a few minutes as he dug in the red dirt around the flagpole, pulling a weed and then squatting there, staring up into the deep blue sky. No hurry. No rush. Collect his money from the Americans for his labors and then off to Saigon to sell his information.

Finally Gerber walked on by and headed for his jeep. Placing his weapon in the back, he climbed into the driver's seat. For a moment he didn't know what to do. Platt was handling everything that he would normally do, such as assembling the men. They would meet at Hotel Three in the morning and then be off—a combat assault to Xa Cat, just as the leg infantry operated.

After unlocking the steering wheel, Gerber backed the jeep out and drove to the gate. He slowed there and looked at the long line of Vietnamese trying to get onto the base for the night shift. These were the men and women who would work the clubs and mess halls and do some of the lowly janitorial jobs.

Gerber had told people for weeks that it wasn't a good idea to have many potential enemies on the base at night, but the brass had learned nothing during Tet. People were hired, those with some kind of political pull first, and then were checked. Gerber didn't know of one person who had ever been fired because a check had come back negative. Anyone who was hired had a job right up until the time he or she was killed storming the bunkers while participating in an assault.

"What a stupid way to fight a war," he said to himself, and immediately thought about what the reporter had said the night before. The Americans didn't know how to win. They were certainly proving it.

Gerber pulled out into the street and joined the traffic. He slowed behind a Lambretta and watched as the two Vietnamese women in it tried to get his attention. One of them stared at him and slowly pulled on the hem of her skirt, sliding it higher.

"Hey, you, GI. Good time. Five hunnert P. You like. You numbah one."

Gerber shook his head, but that didn't discourage them. One of them stood up, balancing precariously, and lifted her skirt to her waist. She wiggled, turned and thrust her butt out at him.

The light changed then and the driver of the Lambretta started off. The woman lost her balance and fell to her knees. Before she fell out of the Lambretta, her friend grabbed her.

Gerber continued along, then turned. He was assaulted from all sides by rock and roll and country music coming from the bars that lined the streets. Men and women walked along, some of them dodging into the bars and some of them diving into the alleys for the little privacy they could catch there.

That was something that never ceased to amaze Gerber. An American soldier who never used the latrine when there were others around to watch would expose everything if he was with a woman. Grab her, pull her panties down and get her into the alley. Quick and dirty. Then out to the sidewalk as if nothing had happened.

He'd seen it all on the streets of Saigon—drug deals and sex, fights that left men bleeding on the sidewalk. It wasn't dangerous enough in the boondocks, so the men had to find new thrills in the Saigon nightlife. They had to do it quick because a three-day pass expired much too soon.

He tried to ignore the sights around him because they were too depressing. There were too many young men away from home for the first time who acted the way soldiers in movies acted. The Army let them down. They weren't taught what they needed to know to protect themselves from the hucksters, the whores and the crooks.

Gerber turned another corner and the traffic thinned out, but the noise was as heavy and the stench was just as bad. There was a parking place on the street, no more than fifty yards from his hotel. He pulled into it and cut the engine of the jeep.

Pedestrians swirled around him—American men and Vietnamese women, all with one thing on their minds. The Americans paid for it, and the Vietnamese were only too happy to take it.

Gerber locked the steering wheel of the jeep, grabbed his weapon and hopped out. Not many of the soldiers on the street were armed. The majority of them were on a pass from the field, and before any of them were allowed into Saigon, their weapons were locked in the armories of their home units. Gerber had his because he lived in the hotel when in Saigon.

The doorman hurried down the three steps that led up into the building. Pretending he hadn't seen the M-16, he opened the door for the captain and held out a palm for a tip. Gerber passed him without giving him any money. Each morning Gerber or Fetterman gave the man a dollar, figuring that was enough tip for the day.

The interior of the hotel was cool, the climate controlled by three tons of machinery installed on the roof at the insistence of the Americans. The lobby was wide, with marble floors and huge marble pillars. There were couches and chairs arranged in conversation areas, potted palms and a few tables scattered around the floor. At the far end was a teak counter with clerks working behind it.

Gerber ignored all the people in the lobby, many of them Vietnamese who had slipped in for a moment of comfort before the bellman and hotel staff rounded them up and threw them out. Of course, if they were young, attractive women, they were allowed to stay.

Gerber reached the elevator, rode it up to his floor, got out and walked down the hall. It was dimly lighted. The carpeting was threadbare and the walls were dirty. When he got to his door, he opened it and stepped into the room. The interior was cool, thanks to the small air conditioner built into the wall under the grimy window.

The room was small, with a double bed that had a tiny ceiling fan revolving above it, a wardrobe against one wall and an old chair pushed into a corner. Off to the right was the bathroom. The door was closed.

And then Morrow stepped out, a towel wrapped around her hair. She wore nothing else. For an instant she looked startled, and then grinned. "You could have knocked."

"Why? It's my room." He felt awkward standing there, looking at her naked body, his M-16 clutched in his hand. He walked to the wardrobe, unlocked it and set his weapon inside. "There."

Morrow moved closer, putting a hand on her hip. "What's the plan for this evening?"

Gerber turned and looked at her. Fetterman would be back in an hour or so, and there were still things that had to be checked if they were going to hit the field. He needed to get back to the radio room over at the SOG building, but couldn't do anything there until Fetterman returned. At the moment everything was in the hands of others. He was as useful as a fifth wheel on a wagon.

Morrow made no move to cover herself. She stood there and grinned at him expectantly.

"I've got a few hours before I have to do anything," said Gerber.

"Hey, don't knock yourself out."

"I simply meant that nothing was planned right now. I've got to meet Tony later and then check in over at MACV. But I don't have to do any of that now."

"Oh," she said, her voice suddenly lower. She reached up slowly and pulled the towel from her hair, tossing it aside. Gerber found the motion strangely erotic, since she was already completely naked.

"I've got an idea," she said.

Gerber nodded. "Let's go with it."

She moved toward him without another word.

6

FORT POLK, LOUISIANA

Major General Billy Joe Crinshaw was bored by the endless slide shows narrated by monotone-voiced officers who likened themselves to the men who had explained the Normandy invasion plan to the waiting armies of World War II. Crinshaw wasn't interested in the historical significance of the recent Tet offensive or why the Khe Sanh siege was a good example of American bravery. He didn't care about the black market operating in Saigon or how the incidence of various venereal diseases was rising as the VC started waging a type of germ warfare by flooding Saigon with infected whores.

Crinshaw sat there in the semidarkness, sipping the coffee that a sergeant was all too willing to get for him, listening to briefing after briefing and wishing he could get home again to Jennifer, who was probably sitting in the living room naked, watching TV and waiting for him.

Finally the current briefer asked, "Do you have any questions, General?"

"Has anyone here bothered to learn that I've already had a tour in South Vietnam?"

"Sir?"

Crinshaw set his coffee cup on the mahogany table in front of him. "I'm already aware of all this. I was in Vietnam a little more than eighteen months ago. I don't have to be told all this again."

"Yes, sir," said the officer, taken aback by the comment. "Anything else?"

"No."

"Then I'll turn the briefing over to Major Johnson. He'll discuss the current logistical problems in Three Corps as they relate to the various fire bases and the lower echelon units."

"No!" said Crinshaw.

"Sir?"

"Sergeant, get the lights," Crinshaw ordered. When they came on, Crinshaw could see the remainder of the small room—the slide projector on a small table, the screen hung on the cinder-block wall and the lectern where the captain in starched khakis waited. Crinshaw stood. "Is there nothing more relevant than what I've already heard?"

"Sir, we have two hours of briefings scheduled."

"I want to see General Wilder."

The captain nodded and hurried to the door. He disappeared through it, and as it closed after him, the sergeant laughed. "You put the fear of God into him."

"But not you, Sergeant?" asked Crinshaw.

The sergeant shook his head. He was an older man, pushing fifty. He'd been in the Army for nearly thirty years, entering it as a young man trying to escape the last of the Great Depression. He'd been in the Army when it had taken three or four years just to get the first stripe and become a PFC. Now there were men who made buck sergeant in three or four years.

But the point was that he'd been through all of World War II and he'd been in Korea and Vietnam. He'd seen the worst of combat and had served under hundreds of officers. One more general didn't scare him. There was nothing the general could do to him. His pension was set, even if he was thrown out of the Army the next day.

"No, sir," he said.

"How'd you like to come to Vietnam as one of my aides, Sergeant?"

"No, sir. I don't think I'd care for that."

"And if I made it an order?"

Now the sergeant grinned. "I can have my gear ready by 0900 tomorrow."

"You don't bluff."

The old sergeant, standing there in slightly wrinkled fatigues, two rows of combat decorations above his breast pocket along with a Combat Infantryman's Badge and jump wings, grinned broadly. He moved over, pulled out the other chair and sat down. It was a breach of military protocol, but it also demonstrated, beyond any doubt, the power the old sergeant felt.

"No, sir. I don't bluff."

"Well, then," said Crinshaw. "How'd you like to accompany me on this trip overseas? That is, if I don't make it an order for you?"

"I think I'd like that just fine, General."

"I'll check with the G-1 and get the paperwork organized. We'll be out of here in two days."

"I suspected I would be getting another tour, but not quite this quickly."

The door opened then and Wilder stepped in. "You tired of these briefings, General?"

"I'm afraid, General, that I'm learning nothing of value in them. I've spent the past few months reading the Intel message traffic, as well as the various assessments written by the CIA, the DIA, NSA and anyone else who can put a pen to paper. Like everyone else, I've been watching this thing, and I don't need some twenty-five-year-old captain telling me that the VC are sending venereal-diseased whores into Saigon."

Wilder laughed. "Germ warfare at its worst, and the networks are staying away from the story. You'd think they'd love to do an in-depth story on it."

Wilder moved into the room, and the sergeant jumped up so that the general could have the chair. "So, what do you want?"

"Unless you've got something scheduled that is important, I'd like to get out of here and spend some time with my wife before I have to get on that plane."

Wilder glanced at the sergeant and snapped his fingers. "You got an agenda?"

The sergeant turned, moved to the projector table and picked up the clipboard sitting there. "There's Major Johnson to brief on logistics, Captain Mitchell on airmobile operations and Captain Hernandez on close air support."

"Nothing there that'll help me," said Crinshaw.

"Nothing at all," said Wilder. "Sergeant, inform those officers that their briefings have been cancelled."

"Yes, General."

Wilder then turned his attention to Crinshaw. "What are you going to do now?"

"Go home and see what Jennifer has on her mind. And pack. Two sets of fatigues, some underwear and one set of civilian clothes. That's all I'm taking, with the exception of my shaving kit."

"Pistol?"

Crinshaw knew that Wilder was referring to the Colt Commander, a 9 mm weapon issued permanently to all Army general officers. Crinshaw had one already, and if he arrived in Vietnam without it, they'd probably issue him another.

"I'm taking the one suitcase and that's it."

Wilder nodded and looked at his watch. It was very late, or very early, depending on one's frame of reference. "I'll take a look at the schedule and see if there's anything that needs to be done. If not, I'll cancel it all."

"I appreciate that." Crinshaw got to his feet. "Sergeant Seneff indicated he'd like to accompany me to Vietnam."

"Does he really want to do that, or was he going along with what you said."

"Do you think Sergeant Seneff would do anything he really didn't want to do?"

"Your point is well taken." Wilder nodded. "I'll get the orders cut for him."

"Then I'm on my way home," said Crinshaw.

HALF A WORLD AWAY, Lieutenant Tuyen Van Thien was sitting in a hut, listening to a political officer talk about the evil of the American soldiers in South Vietnam. It was a lecture he didn't want to hear, but one he had to attend. The political officers took down the names of the men who were absent and then spoke to them on an individual basis. It was not something Thien wanted to experience himself.

Thien didn't like the lectures, especially after he had spent the day in the field, evading the evil Americans. He didn't need some political officer who never got into the field to tell him about it. Thien was the one the Americans were trying to kill. He was the one they had chased that very day.

Then he grinned. It hadn't been much of a chase. They had fled into the jungle as the helicopters had swooped in on the scene of the ambush. Their machine guns had been blazing, the M-60 rounds snapping through the leaves above him.

The men had run, the retreat disintegrating into a rout. Each man had been trying to save his own life. None of them had been worried about the others.

And Thien had led the retreat. He'd kept his AK, unlike some of the others who had thrown away their weapons in fear. He ran forward, leaping over fallen logs and small bushes and dodging around trees. He jumped a narrow stream, slipped on the mud of the bank and fell to one knee. Water soaked through his uniform. He scrambled up and continued running deeper into the jungle.

He ran until his breath came in gasps and his throat was burned raw. He ran until his sides ached and the pain radiated from his chest up into his arms. He ran until he thought he could run no more, and then pushed himself further.

Behind him he could hear the shooting of the Americans—machine guns and M-16s. Nothing was aimed at Thien and his men because the Americans were too far away, still on the landing zone with the remains of the patrol they'd ambushed.

Thien tripped then, catching his foot in the root of a giant teak tree. Sprawling onto his stomach, he lost the grip on his weapon. He wanted to get up but didn't have the energy. Instead he lay there, sucking at the hot, wet air, hoping the pains in his chest didn't signal a heart attack. Finally he was able to get onto his hands and knees. He glanced to the right and saw his squad scattered around him, all of them breathing hard.

"Get to your feet," he ordered, forcing himself to stand. Perspiration poured off him. He moved forward and picked up his weapon. It had fallen among the leaves and rotting vegetation on the jungle floor. Mud was smeared on the stock, but none had clogged the barrel.

"Everyone up," he said again, forcing out the words. As he spoke, he heard the distant boom of artillery. The Americans were trying to find and kill them, but they didn't know where they were. The rounds were exploding somewhere to the south, several miles away.

But that had been earlier, right after the ambush. He'd gotten out faster than he'd wanted, but it was the damn helicopters. They hovered over the landscape like vultures looking for something on the verge of dying. They chased Thien away. Kept him and his men from collecting the spoils.

Now, sitting there, the political officer was telling him the Americans were weak, impatient and stupid. They had been surprised and injured during Tet, and if the NVA and VC could mount a similar operation, the Americans could be driven from the South.

"Vietnam will be a single country again. I'll be able to walk the streets of my home again. I'll be able to live in Saigon where I was born."

"When?" asked one of the men.

"Soon. We're massing for another attack on Saigon."

Thien got to his feet. "Why must we fight in Saigon, Comrade?"

"Because of the Americans. When the fighting is close to Saigon, the American newspapers and television stations cover it. Their reporters, seeing enemy soldiers in the streets, make claims that can only help our cause."

The political officer grinned and continued, "When Americans sitting down to their dinner see our glorious soldiers running down the streets that only hours before were haunted by Americans exploiting the womanhood of Vietnam, they get scared. They won't believe their generals are telling them the truth. They'll think the war effort is on the edge of collapse and they'll call their political representatives, demanding an end to the war."

"But we can't win in Saigon," said Thien.

"It doesn't matter," said the officer. "The pictures of our soldiers in the streets are all that's important."

"When?" asked Thien.

"Soon."

CRINSHAW WALKED into the house as the sun was just beginning to come up. He was tired. His body ached, even though he had done nothing more than attend briefings. He dropped his hat onto the small table in the entryway and then dropped his keys into the center of it, which stretched the material slightly so that when he wore the hat it had the look of the crushed hats the Army Air Corps pilots had worn twenty years earlier.

"Jenny? You awake?"

He walked into the living room and found her asleep on the couch. The air conditioner had been turned off so that it was hot in the room. She was naked and sweaty. Her hair was as wet as if she had just stepped out of the shower. Rather than wake her immediately, Crinshaw looked at her appraisingly. She was a beautiful young woman who looked as good without clothes as she did with them. Some women promised great things when they were clothed, but the moment the clothes came off the flaws were evident. Not Jennifer.

He crouched near her and took one of her hands in his. Suddenly he missed her. He hadn't even left and he missed her. He wished there was a way he could avoid the year in Vietnam. He'd already had a tour. There were other officers who'd never set foot in Vietnam. It was their turn to go.

Jennifer woke up then. Her eyes flew open, and she stared at him and smiled. She uncoiled then, her free hand over her head as she stretched her toes. The muscles in her body tightened, etching themselves under her smooth, lightly tanned skin, giving her the look of marble. "You're home."

"Finally. Time's running out."

"Yes," she said. She rolled over and pulled his hand to her cheek. "Will you be in any danger?"

The answer to the question, Crinshaw knew, was no. As a general, he would be in virtually no danger at all. If she had been a reporter, he would have told her that everyone, every day, was in danger. Sniper bullets and mortar shells were random events that could kill anyone at any time. He would hint that he would be leading soldiers into the field to search out Charlie and destroy him where he lived.

But this was his wife, the woman he loved, and although he wanted her respect, he wouldn't lie to her. He didn't want her to worry about him.

"No," he said. "Very little danger. You'll probably be in more danger here than I'll be in. Drunk drivers and murderers and a hundred other mundane dangers."

She sat up, ignoring her own nudity. "You're not just saying that?"

"No," he said. "I'm not just saying that. I might pretend with others, but not with you."

"Do you have to go? Can't you call someone and stop this? Isn't there anyone you know?"

"This is my job," he said quietly. "I suppose I could get out of it for now, but I'd just have to do it later. Maybe in a year. Maybe less."

"The war could be over in a year," she said.

Crinshaw got up on the couch beside her and looked down at her sweat-slicked body. A bead of perspiration dripped from her chin and landed between her breasts. "Why is it so hot in here?"

"I wanted to meet you naked, and the air conditioner was making me cold."

"I'd better go pack."

She refused to release his hand. "Can't you do anything?"

For a moment, just one moment, he thought about it. He thought about the calls he could make to stop his tour. And he wanted to. He couldn't stand the ache in his gut as he thought of the year without her, thought about what it would be like in South Vietnam while she was still here, waiting. He thought about how long 365 days could be, and he thought about how generals were sometimes required to spend more than a year in Vietnam.

And then a single thought came to him. A single name seemed to spring at him. Gerber. The Special Forces captain was in Vietnam, and now it would be possible to get even with him. Wreck his career completely.

He looked at Jennifer and shook his head. "I have my duty. I've got to follow through on it."

She nodded once and then began to cry. She couldn't help herself.

7

MACV-SOG BUILDING
TAN SON NHUT

When Gerber drove up several hours later, the parking lot was crowded with vehicles, all the lights were on and there was a babble of conversation coming from the interior that was occasionally overpowered by the jet traffic taking off and landing on the airfield. He stood out there for a moment in the wet heat of the predawn and listened to the voices coming from inside the building. He watched a single jet take off, climbing rapidly, the blue-orange of the exhaust glowing brightly. Finally he turned, plucked his weapon from the rear of the jeep and shouldered his rucksack.

He walked around to the front of the building and pulled open the door. Once it had been a screen, but then the Army had bought air conditioners and someone had covered the screen with acetate that was now smeared with dirt. As he stepped into the cool interior the voices stopped. Turning to the right, he saw the men he'd asked Platt to find for him. All of them were there, all dressed for battle, all waiting for instructions.

"Morning, gentlemen," said Gerber.

"Morning, Captain," said Bocker.

Gerber moved into the room. He dropped his rucksack onto the floor, out of the way, and stepped closer. Holding out a hand, he said, "Galvin."

Bocker was one of the older men. He was six feet tall and weighed nearly two hundred pounds. His hair was graying, but age didn't seem to slow him down much. He was the commo man, and Gerber had heard it said that Bocker could put together a radio from tin cans and bits of string. That might not have been true, but it was close.

Next to Bocker was Thomas Jefferson Washington, a huge black man. Now twenty-three, Washington had been trained as both a medic and weapons man. He was a tough young soldier who had grown up in an urban area. The Special Forces had channeled his street-fighting knowledge into jungle fighting. He was a deadly man in a fight who stayed around after it was over trying to save lives.

Gerber moved toward Sergeant Tyme. Justin was a sandy-haired kid with fine features and a spare frame. The Vietnamese diet had done nothing to put weight on him. He was gaunt, and looked as if a strong wind could blow him away. Quiet, and with a love of weapons that bordered on an obsession, Tyme could fix any weapon ever built, regardless of size.

Seated at the table shoved into the corner, drinking a Coke, was Derek Kepler. He glanced up and nodded at Gerber. "Captain."

"How's it going, Derek?"

"Fine, sir."

Last, sitting by himself on the low couch, was Sully Smith. He was a short, stocky man with a dark complexion and a beard almost as heavy as Fetterman's. Smith, the demolitions man, loved blowing things up. The bigger the target, the happier he was.

Gerber shook his hand and then moved back toward the door. He closed it, knowing it wouldn't do much good. The walls were too thin to stop the sound of voices. Leaning against one wall, he said, "Good to see all of you again."

Bocker, the ranking NCO in the room, said, "Thank you, Captain. Now, what in hell is this all about? I had a nice, simple assignment and suddenly I'm on a chopper for here."

Gerber glanced into the faces of each man. "I know, but I've got a deal cooking that requires your help."

"Where's Tony?" asked Tyme.

"I thought he'd be here by now—that was the plan—but I've been told he's still in the field coordinating the strikers. He decided to stay out there for the night."

"Where?" asked Smith suspiciously.

"With Captain Minh's men."

"All right," said Smith.

"So what's the deal?" asked Bocker.

Gerber rubbed his chin and looked at the men he'd assembled. He thought about the men who had been with him at other times. Men who had died doing their duty. The list was getting long now. Longer than he cared to think about, and he was afraid that some of these men would be added to that list. If things went the way they normally did, he could count on it.

Taking a deep breath, he said, "We're going to replay the construction of the old Triple Nickel."

"We're going back there?" asked Tyme.

"No," said Gerber, shaking his head. "We're going to put in a camp where there isn't one now. Right on the infiltration lines, with the hope of inhibiting the enemy." He stopped, then added, "Maybe I should say that we're going to reopen a camp that's been abandoned."

"When?" asked Washington.

"This morning," said Gerber, looking at his watch. "In about an hour and a half."

"Oh, shit!" said Tyme.

FETTERMAN, along with Minh, stood just outside the wire of the old French fort. The strikers, the best company that Minh commanded, were crouched in the knee-high elephant grass, divided into ten loads for the ten helicopters that would be coming in to pick them up. Other members of the battalion who wouldn't be going were scattered farther from the camp, forming a loose ring around the strikers as security. If Charlie tried to sneak up on them, someone would see something. A single shot would be enough to alert everyone to the danger.

Minh was holding the handset of the PRC-25 next to his ear, listening for the message that would announce the arrival of choppers. So far he'd heard nothing other than the static bursts caused by distant thunderstorms rumbling across South Vietnam.

"Perfect weather for this," he said.

Fetterman nodded, studying the lightning flashes that had to be near the Cambodian border. Helicopters always avoided rain and thunderstorms, but the disturbance could give them some cover. Sneak in during the shower, and when the skies cleared, Charlie would find them ready and waiting.

"Ten minutes," said Fetterman.

Minh nodded, the handset still pressed against his ear.

Then, before there was any warning on the radio, they heard the sound of helicopters in the distance. Fetterman turned and scanned the horizon, looking for the choppers.

"Roger, Crusader One Two," said Minh. "We will throw smoke."

Fetterman glanced at the Vietnamese officer and wondered what the helicopter pilot thought of the British accent coming through the radio at him.

Minh pointed at one of his men and ordered in Vietnamese, "Throw a smoke grenade."

The man pulled the grenade from his harness and tossed it out in front of the strikers. There was a dull pop, a flash of flame, and a cloud of purple began to billow, looking mauve in the rising shafts of sunlight.

"ID purple," said the pilot on the radio.

"Roger, purple."

Fetterman moved around and shifted his weapon to his right hand. He looked to the east, squinting into the brightness of the rising sun.

The choppers changed direction, angled to the south and then came back toward the east so that they were moving into the wind. Fetterman watched their progress, and as they started their approach, slipped to one knee. He put a hand up to his boonie hat, holding it on as he turned his back on the choppers. The noise of the engines and the pop of the rotors washed out all other sound.

In a moment there was a swirling cloud of dust and dried grass. It gained strength as the choppers hovered forward before touching down near each of the loads. As the helicopters settled in, the dust and debris blew outward in a dissipating mess. The Vietnamese, not waiting for an order, scrambled forward and climbed into the cargo compartments of the helicopters.

Fetterman, along with Minh, ran toward the lead chopper. Fetterman waited as the Vietnamese officer stepped up on the skid and then hauled himself in. Fetterman followed and sat on the deck, one leg dangling in space. The Vietnamese strikers sat on the troop seat or on the deck, all of them dressed in tiger-striped fatigues and carrying a variety of weapons that had been obsolete by the end of World War II. Each man sat with the butt of his weapon on the floor and the barrel pointed up. It was a measure of discipline instilled by Minh and his officers. The men assumed that position without having to be told.

After sitting there for a moment, the helicopter lifted off and then stopped, hovering a few feet above the ground. The rotor wash tore at the loose grass, whipping it up into the air. Red dust swirled around until it was almost impossible to see the French fort. Fetterman turned his head away from the dust, but the rotor wash caught it all and blew it away from him.

Then suddenly the nose dropped and they were racing across the elephant grass. Crouched in the grass, almost hidden in it, Fetterman saw the strikers who had been put out as security. Two of them were near an M-60 machine gun, and another lay behind a log, his weapon propped against it. Fetterman was sure the man had gone to sleep.

They lifted off, climbing toward the east and then bending around to the west. The thunderstorms were growing and coming toward them. Lightning, looking like the distant explosions of artillery firing, flashed. The air was suddenly cooler as they climbed higher.

Minh was on his knees behind one of the pilot's seats, leaning forward and shouting something at the man. He nodded and then turned to Fetterman. ''What about Gerber?''

''Should be off anytime. They'll have to coordinate on the radio so that we all land at the same time.''

Minh turned and relayed the information to the pilots. He then sat down and stared at the men with him. There was a slight smile on his face, suggesting that he was happy to be away from the routine at the French fort.

THE SINGLE CHOPPER landed on the tarmac in front of the SOG building. It came to a hover, hung there, rocking gently, and then settled to the ground. As the skids touched down, the roar of the engine and the pop of the blades quieted.

Gerber threw open the door and walked across the tarmac. The others followed him. Gerber stopped short and waved them forward. Each man carried his personal weapon and wore his rucksack, loaded with the gear he'd need to survive if, for some reason, they couldn't get the resupply choppers in that afternoon. Each man had enough for a week in the field. Bocker had the added weight of the radios, and Tyme carried an M-60 machine gun, though Gerber had told him they wouldn't need it.

Tyme had the strangest-looking weapon strapped to his back. The young sergeant had told Gerber it was an XM-174, a 40 mm grenade launcher complete with a twelve-round magazine and a small tripod. The types of rounds—HE, willie pete, canister—could be varied. It was an accurate weapon, and when loaded with the HE, it could be very effective at destroying the morale of men in a human-wave attack.

Tyme had grinned and said enthusiastically, "I can't wait to try it out in combat."

"I hope you don't get the chance," Gerber had said.

Washington, along with his medical supplies and bag, carried an M-79 grenade launcher. Not as exotic as the weapon Tyme had, it was still pretty effective.

Smith was loaded down with his explosives, including a couple of claymore mines. He'd already told Gerber that he wanted more of them on the first of the resupply choppers. Trip flares, too. They'd need them to establish the perimeter.

Kepler, who had no specialized equipment, carried extra rounds for Washington and Tyme and extra batteries for

Bocker. He also carried the detonators for Smith because Smith refused to carry both the explosives and the detonators. Kepler didn't mind, figuring he only had to walk out to the chopper and then from the chopper into the camp, a distance of not more than a hundred yards. A simple task. It was unlikely he'd explode before he could get rid of the detonators, or that he'd tire out before he could drop the other equipment.

When the others were on board, Gerber climbed in and then slapped the aircraft commander on the shoulder, holding up a thumb.

The roar in the engines changed, and the rotors began spinning faster, but they didn't move. Two fighter jets took off and climbed out into the threatening weather to the west. A cargo plane landed, followed by an airliner. Then, finally, they lifted to a hover, turned and raced forward.

Tyme closed his eyes, as if he were about to be sick. Bocker grinned and Sully Smith whooped. Tyme leaned forward, glancing down and out at the flashing of the ground under him. Tan Son Nhut fell away and they turned due west. Saigon, a dirty smudge with a golden glow, slipped beneath them.

Gerber sat on the edge of the troop seat and looked out. They flew over rice paddies, which were broken up by clumps of trees. The Saigon River was to the north, but there didn't seem to be defined banks. The river water leaked out into the fields until it looked as if the river was miles wide so that it resembled a narrow, shallow bay.

Slowly the landscape changed until it was drier. The tree lines grew together and the rice paddies faded. They were north of Cu Chi, the giant American base. It was an oval-shaped camp with a column of smoke rising from the northeastern corner. They were passing over forest now, not jungle, scraggly trees only fifteen or twenty feet tall.

They continued north, skirting Dau Tieng, a French rubber plantation. The rubber trees, planted in rows, looked like lines of soldiers marching to the river. And there were clearings, square areas that opened to the sun, surrounded by more trees.

Beyond that the jungle grew. Hills, some of them over a thousand feet high, were covered with dense vegetation, the perfect place for Charlie to hide. Bromhead's camp at Song Be was nestled at the foot of the hills, and Gerber had been told of the problems of operating in that environment. But that wasn't something Gerber would have to worry about.

The door gunner tapped Gerber on the shoulder and leaned toward him. "AC said he's got the flight in sight."

Gerber slipped forward and knelt on the deck between the pilots' armored seats. He tapped the shoulder of the man who wasn't flying. When the pilot turned, Gerber yelled, "We need to take the lead."

"No problem." The pilot moved his foot, depressing the mike button there. Gerber saw his lips move but couldn't hear the words. A moment later the man turned again and said, "We'll be joining the flight in about five minutes. What about an arty prep?"

"Defeats the whole purpose. We want the camp intact as much as possible."

"Suppression?"

Gerber hesitated. He knew that flight crews liked to go in with guns blazing because it kept the enemy dodging bullets. But there could be friendlies in the area. There could be farmers around who didn't like the VC but who didn't like the Americans, either. There was no reason to alienate them further if it could be prevented.

"Normal rules. Return fire for fire received."

"Roger."

Gerber pulled out his map and studied it. He saw the road and the railroad and then looked out, spotting them on the ground. There was a narrow river close to the railroad, and in the distance, the city of An Loc.

To the right, out the cargo compartment door, he could see the rising hills. These were small, compared to those near the Song Be camp, no more than three hundred feet high. And perched on top of one, the vegetation still cut back, was the abandoned camp.

Gerber pointed at it and yelled, "There!"

"I see it."

They turned toward the camp, which looked like a red wound beginning to heal. The hill sloped away on one side, which would make it difficult for the enemy to attack. Trees and bushes grew on the plateau now, trying to reclaim the summit. Tall grass covered most of it, though the remains of the bunkers, the fighting holes and the foundations of the structures that had been there were still evident.

One of the gunships broke off. It dived toward the camp, screaming over it no more than a hundred feet above the ground. It twisted around and came back. A smoke grenade tumbled from the rear, not to mark the landing site, but to show the pilots the wind direction. They were now close to the squall line. Black clouds boiled just across the border, no more than ten or twelve miles away. The wind had picked up, blowing at fifteen or twenty knots, and the last thing the pilots wanted to do was land downwind.

The AC turned in his seat and glanced at Gerber. "You ready to go in?"

"At your convenience," he said.

"Then hang on."

Gerber retreated to the troop seat. He looked at his M-16 and put the safety on. No reason to change that unless they were fired on.

As the helicopters descended, the men shifted around and crouched in the doorway. Smith, with his load of explosives, slipped to the center where he'd have some protection from bullets if the enemy suddenly appeared.

They dropped from the sky, and the abandoned base loomed up in front of them. Gerber studied it closely, figuring out the first moves once they were on the ground. No structures remained, and it looked as if all the usable material had been carted away. That didn't surprise Gerber. Anything the Americans didn't take, the Vietnamese would.

The tree lines were now more than three hundred yards from the edge of the abandoned bunker line. The grass close to the trees was deep, concealing the bases of the trees. The vegetation would have to be cut back or burned away. They wouldn't want to provide cover for enemy attacks.

The nose of the chopper came up then as they flared. Gerber grabbed at the fuselage and held on. As soon as the skids leveled, he leaped out, dropping to the red dirt. He scrambled forward to a shallow depression that had once been a bunker. Rolling down into it, he focused his attention on the tree line in front of him.

Dust from the helicopter's rotors was stirred up into a thick, choking cloud, obscuring the landscape. Gerber closed his eyes for an instant and then opened them. Nothing seemed to be moving in the distance.

An instant later another man dropped into the derelict bunker with him, his weapon pointed out. Behind him the sound of the chopper changed as it lifted off. The blades began to pop as the pilot sucked in some pitch. And then the whole flight was taking off.

Gerber glanced back as the last of the choppers climbed out. The noise drifted away with them. Suddenly it was silent except for the quiet buzz of retreating choppers.

Fetterman ran up, stopped and knelt, waiting as Gerber climbed out of the bunker. The captain brushed the dust from the front of his fatigues and said, "Hello, Master Sergeant."

"Captain."

"Let's get our security established. Half the men on security and a listening post out into the jungle."

"Yes, sir."

Gerber glanced to the rear. There was a slight rise that led to the center of the camp, the perfect place for the fire control tower. And a hole nearby would be large enough for the commo bunker. "Command post over there," he said.

Minh showed up and grinned at Gerber. "Good morning, old boy."

"Captain. How have you been?"

"Just fine."

Gerber nodded. "Good."

Tyme appeared. "I want to get the machine guns sited."

"Go to it." Gerber turned and spotted Kepler. "Sergeant, get a listening post out."

"Yes, sir."

"Captain Minh, I'd like half your men on the perimeter."

"Immediately," said Minh, and he rushed off to get his soldiers organized.

"How long do you figure?" Fetterman asked Gerber.

"We should be able to get the first resupply in before the VC realize we're here."

"An attack?"

"Mortars by dusk, maybe a probe tonight, certainly no later than tomorrow night."

"Then I'd better get busy."

"Hell, we all better."

8

THE ABANDONED CAMP
AT XA CAT

The gigantic Sikorsky Sky Crane hovered fifty feet in the air above the highest point in the camp. Fetterman stood out where the pilot and the sling operator could see him, directing them with hand motions and shouting instructions at Bocker, who held the handset of the PRC-25 to his ear. The rotor wash created by the chopper was ten times worse than a Huey's. It was a hurricane-force wind that threatened to crush everyone to the ground and bury them in the swirling clouds of dust and debris that blotted out the sun.

Under the chopper hung a net filled with hundreds of sandbags, building blocks that could mean the difference between life and death for a new camp.

Fetterman held both hands out flat at shoulder height, telling the aircrew that the sling was right where he wanted it. Bocker said something into the radio, and the huge helicopter began a slow, short descent. The bottom of the net touched the ground and flattened out as the cargo shifted, now that there was support on the bottom.

The roar of the chopper increased and then subsided for a moment. It hung over the cargo net and the pile of sandbags for an instant, and then the supporting cable came loose, falling to the ground.

"That's got it!" yelled Fetterman.

Bocker repeated the message and the helicopter lifted slightly. The nose dropped and the Sikorsky began to slide away from the camp. Picking up speed, the chopper turned south, and in less than a minute was gone.

Minh, with thirty of his men, appeared. "We'll get started on the north wall."

"Good," said Fetterman.

Two of the Vietnamese scrambled up the mountain of sandbags and worked at the ropes in the cargo net, untying them and tossing them aside. They freed the cargo, spread open the net and then slipped back down to the ground. One of them grabbed a sandbag and tossed it to the closest man, who turned and tossed it to the man next to him. They set up a human chain, moving the sandbags from the pile toward the perimeter.

Bocker, carrying the PRC-25 with him, approached Fetterman and the sandbags. "I'd like to get them working on the commo bunker, too."

"Not now," said Fetterman. "We've only got the PRC-25s and a few hand-held URC-10s. We don't need the commo bunker yet."

Bocker shrugged. "Whatever."

Gerber appeared. His fatigues were dirty and sweat-stained now. He'd been down in one of the holes helping Tyme site a machine gun. "Looks like more than enough," he said, pointing at the sandbags.

"They go quickly. I've asked for another load as soon as possible."

"I'd rather have a .50-caliber machine gun and a few mortars."

"Then dig some mortar pits," suggested Fetterman.

Gerber grinned and nodded. That was the one thing that seemed to be missing from the camp. There was no area that might have served as a mortar pit. The remains of the bunkers, the hootches and the dispensary, with its concrete floor, were apparent, but there was nothing resembling a mortar pit.

"Tomorrow," said Gerber, wiping at the sweat. "Where's the concertina?"

Fetterman shrugged. "Hasn't come in yet. Haven't had any word on it, either."

"Shit! I want two barriers up by dusk. At least two."

"I can have Sergeant Bocker make a call and see if he can speed things up."

"I think maybe you'd better do that."

Minh was standing close by. "You think Charlie knows we're here yet?"

"Of course," said Gerber. "He might have missed the combat assault or figured we were using this as an LZ, but with the loads of equipment coming in, he's got to know we're setting up the camp again."

"Patrols?" asked Minh.

"No," said Gerber. "We've got a small enough force here now. I don't want to split the command. LPs, of course. Maybe three of them after dark, but no patrols until tomorrow, and then only daylight ones."

Gerber noticed that several of his men, along with Minh, had gathered around the hill of sandbags. "Let's spread it out, just in case there's some wise guy with a mortar around here."

Minh slipped away, heading off to where his men were laying the first row of sandbags for one of the bunkers that would anchor the perimeter. He stopped, shouted and then ran forward, waving his hand.

"Just like old times," said Fetterman, grinning.

Bocker picked up his radio and drifted off toward the hole in the ground that would become his bunker.

"You know," said Gerber, "we're hanging it out here. Charlie has got to know we're back."

"Minh vouched for the men in his strike force," said Fetterman. "Anyone who's even suspected of being VC isn't allowed in it. All the suspects are in a single company."

"Which doesn't take care of the enemy in the field. Anyone with two eyes should be able to see us here."

Bocker approached again. "Got a Huey inbound with claymores, trip flares and land mines."

"Get with Sully and see where he wants that stuff," said Gerber. Turning to Fetterman, he said, "Maybe we'd better think about getting an ammo bunker built early on."

Bocker was standing near the drop-off to the river valley below. He tossed a smoke grenade out and then retreated, staying away from the boiling cloud of green smoke. It was blown downhill, away from them. Sully joined Bocker and stood with one hand on his hat and the other holding on to his M-16.

There was a crash of thunder and Gerber turned. The black clouds were now closer to them. The wind picked up and the air was filled with the smell of rain.

"That's going to fuck us up," said Gerber.

"Think we should try to get some shelter halves or tents up?"

"Won't do any good."

The Huey appeared, approached and then landed. Both Bocker and Smith ran forward and grabbed boxes out of the cargo compartment. They stacked them up, hurrying to get the explosives out of the chopper before the rain began.

Just as they finished, the first of the fat drops started to fall. The rain stirred the red dust, creating little clouds. Gerber ducked once and looked around, but there was no cover from the rain. Nothing had been completed yet. No structures were up. The foundations of some bunkers had been laid and there were some beams cut to form the tops of those bunkers, but they hadn't been put in place yet.

The chopper lifted off, hovered and then fell away, flying just above the trees until it suddenly pulled up and climbed out to the east.

Smith turned and looked up at the sky. As he did, there was a long, loud rumble and the clouds opened up. The rain poured down, and in seconds everything seemed to dissolve.

Gerber turned his rifle upside down to keep the water out of the barrel and then glanced at Fetterman. The master sergeant, who was no more than two feet from him, was little more than a gray blur. The rain came down with such power that no one could see for more than two or three feet. It came down so hard that it bounced off the ground.

Gerber raised his voice and said to Fetterman, "Let's get to the perimeter."

"Yes, sir."

Together they moved off, their heads bowed. The wall of water was so thick that they couldn't see anything, even the ground at their feet. Gerber stopped and crouched, looking at the water running rapidly toward the hillside.

In this weather there was no chance of an enemy assault. Charlie wouldn't be able to coordinate an attack properly, and he'd just as likely kill his own men as the Americans. The VC would be unable to aim mortar rounds, and snipers, if any were out there, would be unable to aim their weapons.

As the gray sheets of rain savaged the hill, Gerber wondered if the camp would be washed into the valley below. He found himself all alone now. It was as if the rest of the world didn't exist. It was just him and the rain. Heavy, unending rain.

And just when he thought the rain would never stop, it began to slow down. Six or seven feet in front of him he could see Fetterman, standing there like a GI in an old World War II Bill Mauldin drawing—the soldier with his rifle slung upside down, head bowed against the weather, waiting for the war to start again.

Bocker emerged from the pall, carrying his PRC-25 with him. Spotting Gerber, he angled toward him. "Chopper inbound."

"What are they bringing us?"

"Got the concertina and some other supplies. I told them we've got a heavy rain in progress. They're orbiting until it's over, but the rain is going to push them away from us."

Gerber got to his feet and wiped the water from his face. He could make out the bunker line, forty feet away, and thought he could see the trees in the distance.

"Tell them to get in here as soon as possible. We're going to need the rest of the day to get the wire strung."

"Yes, sir."

As he turned, he heard a distant pop—a muffled sound, barely audible over the noise of the rain. He recognized it immediately. "Incoming!"

Gerber dived for the ground, landing in the mud. Bocker did the same, an arm out as if to protect the radio. Fetterman slipped to one knee, head down as he waited for the first of the mortar rounds to hit.

It flashed over them, exploding on the other side of the camp. Then more came down, walking toward the center. Through the curtain of rain, no one could see exactly where they were landing. There were dull pops, not explosions, as if the rounds had been smothered by the mud.

One of their own machine guns began to fire. Gerber twisted around, but couldn't spot it. The rain was still falling too hard for the muzzle-flash to penetrate. A moment later the machine gun fell silent. Then the last of the mortar rounds hit, exploding no more than fifty feet from Gerber. Even that one sounded distant. There was no whir of hot shrapnel, just a dull thunk as it buried itself in the thick red mud.

Fetterman looked down at Gerber and grinned. "You hurt, sir?"

Slowly Gerber got up and brushed ineffectually at his mud-stained fatigues. All he did was smear the red mud around, making it look as if he'd suffered a massive injury to his chest. "No. Just dirty."

Fetterman stood, a single muddy patch on his knee. "Mortars aren't much good in this kind of weather. Mud absorbs everything. They dig out little craters."

"One of these days that attitude's going to get you killed."

"No, sir."

Bocker turned. "I told the chopper we had some mortars, but that the attack's over. They've swung south of the storm and are inbound again."

Tyme appeared. "Machine gunner got trigger-happy. Couldn't see anything but opened fire anyway."

"I'd rather they be a little trigger-happy right now," said Gerber. "That was just harassing fire."

"Means Charlie knows we're here," Tyme said.

"It also tells us," said Fetterman, "that Charlie's already spotted us. We're going to have to keep our eyes open."

Gerber nodded. "I want everyone working to get the perimeter in shape with the exception of one squad for security. We've got to be ready for them tonight."

"Yes, sir," said Fetterman.

"I want a team meeting about 1800 tonight. All the Americans and Captain Minh. It'll be short and to the point."

"Countermortar?" asked Tyme.

"Just what did you have in mind, Justin?"

The young sergeant stood there for a moment, weighing the options. Then he realized why Gerber had said nothing earlier. Given the circumstances, there wasn't anything they could do. They hadn't spotted the tube, they had no mortars of their own yet, and the rain inhibited the choppers. Tyme shrugged and said nothing.

There was a quiet popping to the south. Gerber turned. The rain had abated so that now he could see the trees and the clouds. In the distance he could see the helicopter coming in. The pilots probably figured the rain would give them some cover, so they were making their approach.

Bocker moved out to the point of the ridge line and threw a yellow smoke grenade. The heavy air and the lack of a breeze held the smoke close to the ground. The pilot saw the smoke and swooped in, landing near it.

Fetterman moved over and leaned close to Gerber as they watched the chopper. "Tonight's going to be hell."

"If we survive it, we'll be in good shape for a couple of days."

"Yes, sir, if we can survive."

Gerber shot a glance at Fetterman and knew exactly what he meant.

9

BINH LONG PROVINCE

Thien crouched in the steaming, dripping jungle and watched as the sun came out, drying the American camp at the top of the ridge line. He, along with others from his company, had slipped into position during the heavy rain and had fired their mortars as soon as the rain had slackened enough for them to see the camp. Not many rounds. Just a few to let the Americans know they were around.

Now Thien and his men were watching the activity in the American camp. Men were working to create bunkers. They worked at the corners of the camp, laying a foundation of planks, then sandbag walls, a firing port constructed around a wooden frame and more sandbags. The top was made from a layer of planks covered by several layers of sandbags. It was enough to stop and absorb direct hits from several mortar rounds or from a rocket.

In front of the bunkers, men, stripped to the waist and wearing heavy gloves, worked to set up rows of concertina wire. They uncoiled it and stretched it slightly as it came off the rolls. Two men worked behind those laying the wire, hanging beer cans with pebbles in them.

There was also a crew setting up claymores. The mines, which would fire 750 steel balls, were angled downward slightly so that they would sweep the slopes as the enemy tried to attack up the hill.

"Doesn't look good," one of the sergeants said to Thien.

The Vietnamese lieutenant looked at the man. "A good sapper could penetrate that line in five minutes. A little wire is of no value to them."

"Makes them feel better. Braver."

Thien nodded but didn't say anything. Instead he watched the Americans work. More helicopters came in, hovered and threw off cargo. A few men came in and stayed, joining the work force.

The Americans worked through the evening, completing several bunkers. All those in the corners were finished and had machine guns placed in them. Each time a bunker was completed and its weapons added, the Americans fired several rounds. It was as if they were checking the field of fire of each weapon.

The activity in the American camp never let up. Lines of men tossed sandbags along, dropping them closer to the perimeter. If they didn't use them to build bunkers, they used them to reinforce the holes in the lines, a few rows of sandbags to provide a little extra protection for the men behind them. A low wall, no more than two feet high, was laid, connecting the various fighting positions and bunkers. A man could crawl along behind it if the enemy was attacking.

"They're going to be ready for us tonight," said the sergeant.

"Don't worry about it, Comrade," said Thien. "They won't be able to get everything done."

The sergeant shrugged and continued to watch the activity, wishing for another thunderstorm to slow the Americans' work.

GERBER STOOD near the cargo net that had held all the sandbags, surprised that they had managed to empty it completely. The pile of sandbags had been transferred to the perimeter, and though not all of them had been put in place yet, they would be before dark. The men were working as fast as they could, trying to get ready for the first night on the hill.

Fetterman approached. His jungle fatigues, like those of everyone else, had failed to dry in the tropical humidity. It looked as if the rain had ended moments ago rather than several hours earlier. "You still want to meet, Captain?"

Gerber turned slowly and looked at the exposed hilltop. There wasn't a safe place for them to have a meeting. If they all tried to slip into one bunker, a smartass VC with a mortar might try to wipe out the command structure with a single round. It would be two, three days before they could meet in safety in the camp. It would take that long to get the perimeter built and the other structures up and sandbagged. Once all that had been accomplished, along with the fire control tower, it would be hard for an enemy in the jungle to witness everything going on inside the fence.

"I suppose we should keep this all spread out, just in case," Gerber said. "You have anything to report?"

"I'd like to get some Seabees in here to cut back the grass and bushes and then burn it all off. We'll need help with the fire control tower, and we probably should get another medic. Oh, and we should designate a helipad, grade that area and then either use concrete or a rubberized pad to hold down the dust."

Gerber grinned sarcastically as he looked at Fetterman's rain-soaked fatigues and the two inches of mud that he stood in.

"Yes, sir," the sergeant responded, "but this will dry out and the dust will cause problems later."

Gerber nodded. "Walk with me. We'll talk to each man."

"Yes, sir."

They moved toward the single chunk of concrete that hadn't been broken up when the camp had been abandoned. Washington had set up a tent over it, using the area as his temporary dispensary until they could get a more permanent structure erected.

They found the medic crouched near a cot, looking into the eyes of a prone Vietnamese. T. J. glanced at them as they approached. "Working too hard in the heat."

"He going to be okay?" Gerber asked.

"As long as I can get his body temperature down. I've been giving him fluids and bathing him in water."

"Other than that, how's it going?"

His eyes on the sick man, Washington shrugged. "You can see. I've got six cots in here and a wooden cabinet with my medical supplies. We get anything more serious than a cut finger and we'll have to evac the man. There's just nothing I can do until we get the dispensary built."

"Except hand out aspirin and hope for the best," said Fetterman.

"Except for that." He stood and faced the other two. "I'm not going to spend the night in here. We're too exposed without anything else up."

"You have a dispensary designated?" Gerber asked.

"It'll be in the bunkers opposite the line of attack, if we're hit."

"Fine," said Gerber. "Keep me posted."

"Yes, sir."

They left the dispensary and found Sully Smith crouched behind a sandbag wall, working on the firing controls for several claymores. He was lying on his side, a screwdriver in one hand. When he saw Gerber and Fetterman, he grinned. "I can fire them one at a time or salvo them, depending."

Gerber knelt near him, one knee in the mud. "I take it you're pleased, then?"

"For the moment," said Smith. "We could really use some more of these along with more trip flares and antipersonnel mines. Hell, I could make my own, if we had the ingredients here, but we don't. We need everything."

Gerber nodded. "Get me a shopping list and I'll transmit it to Saigon."

"We could use some C-4, too."

"Fine. Whatever you need. You been running into any problems here?"

"Other than a lack of equipment, no, sir."

Gerber stood. "Keep me informed."

As they walked along the line, Fetterman said, "Seems to be going well."

"If Charlie gives us the time we need here," groused Gerber.

They found Tyme just as he was coming out of a bunker. He stopped and glanced up at them, then wiped his forehead on the sleeve of his uniform, but only managed to spread the mud around. His uniform, like those of the others, was still wet from the morning rain.

"Justin, how's it going?" Gerber asked.

Tyme hooked a thumb over his shoulder. "We need another half-dozen M-60s, and we could use four, maybe five M-2s. I'd like a couple of recoilless rifles to support the machine guns, and I'd like some mortars in here, .60 millimeter, if we can't get anything bigger."

"Don't want much, do you?" Gerber cracked.

Tyme stared up at the captain. "Just trying to get the equipment in here we'll need to hold this place. The more mortars and machine guns we get in, the harder it'll be for Charlie to shove us out."

"Understood."

"We've got nearly everything sited. Each of the machine guns can support at least one other, but we're not ready for the enemy."

"Thanks, Justin." Gerber glanced at Fetterman and they moved on. Kepler, standing near what would become the helipad, was looking out over the countryside. "Derek, what can you tell me?" Gerber asked.

"Not much, I'm afraid. I'd like to get into the field and start setting up the agent network. We've got to start doing that or we won't get anywhere."

"Day after tomorrow at the latest," said Gerber.

"Yes, sir." He turned and came down toward them. "I think we'll get probed tonight. We show any weakness and they'll be on us like stink on shit. They'll come roaring out of the trees to overrun us. We put out enough rounds and they'll wait for reinforcements."

"Tonight?" asked Fetterman.

"Or tomorrow night. No later than that."

"It answers one question," said Gerber. "Half alert until midnight and then full alert to four."

All three of them returned to the middle of the camp. Gerber took a moment to look around. They had been in the camp for under twelve hours, but it was already taking shape. In a week they would have the defenses to withstand an NVA regiment.

As expected, the first of the mortar rounds fell just after midnight. There was the distinct pop of the mortar firing, a pause lasting a few seconds, and then the explosion near the center of the camp. A lull followed, then a volley of rounds fell, walking from the center of the camp toward the area where the helicopters had been landing earlier in the day.

Gerber had just awakened. He was standing in the corner bunker on the southeastern side of the perimeter, staring out into the blackness. From farther to the east came the rumble of artillery, or the crash of thunder. The distance was too great for him to be sure which it was.

"Incoming!" yelled Fetterman.

Gerber tried to spot the flashes, but failed. The rounds landed behind him—dull, quiet explosions, indicating 60 mm mortars.

"Got it!" yelled Tyme. The machine gun in the bunker off the right began to hammer. Gerber could see the muzzle-flash stabbing out into the night. Red tracers lanced out, hit the trees and bounced.

More of the mortar rounds fell. The explosions were coming toward him. Now it sounded as if two or three tubes were operating. The gunners weren't adjusting the range. They were slamming the rounds down as fast as they could.

Gerber pulled the hand-held URC-10 from his pocket and squeezed it. "Zulu Two, say location."

"North side, near the corner."

"Roger, get some artillery in here."

There was a slight pause and then, "Yes, sir. It's on the way."

Gerber wished he had a Starlite scope. It would allow him to get a better look at the open ground in front of him. He was afraid the enemy would use the tall grass to conceal themselves as they crawled toward the bunkers.

Slapping one of the Vietnamese strikers on the shoulder, Gerber pointed. "Shoot low into the grass."

The gunner nodded and grinned, displaying pointed black teeth, an indication that he habitually chewed betel nut. He worked the bolt on the side of the M-60, pulling it back and letting it slam forward. Then he leaned into the shoulder stock and pulled the trigger.

Gerber watched the ruby tracers dance into the night. The gunner hosed down the area in front of them, slowly elevating the barrel until the rounds were hitting about a hundred yards away. Some of them disappeared into the grass while others ricocheted and tumbled upward.

Small fires erupted, bright points of light in the dark landscape. Using binoculars stored in the bunker, Gerber surveyed the ground outside the camp, searching for the enemy, searching for the attackers, but saw nothing.

The gunner stopped shooting and glanced expectantly at Gerber. The captain knew the Vietnamese loved to fire their weapons, even if they didn't have a target. The fire discipline of these men was a tribute to Captain Minh.

"Go ahead," said Gerber. "Put out some more rounds."

Then, from the other end of the line, Tyme began firing his XM-174. Gerber heard it firing, a thunking sound that drifted to him over the noise of the machine guns and the detonations of the mortar shells. The XM-174 rounds landed in the open field beyond the perimeter. The HE flashed with a red-orange fire, setting the grass near it ablaze momentarily. The vegetation was still wet enough to smother the flames.

The willie pete flashed in white-hot detonations. Flaming bits of magnesium scattered, setting other fires. When the weapon was empty, Tyme reloaded, using only HE.

Now there was some shooting from the tree line. The muzzle-flashes sparkled like fireflies on a warm summer evening. Green tracers speared the night, some hitting the ground near the bunkers.

The mortar shells continued to fall. There were detonations around the camp, some of them just behind the bunker line. Gerber could hear the shrapnel slapping on the sandbags outside. He ducked instinctively, though it would have been too late if he had been outside.

At the same time, the South Vietnamese soldier continued to fire his machine gun. Hot brass from it bounced off the sandbags and fell to the floor. The barrel seemed to heat the air around it, making it hotter, more uncomfortable in the bunker. The hammering of the weapon reverberated off the sandbag walls.

Gerber peered out, but there was nothing new to see in the jungle, only muzzle-flashes in the distance. The hammering of enemy weapons was constant, then a new sound joined the bedlam. Bugles. A few wailing notes were picked up by other bugles. These were joined by whistles and finally a low roar.

The first few enemy soldiers burst from cover. Gerber watched them through his binoculars. They were shadowy shapes, running hunched over, weapons pointed at the camp. Some men fired from the hip, the rounds flashing over the top of the bunkers. Others didn't shoot. It was almost as if they were trying to hide in the darkness.

Gerber shoved the barrel of his M-16 through the firing port and aimed low. He didn't use the iron sights. It was too dark and the distance was too great for that. The only thing he could do was fire low on full-auto and put out rounds.

The tall grass helped conceal the enemy soldiers. As the terrain dropped and rose, the VC vanished and reappeared. Gerber watched them, emptied his weapon and jerked out the empty magazine. He dropped it to the floor amid the brass of the M-60 and M-16, then pulled another from his bandolier, slammed it home and worked the bolt. Again he opened fire.

The enemy soldiers were close now. Gerber fired at one man who seemed to be leading the attack. He saw the man stumble, fall to one knee, then stand up. Finally the enemy soldier wavered back and forth, then fell face down.

And then, suddenly, there was a series of explosions. They flashed along the ground just inside the second strand of concertina wire. The sequence started near Gerber with a single, sharp detonation and then walked away. One, two, three, four different explosions.

The attacking wave of VC disappeared. The 750 steel balls from each claymore slashed through the night, killing the attackers. Arms were ripped from bodies, legs from trunks. Those closest to the weapons were shredded, becoming little more than hamburger.

Firing from the attackers tapered and disappeared. Mortar rounds continued to fall, but only to cover the withdrawal of the survivors. If there were any survivors.

The South Vietnamese machine gunner was still firing. The barrel was beginning to glow a dull red. The bunker was filled with the stench of cordite, making it almost impossible to breathe.

"Cease fire," cried Gerber. "Cease fire."

The machine gunner kept shooting a few more seconds and then released the trigger. He rocked back from the machine gun. In the half-light flickering into the bunker, Gerber could see the man's sweat-slicked face.

Gerber leaned forward toward the firing port. A cool breeze blew in, which he welcomed as he stared out into the night. The mortars had stopped now. There was no shooting from the jungle.

And then, too late to do any good, the first of the American artillery shells hit, seemingly in the middle of the enemy staging area. Within moments more shells exploded, their bright orange illumination akin to the strobing of a giant camera flash.

Gerber laughed out loud and glanced at his machine gunner. "Better late than never."

The man nodded.

10

FORT POLK, LOUISIANA

Major General Billy Joe Crinshaw sat in the rear of the small Lear jet and waited as the two Air Force pilots checked the instrument panel and followed the start-up procedure. Crinshaw's suitcase had been stored in the cargo compartment, along with Sergeant Seneff's. Both men were belted into the plush seats of the private jet, waiting.

Air Force Captain Sheila Henrikson, a young blonde wearing a short military skirt and a light blue blouse, moved between them, asking if they wanted something to drink. She knelt next to Crinshaw, displaying a lot of leg and giving him the opportunity to look down her blouse, if he felt the urge to do so.

Crinshaw looked and wondered how it would feel to suck her nipples into erection. Then he turned his head so that he could look out the porthole at the nearly empty airfield. In the distance he could see pine trees and a column of smoke. He knew it was hot outside, but it was cool in the plane.

"You sure there's nothing I can get you, General?" Henrikson asked again.

"I'm fine now."

Standing up, she hunched slightly because of the fuse-lage, then walked away and sat down near the bulkhead that separated the cockpit from the passenger compartment. When she saw that Crinshaw was watching her, she slowly crossed her legs, showing him some more thigh.

Again Crinshaw looked away. He thought of Jennifer sitting in their house and crying as he'd finished stuffing his suitcase. She had hovered near him, touching him frequently, trying to hide the tears. She had tried to put on a brave front and had failed miserably. Instead she had run from the room, returned and then fled again. She couldn't stand the thought of a year's separation.

Crinshaw had demanded that she remain in the house. It would be easier if he left her there. His driver would take him to the airfield where he could catch the special flight. She wouldn't have to face the crowds and wouldn't have the long, lonely drive home.

"But I want to go," she said.

"No," answered Crinshaw. "You stay here. I'll phone you from California."

She leaped at him, clung to him and cried. He held her, rubbed her back and said, "I'll be home before you know it. And we'll be able to meet in Hawaii in just a couple of weeks."

"It's so long. Too long."

Crinshaw held her but didn't say anything. He ignored the horn when the driver sounded it, knowing the plane wouldn't take off without him. He held her until her crying became dry sobs and she hiccuped twice. Finally, when she pulled away from him, he said, "You knew this would happen."

"I didn't think it would be so soon."

Crinshaw shrugged. "They got me a little sooner than I thought, but that's the price we have to pay."

"It's not fair," she said, her voice rough, raw. "Some men haven't even gone once."

"And some have gone three times," said Crinshaw.

Jennifer moved to the couch and sat down, drawing her legs up under her. She seemed to hug herself, her head bowed. It was almost as if she were trying to get used to not having him around.

Crinshaw went into the bedroom and retrieved his suitcase. As he carried it toward the front door, he heard a knock. Crinshaw opened the door and handed the suitcase to the driver. "I'll be out in a few minutes."

"Yes, General."

Crinshaw shut the door and returned to the living room. Jennifer had closed the blinds and now she was sitting on the couch. The room was dark and hot. For a moment he stood there, not knowing what to say. It wasn't a trip to Washington for a week. It wasn't a field exercise where he'd only be out of touch for a couple of days. They were talking about a year. An entire year and maybe a little more. "I've got to go," he finally said.

Nodding, she looked up at him, her face stained with tears. "Go."

"A goodbye kiss?"

Slowly she stood, walked toward him and turned her face up so he could kiss her. There was no passion in it. As she turned away, she sniffed again.

Feeling helpless and not knowing what to say, Crinshaw retreated to the front door. He stopped there and watched her as she fell onto the couch, the tears flowing again. "There's nothing I can do about this."

"I know," she said without looking.

"I have to go."

"I know."

"As soon as I'm settled, I'll write and let you know how I am."

She glanced at him. "I'll be waiting." She hesitated and then said, "Please go. This is hurting too much."

He grabbed the doorknob, but before he opened the door, he said, "You know I love you."

"Come home to me," she told him then, avoiding eye contact.

But now, on the aircraft, as they maneuvered off the taxiway and onto the runway, Crinshaw found himself interested in the Air Force captain. She smiled at him and slowly recrossed her legs, leaving almost nothing to the imagination.

"We're about to take off," she said.

Crinshaw nodded, but didn't take his eyes off the woman. He wasn't interested in watching the scenery flash by or watch as they climbed up into the bright blue sky. Instead he watched the woman as she reached down and scratched her knee. When she saw that he was staring at her, she licked her lips slowly.

In a few minutes they reached altitude. Henrikson unfastened her seat belt, stood and looked into the cockpit. She asked the pilots a question and got a muffled reply. Then she moved down the narrow, short aisle and leaned over Sergeant Seneff. "Is there anything I can do for you?"

"No, ma'am, I'm fine."

Nodding, she turned toward Crinshaw and smiled broadly, then moved to the rear of the plane and through a curtain, which hung there as if the jet were divided into first-class and economy sections. Before disappearing, she winked at Crinshaw.

The general understood an invitation when he saw one. He unfastened his seat belt, stood and walked to the rear. The captain closed the curtain as he moved through it. Crinshaw sat in the only chair and watched her.

She reached down for the hem of her skirt. Suddenly it was clear that she wore no underwear. Crinshaw stared, smiling, all thoughts of Jennifer driven from his mind.

DAN MEYERS SAT in the city room at one of the desks and stared at the darkened band of windows that looked out on downtown Saigon. The room was brightly lighted, almost inviting a mortar shell or rocket, but the enemy never fired at them. Rockets fell on Cholon or Tan Son Nhut, but never in the center of town.

In front of him were rows of desks. Most of them had been scrounged from the military. They were mismatched, painted a variety of unpleasant colors and in bad condition. Some drawers didn't open. Some of them didn't close. The desktops all had typewriters. The veteran reporters had manuals, the newcomers electrics. The problem was the power; it was unreliable, which meant the manual type-writers were the best ones to have.

To one side was a row of glass-enclosed offices, which were used by the editors and senior correspondents. Meyers had a desk and no office. He hadn't been there very long.

The night beat was dull. He could stand in the window and watch the artillery explode in the distance. He could hear the war out there. Sometimes there was machine-gun or rifle fire, but it was always faraway. There was nothing for him to see or report.

He got up from his desk and walked to the rear of the room where there was a bank of file cabinets. They were stuffed with information about Vietnam, Saigon, the American Army and the war. On top was a half-empty coffee pot. Meyers poured himself a cup, dumped in sugar, wished that the air-conditioning worked a little better and walked back to the front of the room.

Robin Morrow sat at her desk, dressed in her usual jumpsuit with the legs hacked off at midthigh and the sleeves rolled up above her elbows. She was reading a story she'd just pulled from her typewriter.

Meyers sat on the corner of her desk and tried to look down the front of her jumpsuit, but failed. "What are you doing here so late?"

"Nothing. Didn't have anything else to do and couldn't sleep, so I came in here."

Meyers sipped his coffee and tried to think of something witty to say. Failing that, he asked, "What are you working on?"

Morrow dropped the story onto the desk and looked up at Meyers. "A nothing little story. Special Forces civic action team. The medic reported treating his two thousandth patient. I figured, what the hell, I write it up and maybe someone somewhere will print it."

"Why bother?" asked Meyers.

"That's a damn good question." She leaned back and locked her hands behind her head. "Damn good. I suppose because there's some news value in it. Special Forces out there treating the sick, helping create a higher standard of living."

"So that we can come along and blow it all up with air strikes and artillery."

"Or the Vietcong can destroy it." She flopped forward, letting her feet slam the floor. Digging through a pile of papers, she said, "VC killed a schoolteacher a couple of days ago. Gunned her down."

Meyers took a deep breath and let it out slowly. "That's the story we're getting. That's the kind of story we always get."

Morrow stopped her search. "Doesn't mean it's wrong or inaccurate."

"I suppose not."

"Just what in hell are you doing here?" she asked.

Again Meyers sipped his coffee. Then, not looking at her, he said, "I'm covering the war. I'm reporting the war. But I'll tell you right now, I'm not going to be fooled by all the bullshit press releases handed out by the military and the embassy."

"Right," said Morrow, nodding. "You know the whole story now. It's just a question of plugging in the facts."

"No," said Meyers, "it's not like that at all. But I'm smart enough not to be taken in by a lot of phony stories about the good we're doing in Vietnam. Hell, I've seen the good. The ruined villages, the maimed men and women and the long line of refugees."

Morrow realized there was no way to argue with the man. He'd made up his mind, based on the negative stories he'd read while still in the World. He knew, as too many of the other journalists knew, what was happening without ever having to investigate it. Because another journalist had written it all out, it had to be right. There was no way that it could be wrong or inaccurate.

She'd seen reporters interviewing each other for stories so that they could get some good quotes. Informed sources were nothing more than other reporters who'd sat around in the same press conference listening to the same facts. Informed sources might not be all that informed. The scramble for an angle, something different or new, sometimes resulted in a distortion of the facts that got printed anyway.

Morrow picked up her story. "There's some good being done here. The farmers, the Vietnamese living in the jungle villages a hundred miles from Saigon, are being dragged into the twentieth century."

"Is that good?"

Morrow grinned. "They've got a way of life that works. Maybe it's not a good thing, but I suppose it's a necessary thing. Infant mortality is down, and they're learning a little preventive medicine. A trade-off."

Meyers realized the discussion wasn't going anywhere. He stood up and stretched, then glanced out the front window and noticed the building across the street was a little more defined than it had been. The sun was coming up.

"I guess I'll go see what's happening down the hall," he said.

Morrow picked up a pencil and drew a line through a sentence. "Go ahead. I'm getting out of here for a while, after I drop this on Hodges's desk."

"He won't do a thing with it."

"You're wrong there," said Morrow. "Hodges will get it shipped to the World. Once there, no one will do a thing with it."

"Then what good is it?" asked Meyers.

"That," said Morrow, "is the question."

11

XA CAT SPECIAL FORCES CAMP

The rising sun revealed the bodies of the Vietcong strung out from the trees to the concertina wire of the camp. The tall grass, wet with morning dew, made it difficult to spot the dead from ground level. By standing on top of a bunker, Gerber could see the paths in the grass cut by the running men. Those that ended abruptly usually contained the body of a dead man. The artillery had prevented the VC from retrieving all the bodies of the dead.

Gerber jumped down from the bunker and walked around behind it. He, along with the others, were still worried about snipers. He'd made a pretty good target, standing there in the growing daylight.

"Patrols, Captain?" asked Fetterman.

"No. I want to get the camp in shape first. Then we'll set up patrols."

Kepler came up. "You want me to take out a patrol?"

Gerber spun around and glared at him. "What in hell's going on here, anyway? We need to get the camp established first."

"Typical leg thinking," mumbled Fetterman.

"Now what's that supposed to mean?" snapped Gerber. Then suddenly he held up his hand. "Never mind. I get it. We're supposed to break out of regular army thinking."

Looking at the two NCOs, Gerber realized he'd fallen into the trap just as quickly and simply as the leg officers he was fond of ridiculing. They moved into an area, erected a camp and then, sometimes, sent out patrols. Most of them were content to sit in their camps and let the enemy come to them. It made good sense in one way. The defenses of the camps, along with the interlocking artillery fire of other camps, made them almost impregnable. If things began to look bad, help could arrive in seconds, sometimes in the form of fighters for air strikes and sometimes in the form of helicopters bringing in another hundred, two hundred or a thousand men.

Gerber nodded and asked Kepler, "What do you want to do?"

"I'd like to take a platoon out, sweep through the jungle where the enemy staged and then out toward the road on the north. Let the people see that we're in the AO and that we're moving around already."

"Tony?"

"Sounds good to me. Anything to get us out of the camp."

Gerber nodded and rubbed his unshaven chin. "I'll get with Bocker and arrange a ride into Saigon this morning. I'll talk with Platt and tell him we need a company of engineers in here to complete the camp. Let them build it while we do what we're supposed to be doing."

"This morning?" asked Fetterman.

"Half the men left here after Derek finds his patrol will work on the camp, and the other half will sleep. Four hours on and four off."

"A single patrol isn't enough," said Fetterman.

"I know," answered Gerber, "but we don't have many people here, and if we strip it down too much, we'll end up being a sitting duck."

"I agree. I'll get on the horn and contact the Twenty-fifth. Maybe they'll be inclined to field a couple of companies for search-and-destroy. That'll boost what we can do."

"I can coordinate with their Intelligence officers," said Kepler. "If they find anything, we'll know about it."

"Tonight," said Gerber. "You have anything else, Tony?"

"No, sir."

"Then let's get to it." He turned and walked toward the center of the camp. Numerous craters, no more than two or three feet across and about eighteen inches deep, were scattered around. There was shrapnel on the ground, but damage to the camp was minimal, mainly because there wasn't anything to destroy. A few sandbags had been ripped apart, and a few of the bunkers had sustained minor damage.

Bocker was crouched with his radio near the area he had designated the helipad. During the night he'd dug a foxhole, and now he sat on the edge of it, staring off into the jungle far below him.

"Galvin," said Gerber as he approached.

Bocker turned and grinned. He looked tired. Black circles ringed his eyes, and there was mud on his face and in his hair. "Sir."

"I want a chopper ride into Saigon today."

Bocker glanced at the radio sitting at his side and then at his watch. "Got a supply chopper coming in this morning bringing us food, ammo and claymores. I suppose you could take it into Saigon."

"I want you to get on the radio and talk to the Twenty-fifth. Let them know we got hit last night and that we want some people to sweep the jungle around here."

"Yes, sir."

"Kepler will coordinate that with you."

"In the meantime?"

"We keep pushing to get the camp finished," said Gerber. "When's the chopper due?"

"Inside thirty minutes," said Bocker. "One of the Crusaders coming off Tay Ninh."

"Hold him when he gets here if I'm not around."

"Yes, sir."

KEPLER·FOUND Minh sitting with his back against the sandbag wall of the command bunker. His rifle was in his lap and his eyes were closed, but he wasn't asleep, just resting and listening.

"Dai Uy," said Kepler as he neared, "I'd like to take a platoon out on patrol."

Minh opened his eyes and nodded. "Good men?"

"The best you have," said Kepler.

Minh stood up and brushed at the seat of his tiger-striped fatigues. "Of course, old boy."

"I want to leave in about twenty minutes. We'll only be out for the day. Food for a noon meal, plenty of water and ammo. That's it. We'll be back before dusk."

"Come with me," said Minh.

Together they walked down the line. The strikers watched them for a moment and then looked away. Each man realized what was happening. A patrol was being formed and no one wanted either Minh or Kepler to think he wanted to go. Suddenly they were very busy cleaning their weapons, checking the perimeter or cooking their breakfast.

Minh pointed to men, saying, "You, you, you." He kept at it until he had designated twenty-four men, including one RTO. At the end of the line, he stopped and looked at Kepler. "That enough for you?"

"Yes, sir. Fine."

Minh moved toward the center of the line then and raised his voice slightly. In Vietnamese he said, "Those indicated, please form here."

The group of men gathered, some of them sitting on the ground, some of them kneeling and some of them standing. All Minh could think about was what a good target they'd make for a smartass with a mortar tube.

"Sergeant Kepler," said Minh, "will be leading a patrol out of here in twenty minutes. You'll form by the corner bunker over there with your weapons, canteens and ammo. You'll bring food for one meal. Questions?"

When there were none, Minh said, "Then get moving." As the group began to break up, he felt better. No more targets for the smartass.

Kepler left the Vietnamese officer and walked toward the bunker. He stopped long enough to find a box of C-rations. Opening it, he found the beans and franks and pulled that carton from the box. He tossed out the things he didn't want—the crackers and the jam—and put the carton back into the box.

Once inside the bunker, he picked up a bandolier of M-16 ammo and slipped it over his head. Then he unhooked his rucksack from his pistol belt and buckled it on. Finally he checked his canteens and discovered that one of them was empty.

Leaving the bunker, he walked back up the hill until he came to the blister bag hanging there. Blister bags held water for the units in the field. This one, unfortunately, had been riddled by mortar shrapnel the night before. Its contents had leaked out and run down the hill.

"Shit."

"My feelings exactly," said a voice behind him.

Kepler turned and found Tyme standing there. "I need another canteen for patrol."

Tyme took out one of his. "Take this one. I'm sure we'll get more water in here before too long."

They switched canteens. As Kepler snapped it into his cover, he said, "Thanks."

"Don't mention it."

He headed back to the bunker, where the Vietnamese soldiers were beginning to gather. They stayed back, using the bunker to shield themselves from the jungle and the trees. They sat in the shadow and waited for Kepler.

When he arrived, he ordered them to stand up. They did, forming a ragged line, still using the bunker to conceal themselves as much as possible. Kepler took that as a good sign. They were well trained enough that they didn't make stupid mistakes.

Kepler walked down the line and checked each man. They carried M-16s and had bandoliers loaded with spare magazines. Each man carried extra equipment. Two of them had spare batteries for the radio. Others carried M-60 ammo for the machine guns. Some had spare rounds for the M-79s, while others carried extra medical supplies for the medic. Everyone shouldered his share.

When he finished the inspection, he moved to the side of the bunker and looked out into the field. Fetterman and a squad were moving around, checking the bodies of the dead and collecting the weapons. They couldn't leave the bodies there to rot because it would cause disease. They had to be buried before they started to decay.

Kepler hesitated, and then saw Gerber coming toward him. Bareheaded, the captain was carrying an M-16 in his left hand and was covered in mud. He didn't look very military.

"You about ready?" he asked.

Kepler nodded. "All set."

"Remember, I don't want you going too far, and you have to be back by dark. Just a short patrol to get the feel of the land around us."

"Understood, Captain."

"Tomorrow we'll think about putting out some ambush patrols, and you can think about starting your agent network."

"Yes, sir." Kepler waited, but Gerber didn't seem to have anything else to say. "We'll be going then."

"Fine. Good luck and good hunting."

Kepler nodded. He moved toward the front of the line and slapped one man on the shoulder. "Point out."

The man turned, walked to the edge of the perimeter and then followed the concertina until he found the opening. He slipped through the wire and out onto the open plain. The grass was knee-high at first, then waist-high and finally about shoulder-high.

Kepler, followed by the squad, used the path created by the pointman. They worked their way out of the camp and through the grass. Despite the rain the day before, it was still hot. A slight cloud rose in the air as they worked their way toward the trees.

The sun was a lot higher in the sky now. With the dust swirling around them held close to the ground by the oppressive humidity, they worked their way to the jungle. Kepler felt sweat blossom before he had gone more than two hundred yards. Forcing his way through the tough grass was hard work, much harder than walking over a freshly mowed lawn in a park. And the dust made it difficult to breathe.

As they approached the jungle, they slowed. The squad fanned out and the pointman slipped forward cautiously. Kepler moved behind him, searching the jungle for any signs of the enemy. He hesitated at the tree line, crouched and stared into the gloom. Overhead birds squawked, while monkeys leaped from branch to branch. All seemed normal in the jungle.

The pointman moved finally and slipped into the trees. Now he walked slowly, his head swiveling right and left as he searched for an ambush. Kepler was right behind him. He held his weapon in both hands. He crouched slightly, head moving as he studied the shadows, the bushes, the ground and the canopy overhead. Too many men had died because they didn't consider the possibility of a sniper hidden in the trees. The enemy could be anywhere.

Twenty yards into the jungle they halted again. Kepler bent to one knee and listened. His men were quiet. From behind him he picked up the sound of one man breathing. There was no sound from any other direction, except for the jungle creatures. There was no sign of the enemy.

After a minute or so the pointman was up and moving again. He stepped over a log, turned, climbed a slight rise and then descended the other side, where he found a narrow stream. The man stopped on the bank, then stepped across the stream.

Kepler and the patrol followed. They wound their way through the jungle, avoiding the paths and game trails, pushing their way through the vegetation, trying to make no sound. Minh had trained his men well. They knew the reasons for noise discipline in the jungle. They didn't want to give themselves away so that the enemy could find and kill them.

Again they stopped. The men fanned out slightly, facing in opposite directions so that no one could slip up on them. Again Kepler listened, but still the jungle was silent. The enemy had gotten out completely. Once the initial attack failed, he had escaped. Kepler was sure Charlie had run back to Cambodia. It wasn't that far, and the invisible line on the ground would be all the protection the VC and NVA needed.

They kept at it all morning. They would move for ten or fifteen minutes and then stop for five. It conserved their strength as the jungle began to heat under the tropical sun, and it gave them the opportunity to listen for anyone else in the jungle with them.

When they reached the edge of the jungle, near Highway 245, Kepler called a halt. They spread out in a loose, defensive circle and began to eat their lunch. Kepler pulled the C-rations from his pocket, used his P-38 to open the can of beans and franks and watched the road while he ate. He knew there would be no VC or NVA on it, but the rice farmers and their families might use it. He hoped to see someone he could begin developing into an agent. Someone to help him find the enemy.

12

XA CAT SPECIAL FORCES
CAMP

Gerber heard the approaching helicopter long before Bocker warned him that it was coming or before he could see it in the distance. He ducked into a bunker, grabbed his pistol belt and a bandolier of ammo and then stepped out. Now the helicopter was visible east of the camp. As he turned to walk toward the helipad, he saw a cloud of purple smoke. Bocker was guiding the chopper in.

He walked to the pad, stopped short and watched Bocker, who crouched near the radio off to one side. "That my ride to Saigon?"

"Yes, sir. Pilot's not happy about it, but what the hell? He'll take you in."

Gerber stepped back down the slight slope and waited as the helicopter grew in size. The noise of the turbine and the popping of the rotors got louder, drowning out all other sound. The chopper dropped out of the cloudless sky, hovered, kicked up a cloud of swirling dust and then settled to the ground. The door gunner and crew chief climbed out from behind their machine guns and began pushing the equipment out of the cargo compartment. Bocker hurried forward to help them.

While they did that, Gerber moved to the cockpit. He stepped up on the skid, leaned in the window and shouted at the pilot, "Need a ride into Saigon."

"No problem, Captain," said the pilot. He pointed toward the northwest. "Looks like you had a little trouble last night."

"Nothing we couldn't handle."

The pilot nodded but didn't speak. It was too hard to communicate by trying to yell over the turbine's roar. Instead he turned and glanced at the instrument panel, as if there were something interesting there.

Gerber stepped down, waited until the cargo was stacked at the side of the pad and then climbed back in. As he buckled his seat belt, the helicopter came up to a hover, hung there and then took off, climbing out.

For a moment Gerber watched their progress. The camp slipped away. On one side he could see the path of the enemy assault. The grass was crushed. Moving among the dead, picking up the weapons, was Fetterman's patrol. Then the helicopter was over the jungle and the camp was lost behind him.

Leaning against the soundproofing, he closed his eyes and tried to figure out what he'd need. The simplest thing would be to have Bromhead move a strike force from Song Be down closer to him. And to get another strike force from Henderson in Moc Hoa. That would give them three camps in the area that could support one another.

Then, if he could convince the Twenty-fifth to patrol his area, that would push the VC and NVA north. He could then drop in on the province chief and suggest that the VC weren't to be trusted. A little diplomacy there, and the VC would find themselves in trouble.

General Platt would agree to Gerber's suggestions because they wouldn't involve moving any large-scale forces. Some would have to be realigned, but that wouldn't cause any trouble. Henderson might bitch a little, but he always did. Bromhead wouldn't complain. He'd welcome the chance to work the Xa Cat area because it would help stabilize the situation at his own camp.

Gerber opened his eyes and glanced out of the cargo compartment. A flight of Hueys was orbiting a mile or two to the north, and beyond them the landscape was fountaining upward, indicating an artillery barrage prior to a combat assault. Then they were beyond the barrage, dropping slightly as they plunged toward the ground.

Gerber's stomach did a somersault. He blinked and saw a small village whose hootches were topped by bright tin roofs. Palm trees partly protected the village, and a highway ran right through it. Gerber knew he was looking at Highway One; they weren't far from Saigon now.

He could see the traffic on the highway—military trucks, jeeps, scooters, Lambrettas and oxcarts. The oxen didn't seem to care about the military vehicles. They plodded along the red dirt shoulders, pulling carts filled with manure.

A few minutes later the Huey climbed again, as a prelude to landing near the MACV-SOG building. They cut across the runways, shooting their approach to the pad there. Gerber watched it all, waiting for an F-4 Phantom to climb up and slam into them. He noticed two of the fighters sitting at the end of the runway, but they stayed where they were until the helicopter was out of the way.

The Huey touched down a few moments later. Gerber unbuckled his seat belt and knelt on the cargo compartment floor between the pilots. He touched one of them on the shoulder and shouted, "Thanks for the lift!"

The aircraft commander held up a thumb.

Gerber turned and jumped out. As he walked across the tarmac, the chopper lifted and took off. At the door he turned and saw it cross the runways again, heading back to Tay Ninh.

Inside the SOG building, Gerber entered the dayroom and found himself a Coke. He opened it and drank deeply. Then, before he could move, an NCO entered the dayroom. "Jesus, you look like shit."

"Thank you, Sergeant."

"No, sir. I mean it. You been out rolling in the mud?"

"I've been in the field. I need to grab a shower and I need a clean uniform."

"Yes, sir. Follow me."

Gerber and the NCO left the dayroom and walked down the narrow hallway. They passed the briefing and radio rooms and entered the supply bay at the rear of the building. The sergeant moved along it, then stopped near the jungle fatigues. He collected a jungle jacket and pants, then found an OD terry-cloth towel. Turning, he handed it all to Gerber. "That do it, sir?"

"Shaving kit?"

"Of course." The NCO moved along the shelves, found one of the VIP kits and handed it to Gerber. It had a disposable razor, a toothbrush, a miniature tube of toothpaste, a comb and a little bar of soap. "That do it?"

"Fine."

The sergeant left, and Gerber headed for the showers. Slowly he stripped off his dirty uniform and dropped it onto the floor. Someone with a big washing machine could probably clean it, but it wasn't worth the effort. He kicked it out of the way, took the shaving kit and stepped into the shower. Pulling the chain attached to the shower head, he stepped under the cool spray with relief. He soaked himself as well as he could, rinsed, then repeated the process. Finished, he moved to the nearby sink and started shaving.

When that was done, he pulled his clean clothes off a hook and dressed. He put on his dirty boots, but figured no one would notice that. Leaving the SOG building, he located a jeep, put his rifle in the rear and climbed behind the wheel. No one had bothered to lock the wheel, so Gerber started it and drove toward the headquarters building.

BY NOON FETTERMAN and his squad had picked up all the discarded weapons. They had also dragged the enemy bodies closer to the perimeter, where a dozen men were now digging a ditch.

Fetterman returned to the perimeter, carrying a dozen AKs with him. As he entered, Washington hailed him. "We'd better burn the bodies."

"You that worried about disease?"

Washington grinned. "Actually, the trench won't be deep enough, and in a couple of days it's going to stink around here. We've got to burn them."

"Then we'll have to get some diesel fuel in here."

"I'll mention it to Bocker."

Minh approached. He glanced out to where the men were working and then turned his attention on Fetterman. "We're a little strapped now, old boy."

Fetterman was about to ask Minh what he meant and then realized. They had Kepler out with a platoon, had a squad out digging the mass grave, Gerber was in Saigon, and Bocker had taken half a platoon to help him stack equipment.

"Captain said he'd arrange more people for us," Fetterman said.

"Just thought I'd let you know we're stretching it mighty thin." Minh smiled. "Didn't expect this when you came for your visit."

Fetterman nodded. "Not much we can do about it now."

Minh agreed. "But we could be in trouble tonight."

THE LITTLE JET touched down at Clark Air Force Base in the Philippines. Crinshaw was wide awake, even though they'd been flying all night. Although there was no bed on the plane, the seats were designed so that a man could stretch out comfortably and get some sleep. Crinshaw had managed that, after Captain Sheila Henrikson had decided she was satisfied.

As the plane rolled to a stop, Henrikson unbuckled her seat belt and stepped over to Crinshaw. "What are your plans now, General?"

"How long is the layover here?"

"We'll switch pilots. Regulations."

"What about you?"

She smiled at him. "I can stay here or go on. The only real problem is South Vietnam. They're supposed to keep all women, except for nurses, out of the combat zone."

"But a quick flight in and out isn't a problem?"

"No, sir." She knelt next to him. "And, best of all, I can put in for combat pay."

"You can do that?"

"Regulations state that the moment the aircraft touches down in Saigon, I'm eligible, even if we just turn around with the engines running."

"Good," said Crinshaw. "Now what?"

"We've got a few hours here. Maybe you'd like to get something to eat?"

Crinshaw looked over at Seneff. The sergeant hadn't said much since they'd taken off from Louisiana the day before. "I'll stay here, General," he said now.

"Loosen up, Sergeant. Get out and live. We're on our way to Vietnam and we might not survive the year."

"Yes, sir."

The plane rolled to a halt. Crinshaw glanced out the window and saw a car racing over the tarmac, heading straight for the aircraft. "Jesus!"

"You have to expect that, General," said Henrikson. "A major general can cause a lot of trouble if he's offended or feels he's been slighted."

As the engines stopped, the hatch was opened and pulled out to form the steps. A young officer, dressed in fresh khakis and wearing a number of combat awards above his pocket, stuck his head in. "General Crinshaw?"

Crinshaw stared at the man, then looked at the Air Force captain. Even after a night on the plane, she looked fresh. It was true that she had changed uniforms as they had crossed the international date line, but it was still a feat. She looked much better than the young officer with his face stuck in the aircraft. "I'll be fine. You can go."

"Sir, I've been instructed to see to your needs and make sure that your stopover here at Clark is one that you'll remember always."

"Don't worry about it. Leave the car."

The man looked as if he'd been insulted. He stood there, the crimson creeping up his neck and spreading over his face. He didn't know what to do. His orders had been clear. And now the general had changed them.

"Captain Henrikson will be showing me around," said Crinshaw.

"Captain Henrikson?"

Crinshaw pointed at the female captain. "She's been assigned to take care of my needs, and her qualifications are much more impressive than yours."

"Yes, sir." He stepped back, as if to leave, and then returned. "If there's anything you need, anything at all, I'll take care of it."

"I'll be sure and let you know. And I'll have no complaints if you can find your way out of here."

"Yes, sir."

As the young officer disappeared, Henrikson said, "You didn't have to be quite so rude."

"Sometimes you do," said Crinshaw. "Everyone's so afraid of insulting you that they won't listen. Rudeness is the only weapon."

Henrikson moved closer to Crinshaw and rubbed against him. He glanced at her, and for a moment he could see Jennifer sitting in the living room, crying. He had a pang of guilt as he thought about her, but then forgot it. Jennifer was in Louisiana and would never know what he was doing in the Philippines. Henrikson was in the Air Force and would never be assigned to an Army base, so there was no chance they'd ever meet back home.

As they reached the hatch, Crinshaw turned. "Seneff, I'll see you in a couple of hours. Find something to amuse yourself."

Seneff nodded. "Yes, General."

"Now," said Crinshaw, smiling at Henrikson, "I hope you have something in mind."

Henrikson grinned and nodded. "I know where there's a bed."

"That would be a change," said Crinshaw, laughing.

13

OUTSIDE THE VILLAGE
OF PHU RON

From the moment they crested the jungled ridge and Kepler could look down into the huge clearing surrounded by rice paddies, he knew something was wrong. It was just after noon, and the fields should have been tended and there should have been people in the village. Women should have been sitting near the cooking fires, using stone tools to crush the rice, and there should have been kids running around outside.

Crouching near the thick trunk of a teak tree, Kepler studied the scene. The men had spread out around him, forming a loose circle. Kepler wiped the sweat from his face and rubbed it on his thigh. He clutched his M-16 in his left hand and pondered what to do. There had to be people down there. He knew they were down there somewhere. The cook fires were still burning, creating thin columns of blue smoke. An ox, tethered to a pole, stood sentinel, as if it had been carved out of stone.

"We go down?" asked one of the Vietnamese strikers.

Kepler nodded, then looked at the man. "We go down, but very carefully." He pointed at the RTO and waved him closer. Taking the handset, he made a call, "Zulu Base, Zulu Base, this is Zulu Two."

"Go, Two."

"I'm near the village of Phu Ron. Something's wrong down here. Inbound."

"Roger. I'll monitor this frequency."

Kepler gave the handset to the RTO and then stood up. He glanced at his weapon and flipped it to single-shot. As the rest of the patrol formed behind him, he took a step forward. Glancing over his shoulder, he saw that the men were ready. Moving slowly, he worked his way into the sunlight and onto a grass-covered plain that sloped down gently. He proceeded cautiously, his head and eyes moving, looking for the first evidence of something wrong. He was watching for a sudden movement that would tip the enemy's hand.

Behind him, the strikers fanned out, making the distance between them even greater. Kepler stopped once and scanned the whole village, but saw nothing out of the ordinary, except the lack of people.

They reached the base of the slope and the edge of the rice paddies. Normally Kepler would have walked through the paddies, avoiding the dikes because of booby traps, but this portion of South Vietnam had been left alone. The VC, if they had planted any booby traps, wouldn't be replacing them. The farmers would only remove them. It should be fairly safe on the dikes.

Keeping his eyes on the village, Kepler stepped up onto the closest of the dikes. The strikers followed suit, spreading throughout the paddy. The burst of machine-gun fire wasn't a surprise. Kepler dived to the right toward a corner of the paddy, landing with a splash. He scrambled up against the dike and peeked over the red dirt.

From the right came a quiet groaning. One striker was down, blood staining his uniform. His weapon had dropped into the paddy, the barrel in the water. The wounded man made no attempt to move, and no one tried to get to him.

Kepler spotted the enemy machine gun. He twisted around and squinted through his sights, but didn't fire. Instead he tried to locate the rest of the enemy. They had to be somewhere.

Around him the strikers began to shoot. There was a rattling of weapons, some on single-shot and some on full-auto. The rounds slammed into the village, kicking up dirt near the machine gun or punching through the mud walls of the tiny hootches.

More firing erupted. From the darkened doorways he could see muzzle-flashes. Rounds snapped overhead, some hitting the water and splashing, others slamming into the dikes.

The hammering of M-16s blended into a single, long detonation. An M-79 blooped out a round. It fell short of the machine-gun nest, exploding in a cloud of black smoke and red dust.

The RTO was crouched in a paddy thirty feet from Kepler. He thought of calling in an artillery strike, but ruled against it. If there were any villagers present, they would be in as much danger as the enemy soldiers.

Instead Kepler brought his feet up under him and glanced over the top of the dike. The firing from the village had tapered off. The machine gun was chattering, the rounds directed at another target.

Without thinking, Kepler leaped over the top of the dike and stretched out in a racing dive. He landed with a giant splash and then scrambled through the muddy water.

Another M-79 round landed, this one closer to the machine gun. It stopped firing for an instant and then opened up again, the rounds directed at the grenadier. The rice paddy around him erupted as the bullets smashed into the dike.

Kepler aimed then. He pulled the trigger quickly, and his rounds smashed into the door of the hootch, peeling away the mud in great dusty clouds. But the machine gun didn't cease firing.

Now the strikers were beginning to advance. Several laid down a covering fire while others moved up—a classic fire-and-maneuver operation.

From the door of a hootch a man sprinted. He wore black pajamas and a khaki-colored chest protector and carried an AK. Kepler tracked him, aimed and fired. Nothing. He fired again and then again. The man stumbled once, as if he'd caught his foot, then took two more running steps and dropped his weapon. His motion was erratic. Finally he stopped, fell to his knees and pitched forward onto his face.

Suddenly the battle changed. The wounded striker, lying on the dike, suffered heavy fire. Bullets landed around him, kicking up clouds of dust. The VC had decided to kill the bait.

A striker jumped up, ran forward and threw himself down into the rice paddy near the wounded man. Kepler saw that and rose slightly, switching to full-auto. "Put out rounds," he ordered.

The grenade launcher fired again and again, as fast as possible. The explosions rocked the village, and black smoke drifted on the light breeze. Rounds from the M-16s, and finally the M-60, began to slam into the hootches. Dirt fountained and mud from the dwellings cascaded.

The striker reached out of the paddy and snagged the foot of the wounded man. The striker sat back and pulled, like a man reeling in a trophy-class fish. There was a wail of pain from the wounded soldier, a shriek that climbed in pitch like a police siren. The wounded man slipped from the dike and into the water, finally protected.

Kepler was up then and running. He splashed through the water, leaped a dike and ran to the edge of the village, where he threw himself to the ground and rolled to the right toward a coconut tree. Enemy gunners fired at him, some of the rounds hitting the tree. Kepler returned fire.

The strikers did the same, maneuvering toward the village. One of them was hit on a dike. He took a step and then tumbled facedown into the paddy.

The machine gun fell silent. Kepler knew what that meant. The VC were withdrawing, getting the important equipment out before he and the strikers could capture it.

Again he was up and running, this time to the left. He rounded the corner of a hootch. Spread out in front of him was the rear of the village. The VC were withdrawing along a dike, heading for the jungle.

Kneeling, Kepler aimed at the last man in the line. He squeezed the trigger, and the VC pitched to the right into the water. Then, from a cluster of hootches, he saw the fleeing machine-gun crew. Kepler sighted on the man carrying the gun. Again he fired and the man fell.

The scramble for safety ended. The remaining two men pivoted and opened fire. Kepler had to dive for cover. An instant later another VC dashed forward and snatched at the machine gun. As that man started running, Kepler fired at him without results. He shot again and again, but the man kept running. Then, suddenly, out of nowhere, there was a single, quiet explosion and a puff of black smoke, which seemed to lift the VC higher and flip him over.

The first of the enemy soldiers reached the trees, but they didn't stop. They kept running. One man fell to his hands and knees, tried to stand up and took a bullet in the back of the head, exploding out the front in a spray of blood and bone.

And then the firing tapered off to single shots, most of them into the trees as the strikers hoped to kill a few more enemy before they got away. Kepler was up and running toward the machine gun. He reached it and saw that the grenade had riddled the wooden stock, but it seemed to be in good shape.

Using his toe, he turned over the body of the gunner. The shrapnel from the grenade had torn up his chest and abdomen. Intestines protruded through holes in his uniform and skin. Blood had pooled under him, and the flies were already beginning to swarm.

As strikers moved from the village to check the bodies of the dead, Kepler retreated, carrying the machine gun with him. He came around a hootch and saw two of his men crouched next to the body of the dead striker. They had dragged him out of the water, while the wounded man had been carried forward so that he was lying in the shade of one of the trees.

"Evac?" asked the senior NCO.

Kepler nodded and turned, looking for the RTO. While the Vietnamese strikers took up positions for security and searched the village, Kepler could get a chopper in for the wounded man. He walked over and knelt next to him. The round had gone clean through his shoulder. The water of the rice paddy had gotten into the wound so that there was a real danger of infection.

"How is he?" Kepler asked the medic.

"He be fine if we get him out of here."

"We'll get that taken care of now," said Kepler. He stood and started for the RTO, who was moving toward him. They met and Kepler took the handset, lifting it to his ear. Squeezing it, he said, "Zulu Base, this is Two."

"Go."

"Need a Medevac at Phu Ron. I have one dead and one wounded."

"Say status of wounded."

"Roger. No immediate danger, but we do need to get him to the hospital."

"Roger. I'll get a chopper on the way. Stand by."

Kepler gave the handset to the RTO. One of the strikers was coming out of a hootch, three people in front of him. All had their hands in the air. Kepler moved toward them.

"What do you have?" When the striker didn't respond, Kepler asked the question in Vietnamese.

"I found them inside. Hiding."

Kepler stared at the three people. Two women and an old man. He'd been in Vietnam long enough to know any of all three could be dangerous. Age and sex made no difference. Seven-year-old girls had taken runs at American units, grenades in their hot little hands. Americans, seeing only a little girl, hadn't killed them, and as a result lost their own lives.

But these people weren't armed. All three wore black pajamas. There was no sign of any weapons. There was fear in the eyes of each one. They knew they were going to die, because the Americans always killed prisoners. The VC had told them that repeatedly.

Then, from the other end of the village, another striker and another three people appeared. Two men, one of them a military-age male, and one girl, no more than fourteen.

"Okay," said Kepler. "Let's get all the people rounded up. Find out what's happening here."

Two of the strikers came forward from the other side of the village, carrying the weapons dropped by the dead enemy soldiers. They came up to Kepler and set the AKs down near his feet. Then, following the orders of their NCOs, they hurried to help clear the village.

Kepler retreated, accompanied by the RTO, and set up his command post near the tree where the wounded man waited for a Medevac. He knelt there, pulled the boonie hat from his head and wiped the sweat from his face.

"We get them good," said the RTO.

"I don't know if we got them good," responded Kepler. "But we did get them."

Standing then and leaning against the tree, he watched as more of the villagers appeared. Some of them came out reluctantly, while others came out with a sense of resignation, acting as if they were about to die. From one hootch a sack of rice was thrown. It was joined a moment later by another and then another.

"You wait here," Kepler said to the RTO. "Anyone tries to reach me, you give a shout."

"Yes, Sergeant."

Kepler walked toward the growing pile of rice. He could see the symbols printed on the front of the bags. There was a shield with a blue field across the top filled with white stars. The bottom of the shield had alternating red and white stripes. Across it were two hands grasping in a symbol of friendship. Along the bottom of the bag were the words To Our Friends in Vietnam from the People of the United States.

One of the NCOs looked up at Kepler. "VC stockpile. They were trying to get it when we walked up."

"Shit."

The Vietnamese sergeant nodded. "Your countrymen are certainly making things tough for us."

Kepler nodded. He wanted to tell the man that the rice had been shipped to the South Vietnamese. If it was in the hands of the VC, then it was stolen from the South.

Instead he said, "Let's get it distributed to the people here. I want that rice handed out. I don't want to see any of it stored."

"Chopper!" yelled the RTO.

Kepler rushed back to the RTO. He took the handset and said, "This is Zulu Two."

"Zulu Two, this is Medevac Two One, inbound your location. Say condition of LZ."

"LZ is cold. We have one wounded and one dead."

"Roger. Can you throw smoke?"

"Roger." Kepler nodded at the RTO, who pulled a grenade from his harness, yanked the pin free and threw it fifteen feet to the right.

"ID green."

"Roger, green." Kepler could hear the chopper but couldn't see it. He turned slightly toward the sound, and the helicopter popped up suddenly over the treetops.

The helicopter descended rapidly. It aimed at the cloud of smoke billowing from the grenade. Rotor wash caught the smoke and twisted it around, swirling it up into the rotor system. The pilot leveled the skids, and the aircraft hung there for a moment before settling to the ground.

As soon as it touched down, two men picked up the wounded man and carried him to the chopper. One of the crewmen leaped out and helped slide the casualty into the cargo compartment. Two other men ran forward with the body of the dead striker. Once the body was loaded on the chopper, they scrambled away. When they were clear, Kepler held up his right thumb, telling the pilot he could take off.

The helicopter lifted off the ground and hung suspended for a moment, kicking up a cloud of red dust. Kepler turned away from it and closed his eyes. An instant later the turbine roar began to fade and the dust settled.

Then Kepler realized he'd failed to get any of the rice sacks onto the chopper. He didn't want to leave very much because the VC would just steal it. The people wouldn't have it whether he took it or not.

Glancing at his watch, he realized it was getting late. They'd have to get out. The VC would probably come back, hoping to catch them around dusk, knowing it would be hard to get support in.

The villagers sat near the rice sacks, watching the strikers, waiting for death. Kepler walked over to them. As he moved, he jerked at the sling of his M-16 and slipped it over his shoulder. A soldier looked less threatening with his rifle slung.

When he reached the villagers, he stared down at them. They were a dirty, tired-looking bunch—people who had nothing going for them other than the rice paddies around them and the assistance from American people.

"Each of you may take one bag of rice," Kepler told them.

They sat there, unimpressed. Kepler grinned, figuring none of them could speak English. He switched to Vietnamese, but nothing seemed to register. Finally he picked up a bag and tried to hand it to one of the farmers. The man stared up, his eyes wide.

Kepler grinned at him, and still the man refused to move. Still grinning, Kepler set the bag at the man's feet. He tried to hand another sack to another farmer and ended up setting it at that man's feet, too.

One of his NCOs came up. "We have cleared the area. All VC are gone."

Looking away from the farmers, Kepler said, "Then let's prepare to move back to camp."

"The rice?"

"We know it's here and we've given it back to the people. We'll have to check here again."

As the NCO moved away, Kepler watched the farmers. The strikers were all moving toward the edge of the village. One villager got to his feet and began to drag off a bag of rice.

As soon as he did, all the others did the same. They had finally realized that Kepler was telling the truth.

Within minutes Kepler and his men had withdrawn from the village and were climbing the slope back toward the jungle. Kepler hoped the VC wouldn't return for a couple of days. He wanted to come back himself. The first of his agents might be recruited from the village, if he could get back in time. It was always a question of time.

14

XAN HOA, CAMBODIA

Lieutenant Tuyen Van Thien watched as the patrol straggled in. They looked beaten. They didn't come in with their heads high, talking about victory. They dragged their feet and looked tired and dirty. Beaten.

Thien, along with several of the other officers, left the small porch of their hut. They had been sitting there, watching the jungle around them, waiting for the patrols to return.

The patrol leader, a small man in mud-smeared khakis, stopped in front of the other officers. He stared at them, almost defying any of them to speak.

"What happened, Lieutenant?" asked the commander.

"The Americans arrived," he said simply.

"What happened?" repeated Thien.

The patrol lieutenant looked at Thien. "They came down the hill, shooting. We didn't want to tip our hand. We halted them and then tried to slip away."

"It didn't work?"

"They came running at us. A hundred of them. We were lucky to get out."

"You'd better see to your men," said the commander. "And then I'll want a full report."

"Yes, Comrade."

The man turned and walked back to where his men waited. None of them were wounded. They were all healthy, and Thien wondered about that. Had they left the wounded, or had there been no wounded to leave? He couldn't think of a battle where there had been no wounded.

"Come with me, Lieutenant Thien," said the commander.

Thien nodded and followed. They walked to the notched log that served as a step up into the command hut. Entering, they stopped in front of the picture of Ho Chi Minh hanging on the wall. There was an old desk with a broken leg, a wooden folding chair and the North Vietnamese flag.

"Lieutenant Tranh didn't distinguish himself today," the commander observed.

"No, Comrade," agreed Thien.

"I think we should move back to the village of Phu Ron. We have too much there to ignore it."

"I can leave at dusk," said Thien. He hesitated and then asked, "What about Tranh?"

The commander shrugged. "It was his first time in the field without supervision. There are many things that can go wrong. If he has learned from the experience, then it was a good mission."

"Yes, Comrade."

"You don't approve?"

"It's not for me to approve or not approve. I believe the men must come first and that the wounded shouldn't be left to the mercy of the Americans."

The commander nodded, then smiled. "A wounded man can be turned to our advantage. The Americans are compassionate. They will hold up their pursuit to care for a wounded man, even when that man is the enemy.''

"Sometimes they just shoot him."

"Sometimes they do, but a wounded man is sometimes a liability that can't be tolerated. Sometimes there's nothing to do but leave the wounded and hope for the best.''

"Yes, Comrade."

"You don't agree?"

"I don't believe in the mercy of the enemy. We must take care of our own, because there's no one else around to take care of us.''

"You'd sacrifice your platoon to save a single man?"

Thien stood quietly for a moment. "If the men know that I won't leave a wounded man in the field, then they'll fight all that harder.''

"There's something to be said for that," agreed the commander. "Now, you'll go to Phu Ron and see what must be done?''

"Certainly," said Thien.

"When you're ready to leave, please stop by to alert me."

"Yes, Comrade." Thien turned and left the hut. He walked slowly past the tiny building that served as a mess hall and stopped at the edge of the jungle, where the men's huts were located. It looked as if the jungle had grown to form a roof over the area, protecting the men from the elements and the cameras of American reconnaissance planes.

Sergeant Ky saw him, left his hut and came forward. Thien nodded at him. "Get the men ready. We have a mission."

"A tough one?"

"Routine. We'll move out in about an hour or so."

"We'll be ready."

GERBER SAT ON THE BED in his hotel room and let the cold air from the air conditioner blow on him. He had unbuttoned his shirt, trying to dry himself. The humidity in Saigon never allowed anything to dry. Walking slowly was enough to create a sweat that soaked the clothes. Comfort was impossible no matter where you were in Vietnam.

Gerber grinned at the floor. The meeting with Platt had lasted no more than fifteen minutes, and the general had agreed to everything he had suggested. It was convenient to have a general who believed in everything you did. It made getting things done easy.

Platt had listened to him as he had outlined his needs, telling the general how he wanted to borrow the men and supplies. A group of engineers to erect the camp. Soldiers from the Twenty-fifth to patrol the area until he could get his strikers trained. Support from the Special Forces camps at Song Be and Moc Hoa.

Platt had nodded, made notes, and when Gerber had completed his shopping list, said, "Engineers can possibly get out there this afternoon. Patrols from the Twenty-fifth probably won't hit the field until tomorrow."

"Will I be able to suggest areas of patrol for them?"

"Hell, Captain, I'd be disappointed if you didn't have suggestions. It's your AO and you should be familiar with it. I'll advise the various commanders."

"What about the artillery?"

Platt nodded and pulled a map out of his desk. There were no American camps marked on it. Just the Vietnamese landmarks and villages. "There are two fire bases that'll be alerted to provide support if you call for it."

"Yes, sir."

Platt folded the map and stuffed it into his desk drawer. "Anything else?"

Gerber thought for a moment. "We could use more heavy weapons. Mortar and machine guns."

"I'll put my supply sergeant on it."

"Thank you, General."

Platt stood and held his hand across the desk. "You keep me informed, Captain. If there's anything you need, just let me know."

"Yes, General."

Gerber had left then. He didn't want to head right back to the camp at Xa Cat. Fetterman could handle anything that happened, and there was little chance the VC or NVA would try anything during the day. They needed the night to mount their attack. Coming out in the daylight made them that much more vulnerable.

So he'd driven back to the SOG building, left the jeep there and taken a cab downtown, checking in at his hotel. Now, sitting there, he felt guilty. Fetterman and the others were working in the hot, humid weather while he tried to freeze himself to death. Had the situation been different, if Fetterman or one of the others had gone into Saigon, he would have taken advantage of everything there. When the chance presented itself, you took advantage of it because you never knew when you'd have the chance again.

He glanced at the wardrobe standing against the wall, but didn't have the energy to get up and fish out the bottle of Beam's inside. He didn't have the energy to do anything at the moment. It was almost as if Newton's First Law of Motion applied directly to him. A body at rest tends to stay at rest. Gerber didn't want to move until sometime in the next decade.

Then, almost as if designed to shake him out of his stupor, there was a knock at the door. Figuring it was the maid, he got up, walked over and opened the door. Surprised, he found Robin Morrow standing there.

"You're here," she said.

"For a little while, anyway. How did you find me?"

She pushed past him into the room. As he closed the door, she said, "I just stopped by on the off chance. Someone told me he saw you over at SOG, so I thought you might be back."

"For a little while," he repeated.

She turned to face him. "How long?"

Unwanted, an old image flashed in his mind. He was in Saigon, summoned by a general named Crinshaw, and while he was eating a luxurious dinner, his camp was being hit by a reinforced enemy company. True, in actuality, Bromhead had held the camp and the casualties had been light, but the image remained. He could still see himself stuffing his face while his men were fighting and dying.

"An hour."

Tugging at the zipper of her modified jumpsuit, Morrow said, "Just enough time."

"Sit down, Robin," said Gerber.

"Sit down? I don't want to sit down."

"I've got an hour to get back to Hotel Three. It'll take thirty minutes to get over there, if I can get a cab. And I don't want to miss the flight."

"You can get another."

Gerber shrugged. What could he say? He was worried about what was happening in the field. He couldn't shake the feeling that something terrible was happening. All he could think about was that if he didn't enjoy himself here, if he just headed directly back to Xa Cat, he'd find everything all right.

He knew it was a ridiculous superstition, but he couldn't shake it. He was like a baseball player who went through a ritual as he stepped to the plate. Knock the dirt from his cleats, swing the bat twice and then slowly step into the batter's box. Break the ritual and he'd strike out. Tell him he was superstitious and he'd deny it, but the next time he went to the plate, he'd do the same thing.

"Ride with me out there," Gerber said finally.

Zipping up, she said, "Sure. Just what the hell's going on?"

Gerber moved to the wardrobe, unlocked it and took out his bottle of Beam's. Uncapping it, he tilted it to his lips and drank deeply. Then, handing the bottle to her, he said, "Nothing much. Just a camp being completed."

"Uh-huh," she said. She took a sip and gave the Beam's back. "This have anything to do with that argument a couple of days ago?"

Gerber grinned. "It might."

"Good," she said. "I want in on it."

Turning and putting the bottle away, Gerber said, "There's nothing to get in on now. We're just reopening a camp."

"Sure," she said. "I know you, Mack. You're up to something else, and I want in on it."

"When we've got things worked out, you'll be in on it. Not before."

Without giving him a chance, she asked, "What about Meyers? He going to be in on it, too?"

"When we're ready."

Changing the subject, she asked, "You sure you have to get back?"

"I'm afraid so," said Gerber. He plucked his M-16 from the corner. "The sooner the better."

Morrow moved to the door. "If you're sure."

Gerber didn't say a word. He just followed her as she walked out into the hall.

CRINSHAW DECIDED that being a major general was even better than being a brigadier general. There wasn't that much difference in the rank, but people thought there was. Most people jumped through a hoop when a brigadier called, but if the general had two stars, they jumped higher and harder, afraid of what he could do to them. A lieutenant general probably had it even better. But for now two stars were more than enough.

After a quick tour of Clark Air Force Base, they drove to the VOQ, where the clerk was only too happy to provide the general with a room so that he could rest and clean up while his aircraft was being serviced. The man stood at attention the whole time Crinshaw was there.

As Crinshaw and Henrikson hurried down the hall to their room, she laughed. "You sure put the fear of God into him."

"No," said Crinshaw, "my stars did that."

They stopped at a wooden door painted off-white. The doorknob was made of brass and had been polished recently. Crinshaw rubbed it, almost fondled it, knowing he was tarnishing it. Someone would have to polish it again within a day.

He pushed open the door and looked at the room. Modern motel was all he could think of. And not even a good motel. There was a single bed with a green cotton spread, a throw rug near the bed, closed blinds on the window, a small refrigerator and a desk with a fan. The door opposite him led into the bathroom, which was shared by the room on the other side.

"You'd think a general would get better quarters," said Henrikson.

"If I wanted to make a fuss, that would be no problem," said Crinshaw. "But that all takes time."

"And we don't have all that much."

"Well," said Crinshaw, "we have as much as I say. The jet can't take off without me."

Henrikson closed the door and leaned against it. "That's true."

Crinshaw pulled his hat from his head and walked to the refrigerator, setting the hat on top. He turned and watched as Henrikson began to slowly unbutton her jacket.

"You sure you want to do that?" asked Crinshaw.

"Isn't it what you want?"

Crinshaw nodded and watched as she stripped off her jacket, the shirt under it and then took off her skirt, letting it fall to the floor and pool at her feet. She stood in front of him, wearing only her bra, half-slip and panties. The garter and stockings had been left on the airplane the night before.

Seeing that Crinshaw was watching her, she finished taking off her clothes. Then standing there naked, she smiled at him and waited for him to make a move.

Crinshaw studied her closely. The night before, in the rear of the jet, he hadn't been able to look at her properly. The close confines and the darkness had made it impossible. Now he could see that she had a good body. She was a damn good-looking woman.

As he moved toward her, he had no thought of Jennifer in Louisiana. He didn't think of her sitting on the couch, crying because he would be gone for a year. He didn't think of her at all. He was interested only in Sheila Henrikson as she reached down and worked the zipper of his pants. That was all he cared about. For the moment.

15

XA CAT SPECIAL FORCES CAMP

Gerber arrived an hour before sundown to a camp that was a beehive of activity. The engineers he'd requested had been there since one o'clock, using their expertise to erect the bunkers and the other structures, many of them prefab and flown in by helicopter. Washington's dispensary was no longer a tent, but a wooden building topped by a tin roof. An air conditioner was built into the side of it, but not working because they had yet to get the generator on-line.

A team house, sandbagged heavily, had been built near the dispensary, and Bocker had gotten his commo bunker, which completed the circle of structures. It looked as if three giant wagons had been parked in a defensive ring to fight off attacking Indians. Small walls of sandbags completed the defense, making a redoubt in case the perimeter was overrun during an attack.

The helipad had also been constructed, right where Bocker wanted it. The engineers had brought in some kind of rubberized mat, staked it down and then ringed it with sandbags to hold it in place. A bright orange X had been painted in the center, and a backstop had been set up to one side to protect the heart of the camp from rotor wash. A net had been hung there, too.

As soon as Gerber got out of the chopper, it lifted and took off. Before he could move from the helipad, Fetterman was standing beside him, beaming like an architect who'd designed a town that was suddenly, almost completely, built in a single afternoon.

"Sergeant Tyme got the weapons sited and ready. We've got three mortar pits, though we don't have the compass rose painted on them. We've got a fire arrow, a commo bunker complete with UHF, VHF and Fox Mike capability. We've got an air-conditioned dispensary, but no power yet."

"What about the radios?" asked Gerber.

"They've got their own independent power. Some battery capability, naturally, but also a small generator that can run them, some electric lights and nothing more. It's all down in the bunker."

"This is incredible," said Gerber. He'd hoped they would get the main bunkers and a couple of the support bunkers completed.

"Yes, sir. Engineer captain said they'd bring in a bulldozer tomorrow, dig us an ammo point and then push the boondocks back for us."

"Christ," said Gerber. "How many of them are there?"

"A full company. Just over two hundred men."

"We can't supply two hundred men . . ."

"Apparently they knew that, too. Brought in tents, but didn't bother with them. Brought in their own food, and their cooks prepared a hot meal. Enough for all of us. They also brought in their own weapons. We've suddenly got another two hundred men here to help defend the perimeter."

"Damn!" said Gerber. "I'm quite impressed. Why don't you show me around?"

They left the helipad area and walked toward the perimeter. Fetterman stopped behind the command bunker on the eastern wall. "We've got a .50 and two M-60s in there, plus radio communications. Just Fox Mike, but you can talk to one of the fire bases in the area. Lima lima back to our commo bunker so that Bocker can call for help. There's a stockpile of illumination flares in there, too. Plus a Starlite-scope, binoculars, M-79 grenades and regular hand grenades. Claymore mines can be fired from a master control panel in the bunker, and each bunker along the line controls the claymores in front of it."

"Jesus Christ in a jeep," said Gerber. "These guys have been busy."

"You don't know the half of it. We've four perimeter wires now, lots of tanglefoot, trip flares and more than our share of bouncing bettys. There are three safe routes through the wire, which I and all the other team members know. Tomorrow I'll show them to you."

"Thanks."

They walked on. Gerber could see that the bunkers built by the engineers were professional structures—straight sides, perfect doorways in the back and smooth, flat roofs to absorb the shrapnel of mortar shells and rockets. He could tell by the placement of the bunkers that the heavy weapons would have interlocking fields of fire, which meant that each bunker could support those on either side of it, and the destruction of one wouldn't open a hole in the defense.

They reached the north wall. It opened on a long field of tall grass that swept all the way to the jungle three hundred yards away. There were a few, huge blackened areas scattered around the field.

"Tried to burn off the grass," said Fetterman, "but we couldn't get the fire going. It was just too wet."

"Well, that'll filter any attack we get tonight. They'll want to stay off the burned areas."

"I thought of that, too," said Fetterman. "That's why we have the pattern we do."

They continued around. The west wall overlooked another drop-off. The enemy, if they attacked from that position, would have to scramble up a slope that was as dangerous to the people climbing on it as the bullets raining down. Not a great avenue for attack. The engineers had erected a single command bunker and a number of smaller fighting positions just in case. Two or three machine guns could wipe everything from the slope. There was no real cover on it and no easy way to get up it. They'd have to guard it in case the enemy didn't see it as impossible, but two squads could probably hold it.

They returned to the south side near the helipad. Here the slope was gentler, the climb not as tough, but it was still a nearly impossible attack approach. Open ground for nearly a thousand yards that finally reached the jungle below them. A mortar crew or two could keep men pinned down there, but it just wouldn't make sense to attack it with any kind of force. A suicide squad, maybe, but even that was a poor risk. Once any fighting broke out, everyone else would know it, and again, a reinforced squad or two would keep the enemy in the jungle and out of the camp.

"I'm impressed," said Gerber.

"Now what?" asked Fetterman.

Gerber scratched his head and then wiped the sweat from his face. "I suppose we need a team meeting now to decide what we're going to do tonight. Is Kepler back?"

"About an hour ago. Ran into a little trouble and had to evac one man. Had one killed."

"I'll want a full report on that," said Gerber.

"Of course. He's preparing it now."

Gerber stopped and turned toward the team house, amazed again at how fast the camp had been put together. It would take a well-coordinated effort to push them off the hill. That and a lot of men. He knew the enemy had the soldiers to do, but he didn't know if they had the finesse.

"Let's head on down to the team house. Who's the commander of the engineers?"

"Guy named Parker. Calvin Parker. On his second tour. Spent the first as a grunt and decided he didn't want to do that again."

"Can't say I blame him."

They reached the team house. Fetterman opened the door and Gerber stepped in. The walls were flimsy, only about four feet high. Above them screening was fastened to the supports. He could see the roof and the rafters. A ceiling fan was mounted in the center, but it wasn't moving. There was little in the way of furniture. In one corner a gasoline-powered refrigerator hummed quietly. Gerber turned and glanced at Fetterman.

"Don't ask me," the master sergeant said. "They brought it in and I wasn't going to refuse it."

There were a few brightly colored lawn chairs, a couple of ammo boxes and a single table. Shelves had been constructed on the back wall, but there was nothing on them.

Tyme entered and headed straight for the refrigerator. Opening it, he pulled out a can of Coke and looked at Gerber. "Evening, Captain."

"Evening."

"I'll round up the others," Fetterman said. "You want Minh here, too?"

"Of course. We'll need his men for the listening posts tonight."

"Can I have one?" asked Tyme.

Fetterman looked at the younger soldier. "Why in hell do you want to volunteer for that?"

Tyme shrugged. "Seemed like a good idea."

"If Sergeant Fetterman has no objections, then neither do I."

Fetterman disappeared and Tyme opened the Coke. "What's on the agenda tonight?"

"We're just going to hang loose, I think. I haven't heard from either Bromhead or Henderson, so I don't know what their plans are. Once we get coordinated with them, we'll get our patrols started and then send someone over to see the province chief."

As Tyme moved toward one of the lawn chairs, Bocker entered. "There you are, sir. Got a call from the Third Brigade, Twenty-fifth Infantry. Wanted to alert us that they've got two patrols out in this area now. One's a company-sized sweep that will be in the field for the rest of the week on a search-and-destroy. The other's a platoon-sized ambush that will be out tonight. They'll shift to the west tomorrow and then set up for tomorrow night."

"Locations?"

"Plotted on the maps, sir."

"I'll want to see that as soon as we're through in here," said Gerber.

"Yes, sir."

Again the door opened, and a man Gerber didn't know walked in. He was big, burly through the chest and shoulders, but with thin legs. His jungle fatigues were dirty and sweat-stained, and his boots looked as if they'd been dyed red. He wore a pistol belt with a single canteen, a first-aid kit and a .45 in a military holster. His hair was black and his face tanned. He had small eyes, pushed close together, and almost no eyebrows. A thin mustache was dwarfed by a huge, reddish nose that made him look like a drinker.

He advanced on Gerber and held his hand out. "Name's Parker. Engineers. You must be Gerber."

"MacKenzie K. I'm glad you and your boys could get in here."

"I'm not thrilled about it myself." He grinned, displaying almost perfect teeth. "We were down at Vung Tau, building an R and R center for the brass. The beach, nurses and no one shooting at us. Suddenly we're all on helicopters flying toward Cambodia. I got to tell you, we weren't happy about it. You got some kind of juice."

"For the moment, anyway," said Gerber. "Justin, why don't you get the captain a Coke?"

"Or a beer," said Parker.

Tyme found one and handed it to the engineer.

Kepler walked in, saw Gerber and said, "Had some good luck today."

"I'll want a full briefing on that a little later."

"Yes, sir."

The rest of the team, Washington and Smith, along with Fetterman and Minh, straggled in. Smith got himself a beer and Washington fished out a Coke. They sat down, while Gerber walked to the refrigerator and leaned against it. "I've taken a quick look at the progress made today and I have to say that I'm impressed. A lot of hard work was done today."

"You can thank the engineers," said Fetterman. "Without them we wouldn't have gotten close."

Parker stood up and nodded. "Thanks." Smiling, he added, "Besides, we want to get back to Vung Tau."

"You need a demolitions expert?" asked Smith.

"As a matter of fact, I need one badly. What are your qualifications?"

Gerber jumped in before Smith could answer. "He likes to see things blow up. The bigger the explosion, the happier he is."

Parker rubbed his chin. "I'm not sure we need someone with that attitude."

"If you're in Vung Tau," said Smith, "I can modify my attitude."

"Then you're hired."

Gerber jerked them back to reality. He glanced at Kepler. "What do you have for us?"

Kepler stood and said, "Most of you know we ran into a quick firefight this afternoon. The enemy ran, leaving us with a stockpile of rice. I distributed it to the farmers, but I doubt they'll hang on to it for very long."

Gerber watched the Intel NCO for a moment, then asked, "What aren't you telling me?"

Kepler shrugged. "I'm not sure how to put it into words. We walked right up there and they opened fire. Any kind of fire discipline, any kind of military tactics and they would have pinned us down in the paddies, so they could chop us up. Instead they ran. They didn't even make a good withdrawal."

"Which tells you?"

"Not frontline troops. Soldiers to frighten the civilians, but not men you'd trust in a fight. They just fired their weapons and got the fuck out."

"Meaning?"

"Well, we know they've got some good people in here. We saw some of that last night. Hell, sir, I don't know. Maybe it just means they're so sure of this place that they flood it with anyone who's lying around, not worrying about the levels of training. They're just not worried about us."

"Gives us an advantage."

"Except they know we're here," said Kepler.

Gerber took a deep breath. "Tomorrow you and I are driving into An Loc to visit the local province chief."

"I think I'd rather go back to the village and see what they're doing."

"Let's send someone else," said Gerber. "I want you with me tomorrow when I see this guy."

"Yes, sir."

Gerber looked at Tyme. "Weapons status?"

"We've got twelve M-60 machine guns and six Browning M-2 .50-calibers. I sited the weapons so that they cover the most likely avenues of attack, but held a couple back for the other two walls just in case. We've got three 60 mm mortar pits in and have a stockpile of ammo near them. I'd like to get a couple of 81 mm mortars so that we can throw some flares up if we need them."

"Any prospects for that?"

"Possibly as early as tomorrow."

Gerber looked at Sully Smith but didn't ask a question. Smith said, "Engineers took care of most of my work. Naturally I'd like more claymore mines and trip flares out there. And I haven't had the chance to review the main bunkers." Smith grinned at him evilly.

Gerber understood. At the old Triple Nickel Smith had mined the major bunkers in case they were lost during an assault. Smith was telling him that with the engineers around he had been unable to do that.

"Anything else, Sully?"

Smith shrugged.

"T.J.?"

"You've seen the dispensary. The engineers threw it up in about an hour. It's a good, solid structure. I'm still getting the various supplies sorted out." He grinned. "Though I don't have that much to sort out."

"Tony?"

"Everything is coming together. I'd like to get more patrols out as soon as possible."

"Recruiting?" said Gerber.

"I haven't thought about it yet. Once you've talked to the province chief, we can start a program of recruiting and training."

"Okay," said Gerber. He sat there for a moment and then looked at Minh. "You've been quiet."

"Certainly, old boy. Just listening and learning. The one question I do have is, do you want me to bring up more of my strikers?"

Gerber thought about that. They had two hundred Americans, a hundred strikers and all the air and artillery support they could use. "I think," he said, "that we need to hang loose on that. Let's get things established first."

"Certainly. I'd also like to return to my camp for a couple of days soon."

"Get with Bocker and he'll arrange transport."

"Thank you."

"Anything else?" asked Gerber. He waited a moment, but none of the men said another word. Finally he said, "I'd like to get two or three listening posts out tonight." He glanced at Tyme. "You still want one of them?"

Tyme shrugged. "Hell, sir, I might be more valuable here for countermortar."

"I'd like to take one of them," said Sully.

"Fine."

Minh shrugged. "I'll take the other one, if you don't mind, old boy."

"Fine. Galvin, have we got enough radios for all this?"

"No problem, Captain. We can get them a land line, too. Plenty of that kind of gear came in with the engineers."

"I want the listening posts to go out after dark. Carefully, slowly, and stay in close contact. Galvin, you and I will brief each of them on the locations of the other American patrols."

"Yes, sir."

Gerber stood for a moment and listened. He could still hear the hum of the gas-powered refrigerator and the buzz of conversation drifting on a light breeze, but even so, there was relative silence. No artillery boomed, though he did hear some jets fly over. The traffic, the people, the sounds of civilization were sixty or seventy miles to the south in Saigon. Around him were the natural noises of the jungle. Finally he said, "Let's get at it. We've got a lot of work to do yet."

16

XA CAT SPECIAL FORCES
CAMP

The listening posts didn't do any good. None of them provided warning that the enemy was near. The first indication that the VC were creeping up on the camp came when the mortar rounds began to fall. Gerber had been sitting on the sandbagged wall around the team hootch, hoping the breeze blowing up from the South China Sea would cool and dry him. Instead it made it seem hotter, as if he were sitting in a steam bath with the furnace running.

He heard the distant pop and recognized it immediately. Rather than diving for cover or jumping up to run for a bunker, he slipped from the wall, bowed his head and listened.

The round landed off to the right in the area where the helipad stood. There was nothing there to get hurt. A second round was fired and it landed even farther away. Obviously the enemy gunners weren't very good.

But then he heard a whoosh and saw a flash as a rocket was fired. Rockets were dangerous. They could destroy a bunker easily.

"Incoming!" yelled someone unnecessarily.

Then, suddenly, there were men scrambling all over the camp. Gerber got to his feet then. There was a distant popping as more mortars fired. He stared into the darkness, but he couldn't spot the flash of the tubes. If the fire control tower had been put up, he might have had better luck. On the ground, though, the lay of the land made it impossible to locate the enemy gunners.

Gerber jogged toward the bunker line, listening to the firing. He reached the command bunker and ducked inside. Fetterman was standing at the firing port, the Starlite scope up to his eyes. "See anything?" Gerber asked.

Fetterman shot him a glance. "Nothing at all. No movement yet."

Gerber grabbed the handset of the land line, spun the crank a couple of times and said, "Bocker, get me a status report."

"Yes, sir."

When he hung up, the jungle seemed to erupt. A dozen mortar tubes fired, and fifteen or twenty rockets came off the rails. Instinctively Gerber ducked. "Shit, here they come."

He dropped to one knee and slipped to the right so that he wasn't standing in front of the firing port. Fetterman lowered the Starlite and sat down on the thick planks of the bunker floor.

Behind them it seemed that the camp was beginning to blow up. The mortars fell with dull whumps, and the rockets slammed into the dirt with loud, flat bangs. Even in the bunker Gerber could smell the cordite. Through the floor of the bunker he could feel the vibrations of the detonations.

"They're dropping a lot of stuff on us," said Fetterman. "Yeah."

There was a hammering then, a slow chugging as one of the fifties began to rake the jungle with heavy fire. The ruby tracers seemed to float out toward the jungle. Some disappeared into the trees while others bounced upward, tumbling toward the sky.

The field phone buzzed shrilly and Gerber snagged it. "Gerber." It was Bocker.

"We have the perimeter manned. Captain Parker reports that his men have filled in along the line. Sergeant Tyme reports that he's ready for countermortar."

"Who's spotting for him?"

"One of the listening posts called in and gave us the coordinates of one of the mortars."

"Hell, we've got all the ammo we need. Tell him to go ahead and see what he can do."

"Yes, sir. Are you going to order the firing?"

"Tell everyone to fire when he has a target. Advise them that there are friendlies out there."

"Yes, sir."

"What about the other listening posts?"

"Nothing from them yet. I don't want to buzz them in case the enemy is close."

"Understood. Keep me posted."

"Yes, sir."

Gerber cradled the field phone. Outside, the popping of the mortars continued. Shells were falling all around the camp. Staring out into the open field, he saw a single explosion that looked like a fountain of sparks fifty yards away. It was almost beautiful.

"I think we've got movement in the trees," said Fetterman. He handed the Starlite scope to Gerber.

Gerber scanned the jungle. He spotted a flash and studied it, but there were no more. Firing began along the perimeter as the strikers and the engineers began to put out rounds, trying to suppress the enemy.

"Think we should slow that down?" asked Fetterman.

"We've got plenty of ammo."

Both of them ducked as a mortar shell fell close to the bunker. Dirt drifted down, shaken from the sandbags above them. Fetterman coughed and then grinned. "I hate this."

"Things will change any moment now," said Gerber. "Be patient."

SULLY SMITH LAY on the jungle floor, his face pressed into the rotting carpet of vegetation. He could smell it. He could almost taste it. And he wanted to turn over and breathe the fresh air of the night but couldn't. Enemy soldiers were all around him. A hundred of them. Maybe more.

Two Vietnamese strikers were with him. No one had heard the enemy as they'd slipped into position. A listening post was supposed to give the camp advanced warning of an approaching enemy, but by the time Smith and the strikers had seen the Vietcong and the North Vietnamese it had been too late. To use the radio or the field phone would give them away. The enemy would hear them.

Instead Smith had stretched out, facedown. He'd smeared his face with camou paint so that his skin wouldn't be visible, but that still left his eyes and teeth. He couldn't even whisper. The only chance he had was to lie quietly and let the war sweep over him.

When he realized what was happening, he'd unhooked the wire for the field phone so that it wouldn't chirp unexpectedly. Then he'd shut off the radios. They were cut off from the camp. There was no easy way to call for help and no easy way to get back to the camp.

Now, lifting his head slightly, he could see the shapes of enemy soldiers moving around him. They detached themselves from trees and bushes and then melted back into the jungle. There were pieces of humanity. A head with a helmet, a back complete with pistol belt and a single arm, or a hand clutching an AK-47.

The enemy didn't make much noise. Two soldiers stopped nearby, crouched and whispered briefly, but Smith couldn't hear the words, only the sound of their voices.

Finally there was no movement around them. The enemy was gone. Smith got onto his hands and knees and picked up the field phone. If the enemy stumbled on the wire, they'd be able to follow it back to his hiding place.

Smith reached out and touched one of the strikers on the shoulder. He pointed to the rear, deeper into the jungle, then pulled his knife from the scabbard and held it up, showing it to the man. He was telling him that they needed to use their knives. Any shooting would bring down the enemy.

Smith got to his feet, stepped to the right and leaned against the smooth trunk of a giant teak tree. Glancing to his left, he saw the strikers, charcoal shadows in the blackness of the jungle. Each held a knife, his M-16 slung over his shoulder. They had the radios and the field phone.

Motioning to them, Smith moved off slowly. He ducked around a bush, hesitated, scanned the area and then continued. The demolitions expert was aware of the two men behind him; he couldn't actually hear them, but he could feel them.

Every two steps he stopped and listened. Firing erupted from the jungle. First mortars and then rockets. There was answering fire from the camp—a few mortar rounds, poorly aimed, and the hammering of M-60s and M-2s with suppressing fire. Nothing was coming near him.

He came to a depression in the ground. Rocks formed one side of it. There was a huge bush and a trickle of water. Smith slid into it, his back against the stone. It overhung slightly, providing protection from the rear and overhead. It was an almost perfect place to wait out the mortar barrage.

With the men in place, he extended the antenna on one of the radios, switched it on and then whispered, "Zulu Base, this is Zulu Seven."

"Go, Seven."

"We have Victor Charlie infiltrating the AO. Maybe one hundred of them."

"Roger."

"Be advised that we have moved one hundred yards southeast."

"Roger. Say intentions."

Smith grinned at the radio. "I plan to stay right here until morning."

"Roger."

THE MORTAR AND ROCKET barrage grew. The jungle came alive with the flashes, and the ground rumbled with the explosions. Shrapnel slammed into the bunkers and punched through the thin wooden walls of the team house and the dispensary. The tents erected by the engineers were riddled. Two of them collapsed and one caught fire, burning rapidly and brightly for several minutes.

Gerber stayed in the command bunker, listening to the hammering of the M-60 machine guns. Hot brass bounced around the interior of the bunker and piled up on the floor. The air was hot and heavy with cordite, making it hard to breathe.

"I don't know what I hate most," said Fetterman. "The mortar attack or the moment it stops."

Gerber understood the comment. When the mortar shells stopped, the ground attack would start. This barrage had gone on too long to be anything but the preliminary to a ground assault.

"They'll be surprised tonight," said Gerber.

"Yes, sir."

A moment later silence descended. The last of the mortar shells fell, and there were no new pops from the jungle, just an ominous quiet punctuated by the sound of machine guns and the crackle of a fire behind them.

Fetterman lifted the Starlite scope and scanned the edge of the jungle. There was movement there now. Shapes seemed to dance around the trees. He could see flashes as the little available light reflected off the weapons held by the enemy. "They're massing in front of us," he told Gerber.

The captain grabbed the handset of the field phone and gave the handle a vicious crank.

"Bocker."

"We've got enemy soldiers spotted in the trees on the eastern side of the camp. Have Tyme put some mortar rounds on them and alert the others."

"Yes, sir."

Gerber cradled the instrument and then stepped around toward the Vietnamese machine gunner. Pointing, he said, "Put some rounds into the trees there."

The man nodded, worked the bolt of his weapon and pressed the butterfly trigger. As the weapon started to fire, he jerked a handful of the linked ammo out of the can. The muzzle-flash stabbed out and the ruby tracers flashed.

All along the line the strikers and engineers began to shoot. At first there was no answering fire. Then, in the distance, came a single wailing note from a bugle, followed by whistles and more bugles as the enemy began to swarm out of the jungle, shouting and shooting.

MINH KNEW he was surrounded even before he saw any enemy soldiers. There had been something in the jungle, some subtle change that he had heard. Quietly he alerted those with him and then used the field phone to alert the camp. He whispered into it, telling them who he was and what was happening around him. Then he jerked the wires out because he couldn't risk someone trying to contact him.

The enemy, a dozen VC, settled into the jungle near him, spreading out quietly. There was a rattling of equipment, metal on metal, and Minh knew someone was assembling a mortar tube, complete with base plate and spare ammo. He also knew that, as they fired their rounds, the ground would light up as if someone had used a camera flash to take a picture. His listening post would be exposed, but the strobe effect would also give away the enemy's position.

He rolled to the right and touched the sleeve of the closest NCO. Minh knew the man well. He'd served with him for six months. Sergeant Phouc was a small man filled with hate. He wanted nothing more than to kill Communists, and now he had the chance. Minh raised his knife and pointed toward the men setting up the mortar tube. Phouc nodded and drew his own knife.

Minh alerted the other two soldiers, Corporal Tam and Sergeant Tri. Both were experienced jungle fighters. They could move among the enemy quietly, slit a throat and escape before the VC knew they were around.

On Minh's order all the men slipped from the LP, leaving their equipment behind them. Minh crawled forward, stopped and stared into the jungle. He saw a shadow move, and by glancing at it and then away, he found an enemy soldier. Moving carefully on his belly, he worked his way toward the VC.

Before he could get close the mortar fired. The yellow-orange flash illuminated the ground. Minh froze, his night vision suddenly wiped out. He dropped flat, his face pressed against the ground, his eyes closed.

An instant later he was moving again, the enemy soldier now little more than a blob in the distance. He skirted around behind the man and hesitated, his knife in his hand. He heard the enemy gunners drop another round into the tube. This time he closed his eyes.

As the mortar fired, Minh was up and moving. He seized the enemy soldier from behind, grabbing him under the chin. Lifting, jerking the head up, he slashed with his knife. He felt a hand grab his wrist. Fingernails raked his skin. He struck again, thrusting the knife up into the man's back. There was an instant of resistance as it penetrated the thick pistol belt and uniform, then the soldier spasmed and his foot kicked out.

Minh let go of the body and rolled it away from him. He froze where he was and studied the surrounding territory. Another soldier shifted as the mortar fired. Grinning, Minh moved toward him. As he approached, the VC turned and looked Minh full in the face. The South Vietnamese captain struck quickly. He grabbed the man at the back of the neck and jerked him forward. With the knife, he thrust upward, the blade slicing through the man's uniform. Blood splashed, washing over Minh's hand. He could smell the overpowering odor of copper as the man slipped to his knees, a cry of pain bubbling in his throat.

Minh stepped back and the man fell forward on his face. He crouched, waited and then saw the mortar crew near their tube. Slipping his knife into its scabbard, he reached behind him and grabbed the butt of his M-16. As he dragged it around, his thumb searched for the selector switch.

He didn't use the iron sights but looked over the top of the barrel. Then, with the selector set at full-auto, he opened fire. The muzzle-flash strobed, lighting the mortar tube in the jerky motion of an old silent movie. The VC crew staggered and fell.

GERBER STOOD in the command bunker and watched as the enemy raced across the open ground. Firing erupted along the bunker line as the strikers and the engineers began to shoot at the attackers. Tracers flashed out. Ruby lances slammed into the oncoming enemy or hit the ground, tumbling upward into the sky.

Next to him the Vietnamese machine gunner began to fire. The bolt rattled as the weapon hammered. Hot brass kicked out, hit the sandbags and bounced off the plank flooring. The bunker filled with the odor of cordite.

"Getting close," said Fetterman.

Gerber nodded and picked up the firing controls for the claymore mines. Smith had been right about that. They were going to need more.

The enemy ran over the open ground, firing and yelling. The black mass seemed to rise up from the ground, rushing at them. It twinkled almost gaily as the VC fired from the hip. Green tracers flashed forward, floating like golf balls.

As the first rank hit the perimeter wire, Gerber mashed the button with his thumb. One claymore fired, a flash of orange-yellow as the ball bearings shot out. He hit another and another, firing the claymores in sequence and destroying the first wave of attackers.

But the VC weren't going to be turned away easily. A few threw themselves on the concertina wire, and the men behind them used them to leap over the barrier. They dropped between the wires, knelt and fired. Rounds slammed into the bunkers. One man stood, a satchel charge in his hand. As he wound up to throw it, Gerber fired. The man flipped backward, losing his grip on the explosive. It detonated in a fountain of white-hot sparks behind him.

All over the bunker line the strikers and engineers were shooting. M-16s on full-auto hammered and hammered. Tracers flashed out, a strobing that sparkled along the perimeter, highlighting the enemy soldiers.

Gerber heard himself firing, but nothing from anyone else, so deafening was the fusillade. He knew others were firing because enemy soldiers were dying in the wire. They hung there like moths stuck on pins.

"Come on you bastards," yelled Fetterman. He was grinning evilly, knowing that the enemy was caught by surprise. The VC didn't know that the size of the camp had nearly tripled during the day.

Then, almost as quickly as it had started, the attack collapsed. Those men still alive outside the wire turned and ran. Bugles sounded again. There were shouts and whistles and cries of pain and despair. The firing from outside began to taper off as the enemy tried to disengage.

Gerber grabbed the field phone. "Bocker, I want you to get the mortars going. To the east, and set them to hit at the tree line."

"Will you spot?"

"Of course."

There was a sudden series of pops behind him, and an instant later the ground erupted.

"Need to add about fifty," said Fetterman.

Gerber relayed the message and then yelled, "Fire for effect."

The Vietnamese gunner let go of the trigger. He fell back, bathed in sweat, breathing hard.

"Fire!" ordered Gerber. "Cut them down."

The man leaped back and pressed the butterfly trigger. The machine gun began to shoot again.

And then, almost magically, the enemy was gone. No more shadows danced at the edge of the jungle. There were no more muzzle-flashes, just the detonations of mortar shells as Tyme and his crews tried to inflict more casualties.

The field phone buzzed and Gerber snatched the handset from the cradle. "Gerber."

"Sergeant Smith reported in. He's got people running all around him. Wants to know if you want him to follow them to see where they go."

Gerber shook his head, started to say no and then thought about it. If Smith was careful, trailing the VC far enough back, he might learn where their main camp was. That was the point of moving into Binh Long Province. They weren't there just to set up another Special Forces camp and sit behind the wire, waiting for the enemy to come to them.

"Tell him to break it off if it gets too hairy, but tell him to go ahead."

"Yes, sir."

"I want him to check in every hour on the hour from this point on with a direction of march. If something goes wrong, we'll know where to start the search."

"Yes, sir."

Fetterman glanced at the captain. As Gerber cradled the phone, he said, "Smith is tracking the enemy."

"That a good idea?"

"Why not? Leave the engineers here to work and take the strikers out. Or put the Twenty-fifth in on the enemy base if we can locate it."

Fetterman wiped at the sweat soaking his face. In the half-light of the bunker, it glistened in his short-cropped hair. He looked down at his hand and then rubbed it on his jungle shirt. "I think I'm beginning to understand this whole thing. We're not in it for the glory."

"Hell, no," said Gerber, shaking his head. "We're in it to prove a point."

17

PHU RON, RVN

Thien and his men slipped into the village long after midnight. The villagers were asleep, having eaten their fill for the first time in weeks. Rice that had belonged in the VC stockpiles had been distributed among them, and knowing that the VC would soon reclaim the food, they had eaten as much of it as they could.

Thien had watched the feast from the tree line that overlooked the village. They seemed to ignore the bodies of the VC lying on the ground. Thien would make a point of forcing the farmers to bury the bodies properly. He would teach the villagers to respect the VC dead.

When things had quieted in the village and the last of the lanterns had been extinguished, Thien slipped from cover. With his men following, spread out in case of ambush, he walked down the slope. He moved steadily, holding his AK at port arms. With his eyes, he swept the countryside around him. There was tall grass, most of it waist high. As they moved through the thick, resistant grass, they kicked up a light cloud of red dust. It hung in the air, following them, marking their progress and threatening to choke them.

As they approached the edge of the village, Thien waved an arm and the men collapsed on the ground. The lieutenant knelt on a dike and surveyed the village. He could hear the soft sounds of a radio playing somewhere. A dog barked once and then fell silent.

Thien raised his arm and waved his men forward. They rose out of the dark and infiltrated the village easily. Moving through it slowly, they peeked into huts, looking at the sleeping forms of the farmers and their families. No one heard or saw them.

When the whole village had been searched and found empty of Americans, Thien called his men together. He knelt in front of them like a quarterback in a huddle.

"Wake everyone and gather them together. Then collect all the rice. Look for any weapons and bring them to the center of the village."

"And then?"

"We'll figure something out. A lesson must be taught."

The men got to their feet and trotted off. They began shouting, slamming the butts of their weapons into the huts as they ordered the occupants out.

As the men rounded up the villagers, Thien turned and faced south. There was a quiet popping there, a rattling that sounded like a firefight in the distance. Small arms, mortars and grenades. A long, drawn-out sound.

One of his NCOs approached, and Thien looked at him. "Sounds like a good fight."

Thien nodded. "Must be someone attacking that new American base not far from here."

"Yes, Comrade. We now have the villagers and the rice. No weapons were found."

Thien turned and looked at the assembled Vietnamese. Old and young. Men and women. Boys and girls. They all stood there in the dim light provided by the moon and stars and a single lantern that someone had brought.

"You helped the Americans today," accused Thien, pointing at an old man.

The old man was stooped and emaciated and had a long white beard. He shook his head. "We helped no one."

Thien pointed at the rice. "You were rewarded."

"Only with what was ours."

Thien nodded and pointed at the sacks of rice. "This belonged to the VC. We will take it now."

The old man said nothing. He stood quietly, his head bowed. He had known it would happen.

"But we won't take it all. We'll leave enough for the villagers," said Thien. "We're not greedy."

His men moved forward and pulled two sacks from the stack, leaving them for the villagers. That done, they pulled the rest of the rice to the right, near where the rest of the platoon waited.

"You have left the bodies of our slain warriors rotting in the fields."

"There was no time to bury them," said the old man.

"The penalty for that is two bags of rice." He nodded, and his soldiers reclaimed the two sacks.

"You leave us with nothing."

"You have your fields, your lives and your homes. Be happy we didn't decide differently. Like the Americans have done, we could burn your homes. We could execute you for supporting the Americans regardless of how little support you gave them."

The old man stepped back without speaking again. He, like the others, waited for the men to open fire with their weapons, but that didn't happen.

"Go to your homes now," said Thien, "and be glad we decided to be merciful."

As the crowd began to slip away, Thien turned toward the American camp in the distance. The sounds coming from it had changed in the past few minutes. The firing was tapering off. Mortar shells were falling again, but this time he suspected they were American weapons directed at his comrades.

"Drag the rice out of the way," he said. "Find cover here. We'll wait for a while."

"It will be light soon, Comrade."

Thien looked at his watch. "I know that. But we might need to support our comrades. We'll wait here."

"Yes, Lieutenant."

WITH CONTACT BROKEN, a few enemy mortar rounds fell on the camp again, but these were directed against them in order to provide cover. Gerber crouched in the doorway of the bunker, listening as the detonations walked away from him. Convinced the enemy wasn't going to attack again, he ran from the bunker and headed for the commo bunker near the center of the camp. Sliding to a halt, he scrambled to the top of the bunker and stretched out near the front so he could survey the damage around him.

Surprisingly there was very little. Merely a hole in the roof of the dispensary, some scattered debris from the exploding mortar rounds and the glowing embers of burned tents in the engineers' area. Wires had been ripped out and most of the claymores and trip flares were gone, but all of that could be easily replaced.

Using the binoculars, he scanned the tree lines around the camp. The enemy was definitely gone, having fled from the hammering of the defenders' weapons. Charlie had gotten out quickly.

Gerber climbed off the bunker. As he dropped to the ground, Fetterman approached. "We've got four wounded and two dead."

"Can T.J. take care of the wounded?"

"He said there was no problem. But he wants them evacced tomorrow because of the risks of infection. However, none of the wounds are life-threatening."

Parker ran up to them. He slid to a stop, a hand on his hat, as if afraid it would blow away. Standing there for a moment, clutching his M-16 in his left hand, he swallowed once and asked, "Now what?"

"We hang loose until daylight," said Gerber.

"They coming back?"

"I don't think so," said Fetterman. "Too close to dawn, and they didn't make much progress against us. The added firepower, that is, your men, surprised them."

"So what do we do?" asked Parker.

Gerber wiped his face. He felt the stubble of his beard with his right hand. "You keep your men on the line. They do know how to fight, don't they?"

"They've been through infantry basic training."

"Then you hold right there. Tomorrow you keep a quarter of the men on the perimeter and the rest can work."

"Where are you going to be?"

Gerber slapped Fetterman on the shoulder. "We're going to be leading the strikers after the enemy, just as soon as we learn where they've gone."

"Who'll be in charge here?"

"Why you," said Gerber. "You'll be the senior officer in the camp. You can do that, can't you?"

"I suppose. Yeah. I can do it."

"Fine. I'll meet with you about dawn and let you know the plan."

"Great." Parker whirled and ran off.

Fetterman watched him go. "We're going out at dawn?"

"We're here to clear the area of VC and NVA, and we can't do that by sitting around on our butts."

"Yes, sir. Then I'd better find Tyme and begin to organize this boondoggle."

"As soon as Minh is in, I'll meet with him," said Gerber.

"Where are you going to be?"

Gerber thought for a moment and then said, "In the commo bunker with Bocker."

"Yes, sir."

Gerber watched as Fetterman returned to the perimeter. When he vanished in the darkness, Gerber turned and walked slowly toward the entrance of the commo bunker. He descended the stairs and stopped in the darkness at the bottom for a moment. There was a glow of red, green and amber in the corner. The radios. Bocker, little more than a black shape, sat in front of the communication equipment, his head bowed as he listened.

Gerber walked across the wooden floor. It was cooler in the bunker. The air was musty already. The bunker hadn't been up more than twelve hours and already it smelled like the inside of a grave. Dank.

"Anything on the radios?"

Bocker looked up with a start. "Didn't hear you come down, Captain."

"What's going on?"

"Captain Minh is on his way in. Said he took out a mortar position and captured the tube for us."

"That'll make Tyme happy."

"Sully is still tracking the enemy retreat. They ran right by him and he fell in behind them. Looks like they're heading for Phu Ron, that village Kepler looked at earlier today."

"Shit," said Gerber. He knew the villagers were going to be in trouble. Soldiers running from a fight would want to feel superior to someone, even if that someone happened to be unarmed civilian farmers. They would take their anger out on the villagers, probably shooting half of them in the process and beating the rest.

"What about the other listening posts?"

"Reported in. Nothing around them. They'll be in about the same time as Minh's."

"Okay." Gerber took a step forward. There was a map sitting on a wobbly wooden table. Nothing had been plotted on it. There was nothing else in the bunker except for Bocker's radios and his weapon. They hadn't had the chance to get things organized yet.

"Where you going to meet?" asked Bocker.

"Team house, if it isn't too badly riddled. I haven't checked it yet."

"I'll relay word to the LPs when they get in."

"Thanks." Gerber moved back and climbed the three stairs that led up and out. Outside, he crossed the compound slowly, looking at the destruction around him, amazed that the enemy could drop so many mortar rounds and rockets on the camp and do so little damage. As he reached the team house, he realized the sun was coming up. Another night gone. Now he understood why he was so tired. It had been a couple of days since he'd had a good night's sleep.

He entered the team house. There was a glow at one end, a Coleman lantern pumped up high. Two men were huddled around it, as if its light would protect them.

"You people need something?" asked Gerber.

"No, sir. Just resting for a moment."

Gerber nodded and hooked a thumb at the door. "Captain Parker is going to need your assistance."

"Yes, sir." Both of them walked toward the door.

When they were gone, he walked over to the gas-powered refrigerator and opened it. There was beer on the bottom shelf and Coke on the top. A chocolate bar sat on top of the Cokes. Gerber left the candy alone and snagged a can of pop. Closing the refrigerator door with his elbow, he opened the Coke and drank deeply.

Fetterman pushed his way in, saw the can and said, "Hand me a cold one, will you, sir?"

Gerber opened the door and pulled another Coke out. As he gave it to the master sergeant, he asked, "What did you learn?"

"We can get out of here in about thirty minutes."

"Sully says the enemy headed toward that village Kepler swept through earlier."

"Great. We going after them there?"

"Yes. Exactly."

Bocker stuck his head in the doorway. "Captain Minh said he'd be here in a couple of minutes."

"Thanks."

Fetterman moved toward the lantern, picked it up off the floor and set it on a table. As he turned it down so that the harsh white light wasn't quite as bright, the door opened again. Tyme, his uniform mud-splattered and sweat-soaked, came in. He set his weapon beside the door and collapsed into the nearest lawn chair.

"Rough?" asked Gerber.

"No, sir. Just hairy. All those rockets and mortar shells dropping around makes me nervous."

"At least they weren't shooting at you personally," said Fetterman.

"Only because they couldn't see me."

Kepler entered, carrying a map. He saw both Gerber and Fetterman with Cokes. As he opened the refrigerator, he asked, "Anyone care if I have a beer?"

"For breakfast?" asked Fetterman.

"Hell, Tony, you're drinking a Coke."

Kepler took out a beer and then sat down next to Tyme. "What's on the agenda?"

Before Gerber could speak, Minh came in. He was dirtier than Tyme and smelled of gun powder, blood and death. Gerber nodded to him and said, "Now that we're all here."

"Hold it, old boy," said Minh. Grinning, he got a beer from the refrigerator. "Now let's have it."

"As you may know, we've got Sully following the VC who attacked us. Apparently they're heading for that village Derek looked at earlier."

"Shit," muttered Kepler.

"My thoughts exactly," said Gerber. "Anyway, I want to take the strike company out now and give chase."

"Into an ambush," suggested Minh.

"No, I don't think so. They've had things their way so long they won't be thinking about an ambush. Besides, the day after an assault and damage, we normally clean up. We never follow up on a victory and give chase to the enemy."

"Who always runs to ground, disappearing, or heads to Cambodia where we can't get them," Fetterman said.

Gerber smiled. "So now, just to throw a wrench in the works, we're going after them. See if we can't inflict a few more casualties before they can cross the border."

"But we won't follow them across," said Fetterman. It was really a question.

Gerber stood for a moment, silently thinking. Finally he said, "Not if we can help it."

18

TAN SON NHUT AIRPORT

Crinshaw's plane touched down as the last of the night was chased from the airfield. Crinshaw had planned it that way, figuring he could sleep on the plane and then have the entire day to get his bearings in South Vietnam. He could arrive at the office before anyone else, set up shop and be ready to go as the staff arrived to begin work. It would give them a rude shock, one they wouldn't quickly forget, and it would provide them with a story to share with those who came to replace them.

As the plane rolled to a stop, Crinshaw stood. He was dressed in a khaki uniform, four rows of ribbons above his pocket and two stars on his collar. It was a tailored uniform that was perfectly fitted to his frame. It would impress those who strolled in during the day.

Henrikson, wearing only a pair of filmy panties, opened her eyes. She turned toward Crinshaw and asked, "Where are you going first?"

"I'm returning to the job I held during my last tour. The office I had, the same building, is being returned to me. I'm going over there."

Henrikson tried to see her watch, but it was too dark in the plane with the shades down. "What's the time here?"

"I don't know. Just after sunup."

"We'll be laying over here," said Henrikson. "We're not leaving until noon."

"You've already earned your combat pay," said Crinshaw evenly.

She raised her hands over her head, letting the single sheet fall away, revealing her body to him. "The combat pay isn't my major concern now."

"I've got work to do."

"You haven't even signed in. How can you have work already? Even the lowest-ranking private gets a week of orientation before he goes to work."

Crinshaw laughed. "But the men who are well trained don't have that luxury. Helicopter pilots can find themselves flying in the war within a day."

"But you have to sign in."

Crinshaw sat down in the swivel seat and faced her. He sat with both feet flat on the floor, his elbows on his knees, hands clasped together. "It's different for general officers. We know ahead of time what we're going to do. I meet with another general who's rotating home. But since this is a job I originated when I was here before, no transition time is needed."

"I have six hours here."

"I'm sorry, but I have work to do. If you were going to stay for a week, things would be different."

She threw the sheet off her, sat up and spun around, putting her feet on the floor. She was displaying her body for him, trying to convince him of his need for her. "I have a wide variety of talents and training. Maybe you can use me on your staff here."

"There are no military women in Vietnam other than nurses. It would be impossible to get you assigned here."

"I thought generals could do anything they wanted to do," she said. Her voice was low and husky.

"Why would you want to be assigned here? Conditions are terrible, the enemy drops mortar shells and rockets on us and there's nothing to do. This is a shit assignment."

"Which looks good on the record," said Henrikson. She had still refused to pick up her clothes. "A tour in Vietnam will help anyone's career, but if I happen to be one of the few women to have been here, then I can get even farther along."

Crinshaw grinned. "Then all this—" he waved a hand "—was just a ploy to get me to reassign you to Vietnam."

"General," she said, "I had a lot of fun. We had fun. Now, if I'm assigned to your headquarters here, that fun can continue. We'll have a whole year together."

For just a moment Crinshaw thought of Jennifer sitting in their house in Louisiana. She was there with the benefit of being a general's wife. If she called the fort and asked for something, letting it drop that her husband was a general, she would get what she wanted. It was almost as if the stars were pinned to her shoulders, too. A general's wife was nearly as powerful as the man himself. No one wanted to offend her for fear he would be offending the general. She had it made.

And he didn't. Not with a year of duty in Vietnam staring him in the face. He didn't like the Vietnamese. They were small people who weren't as civilized as they could have been. They smelled. He wanted as little to do with them as possible. If there was a way to insulate himself from them, he would do it quickly.

But that also meant a year without female companionship. Or easy female companionship. The limited number of possibilities in Vietnam made it difficult. There were nurses in the Army, Air Force and Navy, and there were civilian females working in the embassy, but all of them had been taken. To find one for himself was a difficult task. Here was a woman offering herself to him. All he had to do was make a few calls and suggest that her special talents were indispensable to him.

"You actually want orders to Vietnam?" he finally asked.

"Yes, General. As a career move it can't be topped. What other female officer is going to have that credential in her file? A tour in Vietnam?"

The jet came to a full stop and the engines began to wind down. As the whistling died, Crinshaw could hear voices outside. Probably the ground crew getting ready to service the aircraft.

"Not much time, General."

Crinshaw laughed. "I'll do what I can, but I'm not going to push very hard. If I meet any resistance, I'm going to abandon the idea."

"That's fine. At least I have a chance."

"You come by my office in about three hours and I'll let you know what I've learned. That'll give you enough time to catch the plane. Either way you're going to have to return to the States for a couple of days."

She got off the bed and threw her arms around him, kissing him deeply. With one hand he reached down until he felt the soft skin of her inner thigh. He could tell she was ready for him again. "Not now. I've got some enlisted pukes to scare. Some people to surprise."

"I'll be at your office in three hours."

"Fine." Crinshaw stood up, pushed through the curtain that separated the rear of the plane from the front and found Sergeant Seneff waiting patiently.

"Ready to go to war, Sergeant?"

"I'm right behind you, General."

WITH KEPLER AND FETTERMAN going over the maps and planning a route to the village of Phu Ron, Gerber walked back to the commo bunker. To Bocker he said, "I want you to get on the horn to the Crusaders in Tay Ninh and the Hornets at Cu Chi to arrange for gun support. I want you to contact the Twenty-fifth at Tay Ninh and talk to them about a couple of companies on standby as we begin this operation.

Bocker nodded. "It would be easier to coordinate the aviation assets through their battalion at Cu Chi."

"I don't have a problem with that."

"Twenty-fifth does have some aviation assigned to it," said Bocker.

"I know, but I figure they're booked solid, especially if they have to support the whole division. That's why those other aviation companies are around."

"What time frame are we looking at?"

"Two, three hours."

Bocker shook his head. "I don't know about that. Mission requirements are usually designed a week in advance."

"Yes, but when people make contact, those requirements can be changed. We've had contact and we still have people in contact. That should change things dramatically."

Now Bocker laughed. "That'll help, but it might not be enough."

"Then use General Platt's name. He's given us a blank check. Let's cash it and see what it'll buy us."

"Yes, sir."

Gerber watched as Bocker turned to the field phone first. The network put in by the engineers was a jury-rigged mess that left communications to areas outside the camp questionable. Gerber knew that elsewhere in-country he could place a call to most other bases, though the routing would sometimes be less than straight. After five minutes of watching Bocker work, he knew they'd been lucky to communicate from bunker to bunker.

Bocker cradled the instrument and then looked up at the captain. "Have to use the radio."

"Be careful what you say."

"I know my job, Captain."

With that, Bocker checked the SOI and found the proper frequency to contact the Black Barons, the aviation battalion at Cu Chi. He talked to a clerk there, made his request using the various code words and phrases as published in the SOI and then sat back. "Clerk's going to talk with the operations officer who'll have to check with the CO."

"You talking to hear yourself?" asked Gerber.

Bocker shrugged. "I suppose."

A moment later the radio crackled. "Black Baron Six will have assets available from 0600 until 1000."

"Got the choppers," said Bocker.

Gerber nodded and realized they would be able to fly into the village of Phu Ron. Much better than hiking there. With gun support, they'd be able to engage an enemy battalion with success.

Bocker was already on the radio, talking with the operations officer at the Third Brigade of the Twenty-fifth. It took no time at all to arrange for a company to stand by at Tay Ninh.

Grinning broadly, Gerber said, "Order the Crusaders to stand by with the soldiers at Tay Ninh and then have the Hornets get off to pick us up here."

"Who you going to want in the C and C?"

"Nobody," said Gerber, but he knew someone would have to do it. He wanted to stay on the ground with the troops, but there wasn't anyone else to put in the sky. Kepler would have to stay on the ground. Minh would be needed there, too, and Fetterman, because he was a sergeant, would have a hard time convincing the pilots he knew the score. Working his way through it, Gerber knew he'd have to take the job. Finally he said, "I'll meet the C and C on the helipad. You'll have to warn me."

"Yes, sir," said Bocker.

Gerber left the bunker and discovered Fetterman had the men ready to move out. There was a long line of strikers standing side by side, holding their weapons at port arms. Fetterman, Kepler, Tyme and Minh were moving among them, checking their weapons, ammo and equipment. Each man had his own ammo, squad ammo, batteries, a tripod or extra rounds for the grenade launchers. They all carried two canteens, first-aid kits, knives and machetes.

As Gerber approached, Minh broke away from the men. "We're about ready to move out, old boy."

"Looks good, but we don't have to walk. Lucked into some choppers."

"How we going to handle this?"

Gerber pointed at the open field on the other side of the perimeter wire. "Land the choppers there. I'll take the C and C up, spot our LZ and then direct you into it. With that kind of speed, we might catch the enemy napping."

"And if he has more soldiers there?"

"I've got a company on standby for support. I also have gun support. We should be fine."

"Want me in the C and C?" asked Minh.

"I'd prefer you to me, but I'd better run it. You'll be more valuable on the ground."

"Certainly."

Bocker appeared in the doorway of the bunker and saw Gerber. He turned and trotted toward him. "The C and C is inbound and will land in five minutes."

"Will I have radio communication with everyone on the ground?" asked Gerber.

"That's no problem," said Bocker. "We've got plenty of prick twenty-fives, all set to our team Fox Mike."

Gerber wiped a hand across his forehead and realized just how hot it was already, even though the sun had barely broken the horizon. He couldn't call the day a scorcher, because there was too much humidity. To Minh he said, "I'm going to the helipad now. You get the men lined up in a staggered trail outside the wire."

"Arty prep?" asked Minh.

"Hell, no. We're going into a village that was fairly friendly yesterday."

"Fine."

Gerber slapped Bocker on the shoulder. "Let's get up to the helipad."

As they walked in that direction, Parker ran up to Gerber again. "What are we going to do with the dead?"

Gerber nodded toward the dispensary. "T.J., when he gets the wounded evacked, can have them take out the dead, too."

"No, I mean the VC dead."

Gerber laughed. "Hell, dig a trench downwind, dump the bodies in, pour on diesel fuel and burn them. Cover it all over when the fire dies down."

Parker didn't move. Finally he said, "That's no way to treat the dead."

"It's exactly the way, Captain," said Gerber. "We treat the enemy dead as garbage. It's reported to their Comrades and suddenly the VC aren't as eager to attack. Psychological warfare. Keep the enemy off balance."

"Certainly," said Parker.

Gerber continued toward the helipad, then stopped again. He turned to Parker and said, "Fighting a war is more than just killing the enemy. Too many people refuse to understand that. Fighting a war is taking it to all levels. If the enemy believes that having the eyes of the dead gouged out will

ruin their afterlife, then you gouge out the eyes. If they believe a decent burial is necessary, you stop them from getting it. You fight a war on all levels. So we burn the bodies
and bury them in a mass grave.''

Parker hesitated, then said, ''I understand.''

As Parker walked back to where his men waited, Gerber
said to Bocker, ''Let's go.''

They reached the pad, and Bocker set the radio down behind the net erected to inhibit dust and debris. He knelt next
to it, dialing in the radio frequency assigned to the Hornets.
''Hornet Five, this is Zulu Six.''

''Go, Six.''

''Say location.''

''We're about three minutes out. Can you throw smoke?''

''Roger, smoke.'' Bocker put down the handset and pulled
out a smoke grenade. He pulled the pin and tossed the grenade to the center of the pad. There was a quiet pop, a flame
from the bottom and then a cloud of thick green smoke. ''ID
green.''

''Roger, green.''

Gerber spotted the helicopter in the distance. As it came
closer, it flared, its rotor wash fanning out, picking up dirt
and debris. Gerber turned his back, held on to his boonie hat
and closed his eyes, waiting until the chopper settled.

Turning, he leaped into the back of the C and C Huey. This
one had been modified for command and control. Bolted to
the deck just behind the pilots' seats was a huge radio console. It held a variety of Fox Mike and Uniform radios that
would allow the ground operations commander to talk with
several different units at once. The normal troop seat had
been removed and airline-type seats had been installed instead. On each end the chair would swivel so that the man
there was able to look down on the battlefield. The two chairs
in the center didn't move, but would recline. The ground

mission commander could command his forces while lying on his back. To accommodate that clips had been fastened to the roof to hold maps.

As Gerber settled into the seat directly in front of the console, the chopper came up off the ground. They hovered momentarily, the nose dropping, then took off, climbing out over the six strands of concertina that dipped away from the camp and down the slope of the hill.

Gerber put on the earphone and hit the intercom button. "I'm up."

"I've got the flight about ten minutes out," the pilot said. "Where do you want them to land?"

"On the east side of the camp. Troops are lined up in staggered trail and will throw smoke as soon as the choppers are in sight."

"They lined up into the wind?"

"Sergeant Fetterman will take care of all that. He's fully cognizant of the requirements of helicopter operations."

"Fine."

"Our destination?"

Gerber pulled his map out and unfolded it so that Phu Ron was centered. He looked out of the windshield of the chopper and saw broken clouds and huge patches of sunlight. The ten helicopters of the Hornet flight were dwarfed by the clouds. They were nearly invisible in the distance. "Indications are that the enemy has infiltrated the village of Phu Ron," he told the pilot.

"Phu Ron," repeated the pilot. "This going to be a hot LZ?"

"I'm afraid so."

"Fucking great."

19

THE NEWS BUREAU
SAIGON

Robin Morrow stood at the window and watched as the street below her brightened. All night long it was the same. Thousands of people walking around searching for an evening of companionship, even if it cost a hundred dollars. Or searching to sell an evening of companionship, even if it earned no more than ten dollars. Whatever the traffic would bear, that was what the men paid and the women accepted.

Even with the coming of the sun, the scene didn't change. Soldiers on limited passes were trying to cram a lifetime of living into seventy-two hours, fully aware their lives might soon be cut short. Women, paid well, stayed with them, hoping to suck a few more dollars out of them. Now, with the sun coming up, they were looking for more thrills.

She turned away from the window and wondered why she was depressed, then remembered that Gerber had flown in, spent an hour or so with her and then flown right back out. He wasn't more than fifty or sixty miles away, but he might as well have been on the other side of the moon. That was what was depressing her. The war was passing her by. Life was passing her by. She was spending too much time in Saigon with the other reporters, repackaging the Army's hand-outs in the hope of getting something on the air each night.

She walked to her desk and sat down, putting her feet up on the stack of copy that had been placed there thirty minutes earlier. Meyers came up to her, his face glistening with sweat. His eyes were shiny and he was grinning wickedly. "I think I know where your boy is."

She already had the answer to that question, but asked anyway. "Where?"

"Got himself sent to a small abandoned base near An Loc. He's setting up some kind of Green Beret thing there."

"Why do you think that?"

"One of our boys over at MACV got briefed on who got hit last night. Not much going on, but a company did attack a tiny camp at Xa Cat. Nobody's heard of it before."

Morrow felt her stomach grow cold. That was the problem with MACV. It had more leaks than century-old plumbing. While the American Army griped that the Vietnamese could keep nothing out of the hands of the VC, they talked openly about everything under the sun. Gerber had often complained about the press compromising everything, but all the information came out of the military offices.

"What happened?" she asked Meyers.

"Mortar, rocket and ground assault. They turned it all back without much problem. Today they're going after the VC. I guess they're hoping to hunt them down."

Morrow knew what was happening. Gerber had told her time and again that one of the chief problems was not following up on victories. Once the enemy was beaten, the Americans retreated, too. Now Gerber had repulsed a VC assault and he was going to pursue the enemy instead of sitting back contented.

She glanced at the glassed-in booths that the editors used. Hodges hadn't arrived yet. She turned her attention back to Meyers. "What are you going to do?"

"I'm going to sit down, drink my coffee and read the morning paper. That's what I'm going to do."

"You seen Hodges?"

"Not this morning. Saw him late last night. He'd been out drinking."

Morrow leaned forward and rested her chin in her hand. She stared out the window and thought about Gerber and his tiny camp out in Binh Long Province. There was a story developing out there. Maybe it was time for her to catch a flight out and see what was new in the war.

ALL THROUGH THE NIGHT Thien had watched as the men had straggled in. They came in without their weapons and equipment. They came in mud-splattered and blood-stained. They appeared in groups and one at a time, even as the sun came up.

Thien organized the villagers. He chased them out of their huts and gave the shelter to his wounded comrades. He made the female villagers prepare rice for breakfast and then ordered a water buffalo to be slaughtered to feed the men. When the old man with the gray beard objected, Thien raised his AK-47 and shot the only animal he could see. His fellow soldiers would have beef for breakfast.

As three men dug a pit to roast the meat, Thien stood by and watched. Then a sergeant came up to him. "Comrade Lieutenant, maybe we should get out of this village."

Thien shook his head. "We'll stay through the day and leave tonight. Rest and relaxation is what these men need."

"The Americans will be searching for us."

"No," said Thien. "They'll spend the day in their camp, preparing for our return. They won't have time to look for us."

"You're sure?"

"Of course," said Thien. "It's the way they always operate. There's nothing to worry about."

The NCO nodded, then ran off.

Thien, however, wasn't as convinced of his idea as he seemed. The Americans did stay in their camps the day after an attack, rebuilding and repairing, but there were others who could search for the enemy. During Tet, with everyone involved in the fighting, there had been no one to send, but last night's attack had involved only one camp. There were hundreds, thousands of Americans who could search for them now.

Thien moved among his troops. He found a senior NCO named Suong. "I want you to find three men and move to the top of the hill there. If the Americans are giving chase, I want you to stop them. Your firing will warn us that they are near."

"Yes, Comrade Lieutenant."

"You have ten minutes to get into position."

Suong nodded, whirled and ran off, shouting the names of two other men. They appeared, weapons in hand, and Suong pointed at the top of the hill. All three of them ran to the end of the village and began climbing the slope.

Thien then dispatched another three men to watch the approach from the west. Finally he alerted one squad and scattered them around the outskirts of the village. Now the Americans wouldn't be able to sneak up on them.

Pleased, Thien walked through the village. The soldiers were now almost all hidden in the huts. The wounded were being taken care of by two NVA nurses. The women of the village were using the cooking fires to prepare the rice for breakfast, and two of his soldiers, stripped to black shorts and looking like farmers, were attending the fire and the roasting of the water buffalo. He was certain nothing would go wrong.

Then, as he walked through the center of the village, he heard the distant pop of a helicopter's rotor blades. He turned, and raised a hand to shade his eyes. The chopper was coming right at him, and he was suddenly afraid that he had made a big mistake. The Americans weren't going to follow. They were going to come in by helicopter.

SULLY SMITH HAD FOUND it simple to follow the enemy. The attack had turned into a rout, and no one was worried about noise discipline or slipping through the jungle. They had just wanted to get the hell out before they got killed.

Trailing them was easy. He and three strikers had waited for the enemy to run by and then had fallen in behind them. One of the strikers had waited, taking a rearguard position while Smith had taken the point. Smith and his men moved with the enemy, listening to them as they fled the battle. There were soldiers crying, talking and cursing. They stumbled over vegetation and logs, and crashed through the jungle. They made enough noise for a division.

Moving as quietly as he could, Smith stayed with them. When they reached the edge of the jungle, Smith slipped to the ground and watched as the enemy soldiers ran down the slope and into the village of Phu Ron.

Smith used his binoculars, but it was pretty difficult to see anything. The village was black in a charcoal world. Still, he was certain the enemy had stopped there.

When the sun rose, Smith could see a lot more. Men moved around the village, armed men who forced the villagers out of their hootches. He watched as one of the VC shot a water buffalo. Two men moved toward it and gutted it.

When there was no doubt the enemy would be staying in the village for a while, he pulled out his radio, extended the antenna and whispered, ''Zulu Base, this is Zulu Seven.''

''Go, Seven.''

''I have the enemy spotted. Looks like they're camping for the day.''

''Roger,'' came the reply.

Smith collapsed the antenna and put the radio away. He wiped the sweat from his face as he stretched out on the rotting jungle floor. Taking a deep breath, he listened to the jungle around him. He'd been in places where it had suddenly come alive, the birds and monkeys screaming at dawn. Here there wasn't much noise. A few birds squawked and a couple of monkeys shrieked, but the noise died quickly and it was quiet again.

All he could do was wait. He'd told Gerber and the others where the enemy was, and now it was up to them to attack. From what he could see below he could tell the comrades were going to stay for a while.

Then three men ran from the village, and scurried up the slope. For a moment Smith thought he'd been spotted, but if that was the case, more than three men would be coming, and there would be shooting. He figured the VC were putting out listening posts.

The three men veered to the right. Smith watched them as they slowed and then entered the jungle. They were fifty or sixty yards away, just inside the trees. Smith marked the location, figuring that when the attack from Gerber came, he'd have to take out the enemy LP.

Looking over his shoulder, he saw that the strikers with him had already settled in. In the patchy light of the early-morning sun, he could barely see them. The enemy wouldn't find them if they didn't do anything stupid, and that was all he asked. For now.

CRINSHAW CLIMBED from the rear of the jeep and stood in the parking lot, staring at the building he'd created. The flagpoles had been replaced with larger ones, and the flowers around them gave it an effeminate look. He noticed that the door with the bullet hole from his first tour had finally been changed, even though he'd insisted on keeping it. That was the problem with too many officers. They didn't have any sense of style.

The driver waited, standing next to the jeep. He didn't know what to do. Crinshaw took a step forward, feeling as if he'd never left. The past year or so had never taken place. He knew that eighteen months had elapsed, and yet it seemed that no time had passed. He was coming back to work after a long weekend.

"General?"

Crinshaw stopped and looked back. "You wait here. I'll want you in a little while."

"Yes, General."

Again he started to walk away and again he stopped. He looked at the driver. "You can go get your breakfast if you want. But no more than an hour."

"Certainly, General."

Then, almost as if he were just becoming aware of Seneff, he said, "We'll check in here, look over the offices and then you can go find your quarters."

"On base?"

Crinshaw grinned. "Unless the local regulations have changed, that won't be necessary. You can get a room downtown as long as you'll be into work on time."

"Yes, General."

Crinshaw, feeling his stomach boiling and the chills running up and down his spine, said, "Let's go."

They moved along the sidewalk, separated to maneuver around the flagpoles and then reached the double glass doors that led into the building. Again Crinshaw stopped and examined the doors. He pointed up at a corner and said, "There was a bullet hole there once. A sniper, I think. Everyone wanted to replace the glass, but I made them leave it. I thought a daily remainder that we were in a war was important. Apparently no one else felt that way."

Seneff reached forward and grabbed the door, pulling it open. Crinshaw moved into the building and felt the cold of the air-conditioning wash over him. The poster on the wall to the right looked just like the one he'd had placed there so long ago. It showed a soldier, his head hanging down, ashamed of himself for his liaison with a Vietnamese woman of questionable reputation. It suggested that the soldiers all be careful when dealing with Vietnamese nationals.

Seneff looked at the poster, at the worn green tile on the floor and at the light green paint on the wall, then laughed. "Home again."

Crinshaw peered into the office to his left. Two men in jungle fatigues were sitting behind desks drinking coffee. One of them glanced up, noticed Crinshaw, began to ignore him and then looked up again, staring at the two silver stars there.

"Yes, General," he said, coming to attention. "What can I do for you?"

"Is General Platt in?"

The man glanced at the soldier standing next to him and then shrugged. "I don't know."

"Why don't you take me up to the general's office and we'll see what we can learn?"

"Yes, General." He turned to his buddy. He wanted to say something, but couldn't with Crinshaw standing there. Then, wiping the sweat beading on his face, he whirled. "If you'll follow me."

The man started to push past Crinshaw, realized he shouldn't, then waited for the general to leave the office. In the hallway he glanced at Seneff and raised his eyebrows as if asking for help.

They climbed the stairs to the second floor and walked down it toward the northern end of the building. The closer they got to that end, the nicer the building became. The tile gave way to carpet, the paint on the walls looked fresher and the doors changed from pine to mahogany.

They reached Platt's office and the soldier knocked on it. There was no answer, so he tried the knob. It was locked, of course.

"The general isn't here, General."

"I can see that. Why don't you go find a key and let me in, so I don't have to wait in the hall?"

"I'm not sure I can do that." Crinshaw didn't say a word. He stood there, straight and tall, staring into the man's eyes. Finally the soldier just nodded and said, "I'll be right back, General."

As the man hurried away, Crinshaw grinned at Seneff. "It's nice to have power. Cuts through the bullshit like a hot knife in soft butter. No fucking around."

"Yes, sir."

The soldier returned and unlocked the door. "General Platt should be here in fifteen minutes or so."

"Does the general normally arrive this early?"

The soldier pushed open the door and stepped back so that Crinshaw could enter. He hesitated, then said, "Oh, yes, sir. Every morning."

Crinshaw looked around the office. He noticed the many plants hanging in the corner, the paintings on the wall and the tidy desks. Then he looked back at the soldier. "Thank you. You may go."

Again the man hesitated. "Ah, General . . ."

"I'm not going to steal anything," said Crinshaw.

"No, sir, I guess not. If you need anything, just ask."

"Sergeant Seneff will take care of that."

"Yes, sir." The man moved to the door, then stopped. He looked back at Crinshaw and wondered if there wasn't something more he should do. Finally he left and walked down the hall.

Crinshaw sat there and listened to him retreat. "Do generals scare everyone this badly?"

"New guys who don't know much," said Seneff.

"Right." Crinshaw sat down on the couch and put his feet up on the coffee table. Lacing his fingers behind his head, he asked, "There anything special you want to do?"

"You got me to Vietnam, General. I'll leave all that up to you."

Crinshaw closed his eyes and listened. He could hear the quiet hum of the air conditioner, already working hard to keep the building cool. From the airfield outside came the roar of jet engines. The sound built up as the jets sat at the end of the runway, then faded as the planes took off. Added to all that was the ever-present pop of rotor blades. It was a sound that always made Crinshaw think of Vietnam, no matter where he was. The helicopter was as much a part of Vietnam as was the humidity and the heat and the lying, corrupt officials.

Seneff had been right about one thing. He was home again. Finally.

20

IN THE AIR NEAR XA CAT

Gerber flipped the radio to the team Fox Mike and pressed the mike button with his thumb. "Zulu Five, this is Zulu Six. Say status."

"Zulu Six, this is Five. We're off the ground and climbing out."

"Roger."

Gerber turned in his seat and looked out the cargo compartment door. In the distance was the red slash of the camp at the top of the ridge line. Then there was an almost unbroken sea of green topped by the towering white clouds building over Cambodia. The clouds could mean heavy rain that night. But there was no sign of the ten helicopters carrying his strikers.

Over the intercom the pilot said, "We've got Phu Ron about five klicks in front of us."

"Can you fly over it once so that I can get a good look?"

"Sure. You want high and fast or low and fast?"

"Make it high," said Gerber. "And continue on straight away from it. I don't want the people on the ground to know we're interested in them."

"No problem."

Gerber leaned back and glanced at his map. Kepler had told him there was open ground all around the village. That meant he could land the force anywhere he wanted. The best place seemed to be on the northern side. It would block a retreat toward the Cambodian border.

"We're about a minute out," said the pilot.

Gerber sat up and looked out through the windshield. The village of Phu Ron squatted in a shallow valley. High hills to the west tumbled down to rice paddies and then the village itself. Paddies were also visible on the other sides of the village. The jungle came down close but ended three or four hundred yards from the village, which was an island of open ground in an ocean of two-hundred-foot trees and triple-canopy jungle.

As they crossed over the top, Gerber twisted around and stared down through the cargo compartment door. The village was a large oval-shaped area filled with mud-and-thatch hootches. A few had tin roofs rusted to golden-orange by the heavy rains and constant humidity. At the southern end of the oval there was a huge, smoking pit. Three men, stripped to black shorts, were tending the fire. A few old men and women were standing around; not one of them looked up at the helicopter.

On the northern side of the village was another group of men wearing black pajamas. None of them were armed, but as the chopper flashed over all looked up at the chopper. That told Gerber they weren't harmless farmers. The enemy was in the village.

"Zulu Five, this is Six."

"Go, Six. Be advised we have located the enemy."

"Roger, that."

Over the intercom Gerber asked, "Can you get the flight turned and headed in?"

"Sure. Where do you want to land them?" asked the aircraft commander.

Now that he had seen the village Gerber could use the map more effectively. He studied it again. "I'd like to land east to west on the northern side of the ville."

"Suppression?"

"Full into the trees, but normal rules regarding the village. There are civilians there."

"Understood."

Gerber switched over to the Fox Mike. "Zulu Five, this is Six."

"Go, Six."

"Ah, roger. You'll be turning inbound now. Be advised that there are still civilians in the ville."

"Roger, that."

Gerber stared at the huge block of radios, thinking there should be something else to say, instructions to give, but Fetterman and Minh knew what to do. Fetterman wouldn't allow the men to run into the village firing indiscriminately. He'd keep a tight rein on them while clearing the ville of the enemy. Anything Gerber said over the radio would be useless, and it could give the enemy a clue if they happened to be tuned into his frequency.

Over the intercom the pilot asked, "Where do you want to set up our orbit?"

"Once they start in I guess we can return to orbit right over the village."

"No problem."

FETTERMAN FLIPPED the handset back to the RTO and looked at the faces of the men sitting in the chopper with him. All of them were Vietnamese strikers, men he didn't know. They had performed well during the two probes of the camp's defenses, but that had been sitting in a well-protected bunker with the enemy coming to them. He didn't know if they'd be as brave and reliable when they had to make the assault. Having been trained by Minh suggested they would, but he didn't know for certain.

Looking at them, he used the charging rod of his M-16 and injected a round into the chamber. It was a way of telling them they'd be going into combat soon. He watched as they followed suit, each one trying to keep the barrel of his weapon pointed upward so that an accidental discharge wouldn't hit anyone or do any real damage to the chopper. It spoke well of their training.

The crew chief looked around from his well. "We're about one minute out. Everyone get ready and leave the aircraft quickly."

The Vietnamese spoke among themselves, shouting into one another's ears. Fetterman heard enough of it to know they were relaying the crew chief's words.

Outside, one of the gunships, a heavily loaded aircraft with rocket pods, took up position beside the flight. Its nose dipped slightly and the helicopter fired into the jungle on the northern side of the LZ.

The door guns began to fire, raking the trees. Fetterman slipped to the side of the chopper and looked down. The village was suddenly alive with people, men carrying AKs from one hootch to the next. There was no shooting from the ville yet, but two men were hauling an RPD complete with tripod toward the northern side of the village.

The chopper flared then and Fetterman lost sight of the enemy. He heard a single AK open fire, a loud ripping sound lost in the detonations of the rockets and the hammering of the M-60s of the flight.

As the skids touched the ground, Fetterman leaped from the cargo compartment, letting his eyes take in the whole scene. Men in black pajamas with khaki chest pouches were running through the village, along with men in bright green uniforms, carrying AK-47s.

Fetterman splashed through the knee-deep water, the muck at the bottom of the paddy sucking at his boots. He struggled to the dry ground of a dike and threw himself into the corner as the RPD began to fire. Green tracers, their glow washed out by the sunlight, flashed over him.

The strikers fought to get away from the helicopters as the VC began to put rounds into the aircraft. Windshields shattered and bits of fuselage popped out. Door guns on the side pointing at the village opened fire. Ruby tracers smashed into the hootches, tearing holes in their walls and ripping up the ground.

Fetterman pushed the barrel of his M-16 over the top of the dike and aimed. He spotted a running man and fired. One round. Two. The man stumbled and fell forward, throwing his weapon out in front of him.

The ground around Fetterman was hit. He could feel the impact of the rounds in the soft dirt of the dike. Water splashed as the AK and RPD rounds slammed home, and there was a whining noise as bullets ricocheted.

Around him the strikers began to fire, at first on single-shot, but that soon changed to full-auto. Then, there was the bloop of M-79s. Grenades crashed into the village, sending up tiny black clouds of powder as they exploded around the enemy positions.

Behind him the helicopters lifted off. The door guns raked the village. Ruby tracers struck the ground and tumbled, but the firing from the enemy tapered off as the VC dived for cover.

Fetterman was up then, running forward. He screamed orders at the Vietnamese, trying to get them up and moving. Firing from the hip, he leaped up onto a dike and ran along its edge. Enemy gunners tried to cut him down, but their rounds fell short.

The attacking force was up and running. Fifty, sixty men rushing toward the village, screaming and firing. The hammering increased in volume, while firing from the enemy slowed even more.

Fetterman reached the edge of the ville and took cover behind the thick wheel of a broken-down oxcart. He dropped the empty magazine from his weapon and slammed a new one home. As he used the charging lever, he whirled and peeked over the wheel.

From the blackened door of a hootch came a muzzle-flash, a bright strobing that told Fetterman an enemy soldier was hiding inside. The master sergeant aimed at the center of the flash, then flipped his selector to full-auto. He squeezed the trigger and sprayed the inside of the hootch, trying to put the rounds into the center of the door. The enemy fire stopped abruptly.

Two of the strikers reached the edge of the village and were hit immediately by machine-gun fire. One of them dropped straight down and didn't move. Blood poured from his body so that it looked as if he were floating in it. The other man staggered and fell onto his side. He tried to stand up, pushing at the ground with his right hand, but his strength had evaporated. Then he was hit again, the bullet slamming into the side of his head and blowing his brains out the back. He collapsed, but his legs spasmed, drumming on the ground even though the man was already dead.

Minh raced forward and dived to the ground, rolling behind the trunk of a tree. He glanced at Fetterman and pointed. Fetterman turned and saw that the machine-gun nest was exposed on one side. He aimed at the head of the gunner and squeezed the trigger. The man seemed to flip back, spraying blood. The assistant gunner jumped to his feet and ran. Minh fired at him, putting a round into the middle of his back. The soldier fell and remained motionless.

Firing around them increased as the strikers fought their way out of the rice paddies and onto the solid ground of the village. They took up positions behind the hootches, trees and mud fences, firing at anything that moved.

Fetterman stood and searched the village. He saw another enemy soldier running toward the rear, aimed, fired and missed. The man dived for cover before Fetterman could fire again.

The master sergeant sprayed the enemy positions again. He then reloaded and glanced at Minh. The Vietnamese officer was up on his knees, waving an arm, trying to get his men up and moving. He was firing single-shot.

THE SINGLE HELICOPTER flying over the village could have meant a lot of things. It swooped over the village at three thousand feet. It didn't slow down, circle or turn. The Americans had a lot of helicopters, and Thien wasn't too alarmed at first.

Moments later the noise was back, but this time it wasn't a single ship in the distance. It was a flight of aircraft, coming straight for them. Thien ran to the edge of the village. He knelt next to a mud wall and stared at the sky. The helicopters were descending, and as he watched, the Americans began to fire into the jungle. He and his men were in a lot of trouble. He leaped up, whirled and ran back toward the center of the ville.

"The Americans are coming!" he shouted, but it wasn't necessary. The men were pouring out of the huts, weapons in hand. "To the north," he said, pointing in that direction. "Everyone to the north."

A sergeant stopped near him. "Rear guard?"

Thien glanced at the southern side of the village. He realized he didn't have the forces to cover both sides. If the Americans hit with more than one company, they would be chopped into little pieces.

"No. Everyone to the north. Everyone fire as fast as possible."

"We'll be trapped here."

Thien reached out and pushed the man. "Do what you're told and do it now."

As the man ran off, Thien remained in place, unsure of what to do. He heard the firing of the helicopter door guns, and through the gaps in the village he could see the gunships working over the trees with rockets and miniguns. It seemed to him the Americans thought they were hiding in there. He didn't know the Americans wouldn't shoot up the village unless the VC gave them a reason to do so.

Finally he ran to the eastern side, where the long slope led upward to the safety of the triple-canopy jungle. He crouched at the base of a coconut tree and stared into the trees, but saw nothing.

As he turned, the helicopters flared, their noses rising. His men began to fire, one or two of them and then more and more until they were all trying to bring down a chopper. Thien aimed at the head of a pilot just visible through the side window of a helicopter. He fired at the American, but there was no reaction. He didn't know if the armor had stopped the round, if he had missed or if he had killed the man.

The enemy soldiers were on the ground, fighting their way clear of the rice paddies. Rifle fire filled the air. Nothing else could be heard, just the constant hammering of M-16s, AKs and machine guns.

Thien left his position at the side of the village and ran toward the center. A round snapped by his head and he dived for cover. He rolled over against the side of a hut and then slowly got to his feet.

"We've got to get out of here," yelled a man.

Thien got up and dusted himself off. "We stay and fight now."

"There are too many of them."

Thien ignored the man and ran to the northern end of the building. "Over there!" he yelled at the machine gunner. "Cut them down."

But as the man began to swing the barrel of his weapon, he took a round in the head. He flipped back, blood spurting from the wound and soaking the ground around him. The assistant gunner jumped up and ran away.

"We've got to get out!" yelled someone.

"No!" screamed Thien. "We stay and fight." But then he whirled and ran toward the southern side of the village. He stopped there and leaned against the crumbling mud of a hut. The firing behind him increased as everyone else got into the fight.

The old man stepped out of the doorway, a machete in his hand. It was an ancient weapon, the blade rusty and dull with age. He lifted it over his head and ran straight for Thien. The NVA officer shook his head in disbelief and fired three times, killing the old man.

GERBER, SITTING in the C and C aircraft, watched the fighting below. It was all laid out as if diagramed on a map or a sand table. There were no hiding places for the enemy and no cover for his own strikers. Everything was visible from the air.

He saw his men land and swarm into the village. He watched as the VC and NVA ran to meet the threat. He saw the battle lines drawn and watched as the firing increased. Men fell and died right below him, but it all had an unreal look to it. The whole thing was something from television or the movies.

The gunships broke around and waited, but Gerber refused to let them fire into the village, even when he had a clear view of the Vietcong and NVA. Killing villagers, even by accident, wasn't something he could allow. His plans didn't allow for such an action.

Then the intercom sputtered. "There are men running from the rear of the ville."

Gerber turned and stared out of the cargo compartment. He could see two men, both dressed in black pajamas, running for the trees. They looked scared, as if they were running away from a monster.

"Take 'em," said Gerber.

One of the gunships peeled away and headed for the men. The chopper's nose lowered and a pair of rockets streaked out. As the Huey broke around, the rockets landed between the two men. They were blasted off their feet and thrown into the muddy water of the rice paddy. They'd never move again.

Gerber turned and watched as his men pushed into the village. The strikers split into small groups to attack enemy strongholds. Bit by bit his men were taking the village, pushing the enemy out of it. VC and NVA were fleeing in panic. Two ran up the slope toward the jungle, but before they could get there, gunfire erupted from the trees, killing them. Their bodies rolled downhill toward the rice paddies. Sully Smith and his men had stopped them.

And the gunships began working over the southern side of the ville with machine guns and rockets. Enemy soldiers, fleeing the assault in the north, ran into the paddies, only to be torn to shreds by the gunships.

The radio came on then. "Zulu Six, this is Five."

"Go, Five."

"We've taken the northern end of the ville. We've found four wounded NVA soldiers."

"Roger." Gerber wanted to tell Fetterman to kill the enemy soldiers immediately, but that wasn't the thing to do. Instead, he ordered, "Have them taken under guard to the northern side of the ville for evacuation."

"Roger, that."

"Looks like they're fleeing out of the southern end," said Gerber. "Gunships are taking care of them. Keep up the pressure."

"Roger."

He sat back then, and as he did, the intercom crackled. "Looks like we've got them on the run."

"That we have. As long as we keep up the pressure."

21

PHU RON, RVN

Firing had tapered off to only sporadic single shots. The gunships hovered overhead like predators searching for something else to kill. The villagers were huddled in their hootches, waiting for either the Americans or the Vietcong to leap in and shoot them.

Fetterman moved slowly through the village, his head swiveling right and left. A few fires burned, some of them caused by the grenades or the tracers, and some of them nothing more than morning cook fires that were only now beginning to burn low. The bodies of strikers, VC and NVA were scattered everywhere.

Fetterman walked over to Minh, who was crouched next to a badly wounded striker. The man was bleeding from two belly wounds, and blood was trickling from his mouth and one ear. A medic stood to one side, a field dressing in his hand, but he was making no move to apply it.

As Fetterman looked at the medic, he shook his head. "Should I waste it?"

"We have plenty," said Fetterman.

The medic moved in and tried to stop some of the bleeding from the belly wounds. While he worked, Minh kept up a steady stream of talk, quiet words that were meant to comfort the dying striker.

Fetterman moved back a step and watched as the man died. The striker tried to sit up, groaned once and fell back, blood pouring from his mouth. He coughed, kicked out a leg, reached upward and died.

Minh stood up immediately and glanced at Fetterman. "I truly hate watching my men die."

"We all do," said Fetterman.

Minh picked up his weapon, then held a hand to his forehead to shade his eyes. "Got them on the run, don't we?"

"I think the village is cleared."

"Let's check it out."

They walked toward the south side of the village. On their way they passed two more dead strikers. Minh knelt beside each one, feeling for a pulse. When he found none, he shook his head. As they approached the last of the hootches, they moved more cautiously. Spread out in front of them were the open rice paddies, which swept out toward the triple-canopy jungle. Bodies of NVA and VC soldiers were strewed all over the paddies and dikes.

Kepler appeared and pointed. "A few of them got away from us."

"Good," said Fetterman."

"Good?" echoed Kepler.

"When my great-great-great-grandfather was killed by the Sioux, they eliminated everyone. The battlefield was mute testimony to what had happened, and it was horrifying, but the problem was that there were no survivors, no one to tell how terrible those last few minutes were."

Minh understood. "So the survivors return to their units and let their friends know how the world suddenly turned brown and smelly."

"Exactly."

There was a single shot from an AK. Minh hit the ground. Fetterman whirled as someone else fired a burst from an M-16. He saw the rounds splashing into a rice paddy all around the body of a VC. The enemy slumped forward.

"Haven't gotten them all," said Minh.

As he spoke, a squad rushed from cover. They headed to the closest body, checked it and picked up the weapon. Leapfrogging over the open ground, they took the weapons from all the dead until they reached the trees. Then they returned, each man carrying three or four AK-47s, a couple of pistols and the chest pouches they'd cut from the dead.

The RTO appeared suddenly and gave the handset to Fetterman. Glancing at the man, he said, "Zulu Five."

"Roger, Five, this is Six. Say status."

"We control the ville and the enemy has fled into the jungle. We need Medevac now for the wounded."

"Roger, that. Medevac is on the way. Have you located the villagers?"

"Negative. We've seen very few of them."

"Roger. Keep me posted."

SITTING IN THE C AND C CHOPPER, orbiting the battle irritated Gerber. He wanted to get down on the ground and take part in the action. If asked, he would have told anyone who would listen that part of the trouble in Vietnam was too many officers in too many helicopters watching the war. And while the men were on the ground fighting, those same officers were figuring out ways to put themselves up for combat awards. No longer did a man have to fight a battle to win a Silver Star. He just had to fly over it.

From his perch in the rear of the chopper, he could tell the battle was over. The strikers had swept through the village, pushing the enemy in front of them. The gunships had killed twenty or thirty men as they had tried to reach the safety of the jungle. Smith and his men, hidden on the eastern side of the ville, had killed several more, but now only the Americans and the strikers were moving around.

Using the intercom, he asked, "Can we land?"

"If that's what you want, sure. But I don't recommend it," said the pilot.

"On the south side of the ville, if you don't mind."

"Roger, that."

"What's the ETA on the Medevac?"

"Trail should be here within five minutes to pick up the wounded. We'll take them on to Tay Ninh."

"Good." He pulled off the headphones and hung them on the side of the radio. As he slipped to the right, he grabbed his M-16 and checked the safety.

The chopper came around the side of the village, slowed and then descended. As it approached the ground, Gerber slid to the edge of the troop seat, then stepped out onto the skid. When the chopper touched down in a swirling cloud of red dust and black smoke, he stepped off, holding on to his boonie hat. Once he was clear of the aircraft, it lifted and climbed out rapidly.

"Glad to see you, Captain," said Fetterman, approaching from the village.

"What have you got?"

"We've located a few of the villagers."

"And?"

"They're dead. Four or five bodies. All of them shot once in the head. We also found a few live ones. They're in a state of shock."

"Where's Kepler?"

Fetterman turned. "Over there somewhere."

"Okay," said Gerber. "Let's get this mess cleaned up. Round up everyone who's left alive and we'll transport them to the camp for protection. Then Kepler and I will go visit the province chief.''

''Yes, sir.''

Gerber turned and looked at the open field. The strikers were picking up the bodies of the dead VC and NVA. One man had grabbed the heels of a dead man and was dragging him through the rice paddies. ''We've got to get out of here,'' Gerber said.

Fetterman nodded. ''An hour. No more.''

''I'll count on it.'' With that, Gerber turned so that he could walk through the remains of Phu Ron.

WHEN PLATT OPENED the door, he was surprised to see Crinshaw sitting there. He didn't know who Crinshaw was, but he did recognize the two stars on his collar. Holding a hand out, Platt advanced. ''General?''

''Crinshaw. Billy Joe.''

''Platt. Bruce. How can I help you?''

Crinshaw turned to Seneff. ''Why don't you find us some coffee?''

''Yes, sir.''

Crinshaw moved to the inner door and pushed it open. ''General,'' he said, waving a hand.

Platt shrugged and walked into his inner office. He crossed to the windows and opened the blinds. Turning, he watched as Crinshaw moved to the desk and looked at the swivel chair but then retreated to the couch in the corner. He dropped onto it and said, ''Let's sit down.''

Platt still didn't understand what was happening. He moved over and sat down facing Crinshaw. ''What's happening here.''

''How are things going?'' asked Crinshaw.

''What's going on?'' Platt persisted, a little bewildered.

Crinshaw leaned back and laced his fingers behind his head. "You know that this was my office when I was here last time."

Platt nodded.

Crinshaw grinned. "I've been reassigned to this office and I'll be taking over."

"My tour isn't over for three weeks," said Platt.

"That doesn't mean anything. I'm here now and I'm ready to start work. You don't have to stay around. Go to Vung Tau and relax on the beach."

Platt was stunned, and a little worried that he had done something wrong. It was the first step toward the end of his career. He tried to figure out what he could have done. Everything had been established policy. He'd thrown his weight around to get Gerber his aviation assets, but that had been earlier in the day. There hadn't been enough time to find another general and get him to Saigon. The problem had to be something else.

Crinshaw stood up and walked toward the desk. It was the same monstrosity he'd ordered during his first tour. There had been complaints about it, but no one had bothered to get rid of it. He turned and said, "Your performance has been fine, General. It's just that I'm here and ready to take over. There's no reason for you to stay around."

"There are projects . . ." Platt said, thinking of Gerber up in Binh Long Province.

"Again that's no problem. You have records?"

"There are briefing files available." Platt smiled weakly. "Not everything is laid out in the files. The South Vietnamese tend to tell too much."

"That's the same excuse I've listened to from everyone. I'm getting tired of it."

Platt shrugged. "There are files, and I can verbally brief you this morning if you want."

"No," said Crinshaw. "Why don't you take the rest of the day off, and I'll look through the files and feel my way around in here? Then, tomorrow, if I have any questions, I'll get back to you."

Platt sat quietly for a moment, trying to figure out what to do or say. He'd known that a replacement was coming but hadn't expected him for a few more weeks. He didn't expect someone to show up suddenly, ready to take over.

Standing, he said, "Well, General, I'll be around if you have any questions."

Crinshaw sat down behind the desk, pulled open the middle drawer and looked into it. He didn't say anything to Platt.

After a few moments, Platt stepped to the door. As he reached it, Sneff appeared, carrying two cups of coffee. He held one out to Platt. "General?"

"No, thank you," said Platt. "I've got to get going. Why don't you drink it?"

"Certainly, General. Thank you."

Platt left the office and stopped in the hallway. He turned and looked back at the door. He could see Crinshaw sitting at the desk, drinking the coffee and staring out the window. He didn't like what had happened, but there was nothing he could do about it.

WHILE GERBER WATCHED, Fetterman and Minh got the strikers lined up in the open field in a staggered trail formation so that the helicopters could get in and pick them up. Mixed in with them were the surviving villagers, no more than twenty people. The others had been killed by the VC and NVA before they'd pulled out.

Standing next to Kepler, Gerber said, "I don't understand that. Why kill the people?"

"To send a message to the other civilians in the province. You help the Americans and their allies and you'll be shot, too."

"Okay," said Gerber. "Once we get the men back to the camp, you and I are going to see the province chief."

"What for?"

"Just to see him. Let him know who we are and what's going on around here."

"And then?"

Gerber looked at Kepler and leaned close. "Then we're going to take the war right to the VC. We'll wipe them out."

"Yes, sir."

Fetterman tossed a smoke grenade into the rice paddy. The choppers appeared and descended, landing next to the men.

Gerber watched as the strikers and villagers climbed into the choppers. Some of the villagers carried a few possessions, but most of them only had the clothes on their backs. The little they owned had been destroyed or stolen during the fighting. Poor people caught in the middle of a war.

When they were all loaded, Gerber climbed into the chopper. As they lifted off, the door guns opened fire and the gunships rolled in. This time the target was the village. They wanted to destroy it completely so that the enemy wouldn't be able to use it again—the next step in Gerber's plan.

22

XA CAT SPECIAL FORCES CAMP

Gerber, along with Kepler and Bocker, sat in the commo bunker. Bocker had found a table somewhere and had put it in the bunker. Maps were spread out on it. Bocker was sitting in a lawn chair, Kepler on an upturned ammo case. Gerber stood next to the table.

Pointing at the map, Bocker said, "Captain Bromhead has reported that he has his company in place at Phu Rieng. He told me that it wasn't the best of camps, but they've got bunkers, tents and some heavy weapons. That General Platt sure gets things done."

"When does Bromhead get there?" asked Gerber.

"About dawn. He's got a single striker company, but they can get support from Song Be. He's got the vehicles there to move another company, and they can use their heavy weapons to support Bromhead if he needs it."

"Captain Bromhead down there?"

"Yes, sir. He said that Lieutenant Mildebrandt is in command at Song Be."

"Good."

Bocker pointed at Tonle Cham. "Captain Henderson has got his people in there. Two companies of strikers along with a 105 battery."

"Christ, how did he manage that?"

Bocker grinned and shrugged. "He said they were setting it up as a fire support base. He said he'd be ready to support us by noon today if we needed it."

Gerber pulled the map closer and studied it carefully. With American camps at An Loc, Quan Loi and Loc Ninh, plus the new camps and the Special Forces camps, they suddenly had Binh Long very well monitored. The highways and railroads were covered, and there was a company of Americans at An Loc. There were also small camps with helipads near the Cambodian border. They could hit the enemy within minutes if they decided to. "Did Bromhead or Henderson talk about patrols?"

"No, sir. Captain Bromhead said he'd put out an ambush patrol tonight and begin serious patrols tomorrow. Captain Henderson was going to wait until tomorrow."

Gerber looked at his Intel NCO. "Derek?"

Kepler spun the map around and studied it. "We've taken out a major VC station at Phu Ron."

"How do you know that?"

"I've talked to some of the villagers. They told me Phu Ron was a major stop along the infiltration route. We got the rice yesterday and that pissed off the VC. The raid today caught them with their pants down. Now, after the artillery and guns are finished working over the village, we should swing through and make sure we've gotten everything out that will be of use to the enemy."

"Tomorrow or the next day," said Gerber. He grinned. "You didn't notice anyone missing, did you?"

"Sully!" Kepler said.

"Right. We left him there to watch Phu Ron. He'll be coming in tomorrow. If the enemy shows up tonight, he'll be in position to call in some of that artillery we've been talking about."

"Now, do you want to accompany me into An Loc to visit the province chief?"

"Sounds like fun."

Gerber turned back to Bocker. "Anything else I should know?"

"No, sir, that about covers all of it. Anything else you want me to tell either Captain Bromhead or Captain Henderson?"

"Just tell them we've had a lot of activity in the area. If they need anything, radio us and we'll pass the requests to General Platt in Saigon."

"Yes, sir."

"Okay, Galvin, get on the blower and whistle us up a chopper. Anytime in the next fifteen minutes would be perfect."

"Yes, sir."

Gerber checked his watch. To Kepler he said, "Let's get going."

Together they left the commo bunker and stepped into the sunlight of midmorning. In the tent city, partially rebuilt after the destruction of the previous night, the Vietnamese from Phu Ron were being made comfortable. They were given one end of the tent city so that they'd have a place of their own.

Gerber walked up the hill toward the team house. Fetterman and Minh were already there. Gerber hooked a thumb over his shoulder and asked, "How are the people doing?"

"Fine, sir," said Fetterman. "They seem happy enough."

"But?"

"Well, sir, they've just been burned or bombed out of their homes and they seem to be taking it well. No one's really complaining about anything."

"Maybe they're in shock. Have T.J. take a look at them."

"I planned on that," said Fetterman.

"Captain Minh," said Gerber, "maybe you should have some of your men talk to the villagers."

"Certainly, if you think it'll help."

"Can't hurt. In the meantime Derek and I will head into An Loc to talk with the province chief. We'll tell him what's going on out here and see what we can learn."

From the south came the sound of helicopter rotor blades. Gerber watched Bocker run out of the commo bunker and lope up the hill to the helipad, where he tossed a yellow smoke grenade.

"You ready, Derek?"

"Yes, sir."

"Captain," said Minh, "maybe I should accompany you to An Loc."

Gerber hesitated. He could see it both ways. A Vietnamese province chief dealing with a Vietnamese officer. But, he thought, Americans probably wouldn't intimidate the chief as much. Finally Gerber said, "Let Derek and me do this today. If it doesn't work out, then we can bring you in. Sort of the heavy gun if we need it."

"Fine."

The chopper was getting closer. Gerber glanced at it and said, "We've got to go. Don't want that aircraft sitting on the ground any longer than it has to."

With Kepler he ran toward the helicopter. They reached it, scrambled into the rear, and just as they sat down, it lifted off. The camp fell away as they turned north.

"How are we going to handle this?" asked Kepler, shouting over the roar of the engine.

Gerber laughed. "I was going to ask you the same thing. I figured you'd know more about it than me."

"I'll stay in the background and listen, especially if they start talking to one another in Vietnamese. Remember, most of these guys have delusions of grandeur. They think they control everything around them. Don't insult him, but deal with him from a position of strength. Oh, and remember, if we have trouble with him, there's a nephew waiting to take over."

The crew chief peeked around from his well. "Where do you guys want to land?"

Kepler leaned close to the man. "Let's circle An Loc once and take a look."

"You know what you're looking for?" asked Gerber.

"Oh, yes, sir. The province chief's home or office or whatever will be easy to spot. It'll be bigger and better maintained than anyone else's. There should be a few guards around it. Kind of a makeshift military compound."

Gerber glanced at the crew chief, who nodded and disappeared.

They crossed over An Loc, a dung-colored town of low buildings, some with red tile roofs, some with corrugated tin rusted to a muddy orange. There were a few paved streets, electric power poles and more than a few coconut and palm trees. The streets were even filled with Lambrettas, scooters, cars, trucks and oxcarts, as well as several buses. And there were people, dozens of them, hundreds. An Loc was like a miniature reproduction of Saigon.

"There," said Kepler, pointing. "That's got to be it. Got to be."

Gerber turned and looked down on a square compound that seemed to take up a whole block. There was a wall around it and a long, low building set well back. A road led to the compound, and at the gate were two guard posts. The Vietnamese flag flew from a pole in the center of the complex.

Gerber leaned around and pointed it out to the crew chief. "That's where we want to go."

"Yes, sir." He said something over the intercom, then asked Gerber, "Do you want us to wait?"

"Yeah, I think so."

The crew chief relayed the message, then asked, "Where do you want us to land?"

The protocol of the situation was unknown to Gerber. Normally he'd drive up to the gate. There was no doubt that the province chief would invite him in to talk, but riding in a helicopter he didn't have to stop at the gate. He could fly over it and land near the flagpole. There was plenty of open space. But to do so might offend the man.

On the other hand, there was space outside the compound to land. The flight crew could shut down out there and wait. But that left the aircraft and the men vulnerable to enemy action. Inside, they would be protected.

Finally he decided to err on the side of safety. "Near the flagpole!" he yelled.

As he sat back, the helicopter turned again and they began the approach. They slowed as they descended, crossing the wall about fifty feet above it and finally touching down near the flagpole. The rotor wash tore at the loose dirt, raising a cloud of red dust that faded away as the pilot lowered the pitch and shut down the engine.

Gerber, pulling the boonie hat from his head and taking his green beret from the pocket of his jungle fatigues, slipped to the side of the cargo compartment. He set the beret on his head, adjusted it so that the flash was right above his eye and then jumped from the rear of the chopper. Kepler handed him his weapon, then joined him.

"They should be running out to meet us in a moment," said Kepler.

Two men came from the building then. Both were dressed in modified American-style fatigues, wore side arms and carried M-16s. They looked as if they could have been brothers—the same height, skin color and hair. One of them wore sergeant stripes on his sleeve, and the other had the pips of a captain on his shirt collar.

"You want?" asked the officer as they approached.

Gerber stared at the man. "We would like to see your province chief."

"Colonel Lam no here. Gone."

"Then his deputy," said Gerber.

"No here."

"Dai Uy," said Gerber, "we're here to offer assistance. We don't want anything except to help. Why not stop the games and take us to meet Colonel Lam?"

"No here. Gone."

"When do you expect him back?" asked Gerber.

The Vietnamese officer stood there dumbly. He either didn't understand the question or understood it and didn't care to answer it.

Kepler stepped forward and grinned. He pulled a roll of piasters from his pocket and separated about a thousand P from it. "We have a need to meet with Colonel Lam," said Kepler. "As soon as possible."

The Vietnamese officer snatched the money from Kepler. "You follow."

As they walked toward the door, Gerber whispered, "Changed his tune quickly."

"Had to convince him we were serious."

They stepped up onto a dusty flagstone porch. A single man holding an M-1 carbine guarded the door. His American-made boots were scuffed and dirty. His fatigue pants were torn and baggy, and he hadn't bothered to tuck his shirt in. He looked like a kid playing at soldier who didn't understand the finer points of the profession. As they walked by him, he didn't acknowledge them in any fashion.

Inside, they stopped in a large entryway. A wooden staircase, wide and quite ornate, was off to the left. Its dark wood gleamed. To the right was a wooden bench and a single broken-down couch of Victorian design.

"You wait," said the Vietnamese captain. He opened a door near the couch and disappeared.

Gerber relaxed slightly. He glanced back at the entrance to the building. The door was open, but there was no breeze coming through it.

Before either Kepler or Gerber could comment, the officer was back. "You follow."

They moved toward the door and entered the huge office of Colonel Lam, the province chief. A fat man with a sweaty face, he sat behind a massive mahogany desk. His black hair was slicked down. He wore an immaculate uniform complete with a dozen ribbons attesting to his bravery and importance to the South Vietnamese army. Standing next to him, on either side, were two young women. One was dressed in a light blue and white *ao dai*. The other wore a short skirt, silk blouse and knee-high boots. They both had long, loose black hair, and neither looked to be more than fifteen.

As Gerber entered, he pulled his beret from his head. He moved toward the desk and stopped short before coming to attention. Flipping Lam a salute, he said, "Colonel, I would like the opportunity to speak with you."

Lam turned to the woman in the skirt, and she leaned forward and spoke to him in Vietnamese. When she finished, Lam grinned broadly, then he spoke to the woman.

"Colonel Lam," she translated, her English slightly accented, "says he welcomes the great American warriors to his humble house and asks how he may be of service."

Gerber glanced at the two fancy chairs sitting in front of the desk. Mock Louis Quatorze. A plush carpet was on the floor. Next to each chair was a small table.

"Please," said the woman, "sit."

Gerber, keeping his weapon at his side, sat down. Kepler slipped into the other chair. "Thank you."

"Now, ah . . ."

"Captain Gerber and Sergeant Kepler."

The woman translated for the colonel, who continued to smile, looking as if he didn't understand anything or have a care in the world.

"We've just come from the village of Phu Ron," said Gerber. "The Vietcong and the North Vietnamese infiltrated the village, and we had to drive them out of the area. I'm afraid the village didn't survive."

Again the woman whispered to the colonel, who nodded, the expression on his face never changing. He spoke briefly, then she asked, "Where are the people?"

"We've transported them to our camp. The survivors are safe there."

"You must bring them to An Loc immediately," she told him.

"I'm afraid we can't do that," said Gerber. "Not now. The VC and NVA presence in the area is still too strong, and these people will be targets if they're not protected."

"They are Vietnamese people."

"Yes," agreed Gerber.

There was silence in the room. Gerber heard the quiet ticking of a clock, and then spotted it sitting on a shelf to the right.

The colonel spoke rapidly then. He pointed at Gerber, then northward, toward Cambodia. Finally he fell silent, the smile still intact on his face.

"The colonel says he welcomes the American assistance to his people, but he must point out that it is the American presence that puts the people in danger. If the Americans would take the war to another part of Vietnam, then his people would not be in danger. The Americans talk about winning the war, they talk about helping the Vietnamese, but they leave the Vietcong and North Vietnamese alone because they are hiding in Cambodia."

Gerber knew the man had a point, but he couldn't tell him that. Instead he said, "With his help we can force the VC and NVA from this province. We can destroy the VC power base. That way everyone will be safe."

As she translated, the colonel nodded, grinned and then spoke again. She said, "The colonel says that as long as the enemy is allowed sanctuary in Cambodia, there can be no safety here. As long as the enemy can stand on the other side of the line and watch, all are in danger."

Gerber nodded. "I was hoping we could come to an agreement where we'd work together to push the enemy from your province. Our commitment to that has increased."

For the colonel the translator said, "Even if all VC in the province were killed or captured, there would still be hundreds on the other side of the border."

Gerber rubbed his face. There was nothing to say to that, so he ignored it. "Can we count on the colonel's cooperation?"

"The colonel," she said, "has asked what he can expect in return."

Gerber shot a glance at Kepler, then said, "We'll provide training for his soldiers. We'll provide ammunition, supplies and equipment."

"The status quo," she said, "is most beneficial for us. If we do not inhibit the VC, they do not attack us here."

"I'm hoping to break the status quo."

"Too many VC in Cambodia," she said.

"Would the colonel object to our beginning a training program for his soldiers?"

"There are too many VC around. Too many of them at Snuol, just across the border."

Gerber tried to think of something else to say, something they could discuss, but nothing came to mind. He looked at the quiet, smiling face of the colonel and knew nothing would change, no matter how much he said or promised. The colonel was going to protect himself and his station, and while the VC and NVA held any power, he was going to do nothing to alienate or irritate them.

Still grinning, the colonel said something and the woman translated. "The colonel thanks you for coming to visit him and hopes we can assist each other."

Gerber stood up, hesitated, then saluted sharply. Kepler did the same and then both turned and were escorted from the office by the Vietnamese captain who had brought them in. They walked through the entryway and back out into the bright afternoon sunlight.

"I leave now," said the Vietnamese captain.

Gerber placed his green beret on his head and turned to face the man. "Thank you for your assistance."

"I go." He then whirled and walked off.

As Gerber and Kepler walked toward the chopper, Kepler said, "You know what the old man was telling us, don't you? We eliminate the VC and we'll have him in our pocket."

"Right," said Gerber, nodding. "We do his dirty work and prove we're the toughest guy on the block, then he'll throw in with us. If not, he'll let the VC run wild."

They reached the chopper and found the crew sitting in the back. The pilot was asleep and the AC was reading a paperback novel. "You fellows ready?"

"Anytime."

As the crew scrambled around to get ready, Gerber asked, "Do you think he knows who the VC are?"

"You mean here in An Loc?"

"Here or in the other towns. Those who support the enemy cause or are sympathetic to it."

"I imagine he knows everything that goes on around here. If he didn't, he wouldn't last long as the province chief."

"That's what I thought," said Gerber.

They climbed into the rear of the chopper and buckled in. The AC, now sitting in the cockpit, turned and asked, "Where to now?"

"Back to our camp."

The roar of the turbine built as the blades began to spin. Kepler leaned close to the captain. "What are you planning to do next?"

"We'll see Fetterman and Minh when we get back and try to cook something up. Something the enemy won't forget."

23

XA CAT SPECIAL FORCES CAMP

Fetterman, Minh and Bocker sat around the table in the commo bunker and tried to figure out exactly what they would need for a raid on Snuol. They didn't have much in the way of infantry assets, they couldn't, or rather, weren't supposed to use the helicopters or gunships on the Cambodian side of the border, and they couldn't rely on air strikes and artillery support if they got into trouble. They could use their strikers, as well as Bromhead's and Henderson's men. But all that only added up to five hundred people, most of whom would have to walk to the battlefield.

"If the terrain allows it," said Fetterman, "we should hit the northern side of the VC camp. That way they'll evade to the south, east or west, which means they'll head into South Vietnam.

"Bromhead," said Minh, "could truck his people to the border easily. That blocks that side."

"It would be better," said Fetterman, "if he threw out his men west of the city so that we could funnel the enemy south. Once we got them into South Vietnam, we could use artillery or air strikes to take them out."

Minh rubbed his chin. "Do they have to get into South Vietnam before we can hit them?"

Fetterman shrugged. "The actual location of the border is in dispute. If they're close, I think we can hit them. No one's going to question it." He stopped, thought for a moment, then added, "Well, they might question it, but we should be in the clear."

Minh studied the map. "With my strikers on the ground on the northern side of the village, escape and evasion is going to be limited."

"Yeah," agreed Fetterman, "but we've got to block that out for them. When Captain Gerber returns, we'll have a better idea of what the terrain looks like."

Minh looked at the map carefully. There was one highway entering the town from the west, another from the east and a third to the north. The ground looked fairly flat, and probably had heavy jungle, which would provide cover from the air for the enemy. But it could also work to the advantage of the attacking forces.

Minh had a number of questions, but it would do no good to ask them. Neither Fetterman nor Bocker had seen the village or the terrain around it. They only had the maps he had, so their answers would be speculation. Sitting back, Minh asked, "We'll be in the field for what . . . ten, twelve hours? In and out?"

"Yes, sir," said Fetterman. "Everyone should carry as much ammo, water, first-aid kits and the like as possible. We won't need the rucksacks, though."

Bocker spoke for the first time. "We could have trouble with commo. I don't have enough radios yet."

"Bromhead and Henderson should have radios for their own people," Fetterman said. "You'll have to coordinate with them."

"We going to get aviation support?" asked Minh.

"I think so," said Fetterman. "We're close enough that we should be able to use the choppers."

Minh stood up. "I'll go out and get the men ready."

Fetterman rocked back and put his feet on the table. He glanced at Bocker and Minh and said, "There's not much more we can do until Captain Gerber gets here."

THE AIRCRAFT COMMANDER told Gerber there were two ways to survey the camp. They could either do it very low and fast or very high and fast. The pilot didn't say they couldn't or wouldn't fly into Cambodia, only that they had to do it quickly.

"What I'd like," said Gerber, "is an overflight at altitude and then cross it north to south very low. See what kind of reaction we get."

"And then?"

"We'll get the hell out and run straight for the border." Gerber looked at Kepler. "Anything you want to say?"

"I'd like everyone on board to look at the village. Remember what they see so that we'll have six pairs of eyes looking down there. And I'd like the ride to be as smooth as possible so I can get some pictures."

"I'll do what I can," said the pilot.

They climbed into the chopper and a few moments later took off. Climbing to three thousand feet, they flew north toward the border. Out to the right was a ridge of hills covered with jungle. Bromhead's camp at Song Be was there. To the left was more thick jungle, but no hills.

At three thousand feet it was cooler. And then they began a rapid descent, diving for the ground. In seconds the trees were no more than five feet under the skids of the chopper, and the air was again oppressive.

They crossed the border, and a few minutes later, Highway 13. Sticking to the west side of the road, they low-leveled along, swaying right and left and dodging the treetops. Like a roller coaster, they descended and climbed with sickening regularity. Then, just as they began another climb, the crew chief twisted around and shouted, "We're getting close. Get ready."

Gerber slid to the left side of the chopper for an unobstructed view. Kepler, holding his 35 mm camera, did the same on the right. Both men looked down and studied the terrain. Kepler began taking pictures.

Snuol was a small village, a red tip in the green of jungle vegetation. Sunlight winked from the metal roofs of the one- and two-story hootches. On the northern side of the village was a military camp with some tents, a few low structures and some bunkers. It looked as if it had been modeled on the Special Forces camps built in South Vietnam.

Then, suddenly, they began dropping toward the ground again. They dived toward the trees, leveled out, then banked quickly. Kepler took pictures as fast as he could focus, snap and advance the film.

They flashed over the camp, and Gerber got a good look at the men scrambling around in it. The enemy ran for cover, diving into bunkers or hootches. Each man wore a uniform. One man ran into the open and pointed his rifle up at the helicopter, squeezing off a burst. The tracers flashed by the side of the chopper.

And then they were beyond the camp and over the town. No one there seemed concerned about them. No one ran for cover. No one looked up at them.

As they reached the outskirts of the town, they dived for the rice paddies that surrounded it, now no more then three feet off the ground. The rotor wash created ripples on the surface of the water and flattened the tiny plants. As they approached the jungle again, the pilot hauled back on the cyclic and they popped up. The pilot skimmed the surface of the triple canopy as they ran for the safety of the Cambodian border.

Kepler, ignoring the twisting and turning as the pilots followed the uneven contour of the jungle, slid across the red canvas troop seat. He held his camera in both hands. Over the noise of the wind and engine, he yelled, "I got some pretty good stuff."

"You can use the chopper to take it into Saigon. I need the pictures as quickly as possible."

"Yes, sir."

They continued on like that, dodging and dipping, climbing and diving as they followed the jungle. When they crossed the highway, they began a rapid climb. The crew chief leaned around from his well and shouted, "We're back in South Vietnam now."

Gerber yelled back, "Take us to our camp. Then you'll have to take Sergeant Kepler into Saigon."

The crew chief disappeared for a moment, then struck his head back around. "No problem."

A few minutes later Gerber saw his camp sitting on the ridge line in the distance. They dropped toward it as red smoke began to billow from the helipad. They came to a hover and touched down. As soon as Gerber climbed out, the chopper lifted and headed for Saigon.

As the sound faded, Fetterman asked, "What did you see there, Captain?"

"Let's get down to the commo bunker and we'll go over it." He stopped long enough to look up at the fire control tower. It hadn't been sandbagged yet, and there was no roof so far, but at least it was there now, dominating the rest of the camp.

"Engineers have been busy in the past few hours," said Fetterman.

"They're doing a hell of a job."

"Yes, sir." Fetterman hesitated, then asked, "Can we do it?"

"I think you'll be pleased."

BILLY JOE CRINSHAW had spent the morning sifting through the papers Platt had accumulated and filed. Most of it was routine—supply documents, accounting sheets, morning reports and monthly reports. A lot of paper documenting the conduct of the war, and very little of it classified. A paper trail for weapons, supplies, equipment and ammunition. Nothing very exciting and certainly not interesting to anyone except the people who had to deal with it and the men who had signed their names to various papers to account for it.

But Platt had his hand in a few other pies. No general officer was going to be sent to Vietnam and then do nothing except function as a supply clerk. Besides, a general, because of the power he held, could get things done. Platt had obviously been involved in supplying MACV-SOG with equipment for their covert operations. By coordinating various assets, including aviation, artillery and supply, he was able to change the direction of the war. By allowing men and supplies to be funneled into certain areas, the war could be taken into those areas. Platt had kept himself busy during his tour.

It wasn't that Crinshaw objected to an officer using the tools at his disposal to get the job done. Hell, he'd done the same thing on a number of occasions. He'd initiated actions in the same way.

Most of what Platt had done looked good, at least on paper. And that was what counted. But as he sifted through the mountains of documents, he came across the name he'd been looking for. Gerber.

He separated references to Gerber into one pile and put everything else into another. Then, walking to the door, he opened it and looked out at Sergeant Seneff, who looked bored and hot.

Before Crinshaw could speak, Seneff pointed at Henrikson, who was sitting on a chair. "Sir," he said, "Captain Henrikson to see you."

"Thank you, Sergeant." He looked at the woman, grinned and said, "Come on in." Then he turned and walked back to his desk.

Henrikson came in and closed the door. She glanced at Crinshaw. "The answer is no."

"How can you tell?"

Henrikson took a seat. "You moved pretty fast there, trying to get behind the desk before I could get in here. If the answer had been yes, you would've closed the door yourself."

"To be honest," said Crinshaw, lying, "a number of generals said it was against various regulations to have a woman assigned to my staff in a combat zone."

"What about the nurses?"

"Nurses aren't assigned to my staff, and their job puts them in an exempt category. To do their job, they have to be here. Unfortunately your job isn't as critical."

"I see."

"I hope you do," said Crinshaw.

"Which general?" she asked. "Which generals said I couldn't be assigned here?"

"No one came right out," said Crinshaw, beginning to sweat. "There were suggestions. General Hull was one. General Platt was another."

"I see."

"When do you have to take off?" he asked, trying to change the subject.

"In about an hour."

"Not enough time to do anything," said Crinshaw.

Henrikson got to her feet and smoothed her skirt. "Not really."

Crinshaw escorted her to the door. "Will you be coming back?"

"I don't know. Depends."

"Why not do that? Come back in a few months. Maybe things will change by then."

"You think so?"

"You can never tell."

He opened the door and she walked out, slipping by Seneff without saying a word to him. When she was outside in the hallway, Crinshaw looked at Seneff. "I've got some stuff in my office for you to file," said Crinshaw.

"Yes, sir."

"Then, in about thirty minutes, I'll want you to learn the whereabouts of Colonel Thomas Dawkins. He's the commander or rather coordinates the use of Army Aviation assets in Three Corps."

"Yes, sir." Seneff got up and followed Crinshaw into his office.

"There," said the general, pointing at the papers.

Seneff picked up the papers, started toward the door, then stopped. He looked at Crinshaw. "This isn't what I expected."

Crinshaw grinned. "Wait a couple of days and you'll be surprised."

"Yes, sir."

As Seneff left the office, Crinshaw picked up the massive files that held the information on Gerber. "I've got you cold, you son of a bitch."

GERBER, ALONG WITH FETTERMAN, walked across the compound and entered the commo bunker. Minh and Bocker were still there, sitting around the table and drinking Cokes. Gerber pointed at the red cans and asked, "Where in hell did those come from?"

"Chopper about noon brought us a couple of cases," Bocker said. "Brought in some beer, too."

"Would you like one, Captain?" asked Fetterman.

"God, yes. A Coke, that is. Is it cold?"

"Very. Be right back then."

As Fetterman headed toward the team house, Gerber sat down on an ammo crate. Glancing at the map, he said, "We can get the preliminary plan worked out. Kepler will be back later with the photographs."

Minh leaned forward and outlined the plan he and Fetterman had designed using the assets they now controlled, including Bromhead and Henderson.

"Maybe we should get them here," said Bocker.

"Not yet," said Gerber. "Later, once we've got things worked out."

"What did you see, Captain?" asked Bocker.

"Let's wait for Sergeant Fetterman."

Fetterman entered carrying two cans of Coke. He handed one to Gerber, who said, "Let's get at it."

"From the maps," Fetterman said, "it seems the terrain north of town, where the camp is situated, would be best for our landing."

Minh interrupted. "I've been thinking about that, old boy. If the fields are large enough, what about a parachute drop? Two C-130s would handle it."

Gerber continued to drink his Coke in silence. He closed his eyes as he thought about what Minh had said. Finally he opened his eyes. "I think we'd better stick to the choppers."

"Noise."

"Certainly, Dai Uy," said Gerber. "But if we touch down here, about a klick from the camp, our movements will be masked by a low ridge line and the jungle. We can use the cover of the jungle and the ridge line to sneak into place.''

"They'll still hear us," said Minh.

"Of course they'll hear us," agreed Gerber, "but they'll never suspect an attack. We just don't do things like that, as far as they're concerned. A parachute drop might be quieter, sneakier, but we can count on losing ten percent of our attack force to injuries during the jump, and we could end up scattered over two or three klicks. With the choppers we won't have any injuries, and everyone will be clumped together.''

"How big is the camp?" asked Fetterman.

"Probably no more than two hundred men there. The level of training isn't good." He laughed. "Only one man fired at us as we flew over. The others ran and hid.''

"Keeping their camp a secret," suggested Minh.

"I don't think so," responded Gerber. "It's an open, aboveground camp. Military vehicles, tents and bunkers are all visible from the air. It isn't a secret.''

"This doesn't look like a very good idea," said Minh.

"We're going to do what the VC do to us," said Gerber. "They have the big base. They're complacent. As far as the VC and NVA are concerned, the Americans and South Vietnamese won't attack because of various logistical and political reasons. So, we fly out of the jungle, blow up everything in sight and shoot the shit out of them, then get the hell out.''

"There will be protests by the Cambodians about an invasion of their territory," said Minh.

"Who gives a flying fuck?" snapped Gerber. He looked at the men with him. "If we make enough noise during the attack and we frighten the enemy enough, they should try to get out. We'll put Bromhead's men and Henderson's in position to block that escape.''

"And then?" asked Fetterman.

"We'll get the hell out, using the choppers, then set up on our side of the border. With luck the remnants of the VC will run right into us and be cut to pieces. If not, maybe the artillery, the Air Force or helicopter gunships will get them."

Fetterman finished his Coke and set the can aside. He stared at the map. "Where will the choppers pick us up?"

"Right outside the camp," said Gerber. "We'll want to eliminate the bunkers and weapons on that side. If the enemy breaks as they should, then the choppers will be able to land in a cold LZ." He glanced at the others. "Anything else?" When no one spoke, he said, "We'll have the final briefing as soon as Kepler gets here with the photographs. If there are no snags, we'll hit them in about twelve hours."

24

NEWS BUREAU
SAIGON

Mark Hodges left the tiny glass cubicle that served as his office. Hodges was a short, fat man who hated the tropics, hated Vietnam and hated Saigon. He stayed because he thought that a tour with the news service in Vietnam would advance his career. He stayed so he could send his reporters out to cover the great stories of the war.

And sometimes the not so great stories.

He stopped at Morrow's desk and waited until she looked up at him. "Got a hot one for you, Robin."

"A hot one, yeah," she said.

Hodges parked a hip on the corner of her desk and waved a sheet of paper at her as if it were a banner. "Got a new general in Vietnam."

"Great! Just what we need."

"I'd like you to run over to Tan Son Nhut and talk to the man. See what his background is and what his job is. A nice little story on the new man in the war."

Morrow gestured at the other desks. "Let one of the others do it."

"The others have jobs already. This one is yours."

Morrow held out her hand and Hodges gave her the paper. She glanced at it, then dropped it on the desk as if it were red-hot. She tried to disguise the sudden sinking feeling in the pit of her stomach. She felt light-headed for a moment, and the world seemed to swim around her. Finally she said, "You don't want me to do this."

"Why not?"

Morrow tapped the paper. "I know this guy. He won't want to talk to me. I'll get nothing out of him." She glanced around and spotted Meyers.

"When did that ever stop you?" asked Hodges.

Pointing at Meyers, Morrow asked, "Why don't you send him? It'd be a good story for him."

"I want you to do it."

"I'm telling you this is a mistake. Rather than blow it completely, why don't you send Meyers with me?"

"This is a one-reporter story and it's yours. I'll expect five hundred words on this by nine tomorrow morning. And I don't want to argue about it anymore." Hodges turned and walked away.

Morrow picked up the paper and read the name again. She felt sick. She remembered her run-ins with the man before. She remembered the threats he'd made. And now he was back in Vietnam.

She turned and stared at Hodges, who had reached his office. He walked in and she stood up. She scooped up her camera bag from the floor and carefully placed it on her chair. Then she kicked the side of her desk as hard as she could. The sound seemed to reverberate through the city room. Everyone looked at her.

She grabbed her bag, slung it over her shoulder, whirled, and saw that Hodges was staring at her. Giving him the finger, she stormed out of the office, slamming the door behind her.

KEPLER HAD RETURNED from Saigon with a package of pictures of the enemy camp. Henderson had already arrived and was sitting in the team house drinking a Coke. Bocker came out of the commo bunker and found Gerber and Fetterman sitting in the team house with Henderson.

Bocker entered and said, "Captain Bromhead is inbound and should be down in five minutes."

Gerber stood up. "Tony, let's go meet the young captain at the helipad."

"Certainly."

Gerber turned to Henderson. "If you'll excuse us, Captain. We'll all meet in the commo bunker and look at the plan within the next ten minutes."

"I'll meet you there."

Gerber, Fetterman and Bocker headed out the door. They walked up the slight slope that led to the helipad. Bocker carried a smoke grenade. When they got there, he pulled the pin and tossed the grenade to the center of the pad where it began to burn, pouring out a cloud of yellow smoke.

"Be good to see Johnny again," said Gerber.

"Jack, sir," said Fetterman. "He's Jack now."

"Right," said Gerber. "I forget, but then he'll always be Johnny."

"That's not going to thrill him."

The chopper appeared then, coming from the east. Gerber watched it slip through the increasing cloud cover. He pointed up at the sky and said, "I wonder if those clouds will cause us any trouble tonight."

"We don't have to go tonight," said Fetterman.

"I want to get this taken care of before the engineers are pulled out of here. Those two hundred soldiers give us a real advantage."

"Yes, sir."

The chopper circled around to the south and began its approach. It slowed as it crossed the perimeter wire, hovering slowly forward and kicking up a cloud of red dust. Then the chopper stopped over the pad, its rotor wash beating down the smoke and curling it back through the rotor system. Slowly the Huey settled until its skids touched rubber.

Bromhead leaped out of the rear, and as he did, the chopper rose to fifteen or twenty feet, then spun around and headed away from the camp. As the Huey disappeared and its noise faded, Bromhead came forward. A grin split his face. Although he was now twenty-five, he still had the freckle-faced look of an all-American boy. His hair was a sandy color and his skin was deeply tanned. But after nearly a year as a team commander, he was beginning to take on a haunted look. There were dark circles under his eyes and he was now quite thin. He wore faded jungle fatigues with subdued rank and branch insignia. His jungle boots were black but not spit-shined, and he carried an M-16 in his left hand.

"Afternoon, Captain," said Gerber, trying not to smile too much.

"Afternoon, Mack," said Bromhead. "Tony. Galvin."

"Welcome to our camp," said Gerber. "Such as it is."

Bromhead surveyed the area around him. He looked at the fire control tower that now had a roof, the wooden and sand-bagged buildings, the completed bunkers and the tent city. "It's a lot better than the mess I've inherited."

Gerber glanced at his watch. "Come on, we've got work to do."

Fetterman shook his head slowly. "We don't see the young captain in months and you two act like it's no big deal. Well, hell, how the hell you been, Captain?"

"I've been just fine, Master Sergeant. You're looking very well."

Fetterman patted his stomach. "It's that high living in Saigon. No nightly mortar attacks, good food instead of C-rats, and hot and cold running women. Takes the edge off the combat soldier."

"That'd do it," said Bromhead.

Gerber took his cue from Fetterman. "Hell, Johnny, er, Jack, it's damn good to see you again."

"Thanks. You can call me Johnny if it's easier on you."

"You suggesting I'm not able to remember your name?" asked Gerber.

"Not at all."

"We'd better get down to the commo bunker," said Bocker.

"Galvin," said Bromhead. "I'm not ignoring you. How are you?"

"Fine, Captain."

"Galvin, lead the way," said Gerber.

They walked toward the commo bunker. As they did, Bromhead asked, "What's the status of weapons here?"

"We've got .50s on each wall and each of the .50s is supported by three M-60s. There are enough M-79s for good coverage and we've also got some 60 mm mortars and a half-a-dozen 81 mm weapons. We can keep illumination in the air over the camp all night if it's necessary."

"I could use some of that for my new camp."

They entered the bunker and walked toward the table. Kepler got up and came forward. "Welcome to the camp, Captain."

"Thank you, Derek."

"Captain," said Minh.

"Dai Uy Minh. Hello."

"You're looking good, old boy."

"If we can conclude old home week," Gerber said, "We've got some work to do." He looked at Henderson. "Do you two know each other?"

Bromhead held out his hand. "We've worked together a couple of times in the past." Smiling at Henderson, he asked, "How are you?"

"Good, Jack."

Kepler spread out the photographs. "I'm afraid these didn't come out quite as good as I hoped. Still, they give you an idea of the camp and the terrain around it."

Gerber grabbed one of the pictures and spun it around. He studied it for a moment, then pushed it aside. Looking at the others, he said, "I think it'll work."

Fetterman stood and moved toward the radios where there were a couple of legal pads. He picked one up and returned to the table. Sitting down, he pulled a pen from his pocket and asked, "What do we need to do?"

Gerber gave each man the preliminaries, including the deployment of the listening posts for the night. He told them what he expected and what they were going to have to do. They all listened carefully and agreed that it seemed to be a sound idea.

"If we can pull it off," said Gerber, "this should break the backbone of VC strength in this province. It'll force them to go somewhere else."

"This one base seems to supply the needs of the VC and NVA operating in the area," Kepler said. "We've already hit one of their major supply dumps and eliminated it. Once we get this place, we'll have forced the VC and NVA out altogether."

"How can you say that?" asked Bromhead.

Kepler hesitated, then wiped a hand over his face. He rubbed it on his fatigues, leaving a wet, ragged stain on his chest. "By talking to the province chief we learned that his major concern is the camp at Snuol. He was willing to throw in with us if we could eliminate the VC and NVA camp there. The implication is, now that we've taken out the supply dump at Phu Ron, the only major power source in the region is at Snuol. If it's gone, then it's just a question of mopping up a little resistance from the local groups.''

''The enemy has quite a presence here, don't they?'' asked Henderson.

Gerber took over again. He stood up to pace, as if he were a professor lecturing his students. ''Let's get one thing straight. Our statistics are based on faulty information.'' He laughed at himself, then said, ''Let me rephrase that. Official statistics are based on faulty information. If we don't have a presence in an area, it's conceded to the enemy. If they don't have a presence in the area, it's still conceded to the enemy. We've got thousands of soldiers in and around Saigon so that belongs to us. We don't have many soldiers in Binh Long Province so that belongs to the enemy.''

''And,'' said Kepler, taking over again, ''my investigations suggest there's no real enemy presence other than infiltration through the region into the Tay Ninh, Dau Tieng and Cu Chi areas for staging to Saigon.''

''You mean to tell me the enemy isn't operating around here?'' Bromhead objected.

''Not really,'' said Kepler, ''but it's not quite as cut and dried as that. There are enemy soldiers, just as there are American soldiers, but neither side actually controls the province. You might say with our big bases at Tay Ninh and Dau Tieng that we control the southern and eastern edges of the province, while the VC and NVA with their camp in Snuol control the northern edge.''

''Our job,'' said Gerber, ''is to eliminate that control from Snuol.''

"If we do," said Bromhead, "then the province belongs to us."

"Exactly," said Gerber. "We can then control the movement of men and supplies through it. We'll have the opportunity to begin real civic-action programs. With those, plus medical, financial and social aid, we can undercut any activity by the VC or NVA."

Again Kepler took over. "The VC can operate on two levels. One, by insisting on land reform, ownership of small farms by the farmers, they appeal to the farmers. No longer is the farmer working for a landowner, but working for himself. In South Vietnam, with so many small landowners, that isn't much of a power base, so the VC have to rely on terror." Kepler sat up straight and looked at the men around him. "Charlie can't claim that if he wins he's going to put ownership of the land back into the hands of the poor. But he can tell them that if they cooperate with the invaders from the West, he'll kill them. That makes a real impression."

"So we come in," said Gerber, "and offer protection. You side with us and the VC won't be able to harm you or your family. You can work the land in peace. And we'll teach you ways to make your land more productive. We'll teach you how to make your family healthier. Any power base the enemy has built collapses because the people are content. Satisfied."

"Pretty lofty ideals," said Henderson. "I thought we were here to fight a war."

"Which is exactly what we're doing," said Gerber. "But we're fighting it on all levels. If we push the enemy off the land and destroy everything in the process, we've gained nothing. If we force the VC out and keep the people here, assisting them, then we keep the enemy out. They don't have a power base to build on. If we can do this a province at a time throughout South Vietnam, the VC's power will evaporate.''

Now Fetterman took over. "That will mean the VC will soon cease to exist, and the war will be fought by outsiders from the North. Rather than help the people as we have, they'll destroy everything and erode their support even more. They'll have to import all their weapons, ammo and supplies. And if we chop up their supply lines, they'll wither and die."

"Nice speech," said Henderson. "But what's that got to do with us here tonight?"

"Tonight," said Gerber, "we put another phase of the plan into operation. We lengthen the enemy's supply line so that it's harder for them to fight here."

Henderson laughed. "You can't win at this. One guy with a rifle can keep the fight alive."

"No," said Fetterman. "One guy with a rifle is a criminal and a threat to all peace-loving people. What we have to establish is a base for the people. Give them what they desire most—a farm, their family and a peace that leaves them alone. Keep the enemy out and the war ends. No one will put up with it. Right now there are too many disgruntled people—"

"And rightly so," interjected Henderson.

"Makes no difference," said Gerber. "Our job tonight is to eliminate the enemy base. Tomorrow we'll see the province chief again and try to change some of the old policies. With that, the war begins to wind down."

"It'll never work," said Henderson.

"Why not?"

"Because you'll never have the support of the people. There's always going to be that person who'll hate everything you do. His excuse will be that the changes and benefits were imported by us and therefore are bad. Or that we're tearing the heart out of their culture.''

"But that's going to be a small part of the society, and you'll always have people like that," Gerber said. "Tonight we eliminate the outside influences."

"Or rather the outside influences that are evil," said Fetterman.

"This is crazy," said Henderson.

"If you want out," snapped Gerber, "you're out. I'll call Saigon and have your strike force replaced by the one at Nha Trang."

"No," said Henderson. "I didn't mean I wouldn't go along with the plan. I was merely saying I think your ideals are a bit lofty for a captain in the Special Forces."

"Then we're all agreed on this?" asked Gerber.

"I'm required to move my troops to this point here as a blocking force," said Bromhead. "Then what?"

"If you're not hit," replied Gerber, "you withdraw to your camp and wait for instructions."

"Okay," said Bromhead.

"We'll have to patrol," said Gerber. "We'll have to patrol frequently to keep the enemy from infiltrating again, but I think we can make Binh Long Province as safe as the streets of New York."

"That's not very encouraging," said Fetterman, grinning.

Gerber shot a glance at the master sergeant. He realized Fetterman was trying to relieve some of the tension Henderson's skepticism had caused.

"Okay, then, we'll make it as safe as a farm in Iowa. How's that sound?"

"When do we jump off?" asked Henderson.

Gerber glanced at his watch. "If we don't run into any snags, we should take off at about 0100, maybe 0130. Jack, you might have to leave before that so you can get into position by one. I'd like to hit the enemy camp about half past two in the morning."

"And tomorrow?" asked Henderson.

"We rest," said Gerber.

25

**TAN SON NHUT
SAIGON**

Crinshaw sat with his feet propped on his desk and the phone cradled between his ear and shoulder. He held a file folder in his left hand and a pen in his right. He was waving both of them in the air as if they were on fire and he was trying to kill the flames.

"That's not correct, Colonel Dawkins," he said, his voice steely. "Captain Gerber and the Special Forces at MACV-SOG don't have the support of this office. It's been terminated as of this morning."

"I understand that, General," said Dawkins. "But I can't just terminate his support in the middle of an operation. There are lives at stake."

"Colonel, I don't make it a habit of repeating myself," snapped Crinshaw.

"General, we can't leave the men without support. There are soldiers who are relying on us in the field, and right now it doesn't make any difference to them whether or not Gerber or anyone else lied to get that support. We've got to get them out of the field."

"Does the word *order* mean anything to you, Colonel?" asked Crinshaw.

"Yes, sir, it does. But this goes beyond that. I have a responsibility to the men in the field."

"I could come over there, Colonel." Crinshaw grinned at the documents he held. Dawkins was squirming. He could hear it in the colonel's voice.

"General, what I am supposed to do?"

Now it was time to twist the knife. "You're supposed to obey all lawful orders."

"But—"

"Colonel," said Crinshaw coldly, "I'm aware of your plight. I understand the loyalty you feel for the men in the field, and your desire to obey your orders." Crinshaw stopped talking, letting the silence build.

"What am I supposed to do?" asked Dawkins again.

"Finish the required support functions, but once everyone has been returned to his base, you withdraw that support completely. You'll accept no phone calls, you'll turn away all visitors, and you'll alert this office if there are any requests for assistance or aviation assets."

"Yes, General."

Crinshaw dropped his feet to the floor and leaned forward, elbows on his desk. "I want this understood absolutely. There will be no more support of Gerber or MACV-SOG without the permission of this office. Written permission."

"Yes, General. But—"

"You've been given your orders," Crinshaw interrupted. He knew the colonel was going to say that Gerber's support had been there when the assets had been scheduled. The general didn't want to hear that.

"Yes, sir."

Before Dawkins could say anything more, Crinshaw hung up. That was the trick in dealing with subordinates. Keep them off balance as much as possible. Keep them guessing and they'd be so busy trying to keep up that they'd automatically stay in line.

Crinshaw stood and walked to the outer office. Seneff was there reading a magazine. He closed it as the general approached, and stood up. "Yes, sir?"

"Let's go get something to eat, and then I want to come back here to check on a few more things before we drive over to the SOG building."

"I'll arrange a jeep for that," said Seneff.

"No. I want a staff car. One with an air conditioner that works. You have any trouble with that, you get the name and rank of the man and I'll talk to him."

"Certainly, General."

As they left the office, Crinshaw was pleased with himself. He'd effectively hamstrung Gerber. Without aviation support it was impossible to move soldiers around Vietnam easily. They could always walk, as soldiers had done since the dawn of time, but in Vietnam that invited attack from ambushes and booby traps. Triple-canopy jungle could easily keep men from moving more than a hundred yards a day. Take away the choppers and the men were limited in what they could do.

As they descended the stairs, Crinshaw decided it had been a very good day indeed.

HENDERSON AND BROMHEAD had returned to their own camps. Gerber, Fetterman and Minh moved among the strikers, checking their weapons, ammo and equipment. It was a quick inspection to make sure the weapons were clean and that no one had thrown away any of the extra ammo they were required to carry. As soon as a soldier was inspected, he was allowed to fall out and sit down. Takeoff wouldn't be for three hours.

As they finished, Gerber and Fetterman walked to the team house, where the others waited. Washington had a medic bag sitting on the floor near the refrigerator. Tyme was sitting on a chair. It was tipped back so that he could lean against a wall. He was drinking a Coke and reading a magazine. Kepler was standing in front of the shelves that held canned goods. He looked like a shopper who couldn't make up his mind.

"Three hours to go," said Gerber, "and you people look awfully relaxed."

Tyme looked up from his magazine. "Weapons are ready to go, Captain. In a few minutes I'll make a final check and then review the maps and photos."

Washington pointed at the bag on the floor. "Got my equipment right there, sir. I'll review the plan with Justin after he's completed his equipment check."

"And I know all about the mission, Captain," said Kepler. "I've briefed the strikers on the LPs."

Gerber held up his hands as if surrendering. "All right. You guys win."

"Thank you, sir," said Tyme.

Fetterman opened the refrigerator door. "You up for a Coke?"

"Not now, Tony," Gerber replied. "I drink many more and I'll spend the rest of the night in the latrine."

Fetterman took out a Coke, then dropped into the closest chair.

Gerber sat down, his back to the door, and looked at the men around him. They didn't look like troops about to go into battle. They were as relaxed as soldiers in the World who were waiting for four o'clock so that they could go home. They didn't appear to be nervous.

Tyme finally broke the silence. "I can tell when you want something done, sir, so I'll go out and check on the squad weapons."

"Take a few more minutes," said Gerber.

Tyme sat back, but now he was edgy. Finally he stood up and left the team house.

"Nice going, Captain," said Fetterman.

Gerber nodded, then stood. "I'm going to the commo bunker." He glanced at his watch. "I'll expect all of you to join me there in the next twenty minutes for the final briefing. Tony, I'll want to see Captain Parker as soon as we finish with that. If you see him, let him know."

"Yes, sir."

Gerber left. He stopped just outside the team house, stretched and looked at the sky. The sun had set and the stars were beginning to come out. But even with the sun gone, the heat of the day remained, radiating up from the ground. With the humidity it was still oppressive. He was sweating, and he had done nothing but walk along the line of strikers to inspect them and then cross the compound to the team house.

He listened to the coming night sounds. The helicopters had retreated to their bases and the fighters were gone. It was quiet for a moment, with the exception of the distant boom of artillery and the buzz of the generator the engineers had brought in during the day.

He walked across the compound and reached the commo bunker, which was a little cooler. The gloom had been chased away by the electric lights the engineers had installed. It was better than the Coleman lanterns they'd been using.

"Anything on the radio, Galvin?"

"Captain Bromhead has returned to his camp and they're moving out by truck now. Captain Henderson hasn't reported in yet."

Gerber moved to the table and looked at the materials spread out there. He studied the map again and then inspected the photos Kepler had brought back from Saigon. He laid them out in the path they'd followed during the overflight earlier that day and tried to spot something they'd missed. He looked for indications that the enemy was hiding something in Snuol.

Bocker came around from the radios and joined Gerber. "Looks to be routine."

"Fairly," agreed Gerber. "Not many support vehicles around. I expected something more. And no indication of mortar emplacements or heavy weapons."

"Should there be?" asked Bocker.

"I suppose not." He picked up a picture and held it close to his face. The image had been slightly blurred by the motion of the chopper, but it was clear enough that he could see the staff car, a black vehicle he couldn't identify. It might have been something of Russian manufacture. There were flags on the fenders and two men stood outside of it.

He pointed it out to Bocker. "That's interesting."

"Yes, sir."

Fetterman entered then. He came down, blinked in the bright lights, then said, "Captain Parker will be here in a little while."

"Good."

During the next few minutes the team members slipped into the bunker. Once they were all there, seated around the table, Gerber said, "We'll take it from the top. I'll go over it once and then, Justin, I'll want a quick briefing from you. T.J., I'll want some input from you, too."

Gerber again outlined the plan. He described the assault on the enemy camp and what he expected from the men as they attacked. He talked about the timing and how they'd get the helicopters in to take them out of Cambodia. He detailed the missions of each man. When he finished, he asked if there were any questions, and when no one spoke up, he turned to Tyme.

The sergeant took over, going through the briefing as if he were the commander and everyone else his subordinate. He talked about the specifics of the mission and who had what assignment. He walked them through it from the moment of takeoff at the camp to the moment they'd return after the attack.

Then the field phone buzzed and Bocker walked around to get it. He waited until Tyme looked up and stopped talking, then lifted the handset. "Bocker. This line isn't secure."

The voice at the other end sounded as if it were coming from the dark side of the moon. It was a distant, tinny voice, filtered so that it was impossible to tell if it was male or female.

"Galvin, that you?"

"This is Sergeant Bocker. I repeat, this line isn't secure."

"Galvin, this is Robin Morrow. Is Mack handy?"

"Wait one." Bocker put the handset down. "Captain, it's Robin wanting to talk to you."

"How the hell? . . . I didn't know we had a lima lima to Saigon."

"Engineers got it in by running a line to An Loc and tying into the communications board there. A high wind will knock it out."

Gerber got up and walked to the phone. Before he picked it up, he said, "This is an unsecure line, so let's keep the talk on something else."

When the men nodded, Gerber lifted the handset. "Robin?"

"Mack? Are you sitting down?"

"No, I'm standing here looking at the team. We're kind of busy."

"This won't take long. I've got some bad news." She hesitated, then said, "Crinshaw's back."

"What?"

"Crinshaw's back."

"I heard you." He released the button on the handset and looked at his men. "Crinshaw's back."

"I'm supposed to interview him sometime in the next couple of hours," Morrow continued, "but I'm dodging the assignment as long as I can. I thought you should know he's back in Vietnam. It looks as if he's got his old job again."

"What happened to Platt?"

"I don't know. I'll see if I can find out."

"Okay," said Gerber. "Thanks, Robin."

"When can I come out there?"

"Later. A week. Ten days."

"When are you coming into Saigon?"

"Robin, this isn't the time to talk about this. I've got work to do."

Her voice faded, then came back. "I understand. Call me when you get the chance."

"Of course."

He hung up, returned to the table and looked at the men around him. "Crinshaw is back and that's going to cause us some trouble."

"Shouldn't tonight," said Fetterman.

"I don't know," said Gerber. "Crinshaw is a foxy asshole. He can think of ways to fuck us up that won't be clear for days to come."

"Yes, sir," said Fetterman, "but he won't be able to do anything tonight. If he just arrived, there'll be a transition period."

Gerber waved a hand as if to clear the slate. "T.J., what have you got for us?"

Washington stood up and began to list the problems with the medical side of the team. A lack of antibiotics, a lack of medicines, a lack of everything. "I'd advise you to take the wounded to An Loc if it's a real emergency and to Tay Ninh if we have time."

"Thanks, T.J. Galvin, what time are the pilots arriving for their briefing?"

"Anytime now, Captain."

"Good. Does anyone else have anything he'd like to say before we adjourn?"

There was silence.

MORROW COULD THINK of no reason to stay away from Crinshaw. Anything she told her boss would be thrown back at her, so she found a cab and rode out to Tan Son Nhut. Getting out of the vehicle, she stood for a moment and looked at the building. The memories came flooding back to her. The fighting with Crinshaw to keep Fetterman and Tyme out of jail. Her threats and his eventual capitulation. It seemed so long ago, and yet the events were as fresh as ever.

Without arguing, she paid the driver what he asked and then slowly walked up the sidewalk toward the double doors. She had told herself she'd never have to confront Crinshaw again, yet here she was all over again.

She pushed open the door and stepped into the air-conditioned building. The cold air dried her sweat quickly. Walking to the stairs, she climbed to the second floor, turned and looked down the corridor, but didn't move immediately. Then, steeling herself, she started down the hall.

The building was almost deserted due to the late hour. There were lights on in a few offices, but Morrow hoped

Crinshaw would be gone for the day. That would give her an excuse to put off the meeting.

But Crinshaw was in. His sergeant was sitting behind a desk reading a magazine. When Morrow walked in, he grinned at her. "May I help you?"

"Is General Crinshaw here?"

"Just a moment, ma'am, and I'll see. Please have a seat." He waved at the couch, then watched as she sat down and crossed her legs.

Seneff disappeared into the inner office. Morrow heard the quiet buzz of conversation, then Seneff reappeared. "The general will see you now."

Morrow got up, shouldered her camera bag and entered Crinshaw's office. He was sitting behind it, working on some papers. Signing them with a flourish, he set them aside, looked up and smiled unctuously. "Miss Morrow, it's been a long time. I'm surprised you haven't returned to the States by now." He held out a hand.

Morrow crossed the floor and shook hands. She noticed Crinshaw's palm was sweaty, though the room felt like an icebox. She dropped into the visitor's chair without being invited, placed her camera bag next to her and dug through it, pulling out her pad. "Now, General, what's it feel like being back in Vietnam after a tour in the World?"

Crinshaw took a deep breath and laced his fingers behind his head. "As a soldier, this is where I belong. In the war zone. Naturally I'd rather be home with my wife, but as a soldier I understand the need for my presence here."

"Wife?"

"Yes," said Crinshaw. "I was married six months ago. It's quite a strain being away from her so soon after our marriage but, as I say, a soldier must go where he's told to go."

"What's your role here?"

"Much as it was during my last tour. I'll be coordinating various activities. You'll excuse me if I don't go into too much detail on that. Some of it's classified."

"Sure," said Morrow, knowing Crinshaw was trying to cloak the routine nature of his work.

Crinshaw lowered his hands. "There are definite areas where I can be of value here, and I'm looking into them. Ways to better utilize our resources and ways to prevent the unnecessary deaths of our soldiers."

"Unnecessary deaths?" said Morrow. She knew Crinshaw was shooting off his mouth, but if he wanted to hang himself, she'd let him.

"Well, naturally, we've been very lucky. What I want to do is use our technology to fight the war and keep our soldiers out of it."

"Have there been unnecessary deaths?"

"To my knowledge, no. I want to make sure there are none."

"Just what are your plans?"

Still smiling, Crinshaw said, "Well, you're getting into a classified area again. There are things I need to do to help bring about a conclusion to the war."

Morrow made a note; she knew what the next question should be. Crinshaw was so happy to be interviewed that he was shooting his mouth off. She shrugged and asked the question. "Do you see an end to the war?"

"Well, I know that it's going to end and that the enemy has trimmed down their operations, but that doesn't mean much."

"A real nonanswer," said Morrow.

"Personally I see the war winding down if we push forward. That's the way of war. You put the enemy on the ropes and hammer at them until they surrender. No other way to do it."

"Then the VC are on the ropes?"

"Close to it," said Crinshaw, his smile fading.

Morrow knew he was about to clam up, not that she cared. The story would have to be written not to offend him. They'd go easy on him for the first few weeks, but then they'd nail him if they felt he was being less than honest. She decided she should just get out. "Anything you'd like to add?" She looked up and waited for an answer.

"Just that I'm pleased to be here, serving with the greatest Army and the greatest men."

Morrow stood. "I'd like to thank you for your time, General."

"Thank you, Miss Morrow. Please feel free to come back anytime."

Morrow plucked her bag from the floor, stuffed her notebook in it and got out. She said nothing to the sergeant as she walked through the outer office, and when she reached the hallway, she stopped. Leaning against the wall, she took a deep breath and wanted to scream. It was then that she realized just how much she hated Crinshaw. He could sound so normal, but she knew what kind of man he was. She wondered just how soon he'd do something to get even with Gerber. Gerber would have to be careful, or he'd be in trouble.

26

XA CAT SPECIAL FORCES CAMP

Gerber and Fetterman sat in the bunker with Major Ralph Whitmore, the air mission commander. He would ride in the C and C chopper, coordinating the movements of the helicopters with the troops on the ground. Now he carefully studied the maps and photographs. "Fields here look large enough for the flight."

"No question about it," said Gerber. "But we'd rather put the lift in here. Masks us from the enemy and maintains the element of surprise."

"Fine, Captain," said Whitmore. "I don't care what field we put you into. You want to land there, you got it."

"It'll take us an hour to get into position and then an hour for the assault. That puts the pickup at four, just prior to sunrise."

"We can stand by at Loc Ninh. There's an airfield there," said Whitmore.

"I like it," said Gerber. "Anything else you need to know?"

"Have you got permission to operate inside Cambodia?"

"Did you talk to General Platt?" countered Gerber.

"I've tried. And I'd like to know the size of the enemy force at Snuol and what antiaircraft defenses are available to them."

"None that we've identified. Small arms and .51 cals," said Fetterman. "Nothing radar controlled and nothing larger than the .51s. In fact there's no evidence of mortars, so they're lightly defended."

"Pickup outside the wire, then?"

"Yes, sir," said Gerber. "By that time we'll have neutralized the enemy, so you should receive no fire from the camp during the extraction."

"Other friendlies in the area?"

Gerber pointed at the map. "We'll have blocking forces here and here. They'll be the only friendlies on the Cambodian side of the border."

"All right," said Whitmore. "Flight time in will take about twenty minutes."

"We'll be ready for pickup at 0130," said Gerber.

"Spread the loads farther than normal," said Whitmore. "And set them up in staggered trail."

"Fine. Anything else?"

Whitmore studied the map. "You flew a recon this afternoon?"

"Yes, sir."

"And you saw no evidence of heavy antiaircraft along the border?"

Gerber shook his head. "I know the various maps suggest the border is heavily defended, but the only fire we took was at the camp. Nothing along the border. There's no way to know when you've crossed into Cambodia."

"Then that's it. Oh, escape and evasion?"

"Depending on factors, toward us for extraction or toward the border. We'll have people out and about."

"Fine."

Gerber and Whitmore left the commo bunker and walked over to the helipad. When they got there, Gerber looked at his watch. "We'll be set to go inside of an hour."

"We'll be back," said Whitmore. "Any problems with sniping from the trees?"

"Not tonight. Last couple of nights, yes, but we hit the enemy base and chased them out. We've got listening posts out, and there's no evidence the enemy's around tonight."

Whitmore opened the door to the chopper cockpit, climbed up and strapped in. He glanced to the right, where the pilot was running through the checklist, then turned back to Gerber and said, "See you in an hour."

"Thanks."

"Good luck, Captain. Hope you plan, whatever it is, works."

"Good luck to you, too, Major."

Gerber stepped back and Whitmore closed the door. The major put on his flight helmet, buckled the chin strap and then shouted out the window, "Clear!" With that, the engine began to whine and the rotor started to spin.

When the chopper was gone, Gerber hurried off the helipad. He walked to the team house, but it was empty. The team was getting ready for the assault—Tyme looking at weapons, Kepler studying the Intel, Bocker checking the radios, T.J. gathering the medical supplies and Fetterman overseeing everything.

Gerber walked to the refrigerator, took out a Coke and opened it. Taking a sip, he was surprised at how good it tasted. Sweet and cold. He moved back to one of the tables and sat down.

Gerber was fully aware of what was about to happen. Men would get killed or hurt in the next while. They would die lonely, painful deaths. He wasn't afraid of that. Like most others, he believed he'd come through the battle. His skill, his expertise, would carry him through it. And with the element of surprise, very few of his own men would die. If they executed the plan well, they'd crush the enemy.

He finished the Coke and just sat quietly, letting his mind roam for a moment. It was a luxury he shouldn't have allowed himself. There was always so much to do, and if he thought of fifty ways the plan could fail and corrected them, there were probably another fifty he hadn't thought of.

Fetterman opened the door, stepped into the team house and spotted Gerber. "You busy?"

"No, Tony. Just finishing my Coke."

"We've got a problem."

Gerber couldn't help smiling. He'd been expecting as much. "What is it?"

"Henderson's under attack."

"Shit. How bad is it?"

"Some mortars, and they ran a probe at his perimeter, a small one that was beaten back with no trouble." Fetterman pulled out a chair and dropped into it.

"Is he going to be able to fulfill his end of the mission?"

"I got the impression he called this end to worry us but that he's not concerned. Harassment. I think he'll be there with no trouble."

"Have we heard from Sully?"

"Yes, sir. He picked up some movement in the village, but it was just the locals returning. Those who'd scattered before our fight with the VC."

"Is he going to bring them in?"

"Maybe in the morning. Now he's staying chilly, watching for the enemy. So far nothing."

"What's Kepler make of all this?"

Fetterman wiped a hand across his face. "Derek seems to think it's the last gasp of the enemy in the region."

"He have a reason for that?"

"Yes, sir. He says that if the enemy had any real presence left, they'd have hit Bromhead, Henderson and us tonight. Let us all know Charlie knows we're here. Hell, Jack's camp is so small that the enemy should be mounting an effort to push him out of it. But they haven't even lobbed a mortar round at him yet."

"Maybe they're trying to lull us into a false sense of security."

"I said as much to Derek," said Fetterman. "He told me he didn't think so, not with two nights of attacks here and the raid on Henderson. He thinks it indicates a lack of manpower on the part of the enemy."

"That's good news, if true."

"That's what I said. But Derek told me we could find out easily enough. Just visit the province chief tomorrow and see what his attitude is. If he's overly friendly, it means the VC and NVA have abandoned the province. If he's mildly friendly, it means the VC still probably have some strength."

Gerber closed his eyes for a moment. "It shouldn't be this easy."

"Well, sir, it's not that easy. We've been in contact, on and off, since we got here. We've hammered them pretty good each time."

"True enough." He glanced at his watch. "Guess we'd better get this show on the road." He picked up the empty Coke can and tossed it into the wastebasket.

Together they left the team house. Activity in the tent city was light. The engineers were sleeping. Parker had volunteered his men to man the bunkers while Gerber and the strikers were gone. It was now Parker's job to provide security, though the listening posts and Sully had yet to report any problems.

Minh had his men ready to move out. They were lined up near the gate, each of them crouched down, waiting patiently. All the equipment had been distributed. Each load had a radio and an M-60 machine gun. Each had two men armed with M-79s. Others had loops of M-60 ammo draped around them, or carried extra grenades for the launchers, or spare batteries for the radio. There was a medic with each load, and they, too, carried weapons.

"Everything's set, old boy," said Minh quietly as he approached them.

"Let's get everyone moved into the field and set them up north to south, staggered trail, spread wide," Gerber said.

"Certainly."

"Each load got a strobe light?"

"We're set."

"Then let's do it."

Fetterman moved to the front of the line and opened the gate. It was nothing more than a couple of boards with the concertina nailed to it so that they could get out easily. He moved slowly, crouching low, until he was through the perimeter and out into the field. Then he seemed to vanish. Ten minutes later he reappeared and used his strobe to announce that it was clear in the field.

"That's it," said Gerber.

Minh ran to the front of the line and waved his men to their feet. Slowly they began to work their way through the wire, filtering out over the field.

Gerber brought up the rear and then moved along the line until he came to Fetterman. He was with the first load and had the men formed in a loose circle to protect one another just in case the enemy suddenly appeared.

"I make it ten minutes at most," he said.

Gerber found the RTO and turned on the radio. He held it up so that he could hear its quiet buzz. He was suddenly aware of everything around him. The heat and humidity. The odor of the dirt and the grass and the sounds from the jungle not far from him. Quiet sounds. Night animals searching for prey.

From the camp came the noise of the generator. Gerber turned toward it. A few lights were visible, dim glows that marked the location of the camp. And beyond those loomed the dark shape of the fire control tower. Gerber hoped Parker had been smart enough to put someone up in it. He hadn't thought to say anything because Parker was a regular Army officer, and having a man in the fire control tower should be a natural thing for him to do.

The radio crackled to life. "Zulu Six, this is Crusader Five."

"Go, Five."

"Inbound your location."

"Roger. We have the strobes out. We're in staggered trail north to south."

"Roger, that."

Gerber turned to Fetterman. "We're on time."

The helicopters appeared then, black shapes against the charcoal of the night sky, their lights dim and flashing. A single landing light stabbed out, then disappeared. The roar of the turbines overwhelmed the other sounds around them.

Gerber crouched and waited for the helicopters to land. This wasn't a normal chopper operation. The approach was slower and the form looser.

And then the choppers were on the ground, hovering toward the loads, spreading out even more. The lead chopper came at Gerber, its landing light on now, but as the Huey touched the ground, the light went out. The heat from the lights could start fires.

Gerber watched as the men scrambled aboard. He then followed them, sitting on the end of the troop seat behind the aircraft commander. As soon as he was on board, the chopper lifted and turned so that the AC could look down the flight at the other choppers. When they were all loaded, he turned back and hung there for a moment. Then they began to move, slowly at first, gaining speed but no altitude. The climb started as they raced across the field, aiming at the jungle. As they approached the trees, they popped up until they were four or five hundred feet above the jungle.

Looking back out the cargo compartment door, Gerber watched as the flight assembled. The navigation lights were on dimly, and through the cockpit windshield he could see the pilots illuminated in the dull red glow of the instrument panel.

They flew north until the lights of Loc Ninh were visible. Then they started a slow descent, staying two or three hundred feet above the ground. The door gunners sat behind their weapons, the barrels pointed out as they searched for some sign of the enemy.

They reached the border and crossed into Cambodia. Amazingly no one fired at them. The landscape below was as dark and as dead as the bottom of the ocean. No signs of life.

Gerber watched as the ground slipped under him, a black blur that gave him no indication of what was down there. They crossed a silver ribbon that had to be Highway One and then banked to the west.

"One minute!" yelled the crew chief.

Gerber nodded and chambered a round in his weapon. He held a thumb up, telling the crew chief he was ready. As he did, they began a slow descent, but this time there were no landing lights. The pilots didn't want to give enemy gunners any targets. They'd get closer to the ground before they used their searchlights.

Gerber sat back to wait. He closed his eyes, trusting the pilots to do their job right. He knew he should be watching for the enemy, but couldn't do it. There were so many things that could go wrong now, and he didn't want to see them if they did. He didn't want to know about them.

But then he opened his eyes and stared out. There was nothing to see, just the ground wrapped in darkness with no sign of the enemy camp or any life whatsoever.

The chopper flared, the nose rising. As the skids leveled, Gerber stepped out onto them, and when they touched the ground, he stepped off and went into a crouch. The others followed, and as soon as the chopper was empty, it took off, climbing out to the west, then turning north. They would fly on for another eight or nine miles and then turn to race back for South Vietnam. Gerber didn't think the maneuver would confuse the enemy, but there was no reason not to try it.

"We're ready, Captain," said Fetterman as the sounds of the choppers faded.

Gerber used his compass and got a reading. "You want point, Master Sergeant?" He snapped the compass cover closed.

"Be delighted."

"Let's keep it slow and steady."

Fetterman started off the field and headed toward the trees. He reached them, stopped and let the rest of the company catch up. Then he moved into the trees, leading the men toward the enemy camp.

27

TONLE CHAM SPECIAL
FORCES CAMP

Henderson crouched in the bunker as the last of the mortar shells fell somewhere behind him. A siren still wailed, alerting those who hadn't figured out that they were being attacked. He wished someone would shoot the siren; the noise was driving him crazy.

"Here they come!" yelled a striker, his English surprisingly good.

"Fire!" yelled Henderson. "Open fire."

The machine gunner next to him pushed the butterfly trigger and the weapon began to chug. Brass cartridges bounced off the side of the bunker and rattled to the floor. The odor of burned gunpowder filled the bunker as it became hotter.

Henderson shoved the barrel of his M-16 through the firing port and watched as the first flare burst overhead. In the flickering greenish-yellow light the attacking soldiers looked like phantoms, enemy soldiers created from the bones of those killed in decades past.

He pulled the trigger twice and then stopped firing. Tracers from the automatic weapons in the other bunkers flashed. But the enemy wasn't shooting back. They were running toward the camp, almost as if they thought it was a haven.

A grenade detonated harmlessly near Henderson. Then an enemy soldier stepped on a mine and the explosion flipped him up and over. Two more fell under a hail of machine-gun bullets and the last vanished in a black cloud as three claymores were detonated.

In seconds it was all over. The attackers were dead. There was no movement in the field. The strikers kept firing, but that tapered off and died as the gunners realized they no longer had any targets.

Henderson peered through the firing port, sweat dripping from his face. The heat was trapped in the bunker with only the firing slit and the rear exit open for ventilation. Next to him the field phone chirped. He picked it up. "Henderson."

"We now have negative incoming."

"Roger, that. I want you to pull one company from the line now."

"Yes, sir." The phone went dead.

Henderson stared out of the firing port, but there was no more movement in the field. The attack force had died before they had gotten to within fifty yards of the perimeter wire. A ridiculous sacrifice. Unless...

Henderson picked up the phone and gave the handle a crank. When it was answered, he said, "Give me the fire control tower."

"Martinez here."

"You see anything around the camp?" asked Henderson.

"No, sir. Just made a sweep with the binoculars and then with the Starlite. I've got no movement anywhere around here. The enemy seems to have slipped from the field."

"You see anything, you alert me."

"Yes, sir."

Henderson hung up and looked at the striker in the bunker with him. "You stay alert. You see anything moving out there, you shoot at it first. Then we'll ask questions."

The man grinned, displaying yellow broken teeth. "I shoot first."

Henderson scrambled from the rear of the bunker and was surprised at how cool it seemed outside. The humidity hung in the air, and the heat of late afternoon had yet to break, but it seemed cooler. He wiped at the sweat on his face and rubbed it on his jungle fatigue shirt.

He found the Vietnamese strike force leader and pulled him aside. "We need to get the men ready for pickup."

"We ready now."

"I'd like to put a few patrols out into the trees to make sure Charlie isn't sitting there waiting on us."

For a moment the man was quiet, then he said, "I take care of it. Patrols out in ten minutes."

"Tell them to go no farther than half a klick into the trees. Once the choppers are off they can return."

"I tell."

Henderson moved to the commo bunker and sat down, waiting for word that the helicopters were inbound.

USING FOUR TRUCKS and two jeeps, Bromhead moved his men out of the camp and traveled along Highway 13. One of the jeeps drove on ahead of the column, the men in the back searching for signs that the enemy had slipped in for an ambush. But it was quiet along the road.

Bromhead used his map, watching for signs that they had crossed into Cambodia. The border was open. There were no watchtowers along it. There were no guards or gates, even at the point where the highway entered Cambodia.

Once they were across, he stopped the column for a moment. Then, using his binoculars, he found a point where they could look down on an open area. It gave him a view of several miles so that he could sit there searching for the enemy.

He moved along the line and had the men get out of the trucks. The drivers pulled them off the road, driving into the jungle so that they'd be hidden from view. In Vietnam the jungle had been cut away so that any enemy soldiers wanting to ambush a convoy would have to do it from three or four hundred yards away. In Cambodia that hadn't been done. The men could drive off the road and the trucks were concealed.

Leaving a squad to secure the trucks, Bromhead moved his men into the jungle on the opposite side of the road. They spread out there, half the men watching the road and the other half watching the valley below them. They were now in a position to stop traffic along the road, if that was necessary, or to bring anyone in the valley under fire.

The RTO squatted next to him. Bromhead checked the frequencies, then took the handset. "Zulu Six, this is Cavalier Six."

"Go, Six."

"We're set."

"Roger, set."

Bromhead gave the handset back to the RTO, then knelt on the ground. He used his binoculars and scanned the valley. There would be nothing to see there until Gerber launched the attack, but he needed to familiarize himself with the terrain so that he'd be able to spot the changes.

FETTERMAN KEPT the pace slow but steady. They worked their way through the jungle. The vegetation was light, easy to climb through, and they moved on up the slope to the top of the ridge line. Once Fetterman reached it, he stopped and waited.

The strikers fanned out, forming a loose ring for defense. Gerber climbed to the top and stretched out next to Fetterman. The master sergeant glanced at him and leaned closer so that he could whisper. "I make it another half klick to Snuol."

Gerber raised himself slightly but couldn't see anything through the vegetation. "Shouldn't be any farther than that."

"Thirty minutes until kickoff," said Fetterman.

Gerber glanced over his shoulder, then took a deep breath. "Doesn't seem that anyone knows we're here. Let's press on for another three hundred yards and then you and I'll move forward until we spot the camp."

"Yes, sir."

Gerber slipped to the rear and found Minh. "Pass the word, quietly that we're close. Noise discipline is a must."

"Certainly, old boy."

Gerber moved on until he found Kepler. "I want you to move forward with us."

"Yes, sir."

"And I want Tyme and Washington to hang back as a rear guard."

"I'll let them know," said Kepler.

Gerber returned to the front. Fetterman was crouched next to a palm tree, his weapon held in his left hand. "Ready?" he asked.

"Go," said Gerber.

Fetterman stood and took a step forward. He hesitated, then took a second step, starting the descent. Gerber followed four or five feet behind him, being careful, stepping carefully even though the men in the enemy camp wouldn't be able to hear any noise they made.

They worked their way down to the valley floor, where they encountered a swampy area. Crossing it quickly, they came to the edge of the jungle. Fetterman waved to Gerber, and he passed the word back along the column. As the men fanned out again, Gerber moved forward to where Fetterman waited.

The camp was no more than fifty or sixty yards away. The ground was rough, broken and cluttered with clumps of tall grass and big bushes. Plenty of cover for the assaulting force.

The camp fence looked to be nothing more than a structure designed to define the outer perimeter of the camp. It was flimsy, no more than four feet high, and made of barbed wire. There were guard towers at the corners, but they didn't look occupied.

The camp itself wasn't in much better condition. The hootches were dilapidated. They were set up on posts with notched logs for steps. The roofs were thatched.

There were a few dim lights burning, a couple near the watchtowers and others inside the camp. Gerber could hear the quiet hum of a generator, as well as music from a radio or record player.

Using his binoculars, Gerber spotted a single well-built structure, probably made of cinder blocks. It had a lighted window in it and a half-dozen radio antennae on the roof. Gerber touched Fetterman on the shoulder and handed over the glasses, pointing.

As he looked at the building, Fetterman nodded. "We'll want to take that out first."

"Grenadiers from the fence. Aim for the window."

"Wish we'd brought some LAW rockets," said Fetterman.

"Didn't work worth a damn up at Lang Vei," whispered Gerber. He checked the time. "Twelve minutes."

Fetterman handed the glasses back to the captain and then slipped to the right, disappearing into the darkness and vegetation. Gerber continued to study the camp, looking for signs that someone was awake. Even on a base in the World, where they knew there would be no enemy attacks, the various guard posts were manned twenty-four hours a day. Here the enemy seemed so secure that they didn't bother.

He'd change the attack plan slightly. They'd try to sneak into the camp, use the available cover until they reached the fence, cut the wires and then move in. Then they'd spread out and use knives until the enemy opened fire.

Fetterman returned and dropped to the ground next to Gerber. "We're set."

"Where's Bocker?"

"Off to the right somewhere. Why?"

"Let's take this place quietly if we can. Move in, use knives and set up claymores. Bocker can hit the radio shack and kill everyone in there before he breaks up the radios. That'll give us another big advantage."

"Unless they've got some of the portable jobs scattered around the camp."

"Can't worry about that," whispered Gerber. "We'll just do the best we can."

"I'll spread the word," said Fetterman. "We move quietly."

"Let's hold the main force here while a few of us open up the camp. Then, with the wire down and the radios out, the rest can come forward."

"Yes, sir." Fetterman got up again to pass the instructions on.

Bocker came out of the gloom a few moments later and knelt next to Gerber.

"Galvin, I want you to eliminate the radio shack."

"Where?"

Gerber handed over the binoculars. "There. See the lighted window?"

"Got it."

"Take two men with you and hit it."

"Yes, sir."

Tyme appeared. Gerber hesitated, then said, "I want you to place the claymores so that we can take out as many VC as possible. If they can't get out of their hootches, that's perfect."

Tyme studied the camp and shook his head. "Too many buildings and not enough claymores."

"Do what you can."

"Of course."

Fetterman returned with Minh. Gerber moved closer to the Vietnamese officer. "We've been handed a real plum. A sleeping base."

"I see that, old boy."

"We'll move on it carefully. A small group to cut the wire, Bocker to take out the radios and Tyme to set claymores. Then the rest of the company should come forward. Knives until the first shot is fired, then everyone opens fire."

"Sounds good."

Again Gerber looked at his watch. "Five minutes."

The men spread out, getting ready for the assault. Gerber stayed where he was, searching for a sign that someone knew they were out there, a sign that someone was awake, but he saw nothing.

There was a light breeze blowing that should cover any noise they made as they crossed the open ground. A thin cloud cover had blown up, obscuring the half-moon and stars. That would help them, too.

"We're set," said Fetterman, reappearing.

Gerber took a deep breath and got to his feet. He wanted to charge his weapon but knew there was a round chambered already. He put the safety on, then held his thumb on it, ready to flip it off. Glancing over his shoulder quickly, he started off.

Gerber was the first man out of the trees. There was a slight depression, a ditch at the edge of the jungle. He climbed down, stepped into the tepid water at the bottom, then scrambled up the other side. At the top he crouched and again searched the enemy camp. There was still no sign that the enemy was awake.

When the rest of the first assault force was across the ditch, Gerber started forward. He moved slowly, carefully, using the bushes as cover. Stepping out into the open, he dropped to one knee and listened, but the only sound was the rustling of grass as his men pushed their way through it.

He started off again, aware of the dark line of crouching men who were moving with him. Sometimes he could see them and sometimes he couldn't. They surged and sagged across the open field until they all reached the foot of the fence. Once there, they spread out, searching for cover.

When they found it, Gerber stood and grabbed one strand of the wire fence. It hadn't even been strung tightly. Cutting it wouldn't make any noise. It was a ridiculous fence that offered no protection to the men on the other side of it.

Tyme got to his feet and grabbed a strand of wire. Using his knife, he cut it, snapping the wire easily. Gerber did the same, and in seconds the whole enemy camp stood in front of them, no longer protected by even the fence. The enemy was going to learn something about overconfidence. Charlie was about to learn never to take anything for granted.

28

TONLE CHAM SPECIAL FORCES CAMP

Henderson tried to keep his cool. He didn't want the commo NCO to know he was worried, but he was. He tried to sit still and not pace, but finally succumbed. He walked to the radios and stared at them, as if trying to figure out if they were working properly. He checked the time, sat down and got up again, walking nervously around the inside of the bunker.

"The call will come in when the call comes in," said the NCO.

"Try them," said Henderson.

The man shrugged, then picked up the microphone. "Crusader Operations, this is Quarterback Operations."

He waited, and when there was no response, he tried again, switching to Uniform. When that failed, he glanced at Henderson and shook his head.

"You sure we're transmitting?"

Without a word, he turned, spun the dial and waited for the tuning squeal to die. "Zulu Operations, this is Quarterback for commo check."

"Quarterback, I've got you lima charlie."

"It's not us."

"Try the land line," said Henderson. "I'm going outside to see what's happening there."

"Yes, sir."

Henderson climbed the stairs and stepped into the oppressive humidity. He looked south toward Tay Ninh, but there was nothing to see. Scanning the sky for choppers, he listened for the sound of rotors. Zip. Already they were thirty minutes late. He wondered if Gerber and the choppers had stepped into it, then realized Gerber was fine. If there had been trouble, Gerber's base would have known about it, not to mention the fact that Gerber would have let him know.

"Where are the choppers?" asked Kehoe, one of his NCOs. "They should've been here by now."

"Shit, I don't know."

"Have we got a contingency plan?"

"Hadn't thought about it," said Henderson. "You need a chopper, you call for it and it arrives. If they can't make it, they let you know."

"So what'll we do?"

Henderson turned and looked at the sergeant. He was a young man, like most soldiers in Vietnam. He'd seen some action, but not very much. A young and inexperienced man.

"We can't walk to our position. It would take us five, six hours of forced marching to get into position in time, and we don't have the transport on station to drive there."

"How about another aviation company?"

Henderson shrugged. "I doubt we could get anyone here on time. It takes a couple of hours to coordinate the things." He looked at his watch. "It'll be sunup or later before we can get them here."

He turned and walked back to the commo bunker. Inside, he asked the commo NCO, "You learn anything?"

"Nothing. Nothing on the lima lima, though I did get through to the switchboard at Tay Ninh. From there I got nothing."

"What could have happened?"

"Even if every aircraft they own was shot down on the mission and every crewman was killed, there would still be the operations people there. Somebody's supposed to be manning the radios twenty-four hours a day. They couldn't have suspended operations without us knowing about it."

"How about their battalion?"

The sergeant dug an SOI out of his pocket. "That'd be the Black Barons at Cu Chi."

"Try them."

"Yes, sir." He turned back to the radios.

Henderson listened as the Black Barons refused to answer the call. He stepped closer and looked over the man's shoulder.

"I can't explain it, sir," said the radioman.

"Neither can I. Keep trying. See what you can learn. I'll be back in a few minutes."

"What are you going to do?"

"Christ," said Henderson, "I don't have the faintest idea."

CRINSHAW SAT at his desk, his feet up, and a cloud of blue haze around his head. The smoke was so thick that the air-conditioning was unable to do anything about it. He took the cigar from his mouth, looked at the tip and then pointed it at Seneff. "Too many people around here think they can throw their weight around. They think because they command a unit and because they're engaged in so-called combat operations that they don't have to listen to reason, that they don't have to obey orders when they get them."

"Sir?"

"Don't be dense. Dawkins didn't want to play ball with me. I ordered him to suspend flight operations to Gerber's Special Forces boys, and Dawkins refused. He said that with men in the field he had to complete the mission."

"That sounds fair," said Seneff.

"Don't be an ass," snapped Crinshaw. He put the cigar back in his mouth and puffed up another cloud. "He didn't put anyone into the field. He just wanted the chance to do it, to put the people out and go for some glory. Well, I put a stop to that."

Seneff was beginning to get uncomfortable. He didn't want to know about the infighting and politicking that went on at high levels. Because he was an Army man, he wanted to believe that everyone got along with one another. But he knew that wasn't the way it worked, and it sickened him.

"Sometimes," said Crinshaw, "we find a colonel who thinks of himself as a general. Some of them are on the verge of achieving the rank and the prestige, and some of them just think that way. No matter." Crinshaw waved his cigar, put it back into his mouth and twisted it. "When we find such a man, it's sometimes necessary to slap him down. I had to do that with Dawkins."

"Sir?"

"I made a phone call and Colonel Dawkins has finally accepted his orders." Crinshaw sat up and glared at Seneff. "Dawkins didn't know me, so he thought he was insulated in Army aviation. I'm not in his chain of command, so he figured he didn't have to worry about me, thought I wasn't important."

"And then?" asked Seneff.

"I made a few discreet inquiries. Dawkins might hold an important post here in Saigon, but there are others, with higher ranks, who are in his chain of command. I called General Leat and told him the story. I told the general we've got a renegade Special Forces captain running loose and that he had to be stopped. I told Leat that no more support should be given to Gerber, that we had to make sure nothing was done to damage the Army's reputation.''

"And he went along with that?"

"Certainly," said Crinshaw, frowning. "He understood what was happening. He understood that we can't let the captains and majors or even the colonels run the war. That's the bailiwick of the general staff."

Seneff shook his head.

"Have you got a problem with that, Sergeant?" When Crinshaw said *sergeant*, it sounded like a distasteful word.

"No, sir. I just wonder if you looked into the reason why this Captain Gerber wanted the assistance of Army aviation. Maybe there's a real need."

"In normal circumstances," said Crinshaw, sounding as if he were lecturing a backward child, "I'd have to agree with you. But you've got to remember that I spent a year here earlier and that I know this man. I know the way he operates. Therefore a great deal of investigation wasn't required."

Seneff picked up his coffee and took a sip. "Things might have changed."

"Not where Gerber is concerned," said Crinshaw. He stared at the sergeant, then added, "You've got to understand these Special Forces types. Rules don't apply to them. They go off half-cocked. They cheat. They're not Army. They have no discipline."

"I know a couple of sergeants in the Special Forces. They seem normal to me."

"I'm not going to argue with you, Sergeant. I know what I'm doing."

"I hope it doesn't cost any lives."

Crinshaw snorted. "You're beginning to irritate me, Seneff. Why don't you go find me a cup of coffee?"

Seneff leapt to his feet. "Yes, General."

THIEN WAS HAPPY to be out of South Vietnam. With the Americans pressing them, and their support in An Loc beginning to listen to the enemy, it was time to get out of the south. At least for a few days so that they could get a good rest without having to worry about American bombers, artillery or soldiers.

Once his men had been given a few thatched huts in which to sleep, Thien walked toward the largest of the camp's buildings, a two-story structure that served as both the headquarters and the billet of the higher-ranking officers.

Thien entered through a wooden door that had a hole in the center. He stopped, waited a moment, then looked around. The walls were made of rough wood and the floor of logs. There was a single desk and a picture of Ho Chi Minh on the wall. The North Vietnamese flag hung next to the picture.

Thien heard voices from the back room and walked to the door. He listened, knocked, then entered. "Good evening, Comrades."

"Good evening," said one of the men. He was sitting there in black silk shorts. On his feet were Ho Chi Minh sandals made from truck tires. Around his waist was a pistol belt that held a single canteen. There was a light coating of sweat all over his body. "I'm Captain Van." He pointed at the man next to him. "Major Vo. And next to him is Major Suong."

"Lieutenant Thien."

"Come and join us," said Van. He lifted a brown bottle. "Drink."

"Have you got any cigarettes?" asked Vo.

Thien dug into the pocket of his fatigues and found a sweat-damp, wilted pack. He tossed them onto the table. Vo looked at the pack and shook his head. "Never mind."

Suong, a short, round man who looked as if he were fifty years old, asked, "Where are you from?"

Thien dragged over a chair and sat down. He told them about growing up in North Vietnam and listening to stories of his father's fight at Dien Bien Phu. He told them about his girl back in the North. The beverage in the brown bottle was beginning to loosen his tongue.

"She didn't want me to leave," he said, grinning, but no longer seeing the men in the room with him. "She tried everything she could think of. She told me I had already done my duty, that no one would notice if I didn't return to the South."

"Not very patriotic," said Van. "Each must do all that he or she can to defeat the invaders."

Thien nodded, the motion now exaggerated. "But she wasn't thinking patriotically in those minutes. She was thinking of us and the pain we had already suffered."

"We all must endure until the war is finished," Van said.

Thien ducked his head in agreement, then said, "She left the room and came back wearing nothing. It was a sight to see."

"Have you got a picture of her?" asked Vo.

"No," said Thien. "We can't bring anything personal with us. It provides the enemy with items to exploit in the event of capture."

"The young lieutenant is correct," agreed Vo. He picked up the bottle and waved it around before drinking from it.

"That's too bad," said Suong. "I would like to see a picture." He pulled a sheet of paper from his pocket and unfolded it. Then he displayed a picture of a big blonde who wore nothing at all.

"How long will you be with us?" Vo asked Thien.

"I don't know, Comrade." He glanced around. "As long as I can arrange it."

Vo stood up and staggered to the window. He threw it open, jerked at the fly of his uniform and started to urinate out the window. "Ah," he said. "That's one of the great things that even our beloved Ho can't take from us. He can tell us what to do and when to do it, but he can't take this simple pleasure from us no matter what he does."

"You better be careful what you say," warned Van. "The political officer sometimes hears things that you think are said in private."

"No one here but friends."

Thien watched the show and then took the bottle. He drank from it and slammed it back onto the tabletop. "I'd better go check on my men."

"They can wait a few minutes," Vo said.

Standing, Thien said, "No. I'll take care of it now. I'll see you in the morning."

"In the morning," echoed Vo, unaware that those were the last words he'd ever speak.

29

SNUOL, CAMBODIA

Gerber killed the man.

He came up out of the dark as the man walked by, grabbed him from the rear, his left hand over the man's mouth and nose, and struck with the knife. He lifted the chin and slashed from left to right. As the man sagged, Gerber plunged the knife up over the kidney and into the heart and lungs. The man kicked out spasmodically once, and Gerber lowered him to the grass as he died.

Staring straight ahead, searching for a sign that someone had heard the death of the soldier, Gerber cleaned the blade of his knife on the man's shirt. He wiped it twice on each side. Then he looked right and left and saw the rest of the team moving deeper into the camp.

Gerber stepped over the body and moved toward the center of the camp. He reached a thatched hootch and stopped, his back to the rough vegetation there. Listening he heard the quiet breathing of sleeping men. Tyme or one of the men with him would have to set up a claymore to take them out.

He moved on, listening to the sounds of the camp around him. There was no movement except for his own men. He stopped near the radio shack and saw Bocker moving toward it. The commo sergeant reached up toward the latch while the men with him covered.

Gerber spotted the two-story headquarters building. He noticed Fetterman and signaled him, pointing at the building. Fetterman nodded and began moving toward it. Two strikers joined them. They stopped in the shadows near the side of a hootch. Gerber studied the building, saw no movement at any of the windows and waved the men forward.

Just as they stepped into an open area, a shape appeared in the window. Gerber froze but didn't dive to the ground. It was too late for that. Any movement would draw attention to him. If he didn't move, the man might not see him.

He watched the man center himself in the window, then slide forward. He heard a splashing sound and knew the man was relieving himself. A moment later the enemy soldier laughed and turned away from the window.

As soon as the man was gone, Gerber moved. He rushed forward, crouching low until he reached the front of the building. Fetterman joined him, kneeling on the other side of the door. The two strikers moved to the corners so that they could watch the approaches to the front. Gerber nodded and pointed up at the door.

Fetterman hesitated, then adjusted the sling of his rifle so that it was over his right shoulder. Next, holding his knife in his right hand, he leaned to his left and grabbed the door handle. He looked at Gerber.

The captain nodded. As Fetterman began to open the door slowly, he slipped to his right, his head low, no more than three feet above the floor. A hinge squeaked and Fetterman froze. No one entered the room. There was no sign of life in it.

Gerber eased forward and put his right hand in the center of the door. He pushed it gently and there was no sound. Slowly he got to his feet and slipped around the doorjamb.

Stepping inside, he carefully shifted his weight to his left foot, but the floor didn't creak.

An instant later he was inside the building, his back against the wall. There was a dim light and he could see a picture of Ho Chi Minh hanging on the wall. Next to it was the North Vietnamese flag.

Keeping close to the wall, he moved deeper into the room. Fetterman joined him, working his way along the other side of the office. He reached the flag and stopped. He was near the other door.

Now they could hear voices from the other side of the door. The smart thing would be to kick it open and toss in a grenade, but that would alert the camp. Gerber listened and held up three fingers, telling Fetterman he thought there were three men on the other side.

Fetterman shook his head and held up four fingers. Gerber nodded, agreeing. There was very little chance they could kill all four before one of them raised the alarm.

Gerber held up five fingers, then four, three, two and one. As he pointed at Fetterman, the master sergeant stood and threw open the door, leaping into the room. He kicked once, his toes catching a man in the pit of the stomach. As the enemy collapsed, Fetterman struck with his knife. The blade pierced the man's skin just below the breastbone. Blood spurted, covering Fetterman's hand.

Gerber jumped in to the right. He clubbed the closest man with the butt of his knife and whirled on the other. Before he could strike, the man dived for the window, stretching out like a swimmer starting a race. Gerber leaped after him, trying to snag a foot, but missed.

Fetterman's target tried to grab an AK. The master sergeant cut him off, using his knife. He slashed the man's throat. There was a quiet gurgling and the man slipped to his knees, his hands on his neck. Blood spurted and flowed down his chest, soaking his shirt.

At that moment the last of the enemy soldiers in the room stood up. Gerber grabbed his shoulder, whirled him around and cut him deeply. He jammed the knife into the enemy's chest, upward, toward the heart. Hot blood washed over his hand. The man groaned low in the throat, then fell to the rear, taking the knife with him.

"One got out," whispered Gerber.

"Let's clear the building."

Gerber shook his head. He moved through the room and found the stairs. Instead of climbing them, he pulled out a grenade, worked the pin until it was almost free, then wired it to the side of the stairway, about halfway up. The first man down would kick the wire, the pin would pop free and anyone on the stairs would be caught in the grenade blast. It was an effective booby trap.

Rigging it took less than thirty seconds. As he finished and joined Fetterman, he realized that the man who had escaped had yet to sound the alarm.

WHEN THE ENEMY burst into the room, Thien had been momentarily too stunned to move. He'd watched as one of his comrades had been killed and another clubbed. As that man had fallen, Thien had whirled. Seeing the window, he'd taken a running step and dived, stretching out to reach it. He'd shattered the glass and then tucked and rolled. He'd come up onto his feet and started running full tilt. He knew they wouldn't shoot at him. If they had wanted to use their weapons, they'd have tossed a grenade through the door.

Now he loped through the compound, studying the shadows. There was flickering movement around him. Men dodging in and out of cover. No one paid attention to him.

He ran through the night and ducked around a corner, his back against the rough thatch of a hut.

The breath was rasping in his throat. Sweat blossomed and dripped, not all of it from the exertion. He looked around him, but now there was no movement in the camp, no sound except the humming of the generator.

There were enemy soldiers around. He knew it. He'd seen them. He'd thought that his fellow officers in the room with him would sound the alarm, but there was no noise from there. Nothing. It meant they were all dead.

Thien slipped to one knee, his head down. It was up to him now, but if he went shouting through the camp someone would shoot him. He'd be of no use to his men or the defense of the camp if he was killed. There had to be a better way.

Wiping the sweat from his face, he stood up again. He wanted to move but found himself frozen to the ground, unable to get his feet in motion. It had been the swiftness of the assault. The Americans had come out of nowhere.

Thien took a deep breath and peeked around the corner. Nothing. No shooting. No running men. No firing. It was as if the Americans had turned into phantoms. Ghosts who haunted the land, killing without a sound, their only signs the bodies they left behind.

Thien wanted to move. He wanted to run toward the huts where his men slept, but he couldn't do it. He was stuck right there, sweat soaking his uniform.

WITH THE STRIKERS GUARDING the door and the approaches, Bocker lifted the latch of the radio shack. It moved silently, and Bocker shoved the door open all the way and stepped into the room, closing the door behind him. The radios were humming. Lights twinkled and needles danced.

The radio operator sat with his back to the door, his head slumped as he slept.

Bocker glided across the floor until he was directly behind the seated man. Grabbing the man's hair, he lifted his head and slashed. Blood fountained from the man's throat, spraying the radios in front of him. He spasmed once, rising out of his chair, then twisted to the right and fell to the floor. Blood spread from his neck and pooled next to him.

With the radio operator dead, Bocker moved back to the door and signalled the strikers, who entered the tiny cinderblock building. As they did, one of them knelt next to the door, leaving it open a crack so that he could watch the camp. The other one moved to the window so that he could guard that approach to the shack.

Bocker returned to the radio equipment. The easiest way to destroy it was to shoot holes in it. But gunshot reports would carry too far. For a moment he stood there and looked at the equipment. Russian and Chinese lettering was stenciled on the metal casing.

Finally he reached out and pulled one of the units closer. He ripped the wires from the back, tearing both the antenna and the power cord out. That done, he dropped it on the concrete floor, which dented the case. Then he jumped on the radio, crushing the top, shattering vacuum tubes and twisting the chassis out of shape.

Methodically he worked his way through all the radio equipment, smashing it all and ripping the wires out. When he finished, he moved to the door and looked out. For the moment there was nothing more for him to do except wait. Then he had to get out and help destroy the rest of the camp.

TYME FOUND a place near the center of the barracks. Surrounding him were the enemy soldiers, all of them asleep in their cots. From that point, radiating outward like the spokes of a deadly wheel, were the control cables for the claymore mines. He could detonate all of them at once, spraying the barracks with 750 steel ball bearings. The claymores would shred the building's thatch and anyone inside.

His men had spread out, setting up the mines, pointing them at the door, angling them so that the majority of the ball bearings would burst through about knee-high. When the mines had been set, the strikers had retreated, trailing the wires behind them.

Now Tyme lay on the ground, all the firing wires hooked into a single firing panel in front of him. He could detonate them all at once, or he could fire them in sequence, depending on what the situation demanded.

Lying there, he knew that firing them at the right moment was critical. If he detonated them now, many of the men lying in their cots could escape unharmed. If he waited for the eruption of gunfire, he might be able to catch the men standing up, which would maximize the effect. If he hesitated a second too long, those men who had been standing would be lying on the floor, scrambling for cover.

One of the strikers crawled up to him, leaned close and whispered, "Let's go. Get out."

"Stay," said Tyme.

"We go."

Tyme grabbed his shirt, holding him close. "We stay right here."

At that moment there was a burst of machine-gun fire, a single, ripping sound that shattered the night. Tyme couldn't see who was firing or where it was coming from, but he knew what it meant. Putting a hand next to his mouth, he shouted, "Get them! Get them all!"

One of his men fired two shots and then rolled to the right. Tyme hesitated. He counted silently, almost pushed the button, then didn't. Again he shouted, screamed, hoping to wake up anyone who might have slept through the burst and the two shots.

Finally he did it. He hit the button, firing all the claymores at once. He heard the detonations. There was a rustling as the steel burst through the barracks. Then there were screams. Men in agony. Firing broke out, AKs ripping at the last of the quiet.

"Hose it down," ordered Tyme. "Hose them down."

The strikers began pouring fire into the barracks, shooting blindly. A man appeared at the front door, fired a short burst, then toppled out of sight. Now there were muzzle-flashes in the dark. Emerald tracers flashed overhead.

Tyme threw away the control and jerked his M-16 from his shoulder. He flipped the selector to full-auto, then scanned the dark compound for a target. A man ran from a hootch, wearing nothing and carrying an AK. Tyme tracked him and squeezed the trigger. The man went down as if he had run into an invisible barrier.

Fires erupted. Thatch on some of the hootches began to burn, slowly at first, then faster. Flickering flames grew brighter. Now the enemy soldiers were shadows moving in front of the flames. Tyme shot at them. One man was lifted from his feet and thrown into a burning hootch. He landed with an explosion of sparks that seemed to roll upward into the night sky.

"Now we get out!" yelled Tyme. He got to his knees, emptied his M-16 and pulled the magazine from it. He jerked a fresh one home, then leaped up, running to the side away from the perimeter. "Let's go."

They retreated from the compound. There was more firing. AKs all around them, some of the VC firing at other VC. Random firing. No one had a target. Men screamed, some in pain, others in panic.

Tyme ran past a burning hootch. Through the open door he could see five or six men crouched behind an upturned cot. They had no idea what was happening. As he ran by, he put a burst into the hootch. Two of the men fell and a third began to shriek, the sound like that of tires on asphalt.

He reached the radio shack just as Bocker and the strikers came out of it. Sliding to a halt, he said, "Let's find the captain."

"Who fired?" Bocker asked.

"Who cares? The shit's hit the fan now."

KEPLER, LYING in the grass just outside the tree line, heard the burst of machine-gun fire from the camp. He watched three green tracers float across the ground, disappearing to the right. The rounds hadn't been directed at him or his men.

With that, Kepler was on his feet. "Let's go. Everyone follow me."

As he ran across the sixty yards of open ground, he heard two shots from the camp and then a series of detonations. That had been Tyme and the claymores taking out the men in the barracks area.

As he reached the wire, firing broke out in the camp. He heard a dozen or more AKs, but no one was shooting at him. He crouched there and let the strikers catch up. Then, with fires spreading over the thatched buildings, Kepler waved his men through the gaps in the wire.

They fanned out over the camp, firing into the shadows and the hootches. Kepler ran forward. He came to a man standing near a hootch, facing the radio shack. He held an AK in his hands, but wasn't firing it. Kepler lowered the barrel of his weapon and fired once at the center of the man's back. He saw the hole, a dark splotch, appear on the man's skin. For just an instant the man didn't react, then he dropped, losing his weapon as he fell.

Firing increased around Kepler. Green tracers slashed through the night. In a doorway of a hootch he saw muzzle-flashes. Kepler hesitated long enough to rip a grenade from his harness. He yanked the pin free and threw the grenade at the door like a centerfielder trying to peg a man at home plate. An instant later the grenade exploded. One man was thrown from the hootch, landing on the ground in front of it. The firing stopped.

Washington reached him. "I've got three wounded, now."

"Move them toward the rally points."

Washington hesitated for a moment, stared at Kepler, then said, "Okay." He disappeared into the darkness.

The rattling of weapons increased. Firing all around. Red tracers flashed, slamming into hootches. Fires erupted, the flames shooting into the sky. Now the ground was beginning to take on a flickering life. Shadows danced in the flames, making it harder to spot the enemy.

Kepler leaped to his feet and ran forward. A man came at him, head down. Kepler whirled and put a burst into him. The man straightened, then flipped over backward, firing his AK into the sky.

Kepler and the strikers ran forward, sweeping through the camp, firing into the hootches that weren't burning, searching for enemy soldiers. They ran between two hootches, and a machine gun opened fire. Kepler dived to the right and rolled, his head up, staring at the muzzle-flash.

Two of his men weren't as fast. They took the burst about chest-high and went down. One tried to stand and failed. He slumped to the ground and groaned.

Kepler put a burst into the muzzle-flash of the machine gun. He held the trigger down, emptying his weapon. Then, as he pulled the magazine out and tossed it away, he rolled to the left. As soon as he slammed another magazine home, he rolled onto his stomach, but the machine gun was silent.

Leaping up, he ran toward the weapon. The gunner was dead, his head missing, his blood covering the machine gun and the ground under him. The assistant gunner was groaning, bullets in both shoulders and a wound in the head. Kepler shot him again, killing him.

He ran back to the strikers who had been shot. Both were dead. "You," shouted Kepler, pointing at the closest strikers, "get their equipment and let's get out of here."

Then he was running again, toward the first rally point, firing into the hootches as he passed them.

GERBER HEARD the burst of fire just as he and Fetterman reached the outer office of the headquarters. Now he turned and ran back into the other room, crouching in the doorway that led to the second floor. From the second story he heard men moving. There were shouts and a thud and then running feet.

As the enemy started down the stairs, Gerber moved forward, aimed and fired on full-auto. There were screams. A man tumbled down the stairs. He lost his grip on his weapon, letting it fall.

From the top of the stairs came a burst of fire. In the strobing of the light, Gerber could see one man lying dead on the stairs and a second trying to scramble back up, blood pouring from his side. Gerber fired again and ducked as more AKs joined the first. "That'll hold them for a moment," he told Fetterman.

Then there was a bouncing on the steps. "Grenade!" cried Fetterman.

Both men dived to the rear, facing away from the doorway. There was a quiet pop and a whistling of shrapnel.

"Ow!" yelled Gerber.

"You hit?"

"Nicked in the elbow." Gerber twisted around and looked at the wound. It was just a scratch, with only a hint of blood.

"Good for a Purple Heart," cracked Fetterman.

"If I bother with it."

There was more firing from upstairs.

"Let's get out of here," said Gerber.

Both of them ran to the door. As they passed through it, Fetterman whirled and grabbed the North Vietnamese flag. He ripped it from the wall and stuffed it into his jungle shirt. "Souvenir," he said quietly.

Gerber tipped over the desk and pulled two of the drawers from it, scattering the contents. As he did so, an explosion rocked the building. There were screams and then shooting at the back of the building, AKs and pistols as the enemy tried to fight their way down the stairs.

"Hit the booby trap," said Fetterman.

"Give me your lighter."

Fetterman complied, and Gerber used it to set the papers on fire. "Let's get out of here now."

Fetterman ripped open the door and crouched. No one was moving outside. Fetterman leaped clear and fell to one knee.

Gerber followed and whirled. Fires burned everywhere. He could see men running, but he didn't shoot at them. His own men were mixed in with the enemy.

Fetterman was up again. He trotted to the rear away from the fires and men and headed for the first rally point. Gerber, backing up, joined him.

They reached the far side of the camp and stopped at the fence. Gerber used his knife to snap the wire, just in case they had to get out, then joined Fetterman on the ground.

More of the camp was burning now. Flames were leaping high into the air. There were shapes running. Some men were firing. Muzzle-flashes flickered in the night like fireflies on a summer's evening. There were shouts and screams and the detonations of grenades. There didn't seem to be any organized defense, just VC and NVA firing into the night and hoping for the best.

THIEN DIDN'T MOVE for five minutes. He crouched at the edge of a hut as the enemy swarmed into the camp around him. He saw them moving but was unable to do a thing about it. He could only watch and think about the deaths of his fellow soldiers. He could prevent that if he could work up the courage to act.

A group of enemy soldiers passed close enough to him so that he could almost touch them. He could see their faces and their weapons, and hear the sounds of their breathing. They moved quietly, slipping in to kill and destroy.

When they were gone, Thien knew he had to move. Even though he'd been in fights before, this was different. This was the enemy coming out of the night to kill.

But then he found his feet. He crept along the edge of the hut and found the doorway. Entering it, he felt around on the floor until he located a weapon, a single AK-47 without a magazine. In the dark he couldn't find any ammo. He crawled along the floor, staying low. He found another AK and next to it was an ammo pouch. Using his fingers, he opened the pouch, pulled out a banana clip, then touched the top to make sure there was ammo in it. He loaded the weapon and moved back to the door, where he worked the bolt, chambering a round.

Now, crouched in the door with a weapon, he could no longer see any enemy soldiers. They had vanished into the night like phantoms. Ghosts sent to haunt him.

Finally he stood up, scanned the camp, then fired a burst into the sky. A single, short burst to alert the men that the enemy had invaded their camp. It was answered by two rifle shots, neither round coming close to him.

Behind him, in the hut, the men were shouting questions, demanding to know what was happening.

Thien turned to face them. "Americans in the camp," he shouted. "The enemy's attacking."

"Be quiet and go to sleep," growled one man.

But the others believed him. They scrambled to their feet and started shouting among themselves, trying to shake the cobwebs out of their heads.

"Hurry!" yelled Thien. "They're already in the camp. They're already killing our comrades."

He moved out toward the door, thinking he would guard the men until they were ready to counterattack. They would hit the Americans and drive them from the camp. They would kill them and then display the bodies for all to see.

As he turned, there was a detonation to his right. He was suddenly lifted off his feet and thrown to the ground. Rolling over and over, he lost his grip on the AK. He wanted to stand up, tried to do it, but his muscles wouldn't obey him. Strangely he thought about the political officer talking about taking the fight to Saigon. Attacking Saigon.

But his last conscious thought was that something strange had happened, but he didn't know what it was. He just knew he wasn't in Saigon.

BOCKER AND KEPLER came out of the darkness and ran the last few yards toward the fence. The firing was now behind them. They could see shapes by the wire.

"Four," hissed Kepler.

"Three," said Gerber as he stood up and then crouched.

"Radios are destroyed," said Bocker. "Radio operator's dead and the antennae are ripped out."

"Good."

More of the strikers were coming from the camp now. They were hunched over like men moving through a high wire.

Gerber took a deep breath. "Let's get ready to sweep through one more time."

The men lined up next to the wire. The flood of strikers became a trickle, then stopped. Gerber got to his feet and waved a hand. "Let's move in."

Gerber ran between two hootches, saw one man and fired. The enemy soldier went down without a sound. All around him the firing picked up again. M-16s and AKs. There was an RPD shooting somewhere, but Gerber couldn't find it. Grenades detonated. Tiny, dull pops of the Chicom weapons, and the louder, flatter bangs of the American-made ones.

At the corner of a hootch he hesitated, searching the ground in front of him carefully. There were bodies scattered around now, dark shapes visible in the flickering light of the dying fires.

As he stepped out, a man leaped at him, a knife held high. Gerber rolled with the impact, going down. As he fell, he kicked out, missed and punched with an elbow. There was a single grunt of surprise, and the weight rolled away. Gerber came up, crouched and saw firelight reflect off a steel blade. As the man attacked, Gerber sidestepped and kicked. The man fell to his hands and knees. Gerber pulled at the flap of his holster and whipped out his pistol. He fired at the man, who collapsed without a sound.

Gerber picked up his rifle and holstered his pistol. Then he hurried forward with the rest of the strikers. He passed the headquarters building, which was now burning furiously. Flames leaped high into the night sky. There was firing from two of the upper windows, but before Gerber could shoot back the roof caved in, silencing the enemy weapons.

He continued on, passing more enemy dead and the rubble of burned-out hootches. Equipment was scattered on the ground. The acrid smell of smoke hung in the air, masking the stench of death.

He reached the perimeter and whirled. The strikers and the others were pouring out of the camp. The firing had tapered off until it was sporadic. There were M-16s firing, but only a few AKs. There were no shadows in the camp. No sign of movement anywhere, other than the strikers as they filtered out toward the perimeter.

"Give me a squad," called Gerber. "The rest of you head for the jungle."

Fetterman came forward and knelt next to him. "That should be about everyone."

"We get a good count?"

"We lost a few in the sweep," said Fetterman.

"Then go," said Gerber. All the while he kept his eyes on the camp, searching for enemy soldiers.

"Fall back," shouted Fetterman. He waved an arm, then started to retreat across the open ground outside the camp. There was a burst of machine-gun fire, a single, hammering enemy weapon. Green tracers flashed overhead.

Then the left side of the line opened fire. M-79s blooped out grenades. The explosions rippled among the burning hootches. There were cascades of sparks and flashes of flame. The machine gun fell silent.

"Go!" yelled Gerber.

The line of men rushed from the burning camp. As they did, the squad with Gerber began to hose down the hootches. Everyone fired on full-auto. Gerber burned through a magazine, tore it from his weapon and slammed another home. He emptied that one, too, and reloaded, but didn't fire. The enemy, if there were any left alive in the camp, were no longer interested in shooting back. They were just trying to survive.

As Fetterman and the strikers disappeared into the jungle, Gerber got to his feet. "Let's get the hell out of here."

He whirled and ran toward the trees. Behind him he heard the crackling of the fires and the snapping of ammo as it cooked off. He slowed as he reached the ditch, then stopped and turned. Slipping to one knee, he surveyed the camp. The fires had burned down and there was no evidence of enemy activity. The base had been destroyed. At least for the moment.

Fetterman appeared next to him. "We're all clear. Everyone's accounted for. We left six dead in the camp."

"Get with Bocker and whistle up the choppers."

"Yes, sir." Fetterman looked at the smouldering ruins of the camp. "I guess we can call this a success."

"I guess we can, Master Sergeant. I guess we can."

30

SNUOL, CAMBODIA

"I can't raise the choppers, Captain," said Bocker.

Gerber looked at the communications sergeant. "What do you mean?"

"No response from them on either the Fox Mike or the Uniform."

"Are your radios working?"

"Yes, sir. No doubt about it."

Gerber stared at the burning enemy camp. The fires had burned low. No one in the camp was shooting, and through his binoculars he couldn't see any movement.

"Tony," said Gerber, "keep the camp under surveillance and let me know if anything happens."

"Yes, sir."

Gerber followed Bocker back to where the RTO crouched near a large tree. Bocker took the handset and handed it to the captain. "You can hear the carrier wave and the pops of static, but Crusader Operations won't answer the radio calls."

Gerber nodded and lifted the handset to his ear. "Crusader Six, this is Zulu Six."

He waited, but there was no response. Not from Crusader Six or Crusader Operations, or from any of the pilots in any of the other aircraft. He tried again, and when that failed, asked anyone on that frequency to answer.

"What'll we do, sir?" asked Bocker.

"Switch me over to Henderson." As the tuning squeal faded, Gerber said, "Quarterback Six, this is Zulu Six."

There was a moment of silence, then a quiet voice said through the static-filled handset. "This is Quarterback Six. Go."

"Roger, Six. Say status of aviation assets."

"We have negative assets," said Henderson. "I repeat. We have negative assets."

"Say location."

"We're at home plate with no anticipated chance at bat."

"Roger," said Gerber. He looked at Bocker, then wiped his face on the sleeve of his jungle fatigues, smearing the camou paint slightly.

"Quarterback Six," he said, unsure of what he wanted to ask, or rather how to ask it. He wanted to know why Henderson hadn't moved off station, but he didn't want to compromise himself over the radio. Finally, hoping for more information, he said again, "Say status of aviation assets."

"I have no knowledge of the aviation assets. They failed to appear."

"Roger," said Gerber. "Out." He looked at his watch. It was two hours to dawn. They had to get out and they couldn't wait to learn what had happened to the Crusaders.

Gerber closed his eyes and tried to visualize the map. It would take them an hour, maybe two, to get to where Bromhead had his blocking force. They could ride the trucks out. Even if they had to move slowly, it would double the size of his force.

"Bocker, let's get ready to move out. I don't want to hang around here."

"Yes, sir."

Gerber gave the handset back to Bocker. "Get hold of Bromhead and tell him we're heading for his location. I don't want some trigger-happy striker to open up on us."

"Yes, sir."

Gerber moved off, staying just inside the tree line. He found Kepler and told him they would be moving toward Bromhead.

Washington moved closer. "We've got wounded sir."

"How many and how badly?"

"Three hurt badly and eleven walking wounded."

"Get some stretchers made," said Gerber. "We can't stay around here."

"Yes, sir."

Gerber moved along the line until he found Fetterman. "Tony, we're going to have to walk out."

"What in hell happened?"

"I don't know. I want to rendezvous with Bromhead and use his trucks to get us the hell out of here. We've got to get back across the border by daylight."

"And you want me on point?"

"If you don't mind," said Gerber.

"Give me five solid minutes to get into position," said Fetterman.

"Take ten minutes. T.J. has to get some stretchers made. Once you begin to move, remember that we've got some wounded with us."

"Yes, sir."

As Fetterman moved toward the road and the left edge of the line, Gerber worked his way in the opposite direction, heading for Minh.

"We've got a problem," he told the Vietnamese officer when he found him. "We're going to have to walk out. Tony's got the point. How about you and I hang back here for the rear guard?"

"Certainly."

Gerber again looked into the enemy camp, searching for some sign that the Vietcong or the North Vietnamese were going to try to get out and counterattack, but it was just as if the roles were reversed. In an American camp the soldiers, happy to have survived the assault would wait for morning to assess the damage. They wouldn't send out probes to find the enemy.

But here Gerber didn't see any signs that anyone had survived the attack. He knew some had and suspected they had run off, scattering into the jungle around the camp, hiding from the Americans.

Word filtered down that T.J. had the wounded ready and that Fetterman was moving out. Gerber, Minh and four strikers held back, watching the enemy camp. When the force was moving, they followed.

They moved along the ditch at the edge of the jungle, staying just inside the tree line. The going wasn't bad. The undergrowth was light and easy to push through. They came out onto the highway, then stopped, the men slipping from the roadway to the jungle on either side.

Fetterman appeared and crouched near Gerber. "Sir, we're doing this backward."

"What?"

"Why not have Bromhead bring his trucks to us? Rather than fuck around for two, three hours walking to Bromhead, he could roll up here in fifteen minutes. We pile on, retreat and we're gone."

"I didn't want to bring Bromhead's people any deeper into Cambodia."

"Even so, bring on the trucks and one or two guys to ride shotgun. Hell, sir, we can be out of Cambodia in under an hour, long before sunup."

Gerber couldn't think of a reason not to do it that way. He nodded. "Find Bocker and arrange it. Keep everyone alert."

As Fetterman hurried off, Minh said, "You should have thought of that."

"Hell, Dai Uy, you should have, too. Besides, we'd have had to walk to this point, anyway. Now we've got a chance to recon the jungle to make sure there's no ambush waiting for us."

"You're right," agreed Minh.

BROMHEAD GOT the order and grinned at the radio. He'd wondered why Gerber hadn't thought of it earlier. But then he also knew Gerber had to get to the road first. He probably didn't want to say anything on the radio that would give the enemy a chance to set up an ambush.

Slipping out of the ambush he'd set up in case the enemy had run toward him, Bromhead walked down to where the trucks were parked. He got the men up and in their vehicles and got them started. "You'll have to follow me," he said. Then he climbed into the driver's seat of one of the jeeps.

He turned the wheel, shoved the jeep into gear, then let the clutch out while giving the engine gas. The jeep bounced over the rough shoulder of the road, dropped into a depression that nearly threw him from the vehicle, then accelerated down the road. He stopped for a moment, and looked back over his shoulder.

When the trucks were behind him, Bromhead waved a hand, then started off again. He kept his foot on the gas, aware of his surroundings. There were too many Cambodians and Vietnamese around, so he kept the speed up.

Sticking to the center of the road, he peered over the blackout headlights. They threw only a little illumination on the road. The jungle was a black smear on either side, and if there was something in the road, he'd either have to be on it to see it or it would have to be huge.

The road wasn't smooth. He bounced in the seat, holding on to the wheel to keep himself in the jeep. Behind him he could hear the roar of the diesel engines as the trucks tried to keep up. Bromhead's theory was to make it fast—in and out before anyone could hear him coming.

He slowed down at a corner, then eased around it. There was nothing in front of him except a bridge. He accelerated toward it, slowed as he crossed and listened to the rumble of the tires. The trucks hit the bridge then, the noise of their tires sounding as if someone were pounding on a bass drum at the bottom of an old well.

They hurried away from there, even though there was no sign that anyone was interested in them. The jungle around the road was as deserted as if it were on the moon. Animals, maybe, but no sign of humans. No lights. No men running. Nothing.

They reached the outskirts of Snuol. Bromhead slowed, then pulled off the road. He let the trucks catch up while he studied the road and town. Again there were no visible lights. No sound. No radios, no voices, nothing. Beyond the town he thought he saw a flickering light that could be the fires at the enemy camp, but he wasn't sure. And Gerber had said nothing about traveling through the town.

Knowing he had to get moving, he tried to shift into first, but couldn't get it. He ground the gears, worked the stick and tried again. Finally he took his foot off the brake and rolled back a foot or so. Shoving the stick forward, he got it into first.

Before he could pull off, a shape rose up from the ground to his right. Bromhead grabbed at his weapon, but the man said, "Christ, sir, grind them till they fit."

"You scared the shit out of me."

Tyme got into the passenger seat. "We're down the road a piece. Sergeant Fetterman sent me down here. Said you'd be stopping along here somewhere."

"How in hell did he know that?"

"Figured that as you got close to the town, you'd want to scope things out."

"Where to?"

Tyme pointed. "Down the road about a hundred yards. We worked our way around the town to save that hassle."

Bromhead started forward with Tyme riding shotgun. The sergeant studied the jungle along the road. Finally he held up a hand. "Right here."

"I don't see a thing."

But as the jeep and the trucks behind it rolled to a stop, the men came swarming up out of the jungle. They climbed the sides of the trucks and pressed into them. Washington supervised the loading of the wounded into the last truck.

When that was finished, Gerber appeared by the hood of Bromhead's jeep. "Let's get out of here, Jack."

"Sure thing."

Gerber leaped into the back as Bromhead pulled forward and then turned around. He drove past his trucks, then stopped, waiting as they maneuvered on the narrow gravel road. Once the line was formed, he started off again, this time at a slower speed.

Fifteen minutes later they had pulled to the side of the road and were waiting as Bromhead's men filtered out of the jungle.

"It's going to be crowded," said Gerber.

"Nobody's going to complain."

"Keep it slow and we'll be okay."

Bromhead's men hurried forward and climbed into the rear of the trucks. The men had to stand, jammed in shoulder to shoulder. If they hit a booby trap on the road, the majority of them would be killed. It was a dangerous way to ride, but the only way they could do it without leaving men behind.

As Bromhead watched his men load, he asked, "What happened to the choppers?"

"I haven't the slightest idea," said Gerber. "We couldn't raise them or their operations. Henderson said they never came for his men."

"Then his blocking force was never in place?"

"No, but I don't think it matters. Only a few VC got out, and they scattered in all directions. At best Henderson would have caught or killed only a couple of them."

Dixon, one of Bromhead's men, approached. "We're ready, sir. Everyone's accounted for."

"Hop in," said Bromhead.

Dixon scrambled into the rear of the jeep. As soon as he did, Bromhead popped the clutch. Dixon was thrown back and nearly fell out over the back. Gerber grabbed him.

Over the noise of the engine and the wind, the sergeant yelled, "Thanks, sir."

They drove on, racing for the border. It was a quick trip, the speed reaching forty miles an hour. And then, almost as suddenly as he'd started, Bromhead stepped on the brake. He slowed and rolled to a stop at the side of the road.

"What's the problem?" asked Gerber.

"None. We're in South Vietnam."

Gerber glanced at the surrounding territory. "You sure about that?"

"Of course."

Gerber glanced to the right, then looked up at the sky. Dawn was breaking. There was a sliver of red on the horizon, and the sky was no longer black and filled with stars. There was a paleness to it instead. "None too soon."

"Now where?" Bromhead asked.

Gerber pulled out his map and flicked on his flashlight. Sitting in a jeep on a highway, he couldn't be more exposed. A little light was all he needed.

"Let's stay on this road to An Loc. I want to stop at the province chief's compound there. Get medical assistance for the badly wounded, then see what I can do to shake loose some aviation support."

"And then I'll take the road just north of the town back to my camp."

"I think we've got it," said Gerber.

They rolled on then, the sky brightening around them. The sounds of South Vietnam washed over them. Booming artillery in the distance. Helicopters in the air far to the south. Jets overhead.

They followed the highway through a small village of mud-and-thatch hootches. Again there were no lights, and no one came out to see who was driving by. No one was interested in the movements of soldiers.

They drove around the American camp at Loc Ninh, avoiding it. That was the way Gerber wanted it. The fewer people who knew about the raid into Cambodia, the better it was going to be for him.

The sun finally appeared and the ground became brighter, making it easier to see. They could now speed up without endangering themselves. There were no booby traps on the road. No snipers fired at them. South of Loc Ninh they passed another hamlet, but this time they did see people. A few women outside their hootches were starting cook fires for the morning meal. All of the women watched as the trucks rolled by, and one of them responded to the waving of the soldiers.

"That's odd," said Gerber.

Bromhead looked over his shoulder at the captain but didn't say anything.

And then, after driving another thirty minutes, they came to the top of a small rise. An Loc lay spread out in front of them three miles away.

Bromhead stopped the jeep. "There it is."

Gerber nodded. "I think that's got it. We pulled this off. Pulled it off completely."

"We sure did," Bromhead agreed.

31

AN LOC, VIETNAM

The trucks weren't stopped at the gate of the province chief's compound. They were waved through by the guards, who grinned and saluted. Bromhead rolled to a stop close to the door, and the trucks pulled up behind him. He waved a hand and the engines died, leaving the compound wrapped in sudden silence.

Gerber climbed out of the jeep and saw T. J. leap over the side of a truck. He ran forward and said, "We lost one on the way in. The other two need to get to a hospital as soon as possible. I can't treat them here."

"I'll do what I can." Gerber turned. "Tony, get our people out of the trucks and into some kind of formation. And find me Captain Minh."

"Right here, old boy," said Minh.

"You and I'll go see the province chief. We'll try to get some choppers rounded up and find out what happened to our support last night."

Before they could move, the province chief appeared at the door, flanked by the two women who acted as his interpreters. He was dressed in a pressed khaki uniform, but he looked as if he had just gotten out of bed. "Greetings," he said in heavily accented English.

Gerber moved toward the man. "We've got wounded men in need of medical treatment."

"Officers?" asked the chief.

"Enlisted men. Wounded in battle."

"Come," said the province chief. He turned and entered the building.

Gerber glanced at Minh and shrugged. He followed the man into the building and then into the room where they had met before. One of the chief's female companions disappeared.

"We need medical assistance," Gerber said.

The chief gestured at a chair and rattled off some quick Vietnamese. The remaining interpreter said, "Arrangements are being made for your wounded now."

Gerber sat down but held on to his weapon. The woman moved to a bookcase and pushed on the tops of the volumes, which folded up to reveal a bar. She turned and asked, "What would you like?"

Gerber was going to refuse but Minh said, "Bourbon, if you have it." He turned to Gerber. "And you, Captain?"

"The same."

They were served and the woman stepped back until she was directly behind the chief. He held his glass up and drank from it. Gerber and Minh did the same.

Now he began to speak. He glanced at Minh, then Gerber. When he finished a moment later, the woman said, "It is a wonderful day. If you will step to the window, you will see exactly what I mean."

Gerber glanced at Minh as the province chief stood up. He walked to the window. Gerber and Minh followed suit. They looked out into a walled courtyard. A heavy wooden door opened and three men, their hands bound, were pushed into the courtyard. The bound men were joined by a dozen armed guards. The prisoners were pushed to the far wall, facing the armed men.

Gerber glanced at the chief but didn't say a word. He couldn't stop the execution, even though it was being arranged for his benefit.

The chief spoke and the woman translated. "These three men have been found guilty of inciting a revolt in Binh Long Province. They have been sentenced to death by Colonel Lam. They are the last of the VC infrastructure known to be in this region."

"Then don't shoot them," said Gerber. "Dead men can't tell us anything."

The woman translated, but as she did the Vietnamese outside fired and the Vietcong prisoners died. They were thrown back by the impact of the rounds, bounced off the wall and fell to the dirt. Blood soaked their uniforms and spread over the ground under them.

The chief turned from the scene and grinned with satisfaction. Gerber finished his bourbon. As he did, he heard the sound of helicopter engines.

"The medevac helicopter," said the woman.

"If you'll excuse me," said Gerber. "I need to make some arrangements."

"Of course," she said, then stopped as the chief spoke. Smiling, she translated. "You are most welcome here anytime. Please come back."

As they reached the porch, the helicopter landed. Gerber stood and watched as Washington supervised the loading of the wounded men. With that done, the poncho-wrapped bodies of the dead were slipped into the cargo compartment. Then Washington climbed into the chopper with them. The craft lifted, hovered in a growing cloud of red dust, then took off, climbing out. It had been on the ground for thirty seconds.

Bromhead approached. "I'm ready to head out, Mack."

"Okay, Jack. Thanks for your help last night."

"I'm afraid I didn't do all that much."

"It was enough. Please prepare a report on your activities and forward it to me for review."

"Certainly. You'll have it within a week."

As Bromhead turned away, Bocker approached. "Captain, I just got the strangest call from Sully. He's back at the camp and says it's virtually deserted."

"What?"

"Sully didn't give much in the way of details, but it seems that only a handful of strikers, the villagers and Sully are at the camp. The engineers and all their equipment are gone. Pulled out."

"Shit." Gerber hesitated, then yelled, "Bromhead."

He turned. "What?"

"I need your jeep. Now."

"Of course."

Gerber looked at Minh. "I'll take Fetterman with me. You'll have to arrange transport to get the men back to the camp as quickly as you can."

"Of course."

Gerber ran to the trucks and found Fetterman. "Tony, you come with me. Derek, you and Tyme will have to take your orders from Captain Minh."

"Yes, sir," said Tyme. "No problem."

"What's going on?" asked Kepler.

"I haven't the faintest idea, but I'm going to find out."

CRINSHAW SAT behind his desk, feeling good. A general with a radio was a dangerous animal. He'd laid a few surprises out for Gerber. A few phone calls, a review of a few classified documents, and he knew what was happening. Gerber was building an empire out in Binh Long Province. With his radio he managed to take it apart in a matter of hours. Leaning forward, he yelled, "Seneff!"

The door opened a moment later and Seneff appeared. "Yes, General."

"Get my jeep."

"Yes, sir." Seneff disappeared.

Crinshaw stood up, then opened the right-hand top drawer of his desk. He took out the Colt Commander he'd been given when he'd picked up his basic issue. Loading the gun, he moved to the door where the hatrack stood, holding his pistol belt. Buckling it on, he dropped the weapon into the holster, grabbed his hat, then left the office.

"Jeep'll be here in a minute, General."

"Grab your hat. You're driving."

"Yes, sir."

They left the building and found the jeep in the parking lot. They drove over to MACV-SOG and entered the single-story building. Crinshaw had expected to find a high-ranking officer somewhere, one who could be persuaded to withdraw the support elements of Gerber's tiny empire, but he only found a couple of NCOs on radio watch, a supply sergeant outfitting a six-man team and a lieutenant sitting in the dayroom, listening to the AFVN.

Crinshaw walked into the dayroom and stared at the lieutenant until he opened his eyes. "Where is everyone?"

The young officer got to his feet. "I don't know, General."

"Thank you." He turned to Seneff. "Let's go over to MACV."

They left and drove over to the main headquarters. Crinshaw studied the city as they drove through it, thinking that nothing had changed since the last time he'd been there. There was the same mix of military and civilian traffic filling the streets. There was the same stench in the air—diesel fumes mixed with the stink of open sewers. And the same cacophony of sound. Rock and roll mixed with the noise of traffic. Finally he closed his eyes; he'd seen enough.

At MACV he prowled the corridors, searching for someone who would order Bromhead back to Song Be and Henderson back to Moc Hoa. He tried a couple of colonels who protested that they didn't have the authority to do it. Finally he entered the office of Brigadier General William Rosen Feldman.

Feldman was a short, balding man with a large belly and a slick sheen to his skin, as if he were sweating heavily, despite the air-conditioning of his office. He claimed he was delighted to see Crinshaw and offered him a seat.

Crinshaw sat down and smiled. "I have a bit of a problem, and maybe you can help."

Feldman tented his fingers under his chin. "Anything I can do, General."

"Good. I'm having trouble with the Special Forces."

Feldman frowned. "I don't like those bastards. They think they know everything. They think they're the only ones who ever fought a war."

"Glad to hear that." Crinshaw pulled a sheet of paper from his pocket. "I want these officers ordered to return their forces to their main camps. They've moved off station with no real authority, and that's jeopardizing the stability of their primary camps."

Feldman took the paper and examined it. "Where are their main camps?"

"Moc Hoa and Song Be."

"I don't see these satellite camps as a problem," said Feldman.

"They're not really the issue, General," said Crinshaw. "The problem is that they were established without proper authorization. We can't let these men start running the war themselves.''

''Ah,'' said Feldman. ''Can you give me a day on this?''

''I'd really appreciate it if we could deal with it right now.''

Feldman raised his eyebrows in surprise. ''Certainly, General. Right away. Call me in an hour and I'll give you a status report.''

''Thanks,'' said Crinshaw.

GERBER KEPT his foot to the floor as they rocketed through Binh Long Province. The road had been paved once, but the asphalt was disintegrating so that there were stretches of it that were little more than gravel tracks filled with potholes. They turned off the main road and used another that was in even worse shape. It was a trail through the jungle that Gerber would have avoided if it had been possible, but he needed to get to his camp.

They came to the final turnoff, and Gerber stepped on the brake, sliding to a halt in a swirling cloud of red dust. They sat for a moment, the engine idling. There were sounds from the jungle around them. Birds called and monkeys screamed. He could hear the buzz of insects and the rustling of the wind through the treetops. Sunlight beat down on them, scorching the ground.

Gerber looked up the rutted track. He couldn't see his camp yet. The jungle was too thick, and they had to climb a hill, but he knew it was up there.

''What's the problem?'' asked Fetterman.

''Something wrong here.''

''Nothing's wrong, Captain. Everything's peaceful.''

''I think that's the problem,'' he said.

He shifted, then turned the steering wheel. Slowly they drove toward the camp. As they came out of the jungle, he stopped again. The camp looked peaceful enough. There were a couple of people moving around.

"Here we go," said Gerber.

They drove toward the camp and stopped where the wire crossed the road. Both got out and wormed their way through the perimeter until they reached the gate. As they did, Smith approached from the other side.

"What in hell's going on here?" asked Gerber.

Smith opened the gate, and Gerber, followed by Fetterman, entered. "Let's go to the team house."

"Sully, if you've got an answer, I'd like to hear it right now."

Smith looked left and right, as if he expected someone to sneak forward to listen. "I'm not sure what's going on, but I think General Crinshaw's behind it."

"Why?"

"Captain Parker ordered me back, saying they had to pull out at first light. He wanted to leave the camp in the hands of an American, even if that American was an enlisted man. I pulled in all the other listening posts so that we've got twenty-two soldiers here."

"Why Crinshaw?"

"Shit, sir, I didn't even know he was back in Vietnam. Anyway, Parker mentioned a general in Saigon blowing his stack and ordering them off station as soon as they could get out. He thought the general's name was Crinshaw."

"So Parker just got out?"

"No, sir. He called his headquarters and they confirmed the orders. There was nothing he could do but get out at first light. Either that or get court-martialed. You know Crinshaw isn't above that."

Gerber rubbed his face. He smeared the camou paint and felt the stubble of beard. "I want you to get on the radio and get us a chopper. I don't care what you have to do to get it, but I want that chopper here in thirty minutes."

"Yes, sir."

"Tony, let's get cleaned up and then run down to Saigon."

"What are we going to do?"

"Talk to Crinshaw."

"Just talk?"

"Just talk. For now." Gerber turned and started toward the team house, then stopped. "Sully, have someone retrieve the jeep. It belongs to Captain Bromhead."

"Yes, sir."

Gerber again started across the compound. He felt tired. The plan had been working. They were breaking the back of the VC in the province. Even in such a short time that was evident. The attitude of the province chief was a reflection of it, the first sign that things were swinging around.

He reached the team house and entered. Taking a Coke from the refrigerator, he opened it and drank deeply. Then he dropped into a chair and set his M-16 on the table in front of him. Taking off his boonie hat, he ran a hand through his sweat-damp hair, then touched the cold can to his forehead, letting it cool him slightly.

Smith entered. "Bromhead called. He's been ordered back to Song Be."

"What?"

"Some general in Saigon ordered him to return to Song Be. Radioman was waiting for him to return from the field. Bromhead's waiting to hear from you before he moves."

"What about the chopper?"

"It's inbound. Should be here in about fifteen minutes or less."

"Find Tony and get him over here. Tell him we've got to get to Saigon."

"Yes, sir."

As Smith left, Gerber shook his head. He was beginning to understand the war in Vietnam. He wasn't sure he liked it, but he was suddenly beginning to understand it.

32

TAN SON NHUT
SAIGON

Gerber stood on the tarmac outside the SOG building and watched as the chopper disappeared, crossing the runways and then climbing out. He rubbed his face, realizing how tired he was. It had been a long time since he'd had a full night's sleep.

"I'll see if I can find us a ride," said Fetterman.

Gerber nodded and walked toward the building but didn't enter. He sat in the shade, watching the jets land and take off. As he watched, he thought about the complaints he'd heard from the pilots. Targets that were off-limits. Restrictions on where they could bomb and where they couldn't. Supply lines that remained open only because the politicians had decreed, for some unknown reason, that the supply lines were immune to attack. They were fighting half a war. Gerber now understood that, in a way he hadn't in the past.

Fetterman returned, driving a jeep. Gerber looked at it, then at Fetterman. "Found one?"

"Yes, sir. Anytime you're ready."

Gerber heaved himself up and walked over to the jeep. He climbed into the passenger side, then looked at Fetterman. "I'm getting real tired of this."

Fetterman didn't answer. He shifted and turned, heading back toward the road. As he turned onto it, he said, "I hear Crinshaw is back in his old office."

"Which might explain what happened to General Platt."

"Yes, sir. Word is that Platt is out and Crinshaw is in. So far Crinshaw has made no major changes."

"Other than us."

"Exactly."

They were quiet then. Fetterman drove slowly, passing the barracks, clubs and offices of Tan Son Nhut. They turned once, then entered the parking lot of the headquarters building. When Fetterman stopped the jeep, they both sat there, staring at it.

"I feel we've done this all before," said Gerber.

"Only because we have."

"Makes me wonder if we should have Robin with us. Let her get an interview with the general."

"Won't work this time," said Fetterman. "He's done nothing wrong. He's just arranged the various assets for the good of the service."

Gerber swallowed once, then wiped his face. "It'll probably do us no good to go see him."

"Can't hurt," said Fetterman.

"Let's go," said Gerber. He forced himself up and out of the jeep. Grabbing his rifle from the rear, he turned and stared at the building like a kid who was getting his first glimpse of the White House.

They headed up the sidewalk, opened the double doors and entered. Just inside Gerber said, "I'd forgotten what air-conditioning felt like."

Reluctantly they climbed the stairs and entered the second-floor corridor. The offices were alive with activity. Phones were ringing, typewriters were clacking away, fans were humming and people were shouting.

They walked down the hall and stopped in front of the office that had belonged to General Platt. His name had been removed from it already.

Fetterman raised his hand to knock, but Gerber grabbed the knob and shoved it open. There was a sergeant in new fatigues sitting behind a desk. He glanced up when Gerber and Fetterman entered. "Can I help you?"

"Crinshaw."

"General Crinshaw is busy at the moment. If you'll take a seat, I'll tell him you're here."

For a moment Gerber stood there, feeling the anger choke him. It bubbled over. He'd had to fight with Crinshaw on his first tour. The general had thought that the real war was between him in Saigon and Gerber in the field. He refused to see the enemy as the Vietcong or the North Vietnamese.

"Never mind, Sergeant," said Gerber. "You stay put."

Seneff froze in midstride. He looked at Gerber and was about to protest, then noticed the hard look in his eyes. He stepped back and studied the Special Forces officer. Smeared camou paint at the hairline and under the chin where he hadn't washed it off. Dirty, sweat-soaked and mud-stained fatigues. A bulge for a concealed weapon and an M-16 in his hand.

Gerber moved to the door and glanced at Fetterman, almost as if to assure himself that the master sergeant was backing him up. If he had been worried about it, he saw there was no need. Fetterman was watching Seneff.

Gerber opened the door and threw it open. He had forgotten that Crinshaw liked his office cold. He stood there as the icy blast washed over him. Crinshaw looked up from his work. "You're letting the cold air out, Captain."

Gerber entered and walked across the floor. Dropping into one of the chairs without being invited, he noticed Crinshaw had done nothing to change the decor. Everything was as it had been when Platt had had the office, with the exception of the arctic cold and Crinshaw behind the desk.

"Make yourself comfortable, Captain." He heard the door close, then added, "You too, Sergeant."

Fetterman took the other chair.

Putting his pen down and grinning, Crinshaw asked, "What can I do for you?"

"Tell me why you're fucking around with my operations," said Gerber.

"My dear Captain," said Crinshaw, "they're not your operations, but rather U.S. Army operations. I've merely redeployed some of the assets you misappropriated to build your miniature empire."

"I was doing my job," said Gerber. "I was attempting to force the Vietcong out of the region."

"No," said Crinshaw. "Your job is what your superiors decide it should be. It's not what you decide it should be."

"I had authorization," said Gerber.

"You might call it that, but you expanded it far beyond its original guidelines. No, you didn't have authorization for everything you did. Now I've reassigned the assets and everything is as it should be."

Gerber wanted to argue. He wanted to tell Crinshaw that the man didn't have a clue about the conduct of the war. And then he just sat back, realizing it would do no good. Crinshaw had the power. He could find people, other ring-knockers, who would help protect him. Gerber was the outsider making waves. Too often he'd heard other officers, legs, claim they had to be careful because Vietnam was the only war they had. Crinshaw was doing that: protecting the war so that his colleagues could get their command tickets punched as they moved up what was becoming the corporate ladder.

"You're to close your camp as soon as you can. The Vietnamese forces there are to be reassigned to their original camp, and that's it. I want it done within the week."

Gerber shook his head. "Don't you want a report on what we've accomplished in the short time we've been there?"

"Captain, I don't care what you've accomplished. I want my orders carried out before I lose my temper."

"If you'd just back off this for two weeks," said Gerber.

"No, Captain. You have no time at all."

Gerber glanced at Fetterman, then said, "I'm sorry, General—"

"Sir," said Fetterman, "it doesn't matter."

"Listen to your sergeant," said Crinshaw. "And carry out your orders."

Gerber sat there for a moment. With just a little more time he could have accomplished something. He could have shown them that the war could be won. He would have given them a blueprint for success, but now Crinshaw had jerked the rug out from under him before he'd had the chance to finish.

"You're trying my patience," said Crinshaw. "You're dismissed. I expect you back here within a week to report the success of your new mission."

"General Platt," said Gerber.

"Is on his way elsewhere," snapped Crinshaw. He picked up his pen and got back to work.

Gerber sat quietly, then stood up. He walked to the door and waited for Fetterman to follow. Opening the door, he stepped into the outer office. As he closed the door, he thought he heard Crinshaw laughing.

"Let's get out of here," said Fetterman.

AS SOON AS THE DOOR CLOSED, Crinshaw wanted to whoop.
It had been so easy. He'd waited so long for it. Gerber sitting
in front of him, his plans in ashes and nothing he could do
about it. And Gerber had seen the power. He hadn't complained that much. He had caved in so easily. It had been
beautiful.

He pushed the papers on his desk aside, then stood and
went to the hidden bar. Even though it wasn't quite ten in
the morning, he poured himself a Scotch, drank some of it
and then filled the glass.

He moved to the door and listened, but there were no
voices there. Seneff was alone. Crinshaw opened the door.
"I want you to get General Platt on the phone. I want to talk
with him."

"Yes, sir."

Crinshaw returned to his desk and sat down. He sipped his
drink and let the cold air blow on him. He wanted to call
Henrikson, who hadn't left Vietnam after all, but she would
still be asleep at the hotel. She wouldn't get up before noon.
No, he could tell her about his victory over dinner tonight.

The phone rang and Crinshaw picked it up. "General
Platt?"

"Yes."

"Crinshaw here. I've just had a meeting with Captain
Gerber."

"Yes?"

"He may try to persuade you that he has reasons for es-
tablishing that empire of his out in Binh Long Province."

"Yes."

"I want to make sure you understand that it's been dis-
mantled. He's to get no help with anything, except taking
apart the camp."

"I'm not sure that's a good idea, General," said Platt.

"I don't give a shit what you think. This is the way it's going to be. You give me any trouble, you try to go over my head on this one, and it's going to be your ass."

"I understand, General."

"I'm glad," said Crinshaw. He hung up before Platt could say anything more. Then he sat back and grinned. Gerber had no fallback position. He couldn't do anything except what he was ordered to do. If he didn't, he'd be without supplies, ammo and support. Crinshaw wasn't even yet, but he was getting there.

THE BILLOWING CLOUD of red smoke from the helipad at Xa Cat seemed appropriate. Red smoke often designated enemy positions, and the way things were going, his camp now seemed like an enemy position. Staring out the windshield, Gerber was surprised to see a dozen or more people standing around the pad.

The chopper touched down, blowing the smoke away. The men, standing with their backs to the chopper, turned. Each of them seemed to be grinning. Gerber hopped out and waited for Fetterman. Then they hurried to the edge of the pad. When they were clear, the aircraft lifted, turned and took off. In seconds the sound of the turbine had faded.

Gerber spotted Kepler in the crowd. He moved toward the Intelligence NCO. "Just what in hell's going on here?"

"It's unbelievable, Captain. Ever since we got back people have been streaming in here. T. J.'s been busy treating the sick and the injured."

"I don't understand."

Kepler pulled him aside. "The VC are gone. Totally. They've been pulled out and everyone here knows it. Didn't anyone wave at you as you drove by this morning?"

"Sure, but—"

"That ever happen before?"

"Not too often."

"The point is, the people know. They know things long before we do. And you saw the province chief execute those VC. When was the last time a province chief took that risk? He knows the enemy's liable to retaliate. But the VC are gone from around here."

Gerber wiped a hand over his face. He glanced at the people, then back at Kepler. "Are you sure?"

"Of course I'm sure. The VC have moved out. They realized they were going to have no luck around here, that we'd hunt them down and even chase them into Cambodia. So they packed up and got out."

"Don't you get it, Captain?" said Fetterman. "You proved your point. You showed everyone how to beat the VC at their own game."

Gerber shook his head. "But now we're giving it all back to the enemy."

"What the hell are you talking about?" asked Kepler.

"We've been ordered out of here by Crinshaw," said Gerber.

"You're not going to listen to that, are you?"

Fetterman broke in. "Nothing we can do about it. He moved in and shut everything down before we had a chance to counter. We didn't know we had to fight a rearguard action, too."

Kepler looked at the surrounding men and then beyond at the Vietnamese villagers who were still lined up on the other side of the camp, waiting to enter. "What about them?"

"We'll think of something," said Gerber. "Let's go to the team house."

Fetterman touched his sleeve. "It's all over, Captain. You won. Let it go."

"First, we make sure the Vietnamese are taken care of. Then we'll get out."

"When do we start?" asked Kepler.

"Now," Gerber said bitterly. "Right now."

EPILOGUE

Dan Meyers sat with a group of news reporters, a beer held in one hand, and announced, "There's no way to win this war."

Special Forces Captain MacKenzie K. Gerber watched the performance, then returned to his meal, using a knife to slice off a bit of his steak.

"Aren't you going to respond?" asked Morrow. She stared at the captain.

Gerber put down his knife and fork and glanced at Fetterman, who was eating a baked potato. "There's nothing to be said to the man."

"You're not going to challenge his assertion? You're not going to tell him about the errors of his way?"

"We fuck around," said the reporter, slopping beer from his glass. "We kill people and we can't possibly win the war." He took a deep drink.

"Come on, Mack. Don't just sit there," Morrow said.

Gerber picked up his wineglass and drank from it. He set it down and patted his lips with his napkin. "I have nothing to say."

"I don't believe it."

"The problem," said Gerber, "is that the man is right. We won't win this war."

"Jesus."

"It's not because we can't. It's not because the VC or the NVA are too strong. It's because we won't. I had that demonstrated to me."

"Tony?" said Robin.

"I'm staying out of this," said Fetterman. "Every time I open my mouth I find myself in the field on some mission, so I'm clamming up."

"Robin," said Gerber, "I showed you and anyone else who cared to watch how it could be done. I did it. Maybe for only a week, or maybe just a day, but I showed you. To win, we don't sit in our comfortable little bases and wait for the enemy. To win, we go in search of Charlie. To win, we chase him, no matter where he goes, and if we have to violate the so-called neutrality of another country, we do it."

"You have to get the people behind you to win," Meyers announced.

"He's right to an extent. What he really should say is that you have to keep the people from working against you. If they refuse to help you and they refuse to help the enemy, then we're in good shape."

"But—" Morrow sputtered.

"No buts," said Gerber. "What we're fighting here are the Indian Wars. The Army couldn't win until they got out of their forts and took the war to the Indians. When the Indian strongholds in Mexico were attacked, when they were forced to flee rather than select the time of the battle, the Army began to win. The Army had to keep the pressure up. That's what we don't do here."

Gerber looked at Fetterman and then back at Morrow. "You win this war by taking it to the enemy. You don't sit around. You keep up the pressure. You push, push, push. We can do it because we have a nearly endless supply of technological advantages. Helicopters, jets, trucks, cluster bombs and people sniffers. All sorts of gadgets. And we have good soldiers. Good fighters. Men who'd fight the war, given half the chance. Use all that and the VC and NVA would be overwhelmed.''

"But we don't," said Morrow.

"And that's because we can't attack the real enemy," said Gerber.

"And who's that?" she asked.

"The bureaucrats running the war. We can't win it until we defeat them, and that just ain't going to happen."

GLOSSARY

AC—Aircraft commander. The pilot in charge of the aircraft.

ADO—An A-Detachment's area of operations.

AFVN—Armed Forces radio and television network in Vietnam. Army PFC Pat Sajak was probably the most memorable of the AFVN's DJs with his loud and long, "GOOOOOOOOOOOOD MORNing, Vietnam!" The spinning Wheel of Fortune gives no clues about his whereabouts today.

AK-47—Assault rifle usually used by the North Vietnamese and Vietcong.

AO—Area of operations.

AO DAI—Long dresslike garment, split up the sides and worn over pants.

AP ROUNDS—Armor-piercing ammunition.

APU—Auxiliary Power Unit. An outside source of power used to start aircraft engines.

ARC LIGHT—Term used for a B-52 bombing mission. Also known as heavy arty.

ARVN—Army of the Republic of Vietnam. A South Vietnamese soldier. Also known as Marvin Arvin.

ASA—Army Security Agency.

AST—Control officer between the men in isolation and the outside world. He is responsible for taking care of all the problems.

AUTOVON—Army phone system that allows soldiers on one base to call another base, bypassing the civilian phone system.

BISCUIT—C rations.

BODY COUNT—Number of enemy killed, wounded or captured during an operation. Used by Saigon and Washington as a means of measuring progress of the war.

BOOM BOOM—Term used by Vietnamese prostitutes to sell their product.

BOONDOGGLE—Any military operation that hasn't been completely thought out. An operation that is ridiculous.

BOONIE HAT—Soft cap worn by a grunt in the field when not wearing his steel pot.

BUSHMASTER—Jungle warfare expert or soldier skilled in jungle navigation. Also a large deadly snake not common to Vietnam but mighty tasty.

C AND C—Command and Control aircraft that circled overhead to direct the combined air and ground operations.

CAO BOI—A cowboy. Refers to the criminals of Saigon who rode motorcycles.

CARIBOU—Cargo transport plane.

CHINOOK—Army Aviation twin-engine helicopter. A CH-47. Also known as a shit hook.

CHOCK—Refers to the number of the aircraft in the flight. Chock Three is the third, Chock Six the sixth.

CLAYMORE—Antipersonnel mine that fires seven hundred and fifty steel balls with a lethal range of fifty meters.

CLOSE AIR SUPPORT—Use of airplanes and helicopters to fire on enemy units near friendlies.

CO CONG—Female Vietcong.

CONEX—Steel container about ten feet high, ten feet deep and ten feet long used to haul equipment and supplies.

DAC CONG—Enemy sappers who attack in the front ranks and blow up the wire so that the infantry can assault a camp.

DAI UY—Vietnamese army rank equivalent to captain.

DEROS—Date Estimated Return From Overseas Service.

DIRNSA-Director, National Security Agency.

E AND E—Escape and Evasion.

FEET WET—Term used by pilots to describe a flight over water.

FIRECRACKER—Special artillery shell that exploded into a number of small bomblets that detonate later. It is the artillery version of the cluster bomb and was a secret weapon employed tactically for the first time at Khe Sanh.

FIVE—Radio call sign for the executive officer of a unit.

FNG—Fucking New Guy.

FOB—Forward Operating Base.

FOX MIKE—FM radio.

FREEDOM BIRD—Name given to any aircraft that took troops out of Vietnam. Usually referred to the commercial jet flights that took men back to the World.

GARAND—M-1 rifle that was replaced by the M 14. Issued to the Vietnamese early in the war.

GO-TO-HELL RAG—Towel or any large cloth worn around the neck by a grunt.

GUARD THE RADIO—Term that means standing by in the commo bunker and listening for messages.

GUNSHIP—Armed helicopter or cargo plane that carries weapons instead of cargo.

HE—High Explosive.

HOOTCH—Almost any shelter, from temporary to long-term.

HORN—Term that referred to a specific kind of radio operations that used satellites to rebroadcast messages.

HOTEL THREE—Helicopter landing area at Saigon's Tan Son Nhut Airport.

HUEY—UH-1 helicopter.

IN-COUNTRY—Term used to refer to American troops operating in South Vietnam. They were all in-country.

INTELLIGENCE—Any information about enemy operations. It can include troop movements, weapon capabilities, biographies of enemy commanders and general information about terrain. It is any information that would be useful in planning a mission.

KA-BAR—Type of military combat knife.

KIA—Killed in Action. (Since the U.S. wasn't engaged in a declared war, the use of the term KIA wasn't authorized. KIA came to mean enemy dead. Americans were KHA or Killed in Hostile Action.)

KLICK—A thousand meters. A kilometer.

LIMA LIMA—Land Line. Refers to telephone communications between two points on the ground.

LLDB—Luc Luong Dac Biet. The South Vietnamese Special Forces. Sometimes referred to as the Look Long, Duck Back.

LP—Listening Post. A position outside the perimeter manned by a couple of people to give advance warning of enemy activity.

LZ—Landing Zone.

M-3—Also known as a Grease Gun. A .45-caliber submachine gun that was favored in World War II by GIs. Its slow rate of fire meant the barrel didn't rise. As well, the user didn't burn through his ammo as fast as with some other weapons.

M-14—Standard rifle of the U.S., eventually replaced by the M-16. It fires the standard NATO round—7.62 mm.

M-16—Became the standard infantry weapon of the Vietnam War. It fires 5.56 mm ammunition.

M-79—Short-barreled, shoulder-fired weapon that fires a 40 mm grenade. These can be high explosives, white phosphorus or cannister.

MACV—Military Assistance Command, Vietnam. Replaced MAAG in 1964.

MEDEVAC—Also called Dust-off. A helicopter used to take wounded to medical facilities.

MIA—Missing in Action.

MONOPOLY MONEY—Term used by serviceman in Vietnam to describe the MPC handed out in lieu of regular U.S. currency.

MOS—Military Occupation Specialty. A job description.

MPC—Military Payment Certificate. The Monopoly money used instead of real cash.

NCO—Noncommissioned officer. A noncom. A sergeant.

NCOIC—NCO In Charge. The senior NCO in a unit, detachment or patrol.

NDB—Nondirectional Beacon. A radio beacon that can be used for homing.

NEXT—The man who said it was his turn to be rotated home. See *Short*.

NINETEEN—Average age of combat soldier in Vietnam, as opposed to twenty-six in World War II.

NOUC-MAM—Foul-smelling sauce used by Vietnamese.

NVA—North Vietnamese Army. Also used to designate a soldier from North Vietnam.

ONTOS—Marine weapon that consists of six 106 mm recoilless rifles mounted on a tracked vehicle.

P(PIASTER)—Basic monetary unit in South Vietnam worth slightly less than a penny.

PETA-PRIME—Tarlike substance that melted in the heat of the day to become a sticky black nightmare that clung to boots, clothes and equipment. It was used to hold down the dust during the dry season.

PETER PILOT—Copilot in a helicopter.

PLF—Parachute Landing Fall. The roll used by parachutists on landing.

POW—Prisoner of War.

PRC-10—Portable radio.

PRC-25—Lighter portable radio that replaced the PRC-10.

PULL PITCH—Term used by helicopter pilots that means they are going to take off.

PUNJI STAKE—Sharpened bamboo hidden to penetrate the foot. Sometimes dipped in feces.

PUZZLE PALACE—Term referring to the Pentagon. It was called the Puzzle Palace because no one knew what was going on in it. The Puzzle Palace East referred to MACV or USARV Headquarters in Saigon.

RINGKNOCKER—Graduate of a military academy. The term refers to the ring worn by all graduates.

RON—Remain Overnight. Term used by flight crews to indicate a flight that would last longer than a day.

RPD—Soviet-made 7.62 mm light machine gun.

RTO—Radio Telephone Operator. The radioman of a unit.

RUFF-PUFFS—Term applied to the RF-PFs—the regional forces and popular forces. Militia drawn from the local population.

SA-2—Surface-to-air missile fired from a fixed site. A radar-guided missile nearly thirty-five feet long.

SA-7—Surface-to-air missile that is shoulder-fired and has infrared homing.

SACSA—Special Assistant for Counterinsurgency and Special Activities.

SAM TWO—Refers to the SA-2 Guidelines.

SAR—Search And Rescue. SAR forces would be the people involved in search-and-rescue missions.

SHORT-TIMER—Person who had been in Vietnam for nearly a year and who would be rotated back to the

World soon. When the DEROS (Date of Estimated Return from Overseas Service) was the shortest in the unit, the person was said to be next.

SIX—Radio call sign for the unit commander.

SKS—Soviet-made carbine.

SMG—Submachine gun.

SOI—Signal Operating Instructions. The booklet that contained the call signs and radio frequencies of the units in Vietnam.

SOP—Standard Operating Procedure.

SPIKE TEAM—Special Forces team used in a direct-action mission.

STEEL POT—Standard U.S. Army helmet. The steel pot was the outer metal cover.

TEAM UNIFORM OR COMPANY UNIFORM—UHF radio frequency on which the team or company communicates. Frequencies were changed periodically in an attempt to confuse the enemy.

THE WORLD—The United States.

THREE—Radio call sign of the operations officer.

THREE CORPS—Military area around Saigon. Vietnam was divided into four corps areas.

TOC—Tactical Operations Center.

TO&E—Table of Organization and Equipment. A detailed listing of all the men and equipment assigned to a unit.

TRIPLE A—Antiaircraft Artillery or AAA. This is anything used to shoot at airplanes and helicopters.
TWO—Radio call sign of the Intelligence officer.

TWO-OH-ONE (201) FILE—Military records file that listed all of a soldier's qualifications, training, experience and abilities. It was passed from unit to unit so that the new commander would have some idea about the capabilities of an incoming soldier.

UMZ—Ultramilitarized Zone. Name GIs gave to the DMZ (Demilitarized Zone).

USARV—United States Army, Vietnam.

VC—Vietcong, called Victor Charlie (phonetic alphabet) or just Charlie.

VIETCONG—Contraction of Vietnam Cong San (Vietnamese Communist.)

VIETCONG SAN—Vietnamese Communists. A term in use since 1956.

WHITE MICE—Referred to the South Vietnamese military police who wore white helmets.

WIA—Wounded In Action.

WILLIE PETE—WP, White phosphorus, called smoke rounds. Also used as antipersonnel weapons.

WSO—Weapons System Officer. The name given to the man who rode in the back seat of a Phantom; he was responsible for the weapons systems.

XO—Executive officer of a unit.

ZAP—To ding, pop caps or shoot. To kill.

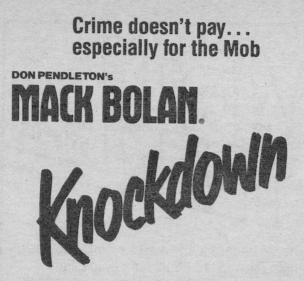

ABLE TEAM ®

DICK STIVERS

Action writhes in the reader's own streets as Able Team's Carl "Ironman" Lyons, Pol Blancanales and Gadgets Schwarz make triple trouble in blazing war. Join Dick Stivers's Able Team—the country's finest tactical neutralization squad in an era of urban terror and unbridled crime.

"Able Team will go anywhere, do anything, in order to complete their mission. Plenty of action! Recommended!"
—*West Coast Review of Books*

Vietnam: Ground Zero is written by men who saw it all, did it all and lived to tell it all

"Some of the most riveting war fiction written . . ."
—Ed Gorman, *Cedar Rapids Gazette*